What People Are Saying About This Book

"Mystical ancient worlds collide with the present...."

—Goodreads

"What a compelling book about a young man's journey of reincarnation into the high rise of aristocracy. His journey through the temptations of life can lead to humility and to trials....'

—Amazon

"Most exciting book I've read in a long time! Very compelling book about a young man's journey of reincarnation into the high position of aristocracy. Something I can identify myself with! How many times have you met someone and felt you know him/her from a previous life?"

—Barnes and Noble

For more on David Francis Cook,
please visit www.DavidFCook.com

ACKNOWLEDGMENTS

Nicole Barrett for her creative input. With her experience in the entertainment industry, she provided colorful feedback, in addition to inspiration.

Kim Biggerstaff for her skill as a teacher of English, grammar, content, and story editing.

FOREWORD

For those of you who may not have read the author's first book, in this trilogy of the "LEGACY SERIES," and for many of you who have already read the first book, the author wants to help you reflect, by giving you an overview of the story so far.

James Bannerman becomes the tenth Earl of Penbroke at the age of fourteen at the untimely death of his father, Collin, in 1958. He is destined to receive at the age of twenty-one a considerable inheritance from his family's estate.

The key element in Book 1, *The Rise to Power*, is the collection of artifacts that lie in the east wing of their English country estate, Penbroke Court. The "Throne," which looks like no traditional monarch's throne, is the prize of the collection, but no one at first understands its origin. These artifacts had been collected from various parts of the world by the seventh Earl of Penbroke during the mid-nineteenth century.

James instinctively understands the Throne, after reading the notes left behind from the seventh earl. He realizes that this "Throne" is not from this age of man, but from the previous civilization of Atlantis, which ended at the end of the last ice age in 10,000 BC. He quickly learns that it is merely a teleportation device, and after having the nerve to sit on the famous throne, he travels through a vortex to a higher dimension to meet his master and guides, where he is told that he too was on Atlantis.

He learns that it was he who had the Throne saved by having it taken to Egypt before the demise of Atlantis and his own life. Now reincarnated 12,000 years later, he works hard against opposition to make sure the Throne is preserved and held for posterity. After restoration, the "Throne Room" is eventually opened to the public as an exhibit to be known worldwide. People now learn the incredible history of the Throne and the story of not only how to reach our guides for our life's direction but also just how advanced the previous civilization of Atlantis was.

James's mother, Phillipa (the Countess), and his sisters, Felicity (Flick) and Rebecca (Becky), play a significant role in the continuing saga. Other characters like Claudia, who was the estate's administrator, Sir Thomas Ringstone, his legal advisor, as well as Peter, his schoolfriend, Peter's sister Kate, and their mother, Sarah, all continue into the second book, *The Temptation to Greed.*

James's girlfriend, Sabrina, also continues with the story. After reaching his twenty-first birthday, James stands at the head of his forefathers' empire in shipping, merchant banking, and property. The second book leads the reader on, to witness James's meteoric rise on the world scene, only to learn his true destiny, purpose, and fortune within the universe, is far more important.

The author weaves a great family tapestry of love affairs, temptation, and greed through this underlying journey of higher vision and spiritual evolvement. The second book continues from 1965 and takes us up to the year 1980.

The first book tackles the age-old question of "Why, are we here?" and the second book answers the very purpose for our being here on Earth, and how we should reach that goal we all desire. These two books hold the key and the gateway for the last and third book in this riveting trilogy, for the very survival of who and what we are.

CHAPTER 1

LIFE IN THE BALANCE

James arrived at Milan Airport to the welcoming arms of his very distraught mother. The shock of the events of the past twenty-four hours had taken their toll. James could clearly see the anguish written all over his mother's face.

"James, I'm so glad you were able to get here so quickly. What a terrible accident to have happened. Antonio decided to rest up at the apartment; he hasn't slept since it happened." Phillipa now looked relieved to have James nearby.

"Tell me," said James anxiously, "What happened?"

They walked through the terminal to where her car was parked. "Let me tell you on the way to the hospital," answered his mother, who was more preoccupied with getting out from the airport. She did her best to remember all the Italian road signs and directions, so it was taking all her concentration.

When they entered the autoroute, she began to relax and relate the story. "Marco had driven up to spend the weekend with Sabrina. What I understand from Antonio, who spoke with Marco's father, was that he was going to surprise her since she had no idea he was coming. He wanted to propose to her. He felt that having waited long enough it was time they made the commitment. You have to understand we are putting the pieces together based on the waiters' testimonies and the police at the scene of the accident. If you ask me, it sounds plausible. It seems they had an argument in the restaurant, and he stormed out with Sabrina running after him. It appears that Marco had more to drink than Sabrina.

"By the looks of the wreck, Marco sped out of control in his Maserati. He wasn't paying attention and they T-boned a garbage lorry. The impact was so severe that even the other driver is in the hospital for minor injuries. Marco, however, is on life support and doesn't look like he's going to survive this. We're still waiting for the final prognosis of all of Sabrina's internal injuries."

"How does she look?" said James anxiously.

"One leg is broken. Her arm is broken and her hands needed a lot of stitches. Her head's been bashed on one side, so she's unconscious. Her face appears unmarked, and her body's a bloody mess. Cuts, bruises...She's going to have scars for life."

"And Marco? What about him?"

"His side of the car hit the lorry the hardest, so he has broken bones all over. Luckily Sabrina got flung out of the car when the car door blew open, or else it would have been much worse for her. Marco was trapped and with the engine moving forward it damaged both of his legs. The worst part is that the car crashed into the side of the lorry between the wheels and hit Marco's head. He's lucky he wasn't decapitated. However, it doesn't look as though he's going to survive."

They arrived at the hospital and Phillipa quickly took James to the room where Sabrina was recuperating. When he entered, he couldn't believe his eyes. That last day they shared on New Years Day at the little cottage in Penbroke was of such profound beauty; how could they have imagined within weeks a terrible event like this could occur? She had one leg held by a sling above the bed and her head was completely encased in bandages except for her face. The rest of her body was wrapped in bandages. It was a pathetic sight and a miracle that she had survived at all. The more he thought about the whole incident, the more upset he grew.

Unbelievable, he thought. *Marco putting the woman he loved in such peril. How could he do this to someone just because he couldn't have his way?*

He sat down silently by her bedside as intense thoughts were rushing through his head.

"James," said Phillipa, interrupting his thoughts, "I'm going to the canteen to get a cup of coffee would you like one?"

"Yes, please."

She left him there in silence gazing at Sabrina. He then started to meditate, wondering why. His anger eventually calmed, and he could then align his thoughts with his masters. As his energy started to increase, he could see all the parts of her body that were racked with pain. The low level of light being emanated from her body told him that she was out of her body and that he was looking at an empty vessel. This experience had been so traumatic that she had sought solace. He could feel that her presence was no longer there.

Suddenly, he felt his hands starting to become warmer. He looked down in surprise to see his palms turning bright red. It was then that he received a message from Serena and he knew that Rachel was there with her. They were feeding him energy for a specific reason and he became so excited that he got up from his chair and instinctively placed his right hand on her forehead and with his left he took her by the hand. It was at this moment that he felt the most intense energy entering his body and it was quickly transmitting all the power to Sabrina.

It was as though he could see her whole body light up with the energy, which now engulfed her completely. It was James's first experience being able to heal someone and an amazing beginning to some of his new powers. He felt her come back into her body and although she couldn't speak or move he knew that this energy he had imparted would heal her completely. Her face seemed alive and the love and compassion he had for her made him feel excited at what he had just done. He released his hands from her as he heard Serena telling him that he had done what was necessary and to now let the miracle slowly work its healing ways throughout the night.

"James, here you are darling. Get some coffee in you. It's been a long day and this will wake you up a bit. Sabrina looks different… She looks restored somehow. I knew just having you here would somehow perk her up. I don't begin to understand the magic of love. I just know it works, even though she looks as though she's not there, she is; I know it. Your presence gives her hope and will make her fight to survive."

"I think she feels me, Mother. And if that can help heal and restore her, that's all I want."

"Antonio has been so heartbroken," said Phillipa. "Can you imagine after losing his first wife and possibly his daughter, how he feels? Poor man. He's going through hell. There's nothing worse than sitting in a room with someone you can't talk to or do anything for. I'm so glad to have you here."

"Look," James said excitedly, "her heartbeat is picking up! I really feel like she knows we're here. She's going to pull through, I know it."

Phillipa decided that it was time to leave and motioned to James to come with her; there was not much more they could do. James was adamant that he remain with Sabrina. His mother relented and shortly wished him good night.

James moved over to the sofa away from the bed, took off his jacket and tie, and popped off his shoes in order to try to get some rest. It wasn't long before he fell into a slumber; however, it was no ordinary sleep. He felt his soul lifting out of his body. He could see Sabrina reaching out to him and, becoming overwhelmed at seeing her, he eagerly moved toward her. "James, you're here with me. Can you see how beautiful it is here?"

"So this is where you're hiding out," observed James. "I thought you were not in your body." The two embraced, filled with joy and comfort at the reconnection.

"James, I don't want to go back. It's so beautiful here. Look at the ocean, the mountains, and all the beautiful wildlife. Our universe has so many places to visit." She looked blissful in her surroundings with a light breeze blowing through her hair and her summer frock.

"Sabrina," started James, "we have too much to do. I know you went through a lot, but you're going to get better and lead a great life. It'll take time for you to be restored to your original self, but it will happen."

"I saw you healing me, so I came back for an instant just to be near you. But that poor body of mine has really been banged up."

"I know. But in a short while you'll see that it's healing quickly. You sustained a lot of injuries, but my masters have worked with me to heal that beautiful body of yours and I, for one, want to be able to kiss those beautiful lips of yours once more."

"James, I know I must return. It's my journey to be with you, and I would miss you terribly. It's so beautiful here, so I'm just enjoying this time before I have to go through the long journey of convalescence."

"You might be surprised at how quickly you will recover," James said comfortingly. "My masters don't have me doing a second-class job, you know!" The two of them rolled with laughter together in the beautiful green grass. It was so real and beautiful to be holding her in his arms. Then, in an instant, he was gone and awoke to the sound of the nurse greeting him with a loud *buongiorno* and coercing him to wake up with an early-morning cup of coffee.

"Signore, signore, come quickly, she's conscious!" James could only remember them being together in his sleep and there, right before his own eyes, were those beautiful big iridescent blue-green eyes staring at him. She held out her hand for his touch.

"Sabrina, my bella! You're back," he exclaimed.

She blinked and had a slight smirk, though it was difficult with all the bandages wrapped tightly around her head. It was hard for her to talk because moving her chin was near impossible. She made noises of happiness and joy at seeing James by her bedside and he could see the fast progress she was already making. James proudly stood by her side as the doctor entered the room. The doctor motioned to the nurse, and asked James if he wouldn't mind leaving for a while, so he could take her down to the examination room to redo her bandages and X-ray her body to review the results of the surgery.

James headed down to the cafeteria for breakfast. He was still thinking about his dream and being with Sabrina. Life has a purpose and it all interconnects in such a meaningful way. It was obviously not her time to go, but the beauty of what exists out there was so comforting to know. He felt that what he had done for Sabrina was all meant to be. He now anxiously awaited her full recovery. On his return to Sabrina's room, he saw that his mother and Antonio had arrived.

"James, you're a trooper staying here all night," said Antonio with his usual upbeat tone. "Sabrina isn't back yet, so hopefully the news is good." No one, not even Antonio, could hide the anxiety of really knowing whether Sabrina had become conscious again for good. They were chatting amongst themselves, when a nurse asked if they would follow her to the doctor's office.

"Please come in and be seated," said Doctor Lorenzo. He then continued, turning to Phillipa, "I have some news to tell you. Your daughter will make a full recovery. Two days ago I would never have been able to even guess how long she would remain in this state, and frankly, the trauma to her head is what troubled me the most. It's an area of the brain that deals with speech and cognitive skills. As for her body, I have never seen a patient heal so quickly. In short, it's a miracle. I wish I could say the same for Marco. We're doing everything we can for him, but even if he survives, he'll never walk again. He'll likely lose the use of one leg, and I doubt that he'll ever be able to function normally after the trauma done to his head. I will say that as long as I've been in this profession, I'm always amazed at how some people come back from near death and others don't."

Phillipa was so emotional at the doctor's news that James and Antonio were near tears.

However, James knew deep down that he had had his first experience of being a receptor of the tremendous powers that had been made available to him. He knew he'd just been an instrument, and was overjoyed at the thought of his beautiful Sabrina making a full recovery. He looked out of the window as if to say a little prayer of thanks to his two female guides, who had shown him the beginning of the wonderful things they could do through him.

Upon entering Sabrina's room, they all stared in shock. There she was, sitting upright, her bandages removed except for a small one placed on the spot where her head had hit the ground. She smiled. "I may look good compared to what I was yesterday, but believe me, I still have a few aches and pains.

"Oh Sabrina, it's truly remarkable to see you like this; it's a miracle. James came to the rescue and I don't know what you two share, but all I know is, it works," said Phillipa, overjoyed.

Antonio walked over to give his daughter a kiss and a hug. "Careful, Papa. I may look good, but don't hug me too tight."

"My Sabrina. I am so happy to see you looking much better. The thought of losing you would have been too much to bear," said Antonio, still stupefied by his daughter's recovery.

"Do you feel well enough to tell us what actually happened that night between Marco and you?" asked an intensely curious Phillipa.

"It's all a bit of a blur, as you can imagine. It all happened so quickly. I just remember he was angry and I know he was bitterly disappointed that I didn't want to marry him… I'm sure in time the events of the entire evening will come back. It was all such a surprise as I didn't expect to see him, especially after I had told him before that I didn't want to make a commitment with anyone until after I finished university. It wasn't the truth, but I thought he would leave me alone. Since meeting you, James, you have been the only person I care about."

James gently walked over to her bedside and sat next to her after giving her a big kiss on the lips. The couple stared at each other longingly and then James broke the silence. "So, out gallivanting around with other men when I'm not around— I just don't know what to think," he said as everyone laughed at the insinuation.

"Speaking of that, how is Marco?" asked Sabrina.

The room went silent, no one wishing to upset her with Marco's condition.

"He's not doing too well," Antonio offered. "The doctors will update us later and then we can give you more news. He suffered more injuries than you, my dear, and the chances of him making a full recovery are slim." Not wishing to lie, he held back important details that might cause guilt.

"Is he going to be alright?" asked Sabrina, anxious.

"Sabrina, I know you're concerned, but focus on your own

recovery for now. You've been through a lot and we're all overjoyed to see how well you're doing. We all hope Marco's recovery will be successful," said James in a calming manner.

"As much as he makes me angry, I don't wish for anything bad to happen to him," Sabrina said.

"Let providence decide. Release him from your thoughts for now," said James, trying to reassure her.

Antonio and his mother said they would go down to the cafeteria and let the two of them have a little time together.

"James, you were in my dream," said Sabrina. "Were you there with me?"

"Yes, I was. As I fell asleep on the couch over there, I felt the two of us connect. I'm so glad you knew that too. It was so beautiful holding you in my arms. We were together in another part of the universe. It makes one wonder at all the places that exist that aren't here on our planet," James mused. "We could have stayed there for a while longer, but something pulled us both back into our bodies somehow."

"I know you healed me. I felt the energy you gave me. It was so powerful that it drew me back into my body for a short while. I wasn't sure how well I would feel, so I drifted back to the place where I was waiting, until I saw you."

"You must understand that my guides gave the energy I gave you. So there is a reason I was able to do that with assistance."

"Can't you do that for Marco?" Sabrina asked hopefully.

"It's not something I can just go around doing for everyone. That kind of intense energy has to be given to me. Besides, I've already thought about that and I'm not receiving any means of direction to change his outcome. Try to focus on yourself for now and let God decide what is appropriate for his life."

"I don't know what would have happened to me without you. I can't wait to walk out of here and spend time with you like we did at Penbroke."

James knew exactly what she wanted and he desired to hold her in his arms again but he knew that now was not the time. "Look. Get better; then we'll discuss it when it will be the right time for either me to fly over to you or you can come see me. I'll arrange everything. You won't have to worry about the cost. I promise we'll take some time together and just talk about us."

"I can't wait. I say a little prayer every night for you. You're always in my thoughts."

Phillipa and Antonio entered the room just then. They all spent some more time with Sabrina to talk further about her unbelievable recovery. James knew he had business he must get back to and calls that had to be made. Antonio and Phillipa drove him back to their apartment first, and then on to the airport to catch his flight.

James called his trusted business partner to get updated on matters at the bank. "How is everything?"

"All is well," Claudia said. "Sir Nicolas called and made an appointment for tomorrow morning at ten, and I said I would confirm if that's okay with you. I wasn't sure how long you would be in Italy. How is Sabrina? Is she alright?"

"She was in pretty bad shape when I first arrived," James reported, "but she's making a brilliant recovery and is now fully conscious. I'll take a flight out tonight and will be with you bright and early tomorrow. I'll tell you all the news when I see you."

James sat down to talk. Both Antonio and Phillipa were intrigued to know what James had done to make Sabrina's recovery speed up.

"I'm flattered to think you feel I had anything to do with Sabrina's recovery," said James modestly. "I believe that love is a very powerful emotion, and with a little meditation, I would like to think I played a role in her recovery. But in truth, you have God to thank for that. Miracles happen and if I played a role, that's great." James paused, and then said, "I couldn't bear to see Sabrian the way she was."

"I'm not so sure that being around Sarah McKenzie hasn't rubbed off on you," said Phillipa. "All I can say is that I was so glad you could come so quickly, and I truly believe you are the reason for this 'miracle.' Just be around when we might need you again."

Antonio joined in laughing with Phillipa while raising his eyebrows in amazement. They felt something had happened, but they weren't going to pursue James any further.

As much as James hated to leave Sabrina, he wanted to get home and have an early night. On the flight back, he couldn't help thinking why he didn't have the urge to help Marco the way he had helped Sabrina. It bothered him that he hadn't done something and so he meditated with Czaur. Czaur's answer came to him very clearly.

"James, you mustn't upset yourself with not doing something for Marco. He was obsessed about being with Sabrina and couldn't bear the thought of her being with anyone else. He will choose to leave this life. Sad as that may be, we are all faced with choices. The karma he has created for himself he'll have to pay off in another lifetime. He has to learn that we don't take people to join with us in life as a possession or trophy. All choices are made by each one of us. Just because a person wants his or her way is not reason enough for this unnecessary car accident. Sabrina was given the gift of healing through you, because she caused nothing. She was forced to make a choice she didn't want. That's her right. You are learning the way our universe works. As much as we want to save everyone, he will find his way into a new life. He must learn the things all of us have to learn. In that way, Marco can advance spiritually and physically."

CHAPTER 2

THE SHEDDING OF INNOCENCE

James entered the office ahead of his meeting with Sir Nicholas. He swiftly hung up his overcoat and put his briefcase down. Then he proceeded to see Claudia.

"Good morning, you look very smart today. Trying to impress Nicholas?"

"Good Lord, no! You're in a feisty mood. Trying to get a rise out of me?"

"Guilty. So what's Nicholas want a meeting for?"

"He has someone he wants you to meet," said Claudia. "A very important civil servant, I believe. He wouldn't give me his name. But tell me more about Sabrina.

James relayed in more detail the story of her miraculous recovery, leaving out the part where he connected with Sabrina in her sleep. "I wish I could say the same for Marco. I don't believe he's going to make it."

"That's dreadful," said Claudia. "His family must be devastated. What a terrible thing to happen! I remember what it was like with Paul. You don't get over incidents like that in a hurry." Death always had a way of making her reflect on her own pain and sorrow.

Rose popped her head round the door. "Sir Nicholas and the other gentleman have arrived. I've taken them to the conference room. Tea or coffee, sir?"

"Oh, a good cup of tea will sort me out. Thanks, Rose," said James.

He made his way down to the conference room, curious to know what Nicholas was up to with this other gentleman. After the introduction to Jeremy Soames, James sat down with an even greater curiosity.

"Your Lordship, I am here for a very important reason. How much are you aware of this country's intelligence community?"

"Call me James, please. You mean the Secret Service with all that cloak-and-dagger stuff you read in spy novels?"

"Precisely," said Jeremy with his tall imposing posture. He was an educated man who had obviously attended some of England's finest schools. In his early forties, he had a suave demeanor and a vibration that James felt was clandestine and was evaluating him more than he needed. This man was at the bank for a very specific reason and wasn't going to play his hand until he was thoroughly sure of just who James was and had become.

"Not much, to be honest, other than what most of the world knows as general knowledge," said James cautiously and starting to become curious.

"I thought as much. So your father never took the time to explain who and what we are?"

"Sir, my father died when I was fourteen," said James, trying not to sound rude. "He taught me a lot about the business but obviously not everything." He was wondering where this was all going to lead. The confidence with which this man spoke was slightly unnerving as James felt he knew far more about him than he cared for him to.

"After I'm gone, Nicholas can fill you in on any details I may have missed. First James, I am aware that you want to give up your banking position, which your family has held for over a hundred years. This is going to present a problem for us. Speaking on behalf of the British government, we have used your bank ever since its inception in 1838. It was because of your family's esteemed loyalty to the British crown that your bank was created in the first place. Your family history is well known for its labors and heroic deeds. That's why the government, through the ages, has always traded with Bannermans as we have done with other notable merchant banks in the city.

"Your bank has played an intricate and trusted role in distributing money to many parts of the world on our behalf. There are private reasons why we use a bank like yours and don't go through the Bank of England." Jeremy pushed his chair away from the table to cross his legs and proceed in a more relaxed manner.

"Forgive me, but you use this bank to send money all over the world for what?" said James, beginning to think he was having an audience with none other than Bond. James Bond.

"Aha! I've got your curiosity."

The two men laughed, interested to see how James was absorbing all this information.

Jeremy continued, "Let me explain how the intelligence service of this country works before we get to the money side of matters." "We have our internal group that takes care of the country we live in, and we have those of the Secret Service who are abroad. Obviously, those who are overseas need to get paid. We have times when we fund various countries or groups. There may be political unrest, famine, and any number of private reasons that may need our focus and attention in order to keep stability in the world. We don't use the Bank of England, because that can leave an audit trail for someone that may use the information for political gain. It's through banks like yours who have proved their trustworthiness over the years that we wire funds primarily to Hong Kong. Jonathan Park distributes these funds to various offshore accounts. In this way, the trail is lost and a very difficult situation gets solved. Is any of this making sense, James?"

"Sure," said James. "I've been of the thought that Jonathan Park was siphoning off money for his own purposes, but now you've made everything crystal clear. The only thing I don't get is that surely, there would be an audit trail through our bank. Having done my time as an accountant, I would be hard-pressed to discover how you'd get around that if someone had a mind to really track these funds."

"Ah, now your mind is working well toward the way in which we do business," said Jeremy with a grin. "We never give you money that has to be wired to Hong Kong, and so on. We use your shipping services to transport our goods to Europe, the Middle East, Africa, and onto Asia. You'll soon learn that we are one of your best and longest surviving customers. We pay you handsomely, in order to include those wired funds, for your shipping services and beyond. When we ask you to transfer funds to an account, you are the one who does it and no money changes hands. You then instruct Jonathan Park with the information we give you. The control of the final account is ours, which is off shore.

"From there we can distribute the funds to the person or persons or nations accordingly." Jeremy Soames stopped and looked at James with a huge smirk on his face, which was mirrored by Nicholas.

James was shocked. He could never have dreamed up such a scheme. His innocence of how the world of governments and businesses operated started to take on a whole new picture and he knew he was going to have to really think all of this through.

"I had no idea that we operated on behalf of the government," he admitted. "How is it that no one has mentioned this clandestine way of operating to me? Who here knows how you operate and takes care of the wire transfers to Bannermans Hong Kong?"

"There's only one person who is part of your organization that has that knowledge and instructs Nigel Thompson with the wire transfers," Jeremy said. "Nigel has no idea what that money is for. He assumes that these are investments made by Bannermans in your Hong Kong subsidiary."

"So who's the person that instructs Nigel?"

"You're looking at him. Sir Nicholas is here today because he would like you to take care of these needs directly. This is the reason why he is a shareholder in your bank as his father was. Since your father's death, we have asked him to increase his investment in the bank until you came of age. The Blythe family is an old and trusted family and has long been part of our inner sanctum. Nicholas's excellent record for job creation and dynamic entrepreneurialism has earned him the elevated position he holds in our organization. He has earned our trust as have all the members we have handpicked from some of the most revered families of this country."

James was getting an education on something he knew nothing about. He was engulfed in the eloquent manner in which Jeremy Soames explained everything. "So this is how it all works? Nations are guided by a select group of people who steer a nation through good and bad times with a civil service that was never elected?"

"Very astute," observed Jeremy. "Democracy is a necessary vehicle for taking care of the basic needs of a nation and more than serves its role as voters elect, reelect, or change a government that performs or not. We are that backbone that guides newly elected officials, through our civil service with people that over the course of decades have become invaluable at what they do. We instruct the leaders of the Secret Service here and abroad, along with the various government bodies that are necessary to run a nation. The heads of these various bodies each report indirectly to our inner sanctum. The best way I can describe our work is this: Have you ever looked at a painting, and then after a while, started to see a painting within the painting?

"We operate completely out of sight, yet we are challenged with some of the most important decisions of the nation. Only the heads of the various bodies of government report to us. That being said, we have a representative that brings a situation to us. That person and only that person contacts one person, whom we have given authority to. Our chosen candidate that represents us will only know one designated person from our team. In short, we've existed for well over one hundred years. No one knows who any of us is."

"You could never dream this up," said James, almost to himself. "No one would ever believe it was true, as there are no names to prove its validity." The more he thought about it, the more sense it all made.

"I've given you my name, but in all reality that might not be who I am. You have Nicholas, who will fill you in on what we expect, should you decide to continue our long-standing relationship." Jeremy paused, and then added, "James, our inner sanctum has watched your progress with great interest. I have met many leaders in the course of my life and I can say this much: Whatever you decide, I know you'll be a great leader one day." He locked eyes with James, making sure he got his drift.

Jeremy Soames asked to be excused and left the conference room. James sat there staring at Nicholas and then burst out laughing. "So this is how it all works, and you've *known* about this?"

"It's how it all works, old boy. Our country and many of the more mature and sophisticated nations have a body of people, namely the civil service and our own directive, the Inner Sanctum, who don't get reelected. Democracy has its weaknesses in that it's always changing. This works for creating new bills, which become law and deals with the day-to-day needs of an ever-evolving nation. It has its place for sure and has proved to be the best system of government in spite of its sometimes-laborious debates and inability to make decisions that are needed swiftly in matters of emergency. It is in these matters that we become involved to assist an outcome. Obviously, the most efficient form of government is a benign dictator, one person who makes the decisions at minimum cost.

"Unfortunately, human nature being what it is, we have developed a democracy. In this way, the views of the elected candidate are heard, and also a view that's supported by the people who have elected that person. However, when it comes to everyday government and services, each one of these has a boss, and if that boss does a good job, he or she can stay in that position for decades. The Brotherhood of the Inner Sanctum, which I am a member of, and hopefully of which you will become a member, runs these services.

"Government is a big business and it needs a boss, too. Not a boss that's here today and gone tomorrow. Only people that have shown excellence in character, example to their fellow man, scholastic achievement, and so on, are watched and then as a need arises, someone dies, or for some other reason, a person is selected to help with the very serious task of helping to run these extremely important branches of government. The intelligence service is one that is scrutinized very closely. Constant direction and decisions have to be made. These decisions often place a great burden on us, and end up in heated discussions between our members before a final decision is rendered. Starting to see how a country works?"

"I think so," said James carefully. "Obviously what you've both expressed is a gross oversimplification. It would take a lifetime of work in order to be truly proficient. After all, the only constant is change and navigating the present-day world has to be an awesome task."

"It's got us to where we are today!"

"Nicholas, what's your future with us if I become a member?"

"I've always believed in Bannermans. You guys have been around a long time and like my business, the same family runs it. So I'm happy to not be involved with the tedious task of making all their wire transfers through Nigel, but as for my shares and investments, if you want to buy me out at any time, be my guest."

Nicholas continued, "I've made money with Bannermans, but since you now have over eighty percent of the company, minority shareholders don't hold much power. My business is privately owned and I can understand anyone wanting that. Most important for me is that we maintain our friendship, James. It took a while to figure you out, but like Jeremy says, for a young man, you've got it together and I'm always up for a bit of a risk."

Nicolas got up to leave. "Call me any time when you've made your decision and I can go into more depth about what will be expected of you. By the way, congratulate me. I'm getting married," he said excitedly.

"Getting married!" repeated James, taken aback. "That's news alright. Who's the lucky lady?"

"It's not, it's a chap I know!"

"Really! Now I know why you haven't settled down." James was almost speechless, but the widening grin on Nicholas's face told him he was being put on.

"It's Davina Samson. Everyone in my business of women's fashions assumes if you're not married by forty, your choices are directed toward the same sex!"

"Good choice. She impressed me at my twenty-first."

"I've got to watch you. All these ladies seem to have an easy eye in your direction. It must be all that lordship stuff."

"You can talk. You had Sabrina under your spell for a while. She likes older men."

"Really," said a bemused Nicolas thinking seriously about the possibility. Then the pair laughingly shook hands and promised to meet soon.

That reminded James. He went to his office to call his mother. "How's Sabrina doing?"

"She's doing great. We've slowly walked down the corridors, so I think she'll be good enough by the end of the week to come back to the apartment. Then Antonio and I will take her home to Tuscany, where she can convalesce. It would be nice if you could come and visit. She does nothing but talk about you, and she's missing you so much."

"I will take a long weekend. The weather's not that great here, but I suspect it's not much better in Tuscany this time of year?"

"Better than England. We get nice sunny days. Anyway, this is your girl. Come and cheer her up."

"I will," promised James.

****

James asked Claudia to come to the conference room; it was time to discuss the business and bring each other up to date. He had thought about including Nigel in the meeting but decided against it.

"Another tea? Or here's some coffee," said Claudia, anxious to hear about his meeting.

James lit up a cigarette, to create a more relaxed atmosphere for an informal discussion. He then continued, "Are you aware of these wires that Nigel sends periodically to Hong Kong?"

"Not really. I obviously see the transactions in accounting. I assumed they were investments that Nigel makes for the bank there. It's all accounted for. Why?"

"I have to share with you something that I want you to be involved with from now on. Nigel has no idea what the wires are for. He thinks that he's being instructed to make necessary investments that Jonathan Park needs to grow the operation there. They seem to end up in offshore accounts that pay a reasonable rate of interest. Other than that, I suppose I should look into this more carefully."

Claudia was growing concerned that she might not be doing the due diligence that James had expected of her.

"And who instructs him to do this?" said James, holding his cards close to his vest.

"I really don't know. Should I?" she asked nervously.

"I think it's a subject we should have discussed before now. I'm not giving you a hard time, but everything must be watched, and don't think twice about turning over something that might not be popular. I realize he's your boss but you are the person I know and the one I trust." James was pushing her buttons. James's father taught him that you have to keep people on their toes.

"I will look into this immediately," she said as though she wanted to run out the door that very instant.

"Now just hold on. I know what those wire transfers are about, thanks to the meeting I've just had. You're going to learn something that is extremely private and for your ears only."

"What can it be? I should know everything here."

"I've just finished a meeting with a top-level official from the British government. Apparently, we have, or more correctly,

Nigel has been transferring funds for the British government for years. The instructions have been coming from Nicholas. Nigel has no idea, but he was led to believe that these transfers were board directives for investments in our bank in Hong Kong. You are the one that knows about the offshore accounts. It seems Nigel is a little naïve on some matters."

"That's weird because I see no incoming source of income to cover these wires."

"You won't. This is an arrangement made between our bank and the British government that dates way back. We've only been in Hong Kong since the early fifties, so this type of transaction has only existed since Nigel came to work here. In the past, my father would have instructed him, but since his departure, Nicholas has been trusted, as he is highly revered by the Crown and British government. However, you probably want to know how we get reimbursed. Well, since we do a lot of shipping with Trans Global for the British government they repay us the amount of the wire, which they include in the shipping costs."

"That's a first for me," said Claudia. "So in a sense, they pay us very well for our services. I've noticed that, and I can vouch for the fact that, they are an extremely good customer and pay like a slot machine." She looked a little off balance as James continued.

"Other than me you're the only one who knows this. From now on I want you to handle these transfers."

"Nigel will want to know why."

"That brings me to my next decision. I believe it's time for Nigel to go."

Claudia sighed. "I think you're right. Since we've released all the brokers, he really doesn't have a lot to do. He's just a figurehead. Everyone likes Nigel. He's been a good and faithful managing director but times are changing. He has a lot of contacts in the city; he'll have no trouble finding a position. It just wouldn't be as prestigious as being the head of Bannermans."

It was a sad moment as Nigel was asked to report to James's office. James politely expressed to him that as the bank had been downsized it would no longer need his services. He took it with dignity. With his hefty severance package he would have time to find another position and not feel the pain too much. Nigel looked forward to the break after nearly seventeen years. With the new direction the bank was taking, he could see the writing on the wall.

James elevated Claudia to managing director of the bank at the beginning of February 1966. This would be with an improved salary and benefits. He instructed her to buy out Sir Nicholas completely. This now left James as a 91 percent shareholder, leaving Peter Hawthorn from Lloyd's Investments and Sir Thomas as his only other shareholders.

The months slowly moved on. James had showed his commitment to remain a bank to the British government and he was awarded the honorable membership that was promised. He was yet to be called to one of their meetings, but in truth he'd been far too busy now preparing for his trip to China. He felt the urge to get straightened out once and for all his prize asset Trans Global Shipping. He decided it was time to take a trip up to his estate at Penbroke. Keith Pruett had kept him abreast of affairs on his visits to the London office. James now wanted to see for himself the progress that was being made.

CHAPTER 3

PENBROKE TRANSFORMED

After resolving all the normal first-of-the-year details at his business, and as it was now fast moving toward the middle of February, James decided to check on the progress at Penbroke. He was excited to see his home as he drove up the driveway to the open set of gates to the courtyard. It was his first chance to drive his new Aston Martin DB6 on the open roads. He kept his little Mini for London driving and Sir Thomas had kindly lent him the use of one of his garages at Hampstead Heath. He was thrilled with the power and refinement of driving his new toy and couldn't wait to show it off to Kate, Sarah McKenzie's daughter, and Peter's sister. It was Friday lunchtime so he would walk on down to the stables after checking out the house.

He was feeling bittersweet, thinking of all the memories this house held, and no one was around to enjoy it. He took time to review the empty rooms. He heard his echo as he walked through the hallways, eagerly checking out whether the house was being kept up in the appropriate manner. His bedroom was just the way he left it. He was looking forward to spending the night there again. After a careful inspection and noticing that all the dust covers were correctly placed on the furniture, he made his way down to the stables.

"Kate," he called out to his racing partner, "how are you, my dear?"

She ran toward him to give him a big hug.

"James, we've been so busy. You can't imagine how many riding instructions we're giving to people. We've got some new 'easy-to-ride' ponies and horses, which Keith helped us buy, and I'm happy to say that we are making a profit, your Lordship."

"Well I knew you'd make this enterprise pay. With your work ethic and competitive nature I'm only sorry that we didn't do this earlier. I'm famished. Let's go and get a bite in Penbroke." James had an idea he wanted to run by her.

"Your wish is my command. Let me take some of my gear off and at least look presentable," Kate said, becoming conscious that she should at least powder her nose.

They walked back over to the main house, and then James remembered Sarah. "What about your mother?"

"Oh. She'll be back here on Monday. She had a doctor's appointment. Will you still be here?"

"I'll make a point of it. I've got to sit with Keith so there's plenty to do."

"Wow! Is this your new toy?" Kate eyed his ride. "What a dream machine! All the women'll be lining up to take a ride with you," she said in her normal provoking manner.

James liked Kate's style and wit. They would never date, but he enjoyed her company and her competitive spirit. She was a winner and he had big plans for her future. The two drove into Penbroke to the little pub now called the Lucky Horse after

Joe's recent wins on Bullet.

"That horse of yours goes like a rocket," said Kate. "Joe and I have been training him and we've both won money on him at the last two steeplechase race events."

After getting a beer and a sandwich they both sat down and James got straight to the point. "Kate, Keith has told me about the things you've done here. Tell me, what level of accounting are you at?"

"I've got my certificates from the chartered institute of secretaries, so I know accounting to balance-sheet level, I can do audit work, and I like finding mistakes. I'm not to tax level or high finance, but I can always learn. Once you know the basics, you can build on that." She sounded proud of her efforts.

"I trust you, and I think you could be a great asset with a little more experience. You strike me as an adventurous person. You don't mind travel. In the business I'm in, we need people to go places and check out what's going on with the various businesses we own. How does that strike you?"

"Like I told you at New Years, I want to move up. You can send me anywhere on the planet and I'll figure it out. If I need help, I'm not too shy; I'll ask."

"That's what I want to hear. In the next few weeks I'm going to China. I'll be going on one of our merchant ships. Would you like to come and help with a financial audit I want to do at our bank in Hong Kong?"

"I would love to go!" said Kate excitedly. "But I don't know if I'm at the skill level you need."

"Don't worry about that. We'll be taking another young man that Claudia works with and he knows exactly what to do. I want you to learn the business. By that I mean experience what it's like out there on the high seas. You'll pick up the financial stuff quickly. This guy, who's a chartered accountant and a very astute auditor, will train you. I have another reason for taking you. As we know each other fairly well, I want you to give me your personal impressions of the staff we have out there. I'm staying here the night, so you're welcome to stay over at the house if you want."

"I think I will, James. Then we can go riding after you've seen Keith."

James dropped Kate back at the stables and then went down to the farm administration building.

"It's good to see you, sir," said Keith. "I knew you were coming up. I've got together all my notes so I can bring you up to date. Shall we go into the conference room?" He had partitioned off a small conference room for discussion purposes.

"Here we are in our fourth year and we have rented almost all the cottages," Keith started. "This is garnering good revenue. Now that the renovations are complete we're earning enough income off those properties to pay off our original loan of seventy-five thousand pounds in one year. Needless to say, we've paid it off and you should know that from your bank records. A three-year payback on the original loan, the Throne Room, and the cottages renovated and rented is, I believe, something that none of us believed would be accomplished so quickly. Of course, the Throne Room was the engine that kicked all this off. The income we're receiving from the Throne Room is close to one hundred thousand annually. So between the cottages and the Throne Room we have more than enough capital to improve our equipment and update the dairy. I believe over the course of this year we can achieve that. This of course will increase revenue again. Matters appear to be very rosy at the moment. I can't tell you how important it is to have almost no debt."

He then continued, "Most farms I've worked for barely manage each year to cover their costs because of the amount of debt they carry. Much still needs to be done but the revenue stream is there. And fortunately, compared with other farms we can go from strength to strength. However, we now have another problem. Due to the rental properties that we've created, our little village is bursting at the seams. A good problem for all the tradesmen, but getting planning permission to expand the grocery store is like pulling teeth. The local council won't allow conversion of greenbelt farmland for commercial use."

Keith was a bulldozer alright. His intense and devoted energy was just what Penbroke needed and James could tell he loved every moment of it.

James nodded, "I'll talk with the local parish and the county and see if we can drum up some support. They always need money for the Cathedral, parks, and so on. With a little influence, I'm sure we can get some help. I know that church isn't big enough either, so I don't think they'll stand in God's way. Do you?"

"Good thinking." Keith chuckled. "It's a good problem. We'll get there. On another subject, Sarah needs to expand her teaching room and the little souvenir shop could do with something a little nicer. We'll get it back on the price of a ticket. Don't you worry."

"Speaking of that, I need to give Sarah a raise. I'll talk with her on Monday, and Keith, you deserve consideration, too. I'll talk with Claudia when I get back down to London."

"Much appreciated, sir. The young'ns are growing and their wants increase as I'm sure you're aware."

James nodded his understanding. "I'll be gone to our business in China for a while...but stay in touch with Claudia and continue to keep her updated. I'm always interested to know of our progress. So how do you like life in Lincolnshire?"

"We couldn't be happier. When the wife's happy, we're all happy. She's closer to her friends now and that makes all the difference."

"Good. Keep up the good work. See you soon." James quickly descended the stairs and, realizing that the day was passing, he went back to the stables to talk with Kate. They both returned to the house to change and go out for dinner. James had booked a table at a pub in Horncastle and he let Kate drive his new car.

"This is fantastic!" she exalted. "You notice I'm not standing it, 'on its ears' yet?"

"Yes, I'm sure you can, but I want to keep it in one piece—thank you very much—and the roads are icy in places." Not that it mattered to Kate.

"I like the color, British racing green with black leather upholstery—very racy." Then Kate grew suddenly serious. "How long shall this trip to China take?"

"With the ships we have today, and depending on how many seaports we have to stop at, I'd say four to six weeks. We own the property next to our bank and I want to start plans for the development of a new high-rise building there."

"How many floors?"

"Around fifty."

"Fifty! That's some project."

"Yes, it's all a race for the sky right now. So many companies are investing there that property is going through the roof. We want to be up there with the big boys towering over Hong Kong Harbor. It'll dwarf our other building, which has only fifteen floors. It'll never handle the business that's coming there. The man in charge of our bank in Hong Kong is a little tricky—I can't quite figure him out. I feel like he's getting money out of the bank; hence the audit you'll be part of. It's been too long since my father visited the bank there, and this will be a splendid opportunity for me to understand our shipping fleet, and what updates are needed."

The next morning James called his mother. He was anxious to know how Sabrina was doing.

Sabrina answered. "When are we going to see each other? I've been waiting to hear from you. I'm good to go! My cast is off tomorrow, so I'm ready to be your dancing partner for sure. I can't believe how quickly my body is healing!"

"Well, I was thinking, why don't you catch a flight to London and I'll pick you up? I'll reimburse you."

"I'm practically on my way. I can't wait to see you. I'll take a flight tomorrow evening. It arrives around 8:30 p.m. at London Heathrow. I'll call if there're any changes."

"I can't wait either. Ciao, bella."

James went to see Kate at the stables for their ride; it was a typical cold winter's day, but the sun was out, and that made all the difference. It had been snowing the day before, but the sun had melted the light dusting that had lain on the surrounding grass lawns.

"James, I was thinking. Why don't you drive me home this afternoon?" she suggested in a provoking way. "You can stay the night, talk with my mother, and then we can do a few laps at our track."

He knew she wanted to get his car out there and hammer the hell out of it. "Want to drive my car, huh? I know what you're up to. So, you'd what—eave your car here?"

"Yes. I can pick it up tomorrow. I'll catch a ride with my mother."

"That's a great idea. Then I can head on to London from your place. It's time I caught up with Peter and see what's going on in the Lloyd family."

James and Kate went for their usual gallop across the beach. Then she wanted to show him how much quicker she was over the fences. James was surprised at the number of people Joe and his friend were taking out for rides. Kate had really got things going in such a short time. She had drive and determination; James knew she was a good bet for the future. They arrived at the Lloyd house late afternoon.

Peter was delighted to see James. "Back up here with all us country bumpkins again? Dad'll enjoy having a chat with you.

He often talks about you and I know you want to see Mom. So let me look at this new machine—classy and beautiful. Want to do a couple laps...before dinner?"

"Hey, I've got first dibs on that," said Kate quite emphatically. "Remember, ladies first."

James and Kate put on their helmets (but not their full race gear), opened the windows, as was common practice, and then ventured out onto the track.

On the first lap she slowly warmed up the tires and tested the brakes to see how well the car stopped and at what points on the track she should brake in order to negotiate the corners. The second lap was quicker and by the third lap she had the car on rails. "Now this is the way you drive a car of this caliber!" she informed. "You see all those wimps out there doodling around in a car like this. This car was made to be driven."

"You surely know how to drive it," said James, feeling a little nervous for his new machine. Admittedly, the temperature had risen to the midfifties by now. He was amazed at her skill of wielding this type of car, but in all reality, it was designed more for high speed driving on the highway. The weight would require stiffer suspension to make it a racecar. That didn't stop Kate. Rain, snow, or shine—she certainly knew how to get the last ounce out of a car. "You should be a test driver. Being a woman, they could shoot some great commercials with someone like you."

She laughed. "That would be a dream come true, but I've got to work for you first, and when I become proficient, maybe you'll let me have time to pursue my passion."

"You're a natural. I believe this is something you could really be successful at."

She brought the car back to the house. "Now, let's have a beer. Those brakes were getting a little spongy after all those laps. I'm sure she'll be safe for the road tomorrow, but have them bled to be on the safe side. You might also want to have them put in a higher-temp fluid for when you drive on the track with me as your instructor."

Peter was observing his bossy sister telling James all the "ins and outs" of driving on track, and was having a big chuckle at his expense. "James, I think she's wiped off fifty percent of your tire life. I bet they could hear the squeals over at Silverstone."

"Don't you start," said James. "I've got to get to London Airport tomorrow."

At that moment, Sarah came out to greet James and asked them all to come inside. It was getting cooler and she had prepared some refreshments for the evening. Mr. Lloyd got up to welcome James and then they all started to talk.

"James has asked me to go on one of the ships to China to do some auditing," Kate said, thinking that they might be assuming she was going on vacation.

"James sounds like an adventurer," said Peter, wishing he could get a break.

"You might say that," said James, "but I'm actually going to learn our shipping business on the way out. Our fleet is getting on in age and with the new shift toward containerization, it's time I did a little research before spending a significant amount of money."

"What kind of goods do you ship around the world?" asked Victor Lloyd.

"Everything. On the way to Hong Kong, we have to make many stops at different ports. We'll be going through the Suez Canal so that'll cut out a good part of the trip. We stop in Portugal, Italy, Saudi Arabia, India, Singapore, and on into Hong Kong. We ship everything from cars, military arms, personal effects, and manufactured goods. It's all over the map.

"So how many ships do you have at present?"

"It's about thirty and they all run from Tilbury, London, to Hong Kong Harbor. Each ship has different stops and carries merchandise based on their capacity and size. We're the biggest shippers of goods between London and Hong Kong in the world. That being said, that's all we do. I'm looking at some other routes, but like everything in life, it takes money."

"So, you're going to learn the business, update the ships, and look for new trading routes," clarified Victor. "Sounds like you've got your work cut out."

"Yes, sir. But that's not all. We've got a bank in Hong Kong, so I have to check that out as well."

"Exciting stuff, but a lot of responsibility."

"How are things working here with the change in the motor cars?" James asked, changing the subject.

"It's not going too well at the moment. The bodies are greatly reduced in size and a lot of the factories have pulled this work in house. It's hard to keep the skills we've developed without more work. The machining is not too bad, but we need to get rid of that labor government and get some more expenditure on defense. We'll survive, but it's been a tough few years."

"I think it's the same for everyone," James sympathized. "Now is a time for regrouping, cleaning house, and preparing for better times."

Sarah had prepared a little snack for the family and said that she would like to talk with James before he left in the morning.

****

James was up early as usual, but when he went downstairs for some tea he noticed that both Peter and Victor had left for work. Sarah soon arrived.

"James, bless you; up with the rooster," she said before pouring herself a cup of tea. "It's the early bird that catches the worm!"

"My father said that often," said James. She seemed to have

some pressing thoughts on her mind. His abilities to now read auras gave him the distinct impression that she had something important to discuss.

"James," she started. "Kate won't be down for a bit. Usually, we go in later to the Throne Room on Mondays as business starts to get busier toward the summer. You may or may not have noticed that Victor is having a very hard time with the business. The change in formula one and the decrease in work from De Havilland and A. V. Roe, our primary customers, have reduced dramatically. Your friend Sandra's father, Francis Cole, is garnering a lot of work from Vickers Brothers at Weybridge and Hawkers at Kingston. He has a much larger facility and he can produce at a faster rate. He's also doing well with the Ministry of Defense on repairs, the kind of work Peter could do in his sleep. I think Victor will survive if he runs a tight operation.

"My fear is after paying off everything we own, he will borrow heavily just to stay in business, which I don't want to happen. Peter has a new process that he wants to implement that some American firm has brought to Derby and will be doing work for Rolls Royce. Here are my thoughts on that: Peter is not a businessman like you. He is more of an artisan and loves working to shape and form metal. I am told this new process goes hand in hand with his abilities. If I can help Peter get on his own, I think that would be a relief to his father, since he doesn't like machining at all. If you could talk with him and understand what it is he wants, I would be so appreciative."

Sarah had bared her soul and James felt an immediate need to help.

"Sarah, you know I'd do anything for you; after all you've done with the Throne Room," said James. "We're more than business partners. We're family. That being said, I know Victor is a proud man and I in no way wish to step on his world and the pride he has for what he's accomplished."

"I'll talk to Victor," said Sarah. "He will, I hope, be relieved at the possibility of Peter having a future, which he believes doesn't lie in the machining business. Any man would want his children to follow in his footsteps. It's natural, but we're not all the same and that's life. We don't always know our parents for our careers. There are many other gifts a parent can give their children as you well know."

"I'll go over to the shop and talk with Peter before leaving, so let's create a plan," said James. "If we can make it happen for the Throne Room, we'll make it happen for Peter."

"China will dramatically change how you think. It'll be exciting, but you'll certainly be challenged. It'll be a good experience and you'll learn a lot. Kate is the perfect person to accompany you; she picks up on people very quickly and although she doesn't make any effort to develop her abilities, much of what I do she could do too. Perhaps you could influence her a little?"

"I can see where Kate gets some of her drive," answered James. "I'm sure she's a chip off the old block. She'll get all the encouragement I can give her. On another note, I'm picking up Sabrina tonight and then I'm driving back to Penbroke. We'll see you there and then we can take a look at what needs to be done for the out buildings." James knew this would please her. He knew he wouldn't be seeing her for a few months and he must make the very best use of his time. He also knew that no one was aware of what had happened to Sabrina and he didn't want to get into that conversation now.

James made his way over to the workshop where Peter was working away. "Good to see you're earning your corn, old boy," he jibed.

"James! Glad you popped over." Peter lifted his head and face guard from his welding.

"Your mother filled me in on everything. I suggest you get a plan together for this new process, what it would cost to buy the equipment, and so on. Let me have a cash flow projection when I return from China. Your mother knows the drill. We did it for the bank on Penbroke, and if you need help, call Claudia. Be thorough. If we go for this plan, it's got to work. I would like you to carefully explain the process and the potential market place. I don't want just a string of numbers that don't relate to anything. Do a market survey; again, Claudia can put you in touch with people that can help," instructed James, exhibiting his business acumen. He thought that if Peter had what it took, he'd step up to the plate. It was one thing to be a master of your trade, but it takes guts, vision, and leadership to make things happen. He truly valued Peter as a friend, but he had to demonstrate that he could run a business.

"Yes, sir, your Lordship," responded Peter. "Seriously though, James, thanks for giving a damn. It'll be a different assignment, but one I need to learn if I'm going to be in business one day. I know we live in a day and age where the old ways of just shooting from the hip won't raise the finances needed to get off the ground. I can see why you took the time to become a chartered accountant; all businesses need someone who is good with the green. Sorry we couldn't have had more time together, but I know those days will come."

Peter looked up to James and wanted to do everything his old friend asked. He was James's trusted wicket keeper and had always made the perfect partner for James.

CHAPTER 4

SABRINA AND JAMES

London Airport was busy as usual and finding a place to park was always a challenge. He couldn't wait until he saw Sabrina cross the entry door after getting through customs.

"James, mio amore, over here." She was carrying her little suitcase and handbag. James couldn't believe how thin she'd become. She was still the beautiful young woman he knew, but he was anxious about how she was doing.

"Let me take your bags," James insisted, taking them from her. "So you feel well? You're up for a drive to Penbroke? We can stay in London if you're tired." The last thing he wanted to do was overtax her.

"Actually, I'm as fit as a fiddle! Brrr...its cold here. Let me tell you, I've been working out like crazy...running, lifting weights, and doing all sorts of exercise. You should know your Sabrina by now." Somehow she looked different to what he remembered.

"Well, don't get too thin. I always thought you looked great the way you were."

"So you're just like all men. You want that sexy, leggy, voluptuous woman that sweeps you off your feet," she said, walking arm in arm kissing his neck every few moments. He noticed that her English was getting better.

"It's also the person inside," James said, trying to sound like he wasn't disappointed by her thinner persona.

"Don't worry. I'll put on a few pounds for my James. Just kiss me—I've waited too long."

James loved her way of saying what she thought. It was her whole presence that gave her sex appeal. Within minutes, he could feel those old feelings flashing back as she had a way of just pulling him into her heart.

"I can't tell you how much I've looked forward to seeing you back on your feet," James said. "To see you in all your colors. I suppose when you're in love it's a feeling that transcends all form and rationality. When I see you, it's that magnetic energy I feel."

"I know I'm almost a hundred percent," said Sabrina, "but I still have a few little aches and pains. I know with your love and your healing hands that I'll be made whole again."

James knew exactly what she wanted and he couldn't wait to take her to his bedroom and adore every inch of her body. He knew she would have sustained some scars from the surgery, but that didn't bother him in the least. Her energy and persona were far and away above any marks she may have sustained upon her beautiful body. He couldn't wait to hold her in his arms again and share the intimacy that made them feel whole.

They arrived at Penbroke close to eleven. He treated her to a glass of wine before retiring, but their passion was so intense neither could wait. The night was spent in soft but warm embrace. James wanted to be gentle with her, knowing all that she'd been through. It was late morning before the two arose.

Sabrina was up first and had breakfast prepared. James loved the way she just took charge and didn't have to be told how to do anything. She was busy analyzing whether the plates, the mugs, and cups were all in the most appropriate place. For most of his life growing up, James had staff take care of those matters. To see Sabrina taking them up reminded him of what Antonio must be missing since she had left home. James had slowly made his way downstairs in his pajamas and was silently observing how she was going about her work to prepare breakfast for them.

"We didn't get much of a chance to talk last night for obvious reasons," he said with a smirk. "Do you remember that night much?"

"I do now," said Sabrina. "It took me a moment to really remember what happened. Marco arrived out of the blue late on a Saturday afternoon. I had plans to go out with a girlfriend to a local wine bar. He just banged on the door and wanted to spend the weekend with me. I said, 'Marco, I have other plans and I wished you could have called.' He said, 'We've had long enough since your father's wedding to get engaged!' He was right in a way...almost eight months. He knew I had been dodging him, but he thought I didn't have anyone else really, so what was the delay? I now had to tell him the truth about us, James. He was quiet at first, and then said we should go to dinner and discuss everything over a bottle of wine. I thought that if he's going to be civil, why not? We've been friends and at one time had some romantic feelings; maybe I should take the time. He'd driven all this way. It was the polite thing to do."

"So what went wrong?"

"He took me to a well-known restaurant in his new Maserati. I could tell he was about to give me the evening of my life. The only problem was that it wasn't what I wanted. After I declined his offer of engagement, he became very angry.

"'You don't know that English aristocrat,' he said. 'He's young, inexperienced, and has got a lot of wild oats to sow! You'll regret being with him. He's not from our culture. The British are very different; they can be very cold and a wife can be very lonely with men of class and privilege. You belong here in Tuscany; these are *your* people and the ones that love you.' So it went on and on. I was becoming more and more angry as well. Who was he to direct my life? If he believed my future with you wouldn't work out, then let time tell. By now we were well into after-dinner drinks and he was going through them like crazy. He looked at the bill, took out his wallet, and threw a huge amount of lira on the table and stumbled his way out of the restaurant, shouting obscenities at everyone. I got up to follow because I didn't think he was in a condition to drive. He grabbed hold of me, pulled me into his car, and the attendant closed my door. He drove off mad and drunk. He was shouting, 'If I can't have you, no one else will! You're *mine*. I'm the only man for you! Can't you see that?' He was driving so fast and so erratically with the car all over the place. Then a garbage lorry pulled out and we went headlong into its side." Sabrina sighed then said, "That's it. That's the whole story."

"Thanks for telling me. And I'm so sorry that Marco died. I would have been devastated at losing you, Sabrina. When my mother called, I came right away. Thank God you're here in my arms again." At these words, Sabrina came over to sit on his lap and tell him once again how much she loved him.

"You know, when you healed me, my mother was there. She knew you would come and she knew what you'd do. It wasn't my time and we were meant to be together. It should never have happened. I've thought about it a lot as I'm sure you have. My mother told me he didn't want to be healed or live if he couldn't have me. I don't believe a man could be happy being with a woman who didn't love him."

"Believe me. My guides would not have given me the healing powers to heal him," said James. "He had to face his own karmic lesson for what he'd done. But when I think what he brought upon you, my sympathy for him fades very quickly."

"I'm sad for his father and sister. The funeral was very traumatic. He lost his only son and heir to the largest vineyards in Tuscany. I suppose his sister Gina will inherit his world one day, but who knows?"

She continued, "The most difficult thing I have to say was in the car, I'm told. As the glove box flew open, there down by the edge of my seat, they found a gift-wrapped box and inside was the engagement ring. There was also a little note in Italian that said, 'Even this stone cannot equal the love and beauty of my Sabrina, but it does show you all of my heart that I want to give you.' It was, of course, returned to his family."

"Life is certainly something," James mused. "You could never dream that up, but you're here now. For me, that's all that's important." James looked at her again as she cleared away the breakfast table, feeling so comfortable being with the love of his life. Then he continued, "Let's pop over to the stables and talk with Kate and Sarah and go for a ride. I have to call the office, so see you upstairs if you're up for it.

"Claudia, sorry," said James on the phone. "I'm taking some time at the farm. It's been a while. Is everything alright at the bank?"

"Absolutely," assured Claudia. "Take a break. You've been going nonstop since you got back from Italy. Sir Nicholas did mention something about a meeting with some people, but he said not to bother you until you got back here."

" I was thinking, would you and Thomas like to come up for the weekend and bring Alex with you?" James asked. "Let's liven up the place a little. Penbroke has been empty for so long and needs some love."

"James, what a lovely idea! I'll talk to Thomas. We were going to play golf, but a change of venue would be a great idea. I miss the place, taking my walks and all. Know what I mean?" Claudia said, remembering the old days.

"Sabrina's here with me, so we can make a foursome."

"You devil! You're so secretive; you never tell anyone what you're up to. It's time you spent some time with your girlfriend. I'll call you."

"I'll be waiting."

Sabrina was busy drying her hair. James put on his casual clothes for a day at the estate. He wanted to devote his complete time to Sabrina before taking his long trip to China. He knew he would be tied up for months and it wasn't something he would say right away, but he would discuss it soon.

"Sabrina, how are you?" Sarah asked, clearly happy to see her. "What's happened to you? You've been through quite an ordeal. Come spend some time with me. Let's talk this out. I feel like this was something that shouldn't have happened."

"I'm doing okay," said Sabrina. "James has been such a help, and I don't know what I would have done without him."

James realized that he should have said something about the accident, to Sarah, but then in all reality, what could she have done?

The two women went off, and in view of the recent traumatic experience, it was probably good that Sarah was able to take the time for her.

James went over to see Kate at the riding stables. "You certainly do stay busy," he said to her. "Since we'll be leaving around the beginning of May, do you think Joe can manage the stables without you?"

"Yes," said Kate. "At least the riding aspect of it. However, I'll prepare one of Keith's secretaries on the financial stuff; I don't think Joe's quite up to that yet. We have a small desk here in the tack room. She can come over once or twice a day and balance up the cash, cheques, and other details. It shouldn't be too difficult. Don't worry. It'll all be organized, and I know

Mom will look in on it now and then. She's a lot like me. As long as the records are left here, she'll figure it out quickly."

"Well, that's good to know," said James. "It just takes someone to keep good records, names with payments. Keith and I will watch things to make sure customers are happy and getting the right attention. Joe has help with the riding lessons, so it'll all work. Don't worry."

It wasn't long before Sabrina was running down to the stables to join him. "James, she's so good! What a jewel you have in her. She went all over my body and helped me with my chakra alignment. She explained to me that I was holding a lot of grief and remorse over Marco's death, which was affecting my third and fourth charkas. She could see an undue amount of energy being used at those parts of my body, which was not giving the energy alignment to the rest of my body. She asked me to talk more with my guides and especially my mother. Through that, I'll release the pain of the experience."

"I appreciate you telling me," said James somewhat relieved, "because I found it difficult to broach the subject the other night. You've healed well physically. But I know that the emotional and mental pain that you had to be carrying inside you had to equal the physical injuries you had. Sarah is the person to help you understand what took place, and can guide you to a complete recovery." Then he added, "Let's go for a walk. I have some thoughts I want to share with you. In a couple of weeks I'm going to see our bank in Hong Kong. It's been a long time since we did an audit there and it's very necessary that I see the operation for myself."

"How long will you be gone?" she asked, concerned.

"I haven't wanted to tell you this, but I could be gone for at least two to three months. I see that you're well on the way to recovery, so my question to you is, are you going back to finish the courses you started at the university or what?"

"I do have a lot of catching up to do. I've now missed out on two terms, so I'd have to start over next autumn. I was thinking this might be a good opportunity to take up the modeling idea. Sir Nicholas convinced me at your twenty-first party. I thought I'd attend a very good studio in Milan and try my hand at it. You'd be surprised how many offers I've had, and with a little practice I might be able to make myself a nice living. It's not what I want to do forever; I want to be with you and be a mother and have a family. And I know that's what you want, right?"

"Yes, it is," James confirmed. "And I think you're good enough at languages already. Look at your English; it's fluent now!

"James, sir, Claudia just called and needs to talk with you," said Keith who was passing him on the driveway. He was introduced to Sabrina and said a few words in Italian. Sabrina was very impressed.

"I better start learning more Italian," said James. "Can't have Keith showing me up!"

"Don't worry. You'll be fluent by the time I get through with you," she said, putting her arms around his shoulders.

James and Sabrina went over to the farm office to call Claudia.

"James," said Claudia, "I've talked it over with Thomas and he has a dinner engagement that I must attend on Saturday evening. He suggested that you come down on Friday and spend part of the weekend with us, then stay at your flat and take Sabrina to the airport on Monday. That way you'll be closer."

"That's what we'll do. See you then."

James spent the next few days driving Sabrina around, to give her the feeling of Lincolnshire. He wanted her to know what the future may hold if they were to spend time there. She seemed to have no trouble understanding the northern dialect and received a lot of stares wherever he took her, not to mention a few wolf whistles as they passed some construction workers in Lincoln.

"Don't worry," she said, amusedly, "I'm used to that. Thanks to you, I'm walking about. I feel glad that I've made a full recovery. I see life with a little more humor. What happened has changed me a lot."

"Really? Tell me about that." He took her into a little coffee shop, as she started to talk.

"When you have a near-death experience, you realize how fortunate you are to be alive. Life must not be wasted. We must live every moment to the fullest. We are young and have our whole life before us. To be in love is the most beautiful thing a person can know. To be with you this week, this moment, makes me realize how precious these days are. I just hope we'll always feel this way, even when we're old and not so attractive."

"We get on so well. When I'm with you it's like time stands still, yet the day passes so quickly. Even when we say nothing, it just feels good walking beside you and knowing that we have a complete oneness between us. James wasn't a person to talk romantically, but when he felt it, it came so naturally.

Then it was Sabrina's turn. "When I'm with you James, I feel so special, especially, since my accident. I've never been with anyone where I just want to give them all the love I have inside me. When we one day have our children, I hope I'll give them as much love as I give you." She became a little emotional and James leaned across the little table to kiss her, to the applause of a few people around them.

They spent the next few days before going to London talking, walking, and riding on the beach. Finally, they walked to the main house and talked about how they would redecorate the rooms with a style that would fit their personalities. The rooms all held a distinct character, which was part of the original architecture. Places like kitchens and bedrooms had become outdated. The kitchen needed new countertops and cupboards, and later, cooking ovens and lighting. The bathrooms and smaller bedrooms could be made into one and then closed off from the main corridor accessing the bedroom they were meant for. Those were the days when there was house staff and a need for more bedrooms. So much had to be done and redecoration was needed almost all over the house. The main master suite was spectacular, taking up one end of the house with an unopposed view of the sea. The furniture was old and well used and the carpet had certainly seen better days. The antiques, which were of great value, were all over the house and needed attention, and in some cases, restoration.

When James's father and mother got married thirty years ago, they had made changes, but not major ones. His grandfather made the biggest changes in the twenties; business was booming then, before the stock market crash. His father had only seen real recovery several years before his death in the fifties. The shipping line and the banking business, however, still continued to grow during the thirties but at a much slower pace. His father saw the largest expansion of the business with the steamships as a young boy. James enjoyed relating his family story to Sabrina. Being a history major, along with her languages, she loved hearing stories. James also related how his father had explained about each one of the earl's paintings that stood in the huge main hallway by the entrance.

Their time together was much needed. James was now making big decisions for his career, and who better to share that with other than the love of his life. He had to know her completely. The accident had brought them closer together, but in reality, outside seeing her with her family, he had spent little time with her alone.

Friday at lunchtime, James and Sabrina packed their bags and headed out of Penbroke toward London.

****

"James, this is a beautiful home for someone that lives in London," said Sabrina, eyeing Sir Thomas's palatial mansion.

"Well, it's not the city, but it's not far away," said James. "However, it is a very prestigious house, even for this part of London. His father, I believe, bought it many years ago." James wasn't sure, but he knew that Sir Thomas had inherited the home.

"I'm looking forward to seeing Claudia again after the wedding," said Sabrina. "I'll see if she's picked up any Italian from her last visit with her mother. I remember, after the wedding, she was going to Rome to see her. Sir Thomas I don't know so well, but he looks like a true English gentleman."

"He's been like a father to me," James explained. "He's our family lawyer and his family has been taking care of our legal business for nearly a hundred years, so we go way back. He's the one that will set up the plans for buying a property and my banking in Geneva."

"James, I came back early to see Sabrina. Sabrina, you look completely recovered, as if nothing ever happened. You must be a quick healer?" responded a surprised Claudia.

Sabrina kept the real secret deep within her and then replied, "I think it's James's magical healing powers that worked. There's nothing like love to solve the wounds of the flesh." Then changing the subject: "I love your house. It's so elegant and large. It reminds me of those beautiful homes you see in the movies."

"Thomas will be here soon and then we can go out for a bite. Let's have a quick cocktail before we go. In the meantime, take your things upstairs to the guest room. You don't mind sleeping together" she winked. "I won't say anything." Claudia was a modern woman, but even in the sixties, customs were starting to change.

They both freshened up and came down to meet little Alex, who wasn't so little. He was walking everywhere, gurgling a few words as he went, holding out his toys, and longing to play with a friend.

Claudia and Sabrina started talking together about her accident. It was pleasant to see Claudia making the effort to speak Italian. James fixed himself a glass of red and sat with Alex on the floor playing with his train set. Moments later Thomas arrived.

"James. Sorry we couldn't join you at Penbroke," said Thomas, "but so glad you came to see us. I see you brought that beautiful Sabrina with you. I've booked a table at a great little place I know, so I'll just get cleaned up and be back down."

Claudia had someone to take care of Alex for the evening. They all piled into Thomas's Bentley. "James, how do you like your new car?" asked Claudia.

"It's a dream to drive after driving the Mini and the old Land Rover for the last five years," bragged James. "I haven't told Mom yet. She'll think I'm really spoiling myself, so I'll let a little time pass."

"You've worked hard getting your accounting degree. You've hit the ground running at the bank as Claudia tells me, so you deserve a car that gets you out and about," said Thomas, who quickly took the time to make Sabrina feel welcome.

"Sabrina, I'm so glad that you've made a complete recovery. We were so concerned when we heard the news."

"Thank you. sir. I feel better than I've ever felt. Of course, being with James makes all the difference."

"That's a nice thing to say. Claudia, you should tell me something like that occasionally," quipped Thomas.

"Thomas, if you were any more pampered than you are now, I'd have to hand you over to the dancing girls," said Claudia.

"You're all I can handle, so no thank you."

They pulled into the driveway to a very old pub that served high-end cuisine. The King's Jouster had been around for hundreds of years. The people who lived north of the city in this part of London had made this a favorite watering hole on a Friday night.

Sabrina loved her time with James at Penbroke, but London had more life. She observed the British fashion and what people wore in a more sophisticated neighborhood of London. It was friendly like she was used to in Milan, but quite different. *How the English love their pubs*, she thought.

Dinner was ordered with a good bottle of wine. Claudia and Sabrina went back to talking, breaking backward and forward from Italian to English.

"So James, if I know you, you've got some more plans up that sleeve of yours, so spit it out, my boy, spit it out," pushed Thomas. He had always liked James's drive and energy. Being a city man himself, he was similar, but James had a way of taking him by surprise, which entertained him enormously.

"Well, I'm glad you're up for it, because what I'm about to share with you is going to do more than surprise you."

"You've got to be kidding! Where on God's green earth are you planning now?"

"Shortly I will be off to China. I want to build that new bank building Father always talked about. It's also high time we did an audit on the bank we have there. All this taxation the labor government is putting on us does worry me though. It's hard to expand our services if all our income is taken away from us. When will governments understand that a nation's wealth lies in the creation of jobs. Heavy taxation in order to pay for debts like World War II doesn't help industry grow, when its hands are cuffed for expansion.

"I don't blame you for your thoughts, but things could change if old Heath gets in at the next election."

"I hope you are right, but I don't think this abusive personal taxation is going to go away soon. When rock stars are paying up to ninety percent, can you blame them for leaving the country? It might reduce, but the writing's on the wall. Eventually, places like Geneva and Monaco are going to be extremely expensive. I'm a Brit through and through, but enterprise is the key to wealth and prosperity; taxation from the lowest to the highest must not be allowed to stagnate growth."

"James, you've got an enormous home up north and a flat that I will sell you in a heartbeat and which you can well afford. What more do you need? The farm is paying its way now. You don't need that much to live on. So leave the money in the company and expense what you can, like we all do," Thomas said, thinking James was overreacting from his enormous ambition to build his shipping fleet and expand his banking.

"You forget, I didn't go through learning all that accounting for nothing. The property we own I want to split off from the bank here, Hong Kong, and Trans Global and charge rent. This will be the beginning of my property business. This will increase cash flow to expand the businesses we own. I want to draw up plans in Hong Kong to build a fifty-story building on the vacant property across from our existing bank there. I know Hong Kong is going to go 'gang busters'; heck, it's already started. Then I have plans later to develop and buy out other buildings. If I don't make these plans now, it's going to get more and more complicated. In a couple of months I'm leaving on our largest merchant ship to China, and when I get there, I plan to audit that bank from top to bottom."

Thomas laughed. "James, you always amaze me. Just when I think you've got everything perfectly on track, you take on these gigantic plans. I wouldn't have your balls for this. Isn't what you have enough, for God's sake?"

James passed over Thomas's words, rooted in the foundation of his forefathers' beliefs, in that it wasn't in what you inherited; it was more about what contribution he would make in his life to that which he was given charge over, and how he could make a difference for the next generation, to honor this proud tradition. He turned to Thomas. "So as my legal advisor, what do you suggest for setting things up with a bank and a lawyer in say, Geneva?"

"Look, if this is what you want, I'll do some research. Let's finish up our meal, then we can go home, have a nightcap, and really think this whole thing through. If I know you, you haven't given me half the story yet," Thomas said, still laughing and shaking his head.

"You boys having fun over there?" asked Claudia, breaking away from her conversation with Sabrina after overhearing Thomas's laughter.

"I think I need another drink before James gives me a splitting headache." Then, turning back to James, said, "I'll never forget it; when you wanted that money for the Throne Room, but you were right. Look how it's worked out. I believed you then and I believe you now. I just don't want you to run so fast that you put yourself into a cash bind, that's all."

The four of them got up to leave and return to the house. Sabrina and Claudia decided to make an early night of it and left Thomas and James to talk it all out.

"James, this is my advice: open an account at a bank in Switzerland or wherever is no difficulty. Incorporate your property business there and we can transfer any amount of funds from Lloyds; you've paid tax on that money already. Make your investments and grow the property business from there. You have to remember, however, that there would be tax implications from evaluating the original share value of today's share value and that would be enormous. What you want to do is not without merit, but my advice is to go at it one step at a time. There are provisions because you are a Peer of the Realm. As an Englishman with a very important birthright, you do have a duty to honor that. Remember the British government, and all that they have entrusted you with over the years."

James nodded his head. "I will move cautiously and evaluate every step." This was a big step and the immediate tax implications could be enormous.

"There's something else you may or may not be aware of," Thomas continued. "The Bannerman family has had a trust for over one hundred years. As tax law started to change with the inception of the Labor Party in 1921, your great-grandfathers, who always had this reserve in the bank here, moved the trust to Switzerland just before the war. The fear of Nazi domination had people investing in Switzerland from all over Europe. This family fund has existed since 1838 when the sixth earl started the bank. So for over 125 years, money has been saved in this account. There was only one time that funds were reduced and that was after the 'Great Depression' of 1929. Business came to a standstill for over two years, and then started to come back. It was really the war that kicked off ours and many other economies worldwide. This is a considerable amount, James. When I checked last time, it was close to three hundred million. You also have money from your father's annual dividends...from his shares in Bannermans since the day of his death. This money has been put into a separate trust account for you. It's over two million, but when you take money out, there will be taxes that are payable. Taxes are a horrible reality, but I will work hard with your accountants to dream up all the best scenarios, knowing what we are faced with today."

****

The next day, after leaving Thomas and Claudia, James was thinking everything through that he had discussed with Thomas. He would talk further with Claudia after taking Sabrina to the airport on Monday.

"James, I like your little Mini, but I think I prefer the Aston," joked Sabrina with a slight prod.

"Aha! You like the nicer things of life; *now* I know all about you," James said, teasingly.

"I would take you in a Mini any day over anyone else in whatever car," laughed Sabrina, putting her head on his shoulder while running her hand up his trouser leg.

"Let's go dancing this evening. I'll book a table at the Fantasy bar. You'll like that."

"Now that sounds like fun. You and I haven't danced since we've been together. I want to see if you've got any rhythm in your bones!"

He drove into the small road behind Harrod's called Walton Place and then into the gated area called Pont Street Mews. He noticed Sabrina taking it all in. "Welcome to my little London pad."

"So you have your own garage?" she asked, thinking that had to be a privilege for this part of London.

He then opened the door to the home that he would buy from Sir Thomas and had been his hangout for the last four years. "Here it is. This is where I've been since we met."

"Compared with my little apartment in Milan, this is like a palace. I love it." She gawked, taking it all in like Claudia had once done. After exploring for a bit, she said, "James, I could live here. You've got all the action of London. Restaurants... shops...and yet you have a lot of space. I love Penbroke, but we are still a young couple and we need to enjoy some nightlife when we're not working." She wondered how many young ladies he knew who wouldn't bend over backward to live in a place like this.

James was amused by her curiosity. "Well, we need to cross over the street and buy you a dress if we're going to paint the town this evening. I'm sure you didn't come prepared."

"The dress I had on last night is good enough, isn't it?" she asked, thinking that maybe he didn't like the way she looked.

James laughed. "I'm joking. I just want to spoil you and I know you didn't come packed for every occasion."

"You really want to buy me a dress?" she asked, exhilarated that he cared.

The couple walked arm in arm to the famous department store and after three hours they walked out with two dresses, two pairs of shoes, and her favorite perfume, in addition to some very sexy stockings that James insisted she had to have. "James, will you always spoil me like this? I know you're a man's man, but when I'm with you, you can be such a gentleman."

"Nothing but the best for my beautiful Sabrina."

"I'll work. You wait and see! I don't want a man to pay for *every*thing, but when we marry, you can spoil me a little more."

She went upstairs to try on her dresses and stockings for the evening. James sat downstairs reading the news, having a coffee, and catching a cigarette on the side. To his amazement, Sabrina had sneaked downstairs in her new stockings and high heels and the scantiest underwear. She silently stood leaning up against the doorway. He sensed she was there because he could smell the fragrance she had bought, and turned around to gawk.

"My God, you look stunning!" he said. She had made herself up beautifully and James drooled to see this very sexy borderline stripper, teasing him with her index finger. He grabbed hold of her in both arms and carried her all the way to his bedroom. "You know how to put a man away. You're my addiction. Just look like this every night before we go to bed, and I'll make love to you forever."

"I know the secret to a man," said Sabrina. "A woman must be his queen by day and his mistress by night. A lot of ladies of the night in Italy are much better at listening to men than their wives."

"Sabrina, you're always beautiful to me however you look, but a little spice is naughty and nice!"

Sabrina laughed. "Now that I've challenged you, what do you think turns on a woman?"

"I'll tell you later."

"You're bad. But maybe that's good," she said, laughing and giggling like a schoolgirl putting on her sexy Italian accent.

They both got dressed up for the evening. James had ordered a taxi so that they could relax and enjoy the Fantasy bar.

"All these places you take me to," cooed Sabrina. "How many times have you been here?"

"Not enough to worry about. But I'll remember tonight because you are with me."

"I think you're too clever with your answers," said Sabrina deductively. "I can see all those beautiful women looking at you. What a place! I can't wait to dance my feet off, mio amore." She was quietly playing with him, but James was cutting her no slack.

"Sabrina, they're not looking at me; they're looking at you. Don't you know by now that women are always checking out other women to see who and what she's wearing and if the competition looks too hot?" James knew he had her there, because it was the truth. When an attractive woman enters the room, men notice for sure, but women secretly stare, and watch for their man's attention.

James and Sabrina danced the night away.

"So now I have you all to myself," relished Sabrina. "I don't have to compete with any other woman in the room!" Women often had to dance with a man that they just wanted to make happy and not hurt their feelings after being kind enough to ask. She had James all to herself, finally, and it felt good. With the new rock 'n' roll music, it was a time where they could laugh at one another but also accomplish a harmony that made them look very much in sync. As the music slowed down, they had developed their own style and people enjoyed watching such a beautiful couple flow to the rhythm of the music.

"You're quite a dominant dancer, and yet now you follow me and I feel completely in time and rhythm with you," observed James.

"I know a man should lead, but so many men don't know how to dance," said Sabrina. "I can only dream of dancing the rest of my life away with the man I love. If we can feel this much harmony on the dance floor, then we should have that harmony in our life together." James could see her aura just bursting out from her with the sound of the music.

"Sabrina, you have such a beautiful way of saying things."

"Now you're thinking. That's a first for most men," she said, putting her head back and letting her beautiful long hair fall back to her waist as she laughed out loud. He picked her up off the floor and took her back to the table.

The couple enjoyed a last drink together. The entertainment and the sharing of an exciting intimate evening together was long overdue.

They were now hot and exhausted and retired to his flat.

James dreaded taking Sabrina to the airport the next day. This was the longest they'd ever been together. Promises and kisses were made at their departure. James knew that what he was about to undertake would be the most challenging test of his career yet.

CHAPTER 5

THE WORLD STAGE

Jonathan Park anxiously waited for his meeting with Andrei Khostov, a talented and upcoming lieutenant in the KGB. It was the end of winter in Russia and the hallways were damp and cold, even for this time of year. A lot of thoughts were going through his mind. He had honorably served the British Secret Service for over fifteen years. During the decisive times after World War II, it was a more defined role of espionage. Now the lines were becoming blurred. Russia was becoming ever more elusive with its new powers over the acquired countries of Eastern Europe; their isolation from the rest of the world seemed more and more apparent. He had enjoyed a high standard of living. His children went to the best schools and without the interference of the now-deceased Collin Bannerman, he had been left to his own devices. As long as he made a good return on the investments made, the shareholders were happy, or at least that's what he thought.

"Comrade, follow me," said one of the officers in uniform as he was ushered down long corridors, past offices of busy secretaries to Andrei Khostov's office.

"Jonathan, come in," said Andrei. "It's so good to see you again. I thank you for making the trip on such short notice." He was still a young man in his late thirties who had been singled out for promotion. His background in the police force and having come from an educated family who taught at the university in Leningrad gave him a leg up in the growing Russian hierarchy. He was fortunate to have had an education not available to most Russians.

Andrei continued, "I will get to the point. We are concerned with China's position in French Indochina. This Chairman Mao is hell-bent on taking both the north and the south regions of the country. Obviously, we agree with his Communist implementation after many years of French rule, and North Vietnam wants that. However, it appears that the Americans are involved and supporting the South Vietnamese. The ruler there, Ngo Dinh Diem, is a staunch Roman Catholic and is culturally French. From all accounts he is willing to fight for what he believes to be a capitalistic society. This poses a problem for us. If someone in the British government could intercede and let Chairman Mao have his way to support the integration of North and South Vietnam, a lot of cost, lives, time, and effort could be saved for all of us. What is a minor irritation at the moment could turn quite a show, if the Americans don't back down. For us and for the Americans, I can hardly see how taking this country is worth the effort. It is, after all, a country of Asian people who are far more culturally aligned with China than its present inhabitants."

Jonathan Park thought his reasoning was more than plausible but somehow it didn't add up. "I'll of course make your thoughts known to our intelligence service," he said, "but after what you've told me, they will ask me why Russia would care."

"China cannot afford this war, even though they have the manpower for it. After World War II, the Chinese are heavily indebted to us for protecting them from the Japanese invasion of their own country, as indeed the United States are, and I would hope the rest of the world."

Jonathan got it. Russia obviously needed to be repaid for its support of China and everyone knew China was militarily weak and was undergoing serious civil war among themselves. "So if I can convince the British government to intercede, what assurances do they have from you that you will not continue this Cold War effort for military superiority?"

"That's another subject and a huge one. The Americans have become extremely powerful since the last war and we do not wish to antagonize anyone in the West. However, we are not going to sit back and watch American imperialism dominate this planet. We have a right, too."

"I'll have a word with my people and see what we can do. No one wants war; the world is trying to heal itself from the cost of the last one."

"After we hear from you, can we meet in Hong Kong? You know we have an interest in peace, but not in the eyes of the Western media. We like Hong Kong and would be prepared to invest with a bank like Bannermans. We like a bank that's privately owned. Business confidences can be held, all these corporate people don't understand the way business is always done, and they take forever making decisions. Your bank has had British owners for hundreds of years and my administration would far rather do business with the British than the Americans. I can see a good relationship developing where the East can meet the West in a private environment. The Americans are still a young country and have a lot to learn about the older world, even if we are all trying to advance. It is always good to retain some of the old values and traditions. You know us Russians; we like some of your ways. I'm sure I can convince my boss to come to Hong Kong and hopefully meet your new lord. We've heard a little about him and what we hear, we like."

Jonathan knew every Russian liked to party. Vodka and the good-looking Asian/European women of Hong Kong always helped reach a deal easier and more pleasantly.

"Keep in touch. There's much at stake here," said Andrei, knowing that he had done exactly what was expected. Make the British stall the Americans long enough to give the Russians enough time to implement their master plan.

****

It was now the beginning of May 1966 and he knew the trip would take him well into June. He would be entering the hottest part of the year in China. James was busy making all his arrangements for his long trip to Hong Kong. Kate would arrive soon for updates on the bank's position in Hong Kong from Claudia and Roger Bell, Bannermans' own chartered accountant. He was now expecting to meet with Duncan Gilmour, the fleet captain who was presiding over the long journey to China.

Rose directed him to the conference room and brought them some tea.

"Well, Duncan, I'm told you are the man of the seas," said James. "I look forward to this journey. I also expect to learn from you and understand all about our shipping business."

"It will be an honor, your Lordship," replied Duncan. "I can't think of anything that makes me happier than to have the very first sea captain of our company traveling with us."

"Duncan, call me James when it's just us, and sir when it's formal. I'm sure for you, this whole adventure is old hat, but for us landlubbers it'll be quite an experience and one that I hope to learn a lot from. In this way, I can understand the needs of our business for the future, and learn a little about our competition," said James, wanting this loyal man of three generations to feel totally at ease. This was the man who was the very heart of Bannermans' history on the high seas.

"James, sir, there's much to discuss in order to bring our shipping fleet up to date," started Duncan, "We've got good engineers, experienced deck officers, and able sea hands, but the equipment is getting dated...and that's where we need to step up to the plate. I understand that you will be visiting our bank there. I think that's a wonderful idea. In my travels I've noticed that someone, like yourself, should take an upper hand. We're all one company and the staff that handles the cargo in Hong Kong, in my opinion, needs a bit of a shake-up." Duncan was not a paper pusher, but any captain that knows how to keep logs and records and run a staff knows a thing or two about the day to day. This voyage would prepare him for what he needed to learn."

"Monday, a week from now I'll be at the ship in Tilbury docks, and I look forward to us getting to know each other better," said James. "I hope Claudia has told you who will be coming on the trip and that you'll have the necessary room. That being said, please don't be kicking anyone out of his room on my behalf. We're all at sea and we expect the same treatment as everyone else."

"Message noted, sir."

James liked Duncan and marveled at how fortunate the company was to have men like him—three generations, and his own son, fourth generation. He was sure there were many other stories of family employment and he wanted to learn about them all.

Claudia rushed into the conference room. "James, before you leave, can we have a word?"

"I'm all yours. Shoot."

"Nicholas called, and the man you met with him. They

would like a meeting with you before you go to China."

"Please set it up," said James. "I'm fairly flexible, so let me know."

Nicholas called him directly and told him that the meeting was urgent and it would take place at the Dorchester Hotel off Park Lane, and to be there by 5:00 p.m. He was told to ask for the Doctor's Club meeting.

James was anxious to meet the group and learn more about this elite society that played such an important role in the country's destiny.

James arrived on time and after giving his name was ushered to a separate room next to where the meeting was being held. Jeremy Soames came in to join him. "James, there are some formalities that we have to go through before you can be received in the meeting. I have to swear you in. I also have something to share with you. I too was on Atlantis and was there with you."

"Really? In what role, might I ask?"

"I was your manservant, Orga, your faithful and educated guide that carried your chair across to Egypt for one of your wives. We waited for you to come and join us. I am fully aware of your Throne Room and have in fact been to Penbroke without your knowledge. I, as a day visitor, traveled through the vortex to meet our master Czaur," said Jeremy, looking more friendly and human in his persona than James had seen before.

"Well, you're certainly full of surprises. I can now see how aptly suited you are for being the leader of this brotherhood. I assume you've been chosen by the masters to lead our nation toward a higher purpose and direction," said James, looking a little shocked.

"Precisely. There will come a day when it will be your turn. I am, in a sense, your guide while you are on this planet. This has been the purpose of my life, to live and prepare a way for your eventual evolvement after me, to continue the work that was started hundreds of years ago."

"People like us have a higher purpose and have been entrusted from above to lead our nation. To work toward the evolvement of other nations, who indeed have their own advanced souls. Our purpose as messengers is to lead our nation toward this spiritual reality. This universe and what we refer to as *divinessence* want us to provide that understanding. There is an opposite force, as I'm sure you're aware. We must do everything within our power to stop it from becoming a reality. You now know who the real Jeremy Soames is. Remember what I told you in our first meeting? My name is Jeremy Soames, but then again, it might not be."

"I think I understand," said James. "So you've known all along?"

"Of course. I knew your father well and the writings in your notebook from the seventh earl. If you hadn't got your loan from the bank, I would have stepped into the equation at an earlier time. Sir Nicholas is not aware of my knowledge, but with time, he will open that door and will be of great assistance to you, but not yet. You must remain silent on the matter and let our masters reach out to those that we must guide in their own good time."

"You and I have a great responsibility, then?"

"Indeed. Now let us continue with the formalities and in time you and I will get to know each other extremely well. Our meetings consist of twenty-seven people who are part of this so-called Inner Sanctum. However, not everyone is present unless it's a meeting of the highest priority. You can understand that we all have other work as well, and we do this without cost, as a chosen person of good standing, for our country." Jeremy enjoyed the astonished look on James's face as he observed how much he was starting to grow.

Jeremy started with the formalities and Nicholas was asked

to join in at that moment as a witness. James had to swear his loyalty to uphold the secrecy and content of all meetings. The names of all the people he should meet and others that he would meet in the future, who may not be present. It was a long and tedious process, but one that was a tradition and had served the country well over the years.

"James, we started a little earlier to discuss some past matters on a previous agenda. We will now enter the meeting room and the people here will now introduce themselves so that they can get to know who you are, and the same for you."

"Ladies and gentlemen, I am honored to introduce James Bannerman, who is now the tenth Earl of Penbroke and chooses to follow the proud tradition of his father and great-grandfathers before him." Jeremy Soames spoke proudly on behalf of his latest member.

Jeremy continued, "I'll start the ball rolling. At present I am the chairman of this committee. You, James, have sworn your allegiance as was necessary to uphold all that is discussed between these walls and to protect the privacy of each one of our committee members. My profession is as a lawyer and judge of this nation's highest court in the House of Lords. Please continue, starting with Your Royal Highness."

His Highness stood up, "James, I'm sure you know me well, as Prince Edward. I was at your father's funeral."

The second person stood up. "I am Linda Burgess, head of this nation's education department."

"I am Rupert Combs, President and Dean of Oxford University."

"I am Robin Forsyte, Archbishop of Canterbury."

James was amazed at the honorable profiles in the room, people from all esteemed positions of authority. He was among the highest in their profession. Engineers, scientists, biologists, doctors, and one person from the current political party's cabinet were all present to debate the most thought-provoking decisions needed to be made for the day. Jeremy Soames then continued to proceed with the meeting's agenda.

"James, it has come to our knowledge through our Secret Service and that of your managing director in Hong Kong, Jonathan Park, that he met recently with a high-ranking official in the KGB at his offices in Moscow. The Secret Service department, based on the information he gave them, has recommended that we intercede in the American involvement in South Vietnam. The Russians believe that supporting South Vietnam against the North will only end up in a long and expensive war to preserve a society that wants to have its own right to democracy and continue on its path as a capitalistic society. The Russians argue that the North Vietnamese are already Communist and the rank and file of South Vietnam is too. So why is America supporting a man named Dinh Diem? He is a Roman Catholic, and a believer of the old values of French Indochina. The Russians believe that most of his people don't really care and culturally, would rather join their allies in the North. So the question is, why would the United States escalate a war in that region if this is the case?"

Rupert Combs, the renowned historian, attempted to answer. "It's possible that the Americans know something we don't. From my perspective, Russia is a Communist country and so is China. Maybe there is an ulterior motive. If communism can spread through Indochina, then what's next? For example, what about Malaya, Indonesia, the Philippines, and potentially, Hong Kong? Maybe Russia is behind this more than China. Japan, or rather, everyone knows that China is militarily weak."

"I'm headed to that region of the world shortly," said James. "Perhaps I can talk with Jonathan and find out firsthand what was discussed. As a family, we are heavily vested over there, and any political undertaking by the Russians and the Chinese is of extreme importance to our long-term plans."

Brenda Mason, who was in charge of the department of customs and excise for the United Kingdom, chimed in. "I believe that we must first discuss this matter with the American embassy and the CIA. I'm sure the Americans are not doing this without good reason. The Russians could be using us as a form of tactical delay in order to muster whatever they can to this region of the world. It's no secret that they would desire a seaport in that region of the world and a Communist region could be a great threat to the Western world. A complete alliance between China and Russia and all the neighboring countries and islands would give the Russians what they've always wanted. For those of you who have studied the location of the USSR, you will know that their desire for a seaport is of extreme importance. The Artic Circle has two outlets, one through the Bering Straights between Alaska and the other between Iceland and Ireland. In all cases, they can be easily monitored. The shipbuilding they have in Leningrad has to pass between Norway, Sweden, and Denmark. Again this can be well monitored. The last is in the Black Sea where they have to pass by Istanbul. In a sense they are landlocked and having access to any ocean unimpeded would be of tremendous strategic importance for their gunboats and nuclear submarines."

The opinions and thoughts were coming in from all directions, but the overwhelming opinion is that more information was needed from the Americans. Russia was trying to use the British as a delay tactic. The Russians wanted to arm the North Vietnamese in the fight for the South.

It was agreed that a meeting with the American ambassador was required immediately and a final decision could be made from there.

Jeremy Soames had urgently contacted the head of the SIS (Secret Intelligence Service) in order to have the prime minister arrange for a meeting with the American ambassador. He also asked James if future meetings could be held at Bannerman's Bank, like the old days when his father was alive. Here there would be less attention drawn to their membership and they would enjoy a more private discussion, which people would consider as being in the normal course of business.

The next morning Jeremy Soames called James to meet him at his office.

"James, I'm here because of your important trip to Hong Kong," he started. "Apparently, the Americans know that the Russians are behind this, and furthermore, they intend to dominate those other islands in the Indian Ocean. It's as we expected; if they had control over the Indian Ocean, they could potentially cut off trade to the East in a big way, which would hurt our economies. It is believed that they want to control entry in and out of the Persian Gulf. Entry into the Gulf is by way of the Gulf of Oman, and through a very narrow entryway known as the Strait of Hormuz. There is no doubt that a plan is underway to dominate the shipping lancs in the Indian Ocean and cutting off our oil supply, or entry into the Indian Ocean, let alone the Gulf region, could play havoc with the Western economy. More importantly, the Americans are taking a controlling effort to support South Vietnam and stop the threat of communism. A united Russia and China could eventually pose a new world threat. Success in this unimportant region of the world would give the Russians what they've always wanted: unimpeded entry from their own seaport to control and disrupt Western trade throughout the world. The outcome of that could be World War III...and no one wants that."

"I had understood that when Khrushchev was in power," said James, "there was a strict difference of opinion about Communist ideology between him and Chairman Mao. So what has brought about a new sense of unity? You were a little younger when the Americans tried to capture Cuba, with American Cubans in the United States. Anyway, this fiasco initiated by President Eisenhower and implemented by JFK ended up as a tragic loss known as 'The Bay of Pigs', off the south coast of Cuba. This was a result of the newly formed regime by Fidel Castro, in order to create an alliance with Russia, as a result of the previous corrupt administration of Cuba being in league with the American government. Anyway, this led to the implementation of defence missiles in Cuba against the US. Kennedy after a very close encounter that could have led to war finally talked Kruschev out of this, but the Russians don't want the US, which has become the number one nation in the world for defense, to gain any further dominance. It's a long story. Read up on it. You will see how touchy this Russian-American relationship is. Hence we now have Vietnam. We will talk further on this matter when you return."

Jeremy then continued, "It appears that due to China's weak economic position, Leonid Brezhnev has regained that relationship. Brezhnev is not as outspoken as Khrushchev, or as opinionated, and rules very much through democratic opinion within their politburo. This has resulted in a new firm resolve to rebuild China. There now seems to be a fanatical desire from within the Russian government to be a world super power, to overthrow what they describe as American imperialism."

"I will talk with Jonathan to try and understand what the Russians want," said James, anxious to know more about the whole situation.

"James, be very careful in revealing how much you know. We have not trusted him for many years. It's unfortunate and happens very frequently to those agents that are far from our daily direction. The seduction of money and influence makes these agents vulnerable to becoming double agents. No doubt the Russians are using him at this stage, but beware, they may want to invest with you and draw you into their long-term plans. Believe me, they have all the power and money to make the world look like a very rosy place. It is our belief that Jonathan owns a couple of nightclubs in Kowloon, and it's Russian money that's made that possible. Take a hard look at your loan portfolio; there may be some connections there, too. We've noticed from our undercover agents who are at the UK's ambassador's office that he has a very high standard of living, something that I don't think your bank pays. Many things to lookout for James; just remember you can always pop over to Alan Archer's office, who's the UK's ambassador there, and news through the normal channels will filter through to us."

James and Jeremy shook hands and then James departed. He had a lot to consider on his journey to the East. It would certainly be a new experience. He now had to carefully think through just what information he should impart to Kate and Roger so that they could look deeply into the bank's affairs.

CHAPTER 6

THE JOURNEY TO CHINA

James had a long conversation with Claudia before making his way to the docks. She knew how to contact him on the ship if necessary and at the bank in China. He had packed a larger than normal suitcase for the long journey. His anticipation grew as he walked up the gangplank to the largest vessel in the fleet, the *Victoria*, named by his father in honor and loving memory of his mother, James's grandmother. It was also appropriate as the name of the harbor for the Port of Hong Kong was Victoria, after Queen Victoria.

None other than Captain Duncan Gilmour, who looked every bit the part, with his old traditional uniform and silver beard, greeted James. The merchant vessels of the day did not require officers or seamen to wear uniforms, but it was normal for a company like Trans Global to want their employees in a uniform that bears their name as well as the company's on the back. They also required their officers to wear traditional navy uniform. It looked professional and set a respectable example within the industry.

He helped him with his luggage to his stateroom, which sat atop the tall tower toward the rear of the ship.

"By God! I've got one hell of a view up here." James looked nervously down from the balcony at the open hull being loaded with containers.

"Yes, sir. Don't be standing out here when it gets a little windy once we get out of here," said Duncan. "My office and quarters are one deck below you, so when you're ready come on down and I'll show you around."

James was surprised by the space in his cabin. He thought that he would be in a bunk bed for the next few weeks and was presently surprised at the bathroom amenities and the size of his bed. He had a magnificent view at the front, side, and rear of the ship.

After unpacking his belongings and changing into something less formal, he made his way down to Duncan's quarters.

"Aye-aye, Captain."

"So let's go take a tour of the old girl, eh!" They started down in the engine room. The *Victoria* was a steamship built in the late forties after the war. There was a control room for the engineers behind the massive twin-engine monsters. The heat down there had to be something, but the lads were used to it. They all wished for the day when the ship could be modernized with diesel engines. From there they went upward to the bridge. This is where the main ship's controls were set out and the deck officers could keep a sharp eye on all the cargo that was on board and steer the ship toward its navigated course. In the hull where the doors to the main deck were now open, they were loading the containers for the voyage. When the hull doors were closed, they would then load the six helicopters produced by Westland. They were being shipped for the coast guard to patrol the islands of Hong Kong. James visited the staterooms for the staff and seamen. The facilities were adequate but needed updating. He saw the kitchens and the main seating area where the lads could spend time in their off-duty hours.

Later that afternoon, Duncan introduced James to the first officer, John Higgins, who was his number one deckhand and his assistant, Jim Hall. The third, in order to complete round-the-clock watch, was on duty. The other first officer was the ship's engineer, Ray Stallings, who also had an assistant. Between them, they constituted the main body of people that ran the complete operation of the ship. Moving this cargo across the world required the best. When it came to hauling high-value goods like helicopters, everything had to be well tied down. Kate and Roger arrived soon after and they were shown to their quarters.

A loud noise was let out from the ship's siren as they left port. James enjoyed watching the crew release the boat from the dock and maneuver the ship out to the waterway and onto the river Thames. It was a new experience for James. They passed Tower Bridge, the Tower of London, and many of the buildings he'd seen from land. The ship slowly made its way out to the Thames estuary and then into the English Channel, and the long journey suddenly lay ahead of them.

That evening after having a drink with Duncan, everyone gathered at the captain's table for dinner, which gave James an opportunity to talk to the staff. He wanted to know how to update the engines and increase capacity, and for some of his fleet they would sell off the older ships to third-world countries and upgrade into newer, larger diesel engines. There was no question that with more speed and more carrying capacity, Trans Global could quickly double its revenues. The business was there, and their ships had been carrying to full capacity for a number of years now. They had the longest history of any shipping line in the business and they were able to offer very competitive rates since all their ships were paid for. It was now a question of morale, having later equipment, and taking advantage of the opportunities that lay in the container business. It would command much bigger ships that could go faster with the same amount of staff. The possibilities were endless and James could see it from all the information he was receiving. Containers were still in their early stages, but positioning the company at this strategic moment could elevate them into becoming one of the largest shipping fleets in the world.

"Sir, what d'ya think of our ship?" asked Duncan, in his Scottish brogue, putting James on the spot.

"I can tell you that I have a lot of work to do. I see we need a lot more facilities. I will try to learn everything I can off each of you, so that I can go home and raid our piggy bank. Shipping has been a proud tradition for the Bannermans, and I want us to remain one of the foremost shipping lines in the business."

Everyone cheered and clapped. It had been a long time since they had the chance to sit with an owner, and to have James with them for the next month was something they'd all been looking forward to.

After dinner, James took a moment to walk out on deck as the sun started to drop in the sky. He lit up a cigar and looked out over the sea. He started to meditate about all that had happened since Sabrina had left and he wondered what lay in store on this journey. He was here to learn. He took time over the week to look at people's auras and energies. He liked the member group of the Inner Sanctum he'd joined; the golden energy that emerged at the Dorchester Hotel made him feel that there was good in the people. Jeremy Soames was truly committed to giving all his spare time to do what was best for the country, and was more than the right man for the task.

He thought about his guides and knew that he would now come in contact with a darker force than he'd known. He would know by their energies. He wondered why people like Brezhnev and Mao wanted to hold others under such control. Did they truly believe that this was for the greater good, or was it a government ideology that allowed them a way of life that they'd never known before? Enterprise and capitalism had to be the way of the world. The wealth of a nation is its people, not the ranting and ravings of an exclusive elite. Hadn't the world under the Nazi occupation of Europe learned anything? He thought that countries like Russia and China had such a vast illiterate and poor electorate, and that was the only way this type of megalomaniacal belief could survive. One day, in their own cultural way, they would have to eventually see that the opportunity for a person to have freedom of choice and have the possibility of making something of his or her life had to win out from a society of such strict autocratic rule.

James noticed, as he was looking out to sea rounding the north coast of France, that the weather in the distance looked dark and carried a heavy cloud cover. It also appeared that the seas were quite choppy as evidenced by the white tips of the waves. The sun had now already set, so he descended to the captain's quarters to ask what measures had been taken to secure everything in the event of a storm.

Not mincing words, the captain declared, "It looks like we're in for some stormy weather. I'm going to the bridge. Care to come?"

"I'll follow."

"These seas in the Bay of Biscay are extremely unpredictable."

As they entered the bridge, Duncan gave orders for all the helicopters above deck to be checked to see that all the ties were good and tight. "All we need is one of those copters breaking loose."

"Aye, Captain. I'm on it. The lads are out there," stated First Officer John Higgins.

"Good. Wish we'd tarp covered those before leaving."

"Well it's too late...now."

The storm was moving at a rapid pace and the first waves could be clearly felt. The wind was starting to pick up and the first officer, John Higgins, gave the word for all deckhands to get off the main deck immediately. It seemed one young lad was not taking the order and was trying desperately to anchor down the cross tubes on one helicopter that was moving about.

"My God! If he doesn't get that strap tightened, he'll never survive!" In the distance was a forty-foot wave. Everyone could feel the swell as the ship was being drawn in like a tiny cork. John called out on the speakers again, but the higher the winds blew, the more difficult it became for the young man to anchor the helicopter. When the wave hit, the wind blew him right up in the air with the man holding onto the strap. The water washed across the deck and pushed the helicopter sideways.

"He's got to let go or he'll be lost," John yelled out on the speakers, but to no avail. To watch this poor person go up and down was a sight no one wanted to witness. Finally, he let go. After smashing his body on the ship's railings, he fell onto the floor of the main deck. No one could do anything. The waves were now coming at the ship with such impetuosity that it would be life threatening to walk out there.

"Leave him where he is. There's nothing we can do until the storm calms," said Duncan.

However, there was another person who had somehow crawled under a lifeboat and was desperately trying to throw him a rope. The young man lay there lifeless as the waves washed over him again and again. Everyone watched in horror as the helicopter kept moving around. It hadn't hit anything yet, but if it broke loose, it would wreak havoc. It took over an hour to traverse this angry storm before the sea began to calm. Men from all over scrambled onto the main deck; the nurse and her aids had a stretcher and they did all they could to get the young man to the infirmary. The others were able to lash down the helicopter, but they all knew there would be hell to pay for such an oversight.

They entered the Port of Bilbao, on the northern coast of Spain, at three o'clock in the morning, and the ambulance was there to take young Stephen Jenkins to the hospital. The nurse on board held out little hope for his survival. When he saw her trying to hold back tears, James realized that he knew her. "Vivian, is that you?"

"James? James Bannerman, I had no idea you were on this ship. I had signed up a year ago so that I could see what it was like aboard a ship with the possibility of working in Hong Kong."

"That young man, will he survive?" asked James anxiously.

"I doubt it. His head has been hit so hard; only a miracle could save him."

"Where was he taken?" he asked.

She gave him all the particulars and James asked Duncan if he could go ashore to see how he was doing.

"James, your Lordship, I doubt there's much you can do," said Duncan, surprised at his request.

"I know. But seeing something like that makes me take it personally. I want to see that he gets the finest care and the best doctor." Against his better judgment, Duncan asked the ground staff to drive James to the hospital.

James went to the emergency operating room and spoke with the doctor on duty. The doctor didn't give him much hope. James said he knew the young man's family and requested a few minutes with him. The doctor reluctantly agreed and James entered. He was alone behind a curtain and James could only imagine what this poor pathetic soul had just gone through to save a helicopter above his own life. His hands started to glow with the heat and he placed his right hand on his forehead and took the other to his left hand and then he felt the force of unimaginable strength enter him. It was the same experience as he'd had with Sabrina. James knew his guides had wanted him to do this for Stephen Jenkins, who had been prepared to give his life. He then withdrew. He knew it had worked and the heart monitor and his vital signs jumped back to life.

"Nurse, I believe with a little patience, this young man is going to recover," James said, confidently.

Her English was poor, but she started to call the doctor and he came rushing into the room. "It's a miracle. He must have a lot of fight in him."

"He's a strong guy and I know he wouldn't give up. We need men like him. He'll become a great seaman one day, if he's not already." James said that he would send orders and compensation. He asked to have him sent home to his people, when he was ready.

James, exhausted, returned to the ship at six in the morning. He quickly went to see Vivian to tell her the news. She broke down with emotion and hugged him for caring so much about the young lad. He left his instructions with Vivian for Stephen Jenkins and made his way to his bed.

It was almost midday when James arose. He went down to the lower decks toward the canteen. To his surprise, he was met with loud cheers and applause. News had traveled fast and many were relieved to know that young Stephen Jenkins had survived the tempestuous storm and the terrible bashing he had received. People didn't know to what extent James had played in his recovery. What he'd done had made a difference. And that was enough for the crew. James saw Kate and Roger sitting at a table together and walked over to join them.

"So while the rest of us were getting our beauty sleep, his Lordship is out there saving the world?" asked Kate with her usual teasing grin.

"Just doing what anyone would have done. I'm so glad he made it. I was there to make sure the best people, doctors, and nurses were making it possible." James didn't want her to assume anything more.

At that moment, a man came over and introduced himself. "Sir, my name is Ron Jenkins. I'm Stephen's father. I work in the boiler room on this ship. I cannot thank you enough for the time and trouble you went to, to see that my son was given the finest care and attention. I can now say that I'm proud to be working for a shipping line where the owner places that much consideration on one employee." The man was quite emotional and his words moved James greatly.

"Mr. Jenkins, no one should die for a helicopter," said James. "Nothing on this ship is worth the life on any man. It was my duty to see that your son or any one of you should have the very best carc and attention. I'm glad I was there to be of assistance."

They were fast making their way down the coast of Portugal toward the Mediterranean Sea. James walked the main deck to look at the helicopter that broke loose. He was happy to see that they had now put tarpaulin over all the six of them to stop any type of weather or wind getting at them. It had been a gross oversight to not do that in the first place. They had been covered with a corrosion-proof liquid, but it wasn't enough to sustain them against the high wind and the waves crashing across the deck.

Duncan was concerned, as captain of the ship. He felt he should have known better. He and his staff were taking a great risk with merchandise of this value, not to mention a potential loss of life.

"As captain, you and your staff should have known better," said James after Duncan had relayed his feelings to him. "In all the years you've been at sea have you not shipped merchandise like these helicopters before? If I was your captain, what punishment would you place upon me?" James was understandably upset and, under normal circumstances, this man should be demoted. James was carefully thinking the matter through.

"The truth of the matter is that the order was given and it was planned to be carried out today," said Duncan, thoughtfully. "It should have been done before leaving the dock. I have questioned all my staff and I am as much to blame as they are. We all had time to secure those helicopters. I believe I should step down as captain and take some shore leave, sir."

"Duncan, with a record like yours and a family history of being at sea, it is unthinkable that this happened," said James. "If all the precautions had been taken and then something unforeseeable took place, I could understand, but I have to agree that this oversight is too great to dismiss. I will give you my decision by the end of the day."

James was in a difficult position. At least one of them should have known better. Yes, Duncan was the captain and it must come from the top, but the fact that no one else had seen this possibility wasn't good either. One man having to take the blame for everyone made the decision much harder. James decided to walk back to the captain's quarters and discuss the matter further.

"James, come in," Duncan said. "I've asked John Higgins to come up if you don't mind, so that if you make the decision of my leaving, he will have to carry on with the duties as captain."

"That's fine, but if you'd told him to carry this out, why didn't he follow your orders? To my mind he's just as responsible as you are."

"Captain, you asked to see me?" John Higgins arrived, cap in hand and very concerned with the outcome of their future career with the ship.

"John, I would like to know if you were told to put tarpaulin over those helicopters and why this was not carried out?" asked James, still feeling he didn't have all the facts.

"Well, sir, I'd checked the radar as we always do," ventured John nervously. "We check for bad weather, so we know where we can slow down or speed up and navigate a course to avoid the possibility of endangering the men and our cargo. There was no sign of any bad weather in the Bay of Biscay, which was a relief, as it is one of the world's best-known trouble spots. I had instructed the men to tarp the helicopters today, as I know we're going to hit some choppy weather before the night's out as we round Gibraltar."

He paused, then added, "Sir, I know how it looks, but we don't normally cover the helicopters or goods of a similar nature because as much as tarpaulin can be helpful in a situation like the one we experienced last night, they can create serious heat problems when we get into the Mediterranean from the sun. That is, the incessant sun without a breeze will destroy the corrosive spray and then the damage could be harmful to the helicopter. After a storm, it's normal practice to take off the tarps and allow the sea breeze to keep the copter as cool as we can. Ideally, the helicopter should be on a deck with a roof. That being said, look at all the planes and helicopters on ships and aircraft carriers throughout the world.

"The problem here was twofold: A storm that we knew nothing about and a loose strap. Had that strap been tighter, I don't think any one of us would be having this discussion. Sir, I would like to thank you for what you did to save that young man's life. A disaster has been averted and I, for one, will never trust the Bay of Biscay when it comes to weather reports. They seem to come out of nowhere and disappear just as quickly. I believe the fate of England would have been different for the Spanish Armada if it weren't for the Bay of Biscay. So I always try to look on the positive side."

"Well, I can't argue with your logic," said James, smirking

a little, "other than we must make more thorough checks, especially on cargo above deck. If you know of risk areas like the Bay of Biscay, don't take chances again. You men are the experts. The unexpected does happen, and we all know that. If it's a result of human error, then we must take measures to check and double-check. I believe your enlightened explanation on the facts at least restores my faith in you, and we have no need to discuss the matter further."

Seeing that the men were relieved, James blew out a sigh of relief and decided to take a quick nap and recharge. It had been a short night and a challenging day with a positive ending. He slept right through to the next morning and got up early to walk the ship. He noticed that John Higgins's prediction of bad weather near Gibraltar had been accurate and now they were out into the sun again. He saw the men undoing the tarps, as he'd said, and now it all made complete sense.

James sat with Duncan that evening and took advantage of the time to know him better.

"So Duncan...tell me about yourself and how you got into this business."

"It's a long story, but my grandfather and my father worked for Trans Global and now my son does. I started out as an oiler and a greaser in the engine room and worked my way up. I've even been a cook when we had one that fell ill. There's not much I don't know about running a ship. My family is from county Durham and we grew up in Tyneside right where the ships are built, so it was a natural direction for all of us. Many of my cousins worked in the collieries, but they had a poor life. They got paid well as time went by, but the health hazards weren't worth it. Today with equipment advances, it's made the job easier but it's still a hard life. My son isn't on this ship but he and I prefer it that way; it's good that he gets his own experience like we all had. I'm fifty-five now and I love sailing the seas and couldn't think of doing anything else."

Suez, the ship entered into the Red Sea and was now on its second leg of the journey.

James then challenged Kate to a game of ping-pong. The name sounded appropriate, playing *ping-pong* on the way to *Hong Kong*. Kate couldn't wait. After practicing for a quarter of an hour where both parties were holding back on their techniques, Kate offered to start the ball to see who would serve. She won the service and off she went like a warrior charging into battle. James let her pull ahead and was quietly observing her tricks. He could see she was an out-and-out attacker. Pulverize the opposition then you can back off, or at least that's what she thought. She was at least five points ahead when James started to slowly close the gap. The more intense she became, the more mistakes she made, and by the time they got to fifteen, it was a tie game.

She then started to risk less and concentrated on maximizing every single point. James could read a lot about a person in sports. He then turned the tables on her and absolutely started to blitz his way into the lead. Over the next five points she could only get one. Then came his defiant, just-over-the-net final point, which Kate couldn't save because he was hitting the ball so hard that she was standing too far from the table.

"So you think you got the better of me. That was only round one," she dared, laughing. "I'll wear you down yet." They played several more games, but James proved to be the dominant player and now he could feel he was at least better in one sport than her. Roger watched with heated anticipation and none of them could stop shouting and laughing.

"I'll buy the beers. I'm too damn hot to play anymore." James had to work hard to beat Kate, who had given him a run for his money.

"I'll get you eventually. Just wait," Kate said in the very quality James loved about her.

The stop in Cochin on the southern coast of western India

was brief and then they were off to their final destination.

That evening James met with John Higgins and felt it was important to review the conversation he had with Duncan before he reached Hong Kong.

"After some discussion with Duncan," James started, "I've learned that you are someone that wouldn't mind having a job on shore to help administrate our shipping fleet. Would you agree?"

"Oh sir, that would be an answer to a prayer," John said, perking up. "My kids are young. When I was single, it wasn't hard being away from home, but now I miss my wife and family. I hadn't said anything to anyone, but I was seriously looking for a post with a company that could offer advancement in the management side of the shipping business."

"Well, tell me about yourself."

"I had a good education at a grammar school in Bristol, and then with the war on, I served in the Royal Navy. Ever since being a youngster, I have had a fascination for boats and all types of ships. I started out as any young lad does in the boiler room on steamships, and at the end of the war I worked in the merchant navy while doing my studies to become a ship's engineer. I passed that exam, and shortly afterward, joined Trans Global as an officer and ship's engineer. I've slowly worked my way up to become a deck officer so I could be proficient in all aspects of running a merchant vessel. My next goal would have been captain. As a first officer I know I could do that without any trouble."

"Duncan says so, too," said James. "He's a great believer in your abilities."

"I couldn't work for a better captain. He trusts me and allows me to make decisions on my own. It's because of him that I've been able to advance. So sir, what is it you have in mind?" John asked with extreme enthusiasm.

"Well, I'm looking for a general manager of the company

and I know you're young at thirty-seven, so I think you could do the job."

"I feel sure I could! As long as I had support in the financial area. Please understand that math was my best subject, but if one is to manage a company well, one must have good, fast, and accurate financial data."

"I couldn't agree more, and that you will have," assured James. "As a chartered accountant myself, I totally believe in having accurate financial information on all areas of the business, so you can track where improvements need to be made." James paused for emphasis, and then lowered the boom: "How do you feel about managing over one thousand employees worldwide?"

"It's a lot of responsibility, but I'm not concerned. I will learn a lot as I go and I know you have some experienced staff in place that can help."

"Good. I want to now share with you some of the plans I have for the future and I would like your opinion. First, I'd like to move us out from London to two places: Felixstowe for the container ships, and Southampton for all our other shipping needs. The container business's growing in leaps and bounds. The next step is to upgrade our fleet. You have an engineering background; that's important. I would like you start working on a plan for upgrading, replacing, and buying merchant ships. It's a rough estimate, but if we can grow at ten percent per annum in ten years, we could be at a hundred ships. I see most of that growth in container ships."

"I like the idea of getting out of London and I know Duncan has mentioned that many times to me. That's a lot to think about. When would you like to start with this change?"

"Now. Nigel Thompson is no longer with us. We need to do this soon, like when you return from Hong Kong. In the meantime, when you have a spare moment, you can be putting your thoughts and ideas together for the future. You'll obviously have a pay review, and there will be a bonus incentive as well."

"I couldn't be more excited, sir. May I contact you directly if I need information?"

"Absolutely. And call me James. When we're on the job, we're a team working for the same cause, so we can drop the formalities."

****

James was impressed with the expansion and new buildings after their last stop in Singapore, which was well on its way to rivaling Hong Kong. Now they were sailing past parts of Indonesia. James had heard a lot about pirates raiding ships in that area, but the coast was clear. Later that afternoon, the Port of Hong Kong was on the horizon and it was a magnificent sight as they journeyed into Victoria Harbor to see the activity, as ships were coming in while others were pulling out. The skyscrapers were innumerable. They were headed to the docks on the northern area of Kowloon. They could now look back and see the island of Hong Kong as the sun began to drop in the western sky.

CHAPTER 7

BANNERMANS IN HONG KONG

James awoke to a magnificent view of Hong Kong Island from his hotel room. He had adjusted to the new time as the slow journey of the ship gradually put the clock forward an hour at a time. People would be asleep back in England. In this part of the world they were now seven hours ahead.

James, Kate, and Roger met up for breakfast before heading over to the bank.

"James, where's the bank?" asked Kate.

"It's over on Hong Kong Island at the corner of Harcourt Road and Tamar."

"Is Mr. Park expecting us?"

"He knows that I'm coming out, but I don't think he's ready to undergo an audit. I didn't want him to be too prepared—nothing like the element of surprise. We're going to be here for at least a couple of weeks, so I think we need to get ourselves a car. That way we can be independent and learn our way about.

It shouldn't be too complicated."

They hailed a taxi and made their way over to the bank. It didn't take long and within twenty minutes they were dropped off outside the bank.

The three of them walked through the doors to a very opulent entrance complete with marble floors, a fountain in the center, and cathedral ceilings. They found assistance at the front desk, which had the directory of all the businesses in the building. Bannermans had the top two floors. They made their way to the fourteenth floor. As they left the elevator, the hallway opened out to a large receptionist desk with Bannermans International Bank in big letters behind it.

"Makes our offices in London look modest." James laughed.

"Definitely. Sitting up here with the gods, I say," said Roger, eagerly waiting to get his hands on some numbers.

James introduced himself, as a secretary appeared in short order. "My name is Fiona Chang. It's a pleasure to meet you, your Lordship."

"This is also Kate Lloyd and Roger Bell."

"Mr. Park is not here yet," said Fiona, "but we expect him shortly. Can I take you upstairs to our conference room and fetch you some of our good China tea...or coffee if you prefer?"

"Certainly," said James. They ascended a staircase between the top two floors. It appeared that all the people that worked for Trans Global were on the fourteenth floor with a few bank people, and all the executives were on the top floor. As they reached the top floor, they could clearly see the view out over Victoria Harbor; it was spectacular. The conference room was spacious and could seat over twenty people. Fiona soon had the tea brought in and another member of the staff entered the room behind her to introduce himself.

"My Lord James, it is an honor to meet you," he said. "I've called Mr. Park and he is hurrying to get here. He wasn't certain of your exact arrival date, but he's asked me to talk with you first. My name is Ling Tak. I have spent many happy times when I was a student in England and have met Lord Collin, your father, at the bank in London. I am the chief accountant here, so if there's anything you need to know I am the one you should ask."

"Thank you for the introduction. Kate and Roger are here to do an audit to understand just where the bank is financially. They'll make a pro forma in order to have a plan to grow the business. As you know, we have the property on the other side of the street. It's my plan to develop this land and put up a larger building than this. I believe the market and the amount of new business coming to Hong Kong will need these facilities."

"There are some temporary political problems on the island," started Ling. "As you know, the textile industry has grown at a phenomenal rate. The amount of labor crossing the border has been severely curtailed, as we don't have the accommodation for these people. It's the problems of success that bring about a demand for higher wages and living quarters. That being said, the amount of investment here is astounding; there seems to be no end in sight! Your plans for future development would be most wise."

"We want to understand the business climate too," said James, "and make the right plans for the future. It's been a long time since any of our staff has been here. If Kate and Roger could be assigned to an office and one of your staff was available to assist, it would make our review and audit go that much faster."

At that moment Jonathan Park entered the room. He eagerly shook hands with everyone, then asked what he could do to make their job as easy as possible. He was informed what was requested of Ling Tak. Ling then departed with Kate and Roger to get them set up.

"James, please come into my office," Jonathan started. "We can continue there."

His office was palatial. It was composed of hardwood floors with Persian rugs, tall Chinese lions in gold leaf, a white lounge sitting area with a teakwood coffee table, and a beautiful mahogany partner's desk. He had, from behind his desk, the same view of the harbor as the conference room. The only difference was he could open his office door to a private balcony and a small swimming pool. Sunshades and tables were off to the side. It was certainly a pleasant environment to conduct business. James thought only in a climate like Hong Kong could one do this. In London, it would be a total waste of space.

"Let's go outside and sit in the shade," suggested Jonathan. "It's such a beautiful day and we can enjoy the view looking back at the harbor and Kowloon."

They took their seats at a small table where James could see in the far distance where their ship had docked. "Well, I understand that you have some contact with the intelligence service in the UK. I was informed that in addition to your duties here at the bank, you're an agent for the British government."

"Yes, James. It's a position I've held for a number of years now and your father was well aware of my responsibility to the government. As you know, I'm limited in what I can share with you. I can say that there has been great concern over the possible escalation of the war in Vietnam. The Americans are supporting South Vietnam against the North. It's our belief that this is an attempt to stop communism. But people are concerned with what exactly America's real position is on the matter. The North Vietnamese are Communist and the South Vietnamese want to continue with the old French regime views for a capitalistic society. It's hard to understand why the United States would intervene in a society that borders China. Chairman Mao is a Communist. The South Vietnamese are of the same culture, except for the ruling few. It would seem obvious that they should go back and live as one in peace."

"Well, let's hope things don't get out of hand," said James. "It's hard to believe that the Americans would want a war in this part of the world unless there was a very good reason. I'm sure the Americans know what they're doing, but that's your area of expertise, not mine."

"Ling Tak knows our business well, so we'll let the accountants thrash it out. While you're here," Jonathan continued, "I would like you to come to my home and meet my family. We're overjoyed to have you in our part of the world. If I can educate you a little, please allow me to do so. My father was English and my mother was a mixture of French and Chinese. I was educated in England at Winchester and spent time learning finance at Cambridge. I guess culturally I'm more English than Chinese. I believe we have grown successfully and we've been able to show a sustained return on our investment over the years."

This, in a way, was true. However, the financial information he had given the London office had been scant and lacking in detail. It was long overdue for a complete audit to understand the reality of what Jonathan Park had expressed. Jonathan was thinking that after being left alone for nearly ten years, James's auditors would never dig back that far and he had already told Ling Tak to make these records difficult to find.

Jonathan showed James around the bank and introduced him to the agent that handled all the administration for Trans Global.

Josh Lee had been handling the shipments in and out of the Port of Hong Kong for years, even before Bannermans had bought the building he was in now. "Tell me, Josh, could we be handling more business if we had the ships?" asked James.

"We could handle three to four times more than we're doing now," said Josh. "Every boat we have leaves here loaded.

We need newer ships, sir, and container ships. With bigger ships we can move faster than the smaller steamships we have now, carry more goods, and increase our trade. I'm asked all the time, 'When will we expand?' After all, we are the oldest shipping line in the world. We give them good service and our ship's captains and staff are experienced. So the confidence is there! Bring it on, boss, and we'll do the rest."

James liked Josh. He looked like a hustler; he had something extra. He wanted to move up, progress, work hard, and make a good buck while doing it.

"Josh, we'll talk more, and rest assured that's just what we're going to do. It takes the team and you're going to see some new energy. There will be some changes at the top, so you'll see people that are really anxious to take us to the next level, including me. We plan to invest and expand our operation here and that takes good people." He was trying to understand what Duncan had told him on the ship about leadership.

James's analysis was that they were more frustrated with the lack of direction and interest needed to be shown by senior management in providing a direction and a future for the staff in Hong Kong. He connected with people and Jonathan could tell that his enthusiasm was infectious. James created an energy, where people felt understood and part of his vision.

James spent the rest of the day going over the business with Jonathan and was anxious to hear about Kate and Roger's first day. They all made it back to the hotel and said they would meet up for supper in an hour.

"Well, I don't know about you guys, but after being on board for nearly a month, I need a good steak," announced James to Kate and Roger's approval. "So how's the audit going?"

"It's not complicated, but the number of offshore accounts is confusing," said Roger, looking perplexed.

"Why? You know who and what they belong to."

"Well, that's just it. I don't. Ling has told me all the accounts are from wires that are sent in the past, by Nigel Thompson, and he just follows instructions."

"So you don't know the offshore accounts Ling is instructed to send the money to?"

"It's such a muddle. I would have to believe Nigel instructs money to be sent to a specific account. He says, 'Nigel just wires the money and Mr. Park tells him where to send it as he acts on behalf of the British government.'"

"I understand that, but Ling must know the accounts that are for the government?"

"That's just it. He says they all are."

"We can check that now. Call Claudia. It's only midday in England. She can give you the exact list of those offshore accounts. If the number of accounts and their numbers match, then we'll know if what he's telling us is correct."

"I'll get right on it."

Roger returned in twenty minutes with a big grin on his face. "I thought as much. Not all the accounts Ling is sending money to are for the British government. That means he's sending money to offshore accounts that are someone else's." Like all accountants, he loved to find someone who may have their fingers in the 'cookie jar.'

"So he must tell us who these accounts belong to and the reasons for the wires," surmised James.

"What if he doesn't know, and Mr. Park is the only one who does?" asked Kate, thinking he could just be doing his job.

"He'll just have to ask Mr. Park, won't he? I don't want to get involved just yet; there may be a perfectly logical explanation. Let's hope there is, because the consequences will be severe if not," said James, suspecting that something had been up for a while. For Ling to not be in on it would be even stranger.

James couldn't sleep that night. He tossed and turned, wondering what else was going on at the bank. If Kate and Roger had picked up on these wires on the very first day, what other things might they find? What of Jonathan Park, as a British agent? What would his plan be if James were to fire him? He finally fell asleep and woke to the sound of Kate asking him if he would be coming with them.

"I've a few things to take care of, first," he answered. "I'll be meeting an architect for the new building, so see you later on."

The architect was a young Englishman, named Evan Ross. He had been with the firm for several years and was enjoying the experience of working in Hong Kong. James knew the company well, having dealt with them in England many times.

Just as they were about to leave the hotel to go to the site, the front desk called out for James. "Sir, it's a call from your office."

James took the phone, thinking it was a call from London, but it was Kate.

"James, I think you should come quickly. Ling Tak is very angry that we've checked out the accounts and says we don't trust him, and the depth of our audit is completely unnecessary. In all his years, he's never had anyone go through his records as we have."

"Ask to talk with Mr. Park and I'll be there shortly. He has to understand that we must have accountability. It's not personal, just business."

"Okay."

James got into Evan's car and they drove to the site. "So sir, you want to build a fifty-story building. That's going to take quite a foundation. It'll be up there with some of the tallest buildings in Hong Kong. Just be aware that someone always comes along and builds a bigger one. Based on what I know in Hong Kong and the typhoons we experience here, I'll work directly with our design team to build something futuristic."

"Remember we're in the shipping business," replied James, "so something that eludes what we're known for in addition to banking would be creative. Evan, I've got to run across the street; I have another meeting. Take your time at this sight. I can look at the plans when I get back to London from your office there."

"We will do an artist's impression first. I can have that over to your hotel in a week, so if you like it, we can then go to work on the engineering side."

"I'll look forward to it. Maybe we can have lunch together."

****

James rushed over to the bank and up the elevator to see what was happening with the audit.

Fiona took him to the conference room.

"What is this?" asked Jonathan Park, looking clearly stressed. "A witch hunt? We've never had to explain ourselves in this manner before."

"I'm a chartered accountant myself," said James. "I can assure you that the kind of audit my staff is conducting is within the guidelines of generally accepted accounting principles. You have all these offshore accounts and we must account for every single one of them. Why do you have a problem with that?"

"All these offshore accounts are controlled by the British government. We're just doing our job."

"We have a list of these accounts and I personally know every one of them. There are, however, accounts that are not accounted for by the British government. All we want to know is to whom these accounts belong to. Is that so complicated?"

"James, with all due respect, that's private information. We can't divulge that to anyone."

"Money is going out of this bank to an account that we can neither account for nor know for whom it's designated. No one is going anywhere until I have those facts. Otherwise, I'm going to assume money is being taken out of this bank without proper authority. I want to hear from Ling Tak just who has authorized money to leave this bank without us knowing about it."

"I have another meeting to attend," said Jonathan, looking a little sheepish. "A lot has happened since your father died. I believe you don't know all the accounts. Nigel Thompson didn't know these accounts. How is it you've come up with a list now?"

"Claudia Ringstone, who's the head of our bank in London, has a complete list of those account numbers from the British government," James confided, though skeptically. "We know that those accounts are for someone else."

"So that's why you're here! To come and snoop around and see what we've been up to?"

"Jonathan, if we find that money has been taken out of this bank fraudulently, we'll have no alternative but to turn you over to the authorities."

"So now it's threats. You can't prove anything; offshore accounts are private," challenged Jonathan.

"If we have funds that have left this bank without us knowing where they've gone, you will be suspended from your job and so will Ling Tak" James scowled, growing irritable. "That's just for starters. If we feel there's criminal intent, then we can have our lawyer validate exactly what these accounts are, since *you* won't. As a civil offense, you're right, but as a willful criminal offense it becomes another matter. So I would advise you to come clean before matters get any worse."

"Fine. I quit. As for Ling Tak, do what you want. He doesn't know anything; he just gets his orders from me."

James promptly picked up the phone and ordered security to the conference room immediately. But just as he turned around, Jonathan confronted him with a right-hand blow to the face. James fell backward onto the conference table, then Jonathan made a beeline for the door. James knew exactly what he was up to and made a rugby tackle on Jonathan as he tried to open the door. Jonathan was attempting to get back to his office for his gun and his book containing all the deals and transactions he'd made over the last eight years. The fight continued. As a British agent, Jonathan Park wasn't afraid of anyone; he knew how to fight. He was fully trained for this assignment. James was able to hold him down long enough until two security guards came to take care of him. He was shouting abusive language at James, calling him a stuck-up freeloader that hadn't a clue what he was doing.

"Don't think you're safe in this town any longer! There'll be a price on your head," shouted Jonathan, hysterically angry.

James picked himself up and went over to the bathroom in Jonathan's office. He washed his face and cleaned himself off. It wasn't the first punch he'd taken and thought it wouldn't be the last. He then locked the door so he could go through Jonathan's office from top to bottom. The security officers had taken Jonathan so quickly that he had no time to get his keys, briefcase, or anything else. James carefully went through his desk. Sure enough, in the side drawer was his book. James fully expected that he would have kept a record of everything. They could use the evidence against the people he had been robbing for years. After further looking he found his gun, and behind a painting on the wall was a safe. The undercover double agent kept meticulous notes, much to his detriment. He had made a fortune squirreling away money from loans he'd made to would-be borrowers, money from Russian and Chinese governments, all to these offshore accounts, and stealing money slowly and quietly from the bank.

James immediately phoned the police and the British embassy since he would need protection. He doubted that he would get any threats from the Russian and Chinese governments or the mafia Jonathan worked with, because the evidence he held was too incriminating. They would sink away into the woodwork and hope to God that they did not get incriminated themselves. James called Ling Tak into Jonathan's office.

"Have a seat," James said when Ling nervously entered the room. "Do you realize, it looks as though, you've been working for a gangster all these years?" James was testing Ling. It was a serious punt, but the facts seemed obvious and Ling had no trouble confirming the situation, now worried for his own future.

"Yes, sir, I do." He couldn't lie. The truth was out and the facts were all around them.

At that moment the police arrived. James had the police escorted to the conference room and said he would join them in a moment.

"Ling, if you talk with Kate and Roger, tell them everything you know; I'll work to help you. I know you must have been afraid of this man, even though he probably took good care of you. In a sense, with a man like that, he would have hunted you down because you knew too much. I've probably saved your life in the long run. Help us out by telling the authorities all you know. Then help us get this man convicted and put him away behind bars."

"Gentlemen, sorry to keep you waiting. We've encountered a very unfortunate event today," said James, approaching the policemen. "The managing director of this bank, Jonathan Park, has absconded funds from this bank illegally and fraudulently. We have offshore accounts to prove it. We have his notebook validating the kickbacks he's been getting from the people he's loaned money to. It's a similar method used by the mafia in collecting protection money. Ling Tak is our chief financial officer. He will attest to all the crimes committed. I hope this man Park can be held, in view of the evidence we can supply, and the testimony of Mr. Tak."

"Sir, my name is Detective Williams; here's my card. We

will go through his office, talk with Mr. Tak, and go from there. Can we use this conference room for questioning?"

"It's all yours."

James went over to Ling, directing him to go to the conference room for his testimony to the police. He then went to speak with Roger and Kate.

"Wow. You guys hit a minefield with those unaccounted for accounts," said James, pleased to finally catch this man who'd been screwing everyone for at least eight years.

"Ling will tell all. He's afraid for his future. He didn't have a choice. Once he had become knowledgeable of who Mr. Park was several years ago, there was no way out. He was afraid for his own life, because the kind of people Jonathan knows I'm sure are linked mafia members," said Roger.

"This is the kind of thing you read about in books. You never believe it goes on in real life," said Kate, who wasn't easily scared.

"To think we're only on the second day of our audit," said James, laughing. "Stay with it. I'll bet we've got a ton of cash to round up, which should help pay for our trip out here!"

"The police want to talk with you again, sir," said Fiona, looking a little shaken after Jonathan's arrest.

"Well, sir, it seems there's enough evidence to hold Mr. Park. He's in police custody in the meeting room of the security office. We've gone through all the papers and personal effects in his office. My team has had a man over to open up the safe. There's a lot of cash and papers in there, which will need your attention. We've left everything as is, so you can audit and process this information for your bank. It would appear that he's got deals all over the place, from sweatshop textile manufacturers, to nightclubs and escort agencies. He's quite the operator. It will be necessary for you to complete a final audit of the whole bank in order to have all the evidence we need for the court. I'm sure that goes without saying, as you came here for just that purpose. It would seem that this man is very deeply connected to both Chinese and Russian people highly placed in government. If those people don't feel threatened, I feel your personal security will be safe. However, a man in your position should have a chauffeur and bodyguard. Hong Kong is a big sprawling city and we don't always know what or who is lurking out there. You're well known by the British Consulate here, so I suggest you talk with them and they can advise you what's best for your own personal safety, at least until things settle down, by which time you'll probably be gone. It seems you know how to handle yourself well, taking on a man like him."

The detective took a long deep breath. "In regard to Mr. Tak, he is, of course, accountable for what's happened, as he worked for this man a number of years. True, he probably didn't have a choice, as that's the way it goes with people like Mr. Park. Nevertheless, when the time comes, it will have to be reviewed. His lawyer can probably get him a good plea bargain, based on the evidence he's given and will give. Hopefully, he'll be pardoned, but the law is the law."

"Many thanks for your prompt attention, Detective Williams. I'll keep you updated as we move forward."

****

Alan Archer from the British Consul's office advised James to swing by immediately to make plans for his continued safety.

"Well, well, well. What a business!" Alan beamed. "Whitehall has been tracking that man for quite a while. What a fool that man was. Lovely wife...and kids, too! A terrible way to end what could have been a sterling career, don't you think?"

"We had our suspicions," said James. "As you know, we do transfer funds on behalf of the government and have done so long before my time. It seems he saw an opportunity to tack on a few more offshore accounts and slowly and prudently bleed the bank. There's been no one since my father died to keep a tight rope on him, so the 'temptation to greed' was too great. What does disturb us is that he's made several loans to sweatshops, nightclubs, and escort agencies, and from his notes, he's been making a tidy sum of money from kickbacks on the side. It appears he gets an upfront commission of ten percent on the loans he makes; then, they pay him protection money after that. This is how he's justified loaning money with virtually no proper accounting facts to support these loans. It's a proper mess and one that won't get sorted out in five minutes. I'm sure the various entities will be happy to see the last of him. However, these are not the type of loans our bank is normally interested in making. We have yet to actually see if he owns these various enterprises, as they're all financially run from offshore companies. It'll take time to know who the real owners are."

Alan poured James a scotch. "Well, people have a high regard for you. No doubt you'll have the place running back in proper order soon. Probably need that after today."

"Indeed. We're about to start construction of a fifty-story building on the other side of the street. It's property we've had vacant for a while. My father always wanted to do this and this way I'll have some sort of memorial dedication, for him."

"By Jove! Quite a project!" exclaimed Alan. "The city will respect your belief in continuing to invest in Hong Kong. Your good name and the shipping line are both highly valued in this part of the world. On another subject, I'm going for a bite. Would you like to join me? I'll have the chauffeur take us to the Coral Club that overlooks the bay."

James wanted to learn his way around Hong Kong, and being with the British Consul who'd been there for twenty years was an excellent opportunity to do so.

"I'm going for the roast beef...always a winner here," said Alan. "A good bottle of wine, and we'll be set. I've been here so long, I'm used to the way of life. There are days when I get homesick. But I know I must make the best of my years while I'm here. There are lots of good Brits you need to meet and Americans, too. I'll have a little gathering before you leave and you can come by and make some friends. All good for business, you know. Can't know enough people. They'll have good advice for you."

Alan was perfect for his ambassadorial role. A typical Colonial Brit. He had the right demeanor to network and build relationships along with the ability to ease through any diplomatic tension, and bring a positive spin to complex situations. James thoroughly enjoyed his evening and the knowledge he was gaining from Alan.

"Now James, my chauffeur will drop you back at the hotel and tomorrow I'll provide a car and driver for anywhere you want to go. You can make your arrangements from there and if you want a bodyguard, I can provide that, too. In fact, I have just the person who can be your driver and bodyguard all in one. When you come back again he will inform you of the best place to hire your own person for the future. Tell Angus, my driver, what time you want to be picked up tomorrow and he'll relay the message."

"I can't thank you enough," said James. "See you at your get-together."

****

"So now we have a chauffeur to drive us to work?" asked Kate, surprised to see the limo pull up.

"Courtesy of Her Majesty's government," bragged James. "It's just for now, in case some nutcase wants to take a pop shot at me. Angus is a driver *and* a bodyguard. So they want to keep me on the planet until we make our own arrangements. Good morning, Angus," he said as the driver stepped out to open their doors. "Let me introduce you to Kate Lloyd and Roger Bell who will be coming with us. They are doing the audit at our bank."

Angus tipped his hat. "Very good, my lord."

Kate whispered to James, "I could get used to this."

Angus drove them to the bank and would return again as needed. The security guard's office at the bank building had laid on temporarily a full-time bodyguard, who would be at the office until James returned to England.

"Okay, let's bring Ling to the conference room to get things rolling," instructed James.

Ling came in and took a seat. "First, what is our bank balance at present with the Bank of Hong Kong?" said James, now trying to narrow down a plan of action.

"We have, as of yesterday, thirty-two million in pounds sterling, earning an average rate of interest around five percent. It appears that about twenty-five million pounds was invested from 1953 to 1955. So compounded over the last twelve years, if none of the money was loaned out, we should have around forty-five million. Now, I understand that the building rental, which is at present fully occupied, more than paid all the staff at the bank and its outgoing costs. Trans Global employees here are paid separately. So I have calculated that at least another million would have gone toward the Bank of Hong Kong for that alone. So in round numbers, if we just took the rent paid to the staff, we should have around forty-six million in our account today. That means that about fourteen million is missing and not accounted for. Ling agrees with my numbers. With all these offshore accounts and the ins and outs from our bank in England, we have narrowed it down to at least five offshore accounts that we know money has been wired to over the years, which accounts for about ten to eleven million. Interest has been paid on this money from these accounts but the loans have just increased and increased. We have several ideas as to what's taken place, but without knowing the exact amounts in these accounts, we have no way of substantiating whether the money that was originally wired is still there."

"Great. The good news is with the rental income from the building we have, plus the value of the building, together with the cash in the Bank of Hong Kong, we're actually ahead. Have you taken into account that it cost around two and a half million for this building in 1953? Did you subtract what it cost to buy this building?"

"No, and that's a good point. So the eleven million that's been wired to these offshore accounts would seem to be a hard number. Ling is not certain that all the money is there; he never saw the bank statements. Well, maybe they're in Park's office. Let's look. As you well know, Park must have loaned the money to the businesses he appears to have been taking kickbacks from. So either he was pocketing some cash from a business he owned or he was getting money over the top."

"The rental income more than paid for all the costs of running the bank," said James. "There had to be a surplus. It appears that he just used this bank as his own personal slush fund to do whatever he liked. He cleverly paid the interest on the eleven million. We know that from our accounting records in England, but he could have been paying us with our own money. So now, Ling, get us a lawyer. Let's set a case for criminal grounds against Park. Then we'll have the reign to acquire the facts."

Deep down, James was satisfied. At least they hadn't lost the original investments his father had made.

****

That evening, Roger asked James if he would join him for a drink. They went out for a walk and stopped at a local club close to the hotel. Kate wanted to watch a show so she retired to her room. When they sat down, Roger started by saying to James, "I would like to tell you a little more about myself and how I think I can help."

"Bring it on, I'm all ears," said James anxiously.

"I've watched you closely over this whole trip, so that I could learn for myself, but also understand the direction you want to take for the bank and your business."

"So, Sir Roger, what's your prognosis after having witnessed quite a week in the history of our Hong Kong enterprise?"

"You and I are very different people. Forgive me if anything I say offends you." He now had James's full attention. "From what I've seen of your style and direction, you like being a hands-on operative type of leader; you like to get into the thick of things, root out any problems, likc any good boss, and make the place pay. You enjoy people and you take the time to get to know them and exchange ideas to make necessary improvements. In my opinion, you are the epitome of the type of person who has the drive and force to run a large corporation and make it bigger. Trans Global Shipping is tailor made for your dynamic and innovative style."

James was listening intently. "Here it comes. What have you got up your sleeve?"

"It's simple, sir. It's the bank. Now I'm getting into the area of my expertise. Not that you don't have that, too. I don't see any innovation to grow and develop the very essence of what was started in 1838, namely a merchant bank called Bannermans, going anywhere. In fact, quite the opposite. We make money with Trans Global, throw the proceeds out toward the bank, and do nothing with it. We have divested all of our investments out of the London Stock Exchange. I totally agree with your strategy there, which isn't the true spirit of merchant banking, anyway. But where are we going now? We don't have a strategy for the bank and its future. We seem completely happy to invest in buildings, collect rent, and make interest on profits made from Trans Global. That could hardly be called merchant banking."

"Wow, Roger, you've come alive. Congratulations. Now tell me, what should we be doing?" James was intrigued.

"First, let me give you some background. I know you're a chartered accountant and have a thorough understanding of those fundamentals, as I do. However, having studied at Cambridge, I had a personal interest in learning everything I could about the oldest institution of banking in the world—merchant banking. The Knight's Templar were bankers. You could buy notes in Europe and convert them into currency in Palestine during the Crusades."

Roger was making his pitch. This was the moment he had patiently waited for. He continued, "So what is the essence of a merchant bank, as opposed to a regular bank? It is an institution that gathers investment and uses that money to invest strategically in up-and-coming companies. This can be in the form of stock options...or short- and long-term loans. There is a planned entry level, when the business needs more money, which is frequently the case in the early stages. The bank, if it chooses, will ask for more shares in order to protect its position. If the company looks as though it's solid, a loan may suffice. The myriad of investment into the world of business, not through the stock exchange, but by making sound and wise investments, is the very essence of merchant banking. The success of the Rothschilds, the Baring Brothers, and Kleinwort Benson, of which the last two I've worked for, has operated in this way. For example, look at the age of the robber barons in America. We had John D. Rockefeller of Standard Oil, Carnegie of Carnegie Steel, CorneliusVanderbilt for the railroads, and other train tycoons. The list goes on."

Roger was now able to make his final point as James listened intently. "However, there was one man who played a strategic role in their development: J. P. Morgan, a merchant banker. Morgan bought out Carnegie for nearly five hundred million in 1901, incalculable into today's money. With other acquisitions he made this company into the biggest steel company in the world—United States Steel.

Morgan became so successful that he bailed out the US treasury in the 1890s with the help of the Rothchilds in order to hold the dollar to the gold standard, with one hundred eighty million plus. Again not in today's money. In simple terms four men took the United States of America from almost financial ruin after the Civil War to being a leading economy in the world by the 1900s. Four men in today's money were worth over one trillion dollars. Morgan then bought out Edison, the light bulb creator and master of DC technology, and then realized he also needed AC electricity and eventually acquired Nikola Tesla's technology, who worked for Edison and afterward for George Westinghouse.

"What did Morgan create with DC electric and AC electric, General Electric! Junius Morgan, a brilliant banker, yet a traditional banker, saw his son's idea as dangerous and away from traditional money-making investments. Junius's vision was exceeded, by his son's guts and brilliance. All this was done from merchant banking. Making investments and working to develop industry and businesses. The number one impact these men had on the economy was in the creation of employment, the words all government wants to hear.

Roger continued, "Today, the goals have changed somewhat; we have a larger world stock market. Our long-term goal is not to run businesses; it's to make money. We seek an ongoing return and financial exit on our investment eventually. The greatest role of the stock exchange is for that prospect. Selling out a company to another buyer, you'd be lucky to get seven times cash flow for its value.

"Take it public to the stock exchange and you can get up to thirty times. It's a whole world by itself and it's the sole reason why I came to join Bannermans! I wanted to be part of that development, which I saw being the new philosophy, after your divestment from the stock exchange." Roger finished by ordering another beer.

"So you believe you can start doing that here?"

"James, this place is bursting with deals that need capital. You're sitting on a gold mine."

"We could be doubling our money in two to three years, and reinvesting, not making a measly five percent."

"This means you want to stay here and mastermind a game plan for what you've just been talking about?"

"I've found my niche. This place has so much opportunity; it's mind blowing. I would work to sort out the matters to get the money back from Jonathan Park. Then I'll be joining all sorts of clubs and committees to network and seek out new prospects."

"Thank you for such an informed history lesson. You are indeed a great student of financial banking and I dare say we are lucky to have you. Now I'm a risk taker, but within certain confines. Your Cambridge education served you well. There's a lot of money in the Bank of Hong Kong and after what we've just experienced, I can't just give signing authority to one person. I believe we need one person to manage the rental property and oversee the construction of our new building, which is somewhere around two hundred and fifty thousand a floor, depending on what we put on it. I want that account to be handled separately. The bank must pay its own way, and the same for the building. We'll keep Ling for now and watch him. I'm going to send out another person who'll be the bank and building accountant and who will be the second signer on the checks."

"Makes sense. So you're offering me the opportunity to run the bank?"

"Yes. I will hold you under review for six months. You will have an automatic rise, of course. Then it's up to you. Make things happen and you'll be making good money."

"James, you won't regret this."

"Well if you can teach us all a lesson over here, then you can come back and teach us all the dynamics in London. I'll concentrate on Trans Global for now and our property development. You concentrate on what you call being a proper merchant bank."

"Thank you, sir. I have one other matter to consult you on and that is for Kate. Will she be staying on?"

"Do we have enough work for her?"

"Not at the moment, but if we do what I think we'll be doing, we're going to need more than Kate. Also, I have to admit what might be a personal issue for you. Kate and I have grown very close over this last month and we have significant feelings for each other." Roger knew if he was going to have James's trust, he had to put all his "cards on the table."

"As long as it doesn't interfere with the job. I don't want to have family gang up against other employees or politics to exist. I know it's not easy. I want you to know that she would have to find something else if it becomes a problem. I believe it's always good to state one's position up front. That being said, let's have another beer. I believe congratulations are in order. Kate is a fantastic lady, and I think you two would make a good match."

The week passed quickly. James now had the artist's impression for his new building, which he would take home, as well as an estimate for the cost.

Alan Archer had called and told him of the date and time of his promise for a get-together.

James came to talk with Roger and Kate. They were getting

closer and closer to tracking the missing funds.

"By the way, I've been invited to the British Consul's party tomorrow night," James said. "I think this would be a great opportunity for you and Kate to come along. You can start your networking there." James was in a good humor. He slapped Roger on the back and made way to his room.

The banquet that Alan Archer had organized was a sumptuous affair. He was an old hand at orchestrating such matters. The governor of Hong Kong was present, as well as the managing director of the Bank of Hong Kong. He'd gathered together all the political brass from the island. They were as anxious to meet the young lord, as he was to meet them. It was a great opportunity for Roger to meet all the right people, too. The word was out about Jonathan Park, and James answered with extreme caution the many questions he was asked. Many women in high-ranking positions wanted to know about the building he was having constructed. It was a great opportunity for him to market their future plans and ideas.

James still waited to hear about the money that Jonathan Park had taken, but there were pressing matters back in England he had to address. He had Fiona book him a flight back to London.

CHAPTER 8

TRANS GLOBAL SHIPPING

James arrived back at his London office. The past six weeks had been an experience he would never forget. He knew that John Higgins would be back in London within the next ten days and he wanted to clearly think out his plans before having the conversation about his future with him. Rose rang his phone. "Sir, it's Roger on the phone.

"Roger, tell me some good news. What's up?"

"Well, we've found the money. The guy had closed all the five accounts in the Cayman Islands and the Channel Islands and transferred it all to one account in Zurich, Switzerland. Thanks to the international aid of Interpol, the Secret Service, and to this lawyer Tak knows, we've found the money. There's roughly almost nine million. 'They're busy wiring the funds to Hong Kong as we speak. Park does own these businesses, and has set up loans after investing most of the money in the textile business he had. Park had owned an escort agency and had investments in other clubs.

Roger had no documented proof that the money that Park had taken from the bank was used for that purpose. It could have been investments Park had made from kickbacks he'd received from other shareholders in these clubs, but no direct connection could be made. Roger wanted no involvement. He decided to treat the loan from the bank as being made directly to Park personally, against the assets of his textile company. The two nightclubs appeared to have received the rest of the money. It was clear that Park had taken the money from the bank. They had all the evidence to substantiate that. "In short, he's used two million pounds out of the eleven million that was missing. My advice is we have two choices: one, we can take control of these businesses, or two, leave it as an outstanding debt that he must repay us when he gets out of prison. That will leave us with some leverage over him for the future. He could one day be a dangerous enemy with his connections, so perhaps it's wiser to keep our enemies closer with the possibility of being repaid. Either way, it's up to you."

"I like your thinking Roger. Let me think it through. Under such circumstances things could have been a lot worse. Well done. I'll be in touch." James knew it wouldn't be long before Jeremy Soames would be calling, and sure enough he was on the other line.

"I heard you had quite a trip," said Jeremy. "That took some guts to corral a fox like that. I'd like to meet tomorrow around ten. Is that good for you?"

"See you then." James knew he was going to hear a lot more about Jonathan Park, who was under police surveillance until his trial.

"Claudia, my dear, how are you? You look exhausted," said James.

"James, you've taken my best man and now I must find a replacement. However, as always, it's good to have you back.

It's quite a challenge running the show when you're not here." With Nigel gone and no Roger, she had gone into overtime.

"You need to get yourself another Roger. He wants to stay out there. In addition, I need another man I can trust to send out to Hong Kong to be our accountant, since Roger will be running the show."

"Wel, you take my best man and then ask me to find two more!"

"You do such a good job. As shy as Roger is, I had no idea how much 'piss and vinegar' he's got. If we're right, I think we have ourselves a true merchant banker for the future. A lot is going to be happening shortly. I've also offered the general manager's position to John Higgins. I believe he'll make Trans Global into what it should be. His knowledge and diversity is just what we need. I asked Duncan, but he's not interested. Having thought about it, John would be more suited to an executive position and knows the business from the bottom up. You'll like him; you'll see."

"So you're at least taking some pressure off me. Without Nigel, I've got all the captains and that administrator Burt Haynes at Tilbury asking me all sorts of questions I haven't a clue about."

"That's how you learn the business: the school of hard knocks."

"I can see that trip hasn't worn you out. If anything, it's energized you. Good job, by the way, with Jonathan Park. That couldn't have been easy."

"We've found most of the money and it's being wired to Hong Kong as we speak. So not a bad start to the week."

"Come over tonight and bring us up to date. You're becoming a wandering vagabond. It's hard to keep up with you these days."

"Thank you. I'll come with you when you go."

That evening James enjoyed telling all his news about the

time he spent on the ship with Duncan, getting to know John Higgins, and the whole episode with Jonathan Park. He told them about Roger having feelings for Kate and his plans for the new building.

"I've checked into your plans of incorporating in Switzerland with the same bank that has your trust fund. There's no problem at all with what you want to do," said Thomas, bringing him up to date.

"Tell me, Thomas, what are we doing with the money in the trust fund?"

"Nothing. It's been accumulating for years. Both your grandfather and father religiously put money back each year, and with the accrued interest, it's grown into a huge sum."

"How about me using some of those funds to build the property business I want to create?" asked James, imagining better usage for some of the funds.

"An excellent idea," said Thomas. "You could transfer funds into the corporation that would be owned by the trust. You are the sole trustee, along with anyone else you care to nominate. I never told your mother about the trust fund since matters were rather sensitive, as you may remember as a young man. Your father never told anyone, and in the will for which I was the guardian for you, there was a private codicil for me to inform you of that at the age of twenty-one or at such time I thought it was wise and necessary. It's time that money was put to use. As a trustee you would be entitled to some remuneration. If you kept the money in Switzerland, you would pay a nominal tax. If it were transferred here, you would of course pay a lot more. That money could be of considerable help to the business. You could pay Bannermans the going market price for all the buildings the company now owns and Bannermans could pay the rent money to the trust. All the accounting for the properties could be done by a separate person for each building and the revenues sent to Zurich."

"This would give Bannermans extra capital to invest in Trans Global," said James, thinking out loud. "Those ships definitely need updating and the fleet needs expansion. Our man in China says he could quadruple the amount of cargo we're doing...if we had the ships."

"Enough business talk, you two," said Claudia as she brought Alex into the room. Alex was now saying a few words and pointed to James saying, "Jam, it Jams!" His mother corrected him but he wasn't listening. James thought of all the expensive pieces he had at Penbroke and how he would have to put them up higher soon.

"How's the family doing? Have you had a moment to catch up yet ?

"I'm embarrassed to say I haven't even called Sabrina, but I will when I get home."

Claudia knew how James felt about his family, and especially Sabrina, after all she had been through. She was feeling much closer to her since their last visit before James went to China.

"Well, I must be getting back to the flat," said James. "By the way, Thomas told me what you want and I'll write the check; I love the place. It's perfect for now and probably for my time when I'm in London, that is, if you still want to sell it to me."

"Of course. I'll check out the market place and see what it's worth."

When James got back to his flat he immediately called Sabrina. "Sabrina! How goes my girl?"

"James, you naughty boy, you never called me from China. I was anxious that you made it there in one piece. Anyway, at least you've not forgotten me. I miss you so much."

"Catch a plane and come over for a few days," suggested James.

"Well, I have some exciting news. I'm already modeling! I'm still going to finish my modeling course that I've taken.

This is a fantastic opportunity and the money is great. I can pay my way now when I come to see you. It's not possible until next week since I have work to do. Believe me, I'm becoming busier by the day. News travels fast once you land that first job, and you get your face in a magazine."

"You must bring me all the news so I can see my bella in all those skimpy outfits."

"James, you bad boy, I wish I was tucked up beside you making love to you this very moment."

"Now you'll make me have dreams about you. Call me when you're free and come over so I can tell you all about my trip. Ciao, bella."

****

Jeremy Soames arrived and was ushered into the conference room. James joined him moments later.

"Good morning, Jeremy. I met our British agent," said James, smiling and raising his eyebrows.

"That man knows how to fight and I wonder how you were able to contain him."

"I threw a good rugby tackle on him and being a little taller I was able to manhandle him to keep him on the ground. I had to give him a pretty good blow to the head though in return for the one he gave me. Fortunately, two security guards came quickly to the rescue. Otherwise, he would've got back to his office. He would have locked the door, collected his records, and with the use of his gun, he could've gotten out of the building. Our evidence would have been hell to obtain; then he would have had an even chance of running off to Russia or China."

"Quite a story!" Jeremy wasn't a man to express much humor, but he certainly had a laugh when James reported the details of the skirmish. "Well, we should recruit you as an agent, as resourceful as you are, you could be a lot of help to our SIS. You ought to take more of our courses over the next few months. You'll be surprised what we can teach you. A man like you has some obvious street smarts. I'm sure you got the better of a lad or two at Sterling Heights. We could teach you how to handle hand guns and all kinds of newly created weapons that our agents are always keen to use."

"That's a good idea. I'll definitely take you up on that."

"I'm here to cover the bank for any losses it may have incurred. Since he was a British agent, we are responsible for his behavior."

"We've recovered most of the money, and we think we're short about two million. So compared with the eleven million we thought we'd lost, that's almost nothing. Tracking down his offshore accounts was no easy task, I can assure you."

"James, in a case like Park always remember that you're completely covered. As a paid British agent, we would have covered you completely for all your losses, and then we would have taken it upon ourselves to recover what we could. We will pay you, of course, for your shortfall and any other costs associated, legal or otherwise, that you may have."

"Well, that's fantastic. You can't imagine the thoughts that were going through my head thinking how much money we could have potentially lost. My father would be turning in his grave. I'll have Roger Bell, who is now acting managing director out there, to send all the details for your review. Again, I'm so glad that you're able to help us set the record straight."

"It still appears that the Russians are behind this operation in Vietnam, and the Americans are going to fight them tooth and nail. Under Leonid Brezhnev, it seems there's a huge drive to dominate trade in the Indian Ocean. If Russia, with China, got powerful enough, that could cripple trade for all of us in the Western world—matters you should be aware of. I hope that your Roger Bell understands clearly about our wires, especially after what you've been through. It's good to have you back with matters in hand. I look forward to seeing you at our next meeting. The dynamics of this new Russian order is making the world take notice. It's going to be an interesting time."

During the next two weeks, James spoke with Roger. Jeremy Soames had paid off the outstanding balance for Jonathan Park and all the legal costs associated with his case. He was now ready to receive John Higgins, who was waiting for him in the small conference room.

****

"John, good to see you again. Had a good trip home, I hope? How is Stephen Jenkins doing, by the way?"

"I had a good trip," John replied, "although we met some nasty weather again as we rounded Cape Town in South Africa to drop off some cargo. The challenges we are all faced with at sea, at least everything was properly latched down, this time. The incident with Stephen was one of a kind. No one wants to ever experience a situation like that again. He's doing well by all accounts, and his dad's back home with him. I'll keep you up to date."

"Ready to hit the ground running?"

"Sir, I'm so excited. My wife is grateful and so are the kids. I'm ready to go to work right away. As you suggested, I've worked up a plan. Here's a copy of my ideas and what I believe we need to take Trans Global Shipping into the future."

"I see some hefty costs here, but they're to be expected," said James, carefully looking through his proposal.

"The way I see it, we must first establish our administrative offices in Southampton. When that's done, we can go about buying, selling, and upgrading our fleet. When Southampton is in place, we can look for a sight at Felixstowe for our second leg of the exercise. Then we can load and unload all our container ships from there."

"So what's your time line to get all this rocking and rolling?"

"I believe if we can get the building in Southampton quickly, I can start on reorganizing the fleet. I would say that you will see a significant change after the building has been acquired within six to nine months. We can then be completely out of Tilbury and the London docks."

"You live in Bristol, I believe," James said, trying to jog his memory.

"Yes, this side toward Newbury. I'm anxious to locate this building in Southampton as early as possible because I would like to move my family during the summer."

"Understandable," said James. "There are some pleasant homes to live in down there. Let's go find a building. I'm ready to go. You check out some likely places and then I'll join you. I would like to buy a building that is modern and can house some of the history of our shipping line in the front lobby. Duncan has all sorts of paraphernalia and so does my father from all the previous generations. Have Duncan ask around. Let's get all the stories and photographs that anyone has that we could copy. When you have time, we can go to Lincolnshire and I'll show you what we've done with our East wing. People come from all over the world to see the artifacts collected by my forefathers. It all helps to add character to what we do. We have a lot of families that have been at sea with us for generations. They all need to be part of this. I want us to get back to having more of a family environment among all those who have earned the right to be an officer. We should celebrate that each Christmas or something."

"Can't wait to hunt down all this history," John said, rubbing his hands together. "I know some of the guys have acquired many things over the years. I'll get a selection for you to choose from, and then we can meet up."

James was happy with his decision to make John the general manager. He had arrived with a plan and had definitely put a lot of thought and time into his proposal.

Within a few days James was having lunch with Claudia at a little pub not far from the bank.

"We haven't had lunch together for ages. It's nice to just take a moment out of our hectic routine and gather our thoughts," she said, sipping on her glass of Chardonnay.

"It's hard to beat pub food when you want a quick bite."

"I'll bet you're not eating breakfast, James. Living the bachelor life, one doesn't tend to eat as often as one should. I noticed you've lost some weight. Don't get too thin."

Claudia was always watching out for James. She cared about him and treated him like family.

"What would I do if you weren't around?" asked James. "You're the best person I have at being able to wear so many hats in the company, and you never complain. I want to let you know you're always appreciated, even though you think I may not notice all the things you do. Hiring that Roger Bell was a smart move. That guy's got it together. How's it going with his replacement and the man for Hong Kong?"

"I'll have it narrowed down by the end of this week, and then I can have Rose make appointments for you," Claudia answered, still blushing from his compliment.

"Sometimes I think we run our place a little too lean. Maybe I need a secretary to take some of the load off you? I know you enjoy all the things you do for me, but don't be shy if things get too hectic."

"From what I see of your future life, you're going to be on the move. The amount of secretarial work you need won't be a lot. We've got Rose and if I get overburdened, I'll get help, but I prefer being the person you want to talk to when you're away. I can use Rose or whomever to book things and make calls. It's not like I do everything as a secretary. I just filter what needs to be done. The essential thing is that I'm in the loop. You and I think alike, and I like to keep up with where you are and then I can act in your best interest." She gave him a big smile.

"Well, that suits me. I'd rather call you because you know what needs to be done, even in your sleep."

"On another note, I spoke to Sabrina. Seems you've got some competition!"

"I didn't think I was in competition with Sabrina." James smirked as she looked at him knowing he was teasing her. "They're lining up to give her modeling work. She's going to call soon and probably will be over here this weekend to stay for a few days. She's trying to impress me with all her opportunities for work, so now she can provide for herself."

"I'm not surprised. She'd lost some weight after the accident and although she's a very stunning young lady, I think she's a natural. You'd better get engaged. She's a hot commodity. Don't leave it too long, Mr. James. Remember what I said at your mother's wedding."

"Okay, Mom. I'm convinced, but just want to be sure. I want to go away to some romantic island and maybe propose, just the two of us; no big fan fare."

James spent the next few minutes telling Claudia how he wants to expand his shipping line. "When John arrives, sit in on our meeting. If you want to be my personal aide—notice I didn't say secretary—I think you should be up on everything we do."

"I'd like that. You do move quickly, and sometimes I find you quite mercurial."

"Then it's good we've had our little chat today. I want you in on everything we do from now on. That way, when I'm not here, you'll know how I'm thinking and what to do. When in doubt, call me. It was unfair of me to let Nigel go and then shoot off to China leaving you holding the bag."

After having their discussion, they strolled over for a coffee at a nearby café then crossed the street toward the bank. Sure enough, John had arrived and Rose had taken him to the conference room.

"John, I want you to meet Claudia. She's the managing director of our bank, and if you can't reach me for any reason, she's the person to contact."

After the introductions were made, John started in. "James, I've been to Southampton and to Felixstowe and there's no doubt in my mind that we should make Felixstowe our main place of operation. For living, the town of Ipswich is close...or Colchester. Whatever poses the best solution for the kids' education and, of course, my wife. I believe that we should rent an office at Southampton and slowly move out of London, and during the course of the year, we can see the necessity of being at Southampton for possibly our bulk cargo ships and tankers if we ever enter into liquid transportation. I know you have some very faithful old customers who ship with you, but I see the direction for us as containerization. If we can increase the size of our ships and pick up more routes, then we'd be in a very strong position to be a dominant player in this market. Felixstowe will be cheaper than London and Southampton, although Southampton certainly has the facilities to also handle all our container business. You could buy several acres close to the port and build and design the building we want for a lot less than we could at Southampton. You live up that way, too, don't you?"

"You plan to move out of London completely, right?" interjected Claudia. "For Trans Global?"

"Yes," James answered, "Mainly because of cost, traffic, and transportation from the docks. We're in a business that's growing by leaps and bounds in shipping containers and this is where we want to build our future. Felixstowe is on the way to becoming one of the largest container ports in England, if not in Europe, and we want to be part of that."

James then directed the conversation back to John. "I agree. Sound thinking. Find you a spot in Southampton. I remember my father and I looked down there when I was a boy. There're plenty of places we can rent on First and Second Avenue close to the port there. I like the idea of having our own building in Felixstowe. I'll use the same architects we have in Hong Kong; their main office is here in London. So John, let's get going and I'll bring Claudia up to date with a copy of your proposal."

John shook hands and left.

"Those are some big changes you're planning," Claudia observed.

"Look, here are his plans. Make a copy and read it over when you have a moment."

"So you plan to upgrade the fleet?"

"Do you realize our man in Hong Kong could ship three to four times what we're doing now?" stated James. "We have a first-class reputation and I would like us to focus more on containers than bulk cargo. We have special jobs, of course, but they are a very small part of our revenue stream."

"There are no flies on you, James. I don't think this place has seen this much action for a long time."

"That's why we divested our money from the stock exchange. We need that cash to buy these ships and it's about time. In the next five to ten years we can quadruple this business. Now's the time to do it before someone else occupies that space."

"Well, this man seems like a good bet. He's young and seems smart."

"We need to do some in-depth thinking now that we have John on board," instructed James. "Our administration, accounting, and management should go to Felixstowe. In other words, we need to keep the financial office here. I know we've held all that here, but I believe it should be at the port. We only need to have here the final numbers. They need to be an autonomous unit that supplies an income statement, writes cheques, pays bills, and so on. I know we've done all this here for years, but I think it's time for a change. This is a bank and a corporate office. As Trans Global grows, we'll never be able to handle it. That's why I've chosen John. We must have Roger Bell to watch the money and police TGS as it grows.

"I agree. When we get this new accountant hired, I'll put him to work on it. We need a system that can be off-loaded and has good controls and accountability, which we can direct from here."

CHAPTER 9

A CHANGE OF PLANS

That evening Sabrina called James to tell him she would be coming for the weekend. He could pick her up from London Airport as usual—same time, same place.

He'd also been thinking about Sandra, his girlfriend from his schooldays, and decided to give her a call. He'd promised to take her out after his dance with her at New Year's, and hadn't gotten back to her.

"I'm so sorry I haven't gotten back to you sooner."

"I understand. I gave our evening a lot of thought after your party."

"Sabrina had an accident...lucky to be alive. She's okay now, but it was a big scare."

"That's terrible. Are you in London now?"

"Yes."

"So am I. I haven't eaten yet. Why don't we get a bite together and catch up? Come over to the Rib Room and we can eat there. I know you like a good steak. Say in about hour?"

"Sandra, you look very pretty tonight. You seem to have a glow about you," said James as he entered the Rib Room. His ability to read auras had continued to grow and he could sense a person's energy and color more quickly than before.

"You're right, I'm engaged to be married." She proudly showed him the ring and he congratulated her.

"Who's the lucky guy?"

"His name is George Hunter. I've been dating him on and off for two years. Since your New Year's bash, we have became more serious. So the wedding is planned for September. I hope you can make it."

"Absolutely! I wouldn't miss it for the world."

"He has his own business in the motor trade. His dealership isn't far from where we live in Cranleigh. He's a distributor for Audi and Volkswagen. He's thirty-one and wants to settle down and have a family. His father is very well to do, and has loaned him some of the money to buy this dealership. He also religiously saved money himself...and proved himself to be a very competent chartered accountant, like you."

"Sounds like a smart man. You seem to like these older guys."

"Well, you're not like a lot of men your age. You're much more mature. For a woman, men take a minute to grow up and mature. I don't think I'm alone in my thinking that a man who's a little older is more appealing and has that experience that a woman likes, or I do. Anyway, I've always loved you, but in a way it was stopping me from loving anyone else. Once I opened my mind to that reality, things started to change for me."

"Sandra, you'll always be special to me. We get on, and I find you so easy to talk to. You do hold some of your cards close to your chest though. When I saw you ride a horse for the first time, it was an absolute joy to watch. Are you still riding?"

"After we get settled and organized I'm going to be working with him in the business doing the accounts. When things are running smoothly, yes, I'll be out there on my favorite horse, Prancer. Riding is just a part of my life. You're not so bad yourself, but teaching George might be a challenge." She laughed. "Anyway, enough about me. What about you?"

They were both enjoying their meal together and then James relayed Sabrina's accident.

"How awful! You must have been devastated. It's a wonder she's recovered so quickly."

"Marco was the only son and heir to one of the largest vineyards in Tuscany. I don't think his father will ever get over it."

"James, I will always recall our time we had at Penbroke, when we left school and that great sense of freedom of waking up in the morning and not having that structure and discipline to deal with. That experience in the Throne Room I still meditate about and it has awakened in me a sense and belief that I will always have...because of you," Sandra said in her sweet modest way.

"It was special," agreed James. "I can now see auras and energy fields around people and that's how I knew there was a special glow coming out of you from your excitement of getting married. You must take time to go see Sarah at our 'Throne Room' and take your husband-to-be. Have a reading. I know you to be a very spiritual person. Keep working to develop and use those skills."

"You're right. I miss that about us. Will I always be able to come and visit and bring some of my like-minded friends?"

"Of course. I believe we met for a very special reason, and that friendship will always be there."

James was happy for her. She'd found someone to love and marry. They enjoyed a beautiful evening together. It was a sad realization that their paths were now moving in different directions, but that love they felt for one another would always be there. *Life takes us on a course we must journey*, thought James. He was in love with Sabrina and he was glad that she'd understood. It hadn't been necessary to discuss the matter any further.

James was sitting at his desk, thinking about taking Sabrina to Penbroke for the weekend. He hadn't been there in a couple of months and he particularly wanted to see Sarah and have a discussion about the many things on his mind. He was feeling the heavy weight of his responsibilities and the huge investments he was about to make. *Life is all about risk*, he thought. *You have to spend money to make money. If you don't, you risk staying on the sidelines or moving backward. Money, in and of itself, is something that deteriorates with inflation. It needs to be put to use. Bricks and mortar*, his father always said, *was a sound investment*. It had made him wonder why his father had originally invested all that money from Trans Global into the stock market. The money should have been carefully reinvested into the business and this huge amount of money he was about to spend would not be necessary.

With the amount of money Trans Global had, with no debt, it was enough to build the company's fleet on an annual basis. A lot of time had been lost in the world's shipping business by not reinvesting on an annual basis. At least he had the money to do it. He supposed his father thought they'd had enough and that building the business any larger wasn't necessary. Even if he wanted to keep the business the same, it still didn't make sense not to keep the fleet upgraded. The older generation must have thought that showing you had extra money made people want higher wages. Although that didn't seem logical, having the money to invest should give confidence, and if a man was worth his weight he should be paid properly. There was a going rate in the market place and most employees knew that already. Perhaps his father was tired of the responsibility. It was certainly an enormous task and undertaking that was before him now. He would just have to work his tail off now and make the money back and never put the business in a position like this again.

"Sir Nicholas is on the phone for you," said Rose, waking James from his thoughts.

"Nicholas, what are you up to? I was thinking of giving you a buzz myself."

"Building your empire. I've heard all about your new skyscraper in Hong Kong. I thought I might be interested in leasing some space from you for my business, when you get this project underway."

"Always interested in taking money," James laughed. "I'm going to need some myself after we've paid that bill for the building. By the way, I'm picking up Sabrina tonight and going up to Penbroke. Why don't you come over and stay with us and bring Davina?"

"Stay in that haunted mansion of yours with spooky old thrones? Sounds like an excellent idea. I know Davina enjoys your company."

"I also know how enamoured you are with Sabrina."

"Who the hell wouldn't be?" asked Nicholas. "Sorry, old boy, you're the one she's got her eyes firmly set on."

"Then we'll see you say late on Saturday afternoon?"

"Splendid, I'll bring the champers. Look forward to it!"

James left the office early Thursday afternoon, as he had one matter on his mind that he wanted to explore before he would fetch Sabrina. Claudia winked at him as he passed her office. "Behave yourself, if that's possible." She laughed, thinking it was about time he took a break.

Sabrina's plane was landing at midday on Saturday. He would take Friday off, look around the estate, and then after the people had left for the day he would make his way over to the Throne Room. The traffic was never kind driving from Claudia's home in Hamsptead on a Friday afternoon to Penbroke, so driving up on Thursday made more sense. Also driving on Saturday morning to the airport from Penbroke would give him some time and he would encounter less traffic. It had been over two months for his long-awaited moment to get his hands behind the wheel of his Aston Martin. At least he'd had the fluid changed as Kate had mentioned and the tires checked at the time of his first service.

CHAPTER 10

THE DARK VORTEX

After making his usual rounds of the estate, he made his way over to the Throne Room. The people had left for the day, and it was still light enough to make the voyage. He was concerned that time on this other place may be different from the time he had experience going to meet with his guides.

He remembered there being another notebook, which the seventh earl had left, referencing an experience he had traveling to the dark vortex. Being younger, he was slightly apprehensive about the thought of traveling to this unknown place, but now, he was ready and his curiosity was getting the better of him.

It was titled the "Dark Vortex." He rushed to read the earl's notes. There at the back of one of the lower drawers, behind some papers, he found the illustrious notebook.

It read…

June 14, 1857

I knew instinctively that there had to be a balancing force to the three-dimensional planet we lived on. So with my usual curiosity I meditated deeply on the subject of there being another reality that lay in the astral plain between the fifth dimension and our life on Earth. In my haste to learn, a number entered my head, two hundred and thirty-two degrees. I immediately rotated the Throne on its circumference to this angle of direction to its base. I nervously thought about the consequences that I might experience as a result of trying to take this trip, but I had to know something about how the material reality of our planet was possible. There had to be another force that existed in the universe that created our dimension and my curiosity got the better of me.

"I sat on the Throne in the usual way as I had before and within seconds I was swirling through a vortex not of complete darkness but of fiery red light with flashes of white.

I arrived sitting on a throne in a great hall.

Two ladies met me on my arrival, and ushered me to the great hall. Sitting there on his magnificent throne was a man of presence and youth, nothing like what I suspected.

"You thought you would be visiting a horned beast surrounded by fire and flames?" He laughed out loud, imagining that this lord thought he had met the devil incarnate.

"The thought had occurred that I was on a one-way ticket to hell, but my curiosity got the better of me," I said, still not trusting that I was seeing the real picture and that he was just giving me a kind introduction before showing me the real horrors to come.

"Understandable, in the circumstances. I am sorry to disappoint you." He again laughed at my suspicious and cautious apprehension.

He took me all around his palace and began to explain who and what they were all about. He was what the Bible would classify as a fallen angel who had lived in the great divine presence of the God light, which he was happy to explain as the source of our reality on planet Earth. Much to my amazement, he was not evil in the sense I had thought. He was part of a number of fallen angels that had broken away from the divine order, to create a reality that they were happy to live in. He told me that many people are not ready for a life that was more spiritual. They had used the dark energy of the universe to create with the light a reality where they could experience the way of life that we now have on Earth.

Far from the writings of religious belief, he convinced me that they served a very purposeful presence in evolving souls. The fact that mankind chooses the path of darkness is a choice of their own making. He convinced me that he and his brotherhood work hard to play a role in the evolution of the universe and have to deal with souls that have of their own volition done evil and heinous crimes against humanity. They can't evolve until they have balanced their karmic debt. He explained that they were part of the architecture of the universe contrary to the way the Bible had explained who they were.

"We take care of those lost souls and attempt to recycle them back to Earth." He also explained how there were many accomplished souls, who wanted to return to Earth for future growth and to many other planets that had similarly evolved.

Needless to say I was fascinated with what I had learned and it would take many more pages to relate the whole experience. I write these notes in the hope that future generations can take the trip and experience the ludicrous indoctrination that I was once taught about heaven and hell.

James was intrigued with what he had found, but decided he would make the trip now. He had a lot on his plate, and wanted to have a deeper understanding of the universe and validate what the seventh earl had written.

He pondered on the thought of travelling through the "Dark Vortex," as his great-grandfather had described, and then nervously made his way over to the Throne. He was again concerned that time could be different in this alternate reality, similar to Earth. Being like Earth it could have a similar gravitational pull in order to distort time, and therefore, he had waited until the crowds had dissipated to make the journey. He told the staff to leave the Throne Room open, as he would close up. The room now had an electronic security system with cameras inside and outside. He had the code in his wallet and so made his way over to take his voyage. He rotated the Throne to 232 degrees as the notebook recommended, and then sat in his seat once again.

The journey was not as quick as going to see his masters—that was instantaneous—but he was moving at a rate that was still fast, by any normal standard. It was strange that the light surrounding him was definitely bright red, but not as white as was described in the notes.

It was then that he arrived in the Palace, but it wasn't like the surroundings described in the book. It seemed darker, more foreboding, and cold. Again, two ladies ushered him away from his throne, down a long dimly lit corridor that opened out into a vast hallway with statues of great historical significance like Alexander the Great, Julius Caesar, Napoleon. *But not Hitler?*

There, before him seated on his magnificent gold and bejeweled throne sat the King or Potentate, described. He looked older, unlike the person he had read about, lacking the energy that his forefather had experienced.

He arose. "Welcome, Lord James. So finally your curiosity for wanting to understand the darker side has been awakened in you?

They shook hands but James did not like the vibration he received. The overwhelming power and force of this being was intense and beguiling. Things must have changed and he wondered why.

"Forgive me, but from the notes I have read from the seventh earl, does it appear that a change has taken place?"

"Your observations are accurate. You must now be aware of the massive population growth on your planet. This has brought about a significant reduction in our energy."

"I don't understand. From the notes I've read, you were in a sense a clearinghouse to reconstruct souls who had lost their way and allow new opportunities for those misdirected souls?"

"This is true, but the ever-increasing amount of lost souls we receive from your planet, and others like your Earth, are seriously draining our resources."

"So why doesn't the divine force increase your energy in order for you to carry out this wonderful task?"

"Your planet and others are nearing the end of a cycle. When this happens your Earth will either move to a higher vibration and restore its own energy supply or will be left with no alternative but to renew itself and continue with a rebirth, such as happened after the last ice age. When this takes place, we have no alternative but to shed those souls that have returned here too many times to a lower dimension."

"So, what you are saying is that those souls who, in a sense, are beyond redemption have to take a step backward?"

"Yes, there are younger planets that have not advanced beyond animal form, so in this way they will have to relearn life in a changed state in order to acquire the values they have lost. Everyone has a chance. Some advance to higher dimensions, while others have to take a step backward. This is how the universe works: the life form of a body is given, and then it becomes our own individual choice to learn the ways of advancement in spirituality or not. It's is then, and only then, that our own energy is renewed."

"As unthinkable as this sounds, it makes sense. The universe is forever trying to advance who we are, but it becomes our own choice as to whether we see through the power of materialism and balance ourselves with values that are there for all of us to embrace?"

"We sadly have to change the material body's DNA for those souls back to their original origin so that they can relearn. We are indebted to those souls that move on passed our dimensions ever striving to be in the presence of the creator. It is then and only then we too receive a renewal of energy. This is how our universe maintains complete balance. In a sense those that pass to a higher dimension heal us, but also give opportunity again, even to those that have to be returned to a lower form of existence. The planets also play their role, depending upon the force of change they must undergo from the results of life upon their planet at the end of a cycle."

"How does one measure this energy needed? Does it depend to a large degree on the advancement and lack thereof from those souls who don't?" asked James.

"Precisely. Your planet has advanced to a stage where four cycles of civilization have already existed. Many have advanced to higher dimensions, like your guides and masters that live in the star system of the Pleiades, but not yet enough to advance the planet as a whole. As your planet is only halfway through its life cycle and expendable energy, it can renew itself, so there's still time. Other planets will die and become like other dead planets that circle your Sun with no atmosphere, as the driving force of its central magnetic field has dried up. We must all understand that by our own advancement, we in turn energize the very planet we live upon. This is a profound subject and yet a mathematical balance that is known only to the highest levels of those within the light of the divine creator."

"These actions are then of particular importance, and gives me a greater understanding of how important it is for all of us to work harder to recognize what our planet so unselfishly, gives, allows us, to do and be. It now remains for us as human beings to have a greater love and awareness for the great gift we have been given and to live life on such a beautiful place." James was becoming tired. He could feel the great strain this man was under, and then he asked his name."

"Why, I am Lucifer of course! The fallen one. Maybe one day you will come to respect all the hard work we do on your behalf. Perhaps you, James, could put in a good word for me." He laughed out loud to what appeared to be long overdue. "Your presence today gives me hop...and your questions even more so. However, go easy on claiming me as a savior. It may not be well received, as yet. Who knows in time?" The pair of them laughed and then opened their arms to give each other an unlikely hug. To think he had been talking to Lucifer all this time, only to realize that he made complete sense. Some would say, the arch deceiver had won again. James did not see it that way.

****

James returned to the house after closing up the Throne Room. He had been right about the time change; it was dark; he had to have been gone for at least four hours. He pondered over all that had been said by Lucifer. It seemed possible that he served a role somehow in the universe. God had made it very clear that he was the Alpha and the Omega in Genesis, the first chapter of the Bible. It also made sense that we all die, and not everyone goes to heaven, or at least not right away. It also made sense that our physical form or body dies and the spirit must learn and work toward a higher purpose. Taking on a new body was like having another chance to evolve.

However, if we didn't learn the laws of spiritual guidance and love and from our teachings to increase our understanding, then the possibility of us digressing had to exist. James's mind was thoughtfully analyzing all these points over a cup of tea before retiring to bed.

It also made sense that if we were completely devoid of any spiritual knowledge we would digress to a lower understanding and therefore require a physical body to reexperience life in a lesser form. The divine respects all creation. We just have to learn our own journey in our own free time. If life on Earth was everlasting, he thought, then maybe we would have the freedom of choice to remain there, but life is not. The only true constant is change and we have to in our own way move with it. He would sleep and meditate with his masters to receive more answers; it was a lot to absorb completely. He would also talk it over with Jeremy Soames in time and ask about his own understanding of the way life evolved and digressed.

CHAPTER 11

SABRINA'S EXCITING NEWS

Sabrina was standing at the entrance as he crossed from the parking lot.

"James, mio amore." She looked fabulous, with her large charcoal-rimmed hat, her long flowing hair, and a tiny charcoal matching jacket over her bright pink summer dress, which had a lace-embroidered pattern showing some of her skin. Her matching hot pink open-toed high heels certainly helped to make her look irresistible.

"My lovely Sabrina! I see you're getting quite a flair for wearing eye-catching finery." James took her suitcase and was proud to be walking the love of his life to his car.

"James, you forget, I'm a model now and I must promote fashion; it's what pays my bills."

"Well, that's a relief. Now I can become a kept man, since my girlfriend can keep me in a manner I'm used to!"

"I have all I can to pay for myself, but believe me, I would love to." Then she whispered in his ear, "I want all of you right here and now, but I'll be a good girl and wait."

She looked so beautiful that he decided to stay the night in London. The traffic would be easing up as commuters were on their way home. They could go out to dinner at a restaurant he knew well, where he would be so proud to show her off.

They parked the car and walked over to The Brass Bell, one of James's favorite places to have the very best cuisine. They all knew him well and certainly the Friday night crowd was looking attentively at Sabrina.

The owner came over and enjoyed having a conversation in Italian with her. He was from Florence too, and knew exactly where she lived and the vineyard her father owned. She was already selling him her father's wine.

"So this is where you hang out when I'm not around," said Sabrina when the owner had left.

"I thought this would be an appropriate way to kick off our weekend before we're eating at the pubs in Lincolnshire."

"I'm happy just eating a cheese sandwich at the kitchen table as long as I'm with you."

"This weekend we'll be seeing Sir Nicholas and Davina at my home in Penbroke. They're coming to stay the night and we can all go out for dinner tomorrow."

"Nicholas is a handsome guy. He was quite confident when I met him at your twenty-first. I told him that there was only one man in the world for me and that was you, but he doesn't take no for an answer. He's a lot of fun though, and I like Davina. He should marry her. He would be a lucky man to have her."

"Well, you'll be happy to know that they are going to do just that."

"Oh, really! That's so exciting. I also want to talk to her about modeling. Maybe I could get some work over here and you and I could be closer to each other."

"It's funny you say that. I was just thinking the same thing."

"It shows we're meant for each other, I guess. Great minds think alike!"

They both ordered pasta and her favorite bottle of wine from Villa Antinori. Everyone in the room noticed the magnetic attachment they both felt for each other. They, however, were completely oblivious, lost in their own little world.

After dinner they strolled outside for a look at the shop windows, just holding hands, and then they went back to the flat. They spent the rest of the evening wrapped in each other's arms, adoring the completeness they felt of being together again.

James got up early, but he noticed that Sabrina had beaten him to it. She had breakfast ready as he entered the kitchen.

"My Sabrina, you take good care of me," he said, giving her a kiss.

"See what you could get used to, if I was around," she said, looking very sensual in her light silk nightdress and slippers.

"Let's finish breakfast and get on the road before all the traffic hits."

"Just because you want to open up that car of yours. I know you, James. You like speed."

"Can you always read my mind?"

"Most of the time. It's funny when one has a near-death experience, I do have perceptions and senses about things that I didn't have before. What has helped me trust my intuitions is having had that experience with you in the Throne Room. I believe everyone has these abilities; they just don't develop them and trust what they may feel. I love that we can talk about the wildest things and be in sync. Most men don't believe in those things, but I've found that many girl friends like to talk about what's out there in the beyond. It's so nice that you and I can learn from each other."

But James's mind was clearly elsewhere. "Thinking what I'm thinking?"

"James, let's finish breakfast. We have all day for that. Drink your coffee. You're still half asleep."

"Dreaming about you."

James packed lightly since he had everything he needed at his home in Penbroke, and before eight o'clock they were burning their way up the north circular for the weekend.

Sabrina broke the silence as they turned off onto the A1 motorway.

"James, will you always love me like you do?"

"Why? Having second thoughts?"

"That's not an answer."

"I don't think I could ever stop loving you more and more every time I see you. Ever since we met, I feel this electricity when I'm with you, and I just work when we're not, because it shuts out the pain of not seeing you."

Sabrina sighed. "We must be together. I'm not talking marriage. We've been seeing each other on and off for over three years. The pain of us not being together is too much."

"Look, after this weekend let's take a holiday and get away to some Caribbean island where I can surprise you and from then on we shall be together for as long as we have breath in our bodies. Let's organize our lives so that you can work over here and then help me get Penbroke Court renovated for our new life together."

"I can't wait. I know you have work; I will have work and it's part of our life having to travel. Living together and sleeping together is all I care about."

It was getting close to eleven o'clock when they turned into the gates of Penbroke Court and Rodney was around at the garage to open up the door for the young couple.

James and Sabrina decided to walk over to see if Sarah was around.

"Sarah, how lovely to see you," exclaimed Sabrina when they ran into her.

"I just heard from Kate and she seems very happy out there in Hong Kong. She's madly in love with this Roger and she's quickly adapting to the way of life. She misses all of us, but she loves the weather out there. In their spare time they're exploring all those islands and new places outside the island of Hong Kong itself. But tell me about Roger. What's he like?"

"Tall, dark haired, and handsome. If I didn't know him better, I'd think he would have women lining up, but he's shy, except when it comes to work, and then he changes completely. He's extremely well educated and comes from a good well to do family, and I believe Kate is perfect for him. She beats him in everything from table tennis to snooker and he doesn't mind at all. He loves her self-confidence and competitive nature and I believe she brings out the very best in him. A perfect match, I'd say."

"I'm so excited for her. We all know she's a bossy knickers, so he sounds like the right person. It's always a relief when your kids find the right one, so we'll keep our fingers crossed. And Sabrina, look at yourself, you become more and more beautiful every time I see you. James, you can't leave this woman on the market any longer."

"Just what I've been telling him," said Sabrina. "He needs to get his head out of those numbers and check out the catch he has. You know, I'm a model now and I'm earning some money, so I'm not a kept daughter or girlfriend any longer."

"A model! That's not hard to believe. You're a natural with that sparkling personality and that lovely Italian accent. I can't wait to see some photographs."

"We're seeing Sir Nicholas later today," said James, "so she might be able to get some work here and then we could be closer together."

"I can see that happening," Sarah surmised.

"I'd like to spend some time with you alone when you're free," James said to Sarah.

"Sure. Come over after lunch, say one o'clock and we can talk about everything."

Sabrina and James went off to have lunch at the little pub in Penbroke now renamed The Flying Bullet. James's horse, Bullet, had become a local hero, so the publican had renamed his pub in honor of Joe's successes in riding Bullet to victory.

"You want to have a talk with Sarah after lunch?" asked Sabrina curiously.

"I do. She needs some new buildings. We're replacing the temporary buildings that surround the Throne Room with permanent ones that match the architecture of the house. With the expansion of the business and the amount of visitors who come each year, we now have to expand, mainly thanks to Sarah's efforts. Also, I have a lot on my mind with the expansion of my own business in London and around the world. I don't have a mother or anyone to really bounce off ideas with. Claudia is my closest confidant but it's sometimes good to have an outside perspective."

"I hope one day you'll share more about your business so that I can understand it all. I'm pretty good with numbers, but I don't believe the world of business would be for me. I can only give you what I feel from my own intuitions about people."

"Just being with you is enough," cooed James. "Loving someone like you is a power that elevates a man like me to be successful. I believe in love and the transcending power that it has. All this without someone to love would be an empty existence. I want my time with you to be about us, and our children one day. A place where we can draw the shutters on business and be the human beings God intended. For me, you completely fulfill that role and I would never ask anymore of you than that."

They finished their lunch and James took Sabrina into the house.

"Now go and explore everywhere by yourself and tell me all about it when I get back," instructed James. "Rodney is around if you have any questions." He walked down the long corridor to the east wing where he saw Rodney. "Rodney, I would like you to make up the guest room and see that it's clean and also, see that the master bedroom is up to par as well. Get some help if you need from Keith Pruett. Sabrina is looking around so don't be startled if you find her in some place you think she shouldn't be."

"Yes, my lord." Rodney was from the old school of house staff, well into his sixties, but faithfully performing his duties with impeccable responsibility. He'd always been a quiet man. James thought he should make the effort to talk with him more often.

James continued his walk to Sarah's office. "There you are. I have an hour and my staff is now better trained, so it frees me up a little more. The weekends are always busy this time of year. I've made some herbal tea, so come and sit at my table here and make yourself comfortable."

Sarah then continued to hold his hands to feel his energy and tune herself into his aura. She liked to use her Tarot cards as they were her way of being able to collect her thoughts of what she was seeing and hear what her guides would communicate to her. She had him pick out the cards and she turned them over and placed them between the two of them as she had done before.

"James, there's a lot of activity going on in your life. I see action all over the place: ships, buildings, airplanes, and big lorries; there's no end to it. So much change and you are wondering how to manage it all. It's all meant to be and you are doing an incredible job with the hiring of new people and changing the way things had been done in the past. It's a new age and your businesses have been run well, except for the one in Hong Kong, which I will get to later. They have not had the investment that should have been made at an earlier time.

"Now the burden is placed on you. I see the shipping business growing, and not to talk badly of your father, he saw that too. He was comfortable in his latter years. He decided to leave that decision to the next generation: to take the business forward or reinvest, expand, or sell. You have chosen the most courageous direction and that is to build on what you have, honoring and respecting your forefathers. Your guides love you for this and I can only see tremendous success. You know you must do this or alternatively sell the business to someone who will. This business has to be put right and grow. It will all come to pass, and don't have fear about the money; it will all be there. You have good guides working with you to that end. Think of all the jobs you'll create and the hopes and dreams that'll be given to so many.

"The man you have in Hong Kong, this Roger, is very smart. He's going to do something with the bank that hasn't been done for some time. Trust him. He's sharp. This man will not only make himself rich, but the bank as well. You'll learn from him. You like risk, but you are not sure when it comes to investing in people you don't know. You like to invest in what you can control. I feel you are watching him very closely; he wants to show you what he can do. I believe he's Jewish. He's afraid to tell you though."

"It's funny you should say that," James cut in. "I thought so too, but I didn't want to bring the subject up unless he did. I have many Jewish friends; I'd actually have more faith in his handling of money if that's the case. I've always believed in the genius of Jewish people. They can start out anywhere with so little and make a success of their lives. I believe they have a gene we don't have. Banking would be perfect for him, then."

"This man you just let go from the bank...a horrible man," Sarah continued. "He works with other countries. Watch him when he surfaces again. He's a very dangerous man. Other countries that don't share our values like China and Russia will test you. Of course, there are good people there, but those who are in power are now not good souls; they think by abolishing the privileged they can help the workingman. The only person they want to help is themselves. There will be countries with different ideals that will want to invest in your bank. It's okay, but tread very carefully. Roger is your man for that. You yourself will visit these countries. You will learn a lot about them and so they will about you. Tell me; you have some new abilities, don't you?"

"Well, I can see auras now," answered James, "and I'm learning what they mean. They help me understand a person when I'm talking with them. I've also healed two people that nearly died, but I only do this when I'm called upon to help."

"Who were these two people you saved?"

"Sabrina and a young man on our journey by ship to China. I haven't told anyone else about this."

"I wasn't able to pick that up from you because my guides wanted you to tell me. It was such a selfless act you did, where you were given the power to bring people back to life. It now makes me see that they were testing you to see if you would talk about this...or just keep it to yourself."

"Obviously, Sabrina knows I did this for her after her accident, which you and I have never discussed." James brought Sarah up to date with the reason why he was not able to help Marco, and how he could only help those his guides empowered him to heal. The divine essence made the decisions for some people moving on to the afterlife and he wasn't empowered to alter those outcomes.

"Interesting. I can now tell you that you'll have other abilities because of your discreet and modest behavior. For example, you can heal and receive information on what's about to happen from your masters and you can read thoughts when you have to. Your psychic powers have grown as you have worked to use them. These abilities are there for times of great need to protect yourself, help others when guided to do so, and guard you against forces that are not good. Now Sabrina, I thought she had a glow about her that was different. So she knows what you did?"

"Yes. She could see me pulling her spirit back into her body when I was alone in the hospital room. Not even her father or my mother knows what took place. They do suspect that it was a miracle because the doctor held out very little hope. At best, she would have been an invalid."

"She wasn't meant to go. It was Marco's jealousy of wanting her that put both their lives in danger and he died for it. He knew he didn't want to live unless he could have her. The senselessness of such possessive love is not a love from the light. It is a control for lust, like possessing a toy or trophy. Thank God you saved her life."

"I fell asleep in her room and that night we talked in my dream," continued James. "She loved the place where she was so much and didn't want to return to such a mutilated body. I think she would have come anyway because any chance of us having the love we have together was worth the risk."

"It seems only right that you two are together. So now Sabrina, having had an experience like that, will see life differently. She was attractive before, but there's something quite magnetic about her, and now I can see why."

"I have something that has concerned me for a while and I keep forgetting to talk to you about it. The vortex on the Throne is very powerful. Have you ever had anyone actually get hurt or physically suffer as a result of its power?"

"I remember telling you that someone could get hurt as a result of trying to travel the vortex if they weren't ready. The answer is the vortex somehow knows not to transport a person who is not aligned. A person doesn't have to be perfectly aligned to a high degree of spirituality within themselves for the vortex to receive a person. What has happened is a person gets a glimpse of some negative experience and their fear, in a way, protects them and then the vortex rejects them. The creator of the Throne knew this, and somehow there is something built into its design that knows when a person is ready or not. In answer to your question, no one has suffered physically so far. I am always acutely aware of whether a person is ready to take the Throne or not. It does lead me to the thought that we should have more security around the Throne, in case someone tries to sit there without the proper instruction or permission.

"I know you'll do all that's necessary to make sure we protect not only ourselves from some legal action, but also the person themselves," said James. "Sarah, thank you. It's always such a gift to have you with us. I will tell Keith to get the architect to work on your new buildings here. These temporary ones have more than done their job and you deserve the best. So please, work with them to see you get what you want."

"James, a word of warning. Your business is very important to you, and it's quite natural in your young years to want to be successful, because you are competitive by nature. Know the time when to step back and let others take the lead. It's not yet, but there will come a time when the greater purpose for your life will become all too clear. Remember all material things are transitory; it's the legacy of our lives that's left behind, which will speak far and above what you are doing now. I don't mean to lessen your honorable efforts toward the business now; just keep those thoughts in mind." Sarah thought he had an idea of the advice she was giving, but James was far from giving up his frenetic drive for worldly success yet.

They gave each other a big hug. "How's Peter doing these days?" asked James.

"Oh, his father and he are rocking along."

"He needs to get those plans to me for the metal-forming

process known as shot peening."

"I'll bring him along with the plans tomorrow."

"Good. Then we can all have a beer at the pub in Penbroke?"

"I'll look forward to it."

****

James returned to the house and went looking for Sabrina. It was getting late in the afternoon and he knew Nicholas and Davina would be arriving soon. He found her combing her beautiful locks in front of the bedroom mirror.

"James, I like this room. It has a good energy about it. A lot of happiness has been shared here. The view looking out to the sea is spectacular. Can I work with you to help make this house the lovely place I'm sure it once was? It's not that it's not beautiful now; we just need to put our stamp and personality on it."

"I agree. I wonder what the world will say about us one day. Will it even matter?"

"Speak for yourself. It matters to me!" said Sabrina emphatically.

CHAPTER 12

NICHOLAS AND DAVINA

James could hear a car coming up the driveway, so he quickly hopped into another pair of slacks and put on his favorite shirt and sweater. Sabrina was busy making herself look gorgeous; she wanted to impress Nicholas for her future possibilities.

"James, old boy, I brought two bottles of Moët et Chandon. And after we polish those off, we can go get a bite," said Nicholas with his usual flair for entertainment.

"I've booked us a table at the Armoury in Lincoln," informed James. "It's the best I know round here for good food, and the least I can do for a couple that has taken the time to drive all the way from Cheshire to see us."

At that moment Sabrina descended the staircase and Nicholas watched intently. "Now that looks like a model to me; don't you agree, Davina?" He was careful not to create any jealousy. He knew Davina was very pretty and James had certainly noted that on the night of his twenty-first.

"James, now you can show me around your old home," said Davina. She then whispered to him, "Let Nicholas do his thing with Sabrina. He's actually harmless."

James liked Davina. With long flowing dark hair, tall as a model should be. She certainly had all the natural good looks to make a woman stand out: large dark brown eyes, petite features, and high cheekbones, combined with long strides, which gave her a graceful deportment. She knew how to walk the catwalk and make any woman want what she was wearing. It was her confidence. Now at twenty-seven and the future wife of Nicholas, she possessed all the confidence a man like Nicholas would want.

"James, I think we make a good dancing couple, don't you?"

"You're too kind, but I do like to dance with a person of your natural ability. Makes a man's job a lot easier."

"Nicholas hasn't a clue. He steps all over my feet, but I love him anyway. It's certainly not given to us all. So now I have the chance to know you a little better. You look more mature than your years."

"Well, when you lose a parent at fourteen you tend to grow up in a hurry."

"Nicholas had a tough father, but he probably deserved it with all the gallivanting around he's done. You look more stayed, but don't forget to let your hair down and run across the lawn stark naked and scream at the world occasionally!"

It was impossible to not like Davina. She reminded James of a Lauren Bacall—a classy flair, with an outrageous sense of humor. She'd keep old Nicholas on his toes. She'd been modeling since she was seventeen and there wasn't a magazine in the world that hadn't photographed her. She was a wealthy woman in her own right and had to be respected for all those hours and dedication she'd put into being the best.

"Let's go down to theThrone Room. Nicholas has told me all about it so I must see it for myself."

James was delighted to get her down there before Rodney locked up.

"Wow, this place could take a person's breath away. No wonder you went to all that effort. These are great pictures of your grandparents. So here's the Throne. Look at those gemstones! Every woman dreams to own a collection of rocks like that, don't you think?"

"They're worth quite a lot, that's for sure," said James, laughing to himself.

"Have you sat on that throne and gone to wherever?"

"I certainly have."

"I don't think I've got the nerve, but I am intrigued. So tell me what happens."

"Well, you can meet your guides, and maybe your master. It's a different experience for each person. All I know is I've never met a person who wasn't emotionally moved by the experience."

"So there's really something up there for all of us to believe in. Isn't that amazing?"

"Over there are classrooms, which we are about to make into permanent buildings, including the souvenir shop and tea rooms."

"I will do this one day, I promise. Let's go to the souvenir shop; I want to take something back with me." They went in and walked around and the attendants there were excited to see his Lordship and Davina whom they recognized from magazines. They welcomed them both and extended their best wishes to the couple. Davina bought a little book that told her the whole story of the Throne Room and the history of the Lords of Penbroke. James quietly walked over to the shelf next to the register and pulled out a small keychain that had a replica of the Throne attached. He then walked back and gave it to Davina and said, “I realize the rocks aren’t as big as the ones on the Throne, but it should give you inspiration enough to tell Nicholas that you really need the real thing!”

“Thanks, and I will certainly relay the message. He truly owes me that much, and a car to go with it!” she said, laughing and giving James a little hug. The staff was all laughing at her remarks, knowing they could only dream of such a thing. “Should we put that on your account, your Lordship?” asked a member of his staff.

“The key chain or the real thing?” he asked with a sly smirk.

James was secure in knowing that the little key chain would be highly valued. He hoped one day she would possibly take a lesson from Sarah McKenzie and make the trip into the unknown. Davina, beneath her classy image and upfront humor, was a very feeling person. James could read that from her aura. In the world of fashion she had to get tough and stand out. That’s the world that made her, but inside was this little girl that was fascinated learning about the things that James had shown her.

“Well, we ought to walk back and hook up with the others and have a drink of that champagne that Nicholas brought,” suggested James.

“Thank you for showing me all this. I promise I’ll return and in the meantime I’ll cherish my key ring.”

James and Davina returned. Nicholas already had Sabrina striding backward and forward, up and down the staircase, and then decided that she definitely had what it took.

“Come to my office on Monday and we’ll sign you up, young lady.”

“So you can use her for your line of clothes?” asked James anxiously.

“I can. Our styling is more sophisticated and is totally suited to her disposition. I know Darlene Jenson of Fashion World will definitely help her, as she did Claudia. Sabrina is a natural for swimsuit wear. Sporty…sophisticated—she can do it all. She'll be a very busy lady by the time I get through with her."

"I didn't know Claudia did modeling. I'd like to talk to her when we can."

"You still use her?"

"Claudia? Absolutely. Women love the way she looks. She's got that sophisticated style that sells my clothes off the rack."

Nicholas poured everyone a glass of champagne as they all sat down in the drawing room. They laughed about the last time Nicholas was there and Sabrina was teaching him some dance steps at James's twenty-first birthday party. Deep down, James wanted to get engaged when he took Sabrina on holiday. He would of course ask her father, Antonio, as was the custom in the older, more respected families.

"James, we're here to ask you and Sabrina to come to my place for our wedding. I've brought the invitation; I warned you some months ago in London. It will be near our home in Cheshire, not far from where our main factories are, around Manchester and Leeds. Put it on your calendar for Saturday, September twenty-fourth at 2:00 p.m. at the old vicarage in the village of Tarporley."

"So you're on the doorstep to the Duke of Westminster who has some ten thousand acres at his country home. Eaton Hall? I've not had the occasion to visit," said James.

"Well, our home is not quite as large, but there will be room at the inn if you want to stay," said Nicholas modestly. "James, I want you to be my best man. Davina's school friend will be her maid of honor and her sister will be her bridesmaid, and you too, Sabrina, if you would," said Nicholas, with the nodding approval of Davina.

"I would be delighted to be a bridesmaid," said Sabrina without hesitation.

"I don't know you that well," said James, shocked.

"Well, it's not a question of that. You're the only man I

know. I've spent my whole life surrounded by women and I would have had a best woman, but Davina wouldn't approve, so it's down to you, old boy. Just dream up some rubbish about me; they'll all be sloshed by that time and won't remember a damn thing anyway."

The four of them packed into Nicholas's Rolls and sped off to Lincoln for the evening.

The Armoury Hotel had always been impeccably run. The headwaiter, after checking the booking, personally escorted the ladies, one on each arm, with a tremendous sense of importance in front of a staring Saturday night crowd.

"James, you chose well," admitted Nicholas. "I don't know Lincolnshire well, but this looks like the place to go for a decent meal. Many people were looking over at the table placed strategically in the center, recognizing Davina from her modeling, and were busy gossiping as to who the other guests might be. No doubt the headwaiter would inform them all on his rounds. Having important people to dinner was the finest form of marketing for the hotel."

Between Nicholas, Davina, Sabrina, and James, they were all in continuous fits of laughter, thanks mostly to Davina. The room got louder and louder as everyone started to get into the spirit of having a good time. Sabrina was quietly watching the British well-to-do enjoying the evening. It was opposite of all the things she had learned growing up.

"James, I want to go to Hong Kong the next time you go," said Nicholas. "I've got some contacts with the Swires Group; they own a big chunk of the airline Cathay Pacific. We should get a first-class seat for both of us. Hong Kong has a future for us and nothing would make me happier than to have a showroom there. I want to tailor our fashion for the up-and-coming Asian women. I'm also looking at manufacturing there. Costs are going up here and if we're going to maintain our competitive position in the upper-class community against all these Italian, French, and German designers, I've got to start getting creative. Heard about your escapade with your bank manager out there from you-know-who. That took some guts. People in high positions are taking a lot of notice of a man that's going places. You're an inspiration. You get out there and get involved. That's what it takes. Things don't run themselves; they end up running you."

Nicholas's admiration for James was growing rapidly. Even though he was a lot older, he felt very close to James. James's maturity made them a good pair. James thought he would get to know Nicholas better and start bouncing ideas off him. They weren't competitors and they could help each other. He was glad that he'd invited him for the weekend and could see that Davina would be a great asset as well as a friend to Sabrina in helping her with her career.

"Do you ride?" James asked Nicholas.

"Not my cup of tea, but I know Davina does. Want to go riding tomorrow with James?"

"Absolutely! I would love to, and you too, Sabrina. Nicholas will you ride, as well?"

"No. I'm going over there to see Sarah tomorrow. I want to start to open up my stuffy old mind. You guys hit the beach. Let this old timer have some peace and solitude and learn how to meditate."

"Actually, that would be great for you, Nicholas. Sarah would love to work with you. It would be such a complement for you to go and see her," said James, thinking Nicholas was really trying to make an effort. He thought Davina must have had something to do with that. Nicholas had always felt sorry for saying what he did that day to James, about his disbelief in Atlantis, and the whole realization that another dimension did exist. Now this was a moment to take a different type of risk and see where it would take him.

James picked up the tab. They all drove back to Penbroke.

Nicholas was trying to scare Davina into believing one of the earls was a complete crackpot and goes stalking the hallways and corridors in the middle of the night. Sabrina then said, "James, is this true?"

"It's only an apparition."

"Tell me this isn't true!"

"Yes, James, tell me it isn't true!" Davina joined in the hysterics.

"I'll tell you what. If any of you hear something come get me and I'll take care of it."

"Not bloody likely! You're not ending up with two women in your bed, James," said Nicholas.

"You started it. I can't say I've experienced anything, and I've slept here since I was a baby. But different people sense and see different things!"

"James, stop having us all on," said Sabrina, thumping him in the ribs.

They all had one last glass to celebrate a fabulous evening and Davina had to be sure there wasn't a ghost in the house. So she cross-examined James again. Then the hall clock struck twelve and they all nervously ran to their rooms. James initiated it, just for a laugh.

In the early hours of the morning, James awoke to a huge boom that seemed to come from the living room.

"James, I'm going with you," said a frightened Sabrina. "If that's the ghost, I want to see for myself."

Nicholas and Davina had heard the same sound and the whole gang followed James down the main staircase to the living room. There, on the floor, was a brick with a note tied around it with a piece of string. James nervously prodded the brick in case it was some kind of explosive device. After he was sure it was only a brick he untied the string and read the note.

If you're going to throw a party and talk about me, the least you could have done is invite me!!!
From:
You Know Who

The four of them stood looking at each other. "I'll call the police. Whether it's a ghost or a prank, this has to be reported. There doesn't seem to be any obvious damage, but then the police can patrol the whole house," said James, looking rather shocked.

"I agree," said Nicholas, just as concerned. "You don't have a choice."

James cautiously walked out of the room toward the front staircase to pick up the phone in the main hallway. As he picked up the phone and began to dial the number, a voice behind him started to laugh his head off. James turned around in astonishment to see sitting on the staircase none other than Antonio laughing himself to tears.

"How in God's name are you here and why did you do that?" asked James, dumbstruck.

Then James's mother, Philippa, followed Antonio down the stairs as they all started to gather at the front entrance. She was laughing along with Antonio.

Then Antonio started, "We knew Sabrina was coming over to see you, but we weren't sure you'd come to Penbroke. We wanted to get out of the heat for a week and stay at the house in London. Then we decided to drive up in case you might be here. You had all gone out to dinner, so we saw Rodney and your mother knew where your father kept an old shotgun, as I wanted to get up early and go out and shoot. Rodney got us a room at the other end of the house because we didn't want to disturb you. When you came back we were going to surprise you with our visit, and then we overheard you talking about ghosts. So forgive me, I couldn't resist the temptation. I had to fire a round after I'd put the brick in the living room with the note."

"Papa, you're so bad," and then Sabrina went off in Italian, and everyone started to join in laughing their heads off at how easily they'd all been fooled.

"Well, Nicholas, you started this whole ghost story business and look where it's got us all in the middle of the night," said Davina, laughing at him.

"I don't know about you all, but I'm going to have a drink. Anyone coming?" asked James. "And Antonio, consider yourself invited. Mother, are these the kind of antics you have to put up with in Tuscany?"

"Oh, he's always up to something. Sabrina knows her father and what he can do."

The whole group enjoyed the informal gathering and after a good scotch, slowly made their way back to their bedrooms.

The next morning everyone was feeling a little sleepy from the night's interruption. At least it was Sunday.

Antonio came over to see James. "I'm still amazed at the recovery my Sabrina has made and now she makes good money. I can never thank you enough for coming to see her. What happened to me was a miracle, and I know only a loving God could make that possible and you were his instrument, James. Love is a powerful thing and it doesn't always give us what we want but what is right. In Sabrina's case, it was what we all wanted and it was right. When that happens, it's truly special." He lovingly patted James on the back in a way that a father would to a son.

"Life without Sabrina would be an uphill battle for all of us."

"I'm going for my walk and see if I can shoot something. I know you'll take the girls riding."

Nicholas was busy chatting with Phillipa as the girls got up to leave with James.

"Phillipa, I'm going over to have a chat with Sarah. I've thought a lot about that throne room and how well James has done with this project. I'm curious to see how it all looks." He then slowly made his way down to the east wing to Sarah's classroom.

"Sarah, do you remember me?" he asked.

"Of course. How could I forget?"

"Can I take a few moments from you? I'd really like to take another go on that throne. Do you think I'm ready?" he asked nervously.

"Come and sit over here. Let me analyze your aura and your field of balance." Sarah looked at him as though she looked past him and slowly she could see his energy level emerging. His third chakra was so powerful that he'd not developed enough of his heart chakra. It was as though the light that came into him from his base only went as far as the first three chakras and the energy that came from his head again went to that central ego of the third chakra.

"Nicholas, I would have to talk with you to help open your fourth chakra, which is your heart." She explained all the chakras in detail to him and showed him where the concentration of energy was and where it wasn't. "It's only when we can evenly distribute that energy that we can have balance. Experiences in your life have made you very strong and you have a lot of self-belief. To balance yourself, you must open your heart. The painful experiences of your childhood and the drive and determination are all the things that you've mastered. In order to evolve, you must go back and revisit those painful experiences and let them go. It's funny, like all the difficult challenges in life get redirected to an area that gives us control over self which is predominantly the first three chakras. It's the other chakras that you must now work on. This woman you are with now you love very much. You've had other women." She laughed and he did too, because she didn't want to tell him, *It's about time you settled down.* She delicately worked to tell him in a way he'd receive her advice, and then she continued, "But this one somehow understands you and it's her humor and the way she looks at life that's working to change the way you see your life."

"You can see all that and you've never met this woman ever?"

"No. Who is she?"

"She's one of the most famous models in the world, and you've exactly described what I see in her."

"Well, it's through you that I see this."

"I can tell you that this woman loves you and I can feel your love for her. You admire her courage and her way of being natural. The list goes on. It's all these things that have helped her be who she is, and that's what you see in her. Now the fascinating process of love is that it's free. The development of your relationship and the children you'll have will change you and help you to see the world in a way that you've never seen it before. This will allow you to heal those wounds of the past and open up all your chakras for a complete alignment. Then you'll be ready to take your trip to the stars. Incidentally, she too is being healed by your love for her. It's funny. I see you doing this together and you'll both talk about your experiences in detail afterward."

"Sarah, I've never met a woman like you in my life. How do you know all this stuff? It's mind blowing," said Nicholas, thrilled at the conversation they were having.

"There are others like me, but you haven't been ready and that's okay. Each one of us comes to a point of understanding in one way or another. That's why you're here today, to take that first step in an area you've waited many lifetimes to embrace. When are you getting married?"

"You can see that? At the end of September this year."

"This woman is the one for you and you've waited a long time, haven't you? After you've been together, say six months, come and visit me, and I will look again at your energy field, your aura, and then we'll see whether you're ready. It's my belief you'll be ready to know things you've waited to know for a long time."

"I don't know how to thank you. I must give you something for your time."

"Not at all. You're a friend of James and to see you here again is payment enough."

Sarah showed him around the Throne Room as it was. He was inspired to see all the new developments that had taken place and would take place. He was also pleasantly surprised to see the people busily working their way toward the tearooms with the patio outside to talk about their day.

James remembered that Sarah had promised to bring Peter over. He wanted to see his plans for the new business he wanted to start, so he made his way over to her office.

"I'm sad to say he's not pursuing it at the moment," said Sarah. "His father wants him in the machining business. Although Peter is not happy about that, unless he goes off on his own, he doesn't have much choice. I've tried to talk with Victor, but he's adamant. He feels Peter doesn't have the skills to run a business like that, and at best, he would end up being an employee. There is some truth to that," she concluded, sounding frustrated with the whole situation.

"I understand," said James.

"I feel in time, something will come of this. It's just not now," said Sarah. "On another note, I enjoyed talking with Nicholas. He's come a long way. We'll get him on that throne soon. He's not quite there yet, but he has the will."

"Thanks again for taking the time," said James as they parted.

Nicholas had made his way back to the house and could hear everyone chatting again about last night's caper.

"So did you enjoy your visit with Sarah?" asked Davina, curious to see what his reaction was.

"That woman is incredible. A year ago I would have said all that stuff is hogwash. What she told me really hit home. She could see us getting married. She told me a lot of insightful things about myself, which I will share with you later. I have to say, James, what you've developed here for the public is truly special."

"So you've been converted?" asked Phillipa, intrigued by his change and sudden acceptance of something she'd thought he'd never believe in.

"It's all about these seven chakras or energy points we have in our body and learning to align them. She could actually see the colors of my energy from my aura. From that, she was able to tell me some very personal things in order to achieve that alignment. James, you know that already, but until you really give it some thought, it all sounds gibberish. It's what she could tell me from seeing the energy I project that amazed me, since it was all true."

"Well, I can see I'm now the last of the doubters," said Phillipa, thinking it was time she opened up her mind. "You've thrown down the gauntlet. Now I'll have to experience it for myself the next time I come over when things are a little quieter for her. I know this is her busy season during summer." She didn't have to believe anything Sarah might say, but there was no harm in seeing what she might advise.

Antonio was entertaining the idea himself. He was not a man that would be into that sort of thing, being brought up as a strict Roman Catholic from a faith handed down to him from generations. He would see how Phillipa's experience went and take it from there.

"Davina, we must be off," Nicholas said. "I have to be in London bright and early tomorrow and you have to get ready, too." After saying all their good-byes and thanks, their car could be heard driving out of the front courtyard and down the asphalt driveway.

CHAPTER 13

TOGETHER AT LAST

James, his mother, Sabrina, and her father had a late lunch at the pub and then they all headed back to London. Sabrina had to see Nicholas at his office to work out her contract and James needed to be at his place of work.

That evening Sabrina arrived at the flat with some news. "James, it's done," Sabrina said as she ran into the London flat to give him a hug. "I have a contract and he will help me with my residency status on a temporary basis. Then we can work together to get my permanent residency."

James opened a bottle of champagne to celebrate the moment, as he had something else to offer her. "Sabrina, I have something for you. Open this box."

"You bought me something? You're always spoiling me. You shouldn't have." She eagerly opened the box sitting on the kitchen table and all she could do was to keep removing paper and more paper. "James, is this an empty box? Is this some kind of joke you're playing on me?"

"Keep digging."

There, at the bottom, was a small box, which she eagerly opened and there, to her stunned silence, stood a giant diamond solitaire ring.

"Does this mean what I think it means?"

"Yes. It means that the only way I can get someone as beautiful as you to spend the rest of my life with is to buy you the biggest rock I could find. So will you become engaged to me so that we can get married, mia amore bellissima?"

"James..." She broke down crying. Her voice was trembling with emotion and all she could do was to give him a huge hug.

"Well, I'm still waiting."

"Of course! Yes, yes, yes! I love you with all my heart forever and beyond."

"Thank God!" He laughed. "You haven't finished yet. Look in the box again." As she pulled the last papers from the box she found an envelope with two airline tickets and a hotel reservation for a trip to Barbados.

"James, when is this?"

"Tomorrow."

"I've got to be at work."

"Don't worry. Nicholas knows. Your office and agent in Milan know. The whole world knows, including your father. I've already asked his permission. So it's up, up, and away!"

So much had happened during the first six months of 1966, from Sabrina's accident, James's trip to China, the incident with Jonathan Park, and now James's engagement with the woman of his dreams.

****

James and Sabrina swam in the calm clear waters of the Caribbean and scarcely left each other's side. They slept, relaxed, and made love on the silent private beach all to themselves, looking at the stars. In this oasis of peace and splendor, they could read their books and eat the finest food. They knew that the next few years would be frenetic for them both. Sabrina's modeling career was beginning to take off in a big way and James had his work cut out for him to rebuild and expand his shipping fleet. They had to make the best of this time alone since they would be traveling frequently. They both knew they would take care of business first and then settle down to marriage and family life.

CHAPTER 14

A JOYFUL WEDDING

Later that year James and Sabrina prepared for their journey to Nicholas's home in Tarporley. It was Friday after lunch and James had packed his morning suit. Sabrina knew that Nicholas would have her bridesmaid dress ready when she arrived at his home. Driving from London was so much easier since they took all the main motorways and were now entering the village of Tarporley close to teatime around 4:00 p.m. James knew Nicholas's home was out in the countryside away from the village because he owned a farm. He was busily looking for the entrance to Barrington Estate. He knew Nicholas had purchased this property after his father died. He'd sold his family home, which was closer to Manchester, to live further out. He had no clue what kind of place Nicholas had, but was eagerly watching for a sign that would lead him down Barrington Lane.

"There it is, James. Turn right here," said sharp-eyed Sabrina.

"I see a place in the distance, but it's a castle. That hardly looks like an estate to me. Anyway, let's keep going," said James, slightly confused.

As they drew closer, they could see a high stone wall that seemed to line the side of the road for a good mile. They arrived at what looked like an entrance to the castle. The pair looked up and there, written on a wrought-iron arch above the large oak and metal studded gates, were the words Barrington Estate.

"This must be it. Nicholas lives in a bloody castle!" said James, completely shocked.

They drove up the long tree-lined driveway, which was completely straight and wide enough for two cars to pass each other. The driveway had to be over half a mile long as the couple was busy soaking in the surroundings.

"This place is massive. It's got turrets, a drawbridge, and a portcullis. I suppose we just drive straight across," said James, still not quite sure.

As they entered the huge cobblestone courtyard, their eyes wandered over to the majestic stone entrance. It was then that they could see Nicholas's Rolls.

A man dressed in a suit descended the steps to meet them. "My lord and Lady Rossi?"

"Yes," said James.

"Let me take care of your bags, my lord. Sir Blythe is waiting for you both in the main hallway."

James and Sabrina mounted the steps and walked through the main entrance to an enormous hallway. It had two staircases opposite each other that went up to a gallery that encircled the entire hall. In front of them, between the two staircases, stood a tall and imposing fireplace. The stone floor they stood on had beautiful rugs and refectory tables. James imagined that this main hall would be a perfect place to hold a huge dinner party. Above them he noticed a cathedral arched roof fifty feet above them, which had to have been built around 1500.

Tapestries and all sorts of spears and finery decked the walls and massive wrought-iron chandeliers hung above them. It was truly a sight to see.

Sir Nicholas then made his grand entrance walking down the wide staircase. "James, you finally found my little inn?" he said with his usual dry wit.

"My God, Nicholas, you could have told me you lived in a castle," chided James. "You had me believing I was completely in the wrong place."

"Bad form, old boy. Can't tell people these days you live in a castle. First, they won't believe you and second, I don't like to brag when it comes to my personal life. I save all that hoopla for the business. Let's go and have some afternoon tea in the drawing room while Reggie and Jenna get things ready."

"This castle is spectacular. How on earth did you get this place?"

"I've always had my eye here. It was on the market for some years. I had to do quite a bit of renovation. They finally let it go for a decent price and so I jumped at the opportunity. There aren't many people that want to buy a castle so I had an advantage. I have around a thousand acres of arable and dairy farming. So I enjoy coming up here and getting away from London. It gives me time to think up new designs and fashions that I draw in my study."

They sat on the comfortable large sofas in the drawing room off the main hallway. The room opened out to a beautiful veranda patio with an uninterrupted view toward the lake and surrounding woodland. Jenna brought in the afternoon tea and biscuits as they continued the conversation about Nicholas's home.

"Later I'll take you on a tour and then you can see why I have such a passion for this place. Now you guys, let Reggie take you to your room so you can unpack and make yourselves comfortable. Then come down and we'll take a little tour. Tomorrow will be a busy day for all of us."

James and Sabrina were escorted to their room and enjoyed ascending the wide carved oak staircase to the gallery above. Reggie opened the double doors to the guest room and there in front of them stood a magnificent four-poster bed. The beautiful oak wood floors, the quilts, and the chairs were all of excellent taste and gave one the feeling of stepping back to Tudor times. From the windows they could see for miles much of the property that Nicholas owned. The adjoining bathroom had all the latest conveniences.

They returned to the hall after arranging their things to take a tour of the estate. Nicholas drove them around the perimeter of his castle. It had four turrets, which could be entered separately or by a hallway from the second floor. The narrow slits in the walls defined the weapons like the crossbow that was used at the time of its construction. The moats that surrounded the exterior had now been grassed in; only the drawbridge remained and had been preserved to keep the castle's heritage. The property had wide open spaces with the occasional wooded copse. The main part the land was flat with small undulations giving the viewer opportunity to see great distances. James was struck with the smooth roads that Nicholas had laid to navigate the property and the cleanliness of the buildings and farm administration building. Nicholas was a perfectionist in all that he did, and his attention to detail was the earmark of his trade.

That evening they had a small dinner prepared in an alcove off the kitchen and there they discussed the events of the following day.

James was thinking through his speech and what he would say when it was time for him to speak. Sabrina had been silent. She was in awe of all the surroundings, taking in her first experience of being in an English castle.

"With such a beautiful place, why on earth wouldn't you

hold your wedding here?" James inquired.

"I'm flamboyant and openly extravert in my business activities," Nicholas started, "because that's the world I'm in. When it comes to the personal side of life, I'm private. Can you imagine how many newspapers and photographers are going to be present at tomorrow's wedding? The last thing I want is everyone breathing over my personal life. I have enough of that in business. This place is my retreat and I cherish that. James, you've become part of that personal side of my life. My respect for you and what you're doing as my best man speaks volumes about our friendship."

The day of the wedding was smartly chosen. The late September mornings with the crisp air and the dew on the lawns in front of the castle sparkled with a clear morning sky as the sun started to rise.

Sabrina was busy preparing herself after a late breakfast for the day by trying on the beautifully designed bridesmaid dress that would match Davina's sister and best friend. Davina's wedding party had all stayed the night in Chester where the reception would be held. This was appropriately far enough away from Nicholas's private life. After the wedding the couple would fly to their yacht harbored in Monaco on Nicholas's Learjet from Manchester's Ringway Airport.

It was now 1:30 p.m. Nicholas, James, and Sabrina made their way to the old vicarage in Tarporley in his Rolls, driven by his chauffer/handyman, Reggie.

The people started to arrive and it was then that Sabrina separated herself from James to meet up with Davina and the others in the vestibule adjoining the entrance. James helped organize the usher who was busy handing out the programs for the service. He, the usher, was none other than Jeremy Soames himself, an old Etonian, and a close school friend of Nicholas and his family through the years.

The attendance was not more than fifty people. Nicholas and Davina had wanted it to be a close and private affair. There would be enough fanfare with reporters and photographers after the service. The service went smoothly as Davina's father walked his daughter to the altar. Between the fair hair of Sabrina and the darker hair of Davina's sister, they made a beautiful pair. They proudly carried the trail behind the ravishingly embroidered ecru wedding dress. Davina, who could not go unnoticed, was wearing the dress with her usual flare and stature.

The congregation was composed of many of the people who were part of the Brotherhood of the Inner Sanctum. James stood anxiously by Nicholas and had strategically placed the ring in his waistcoat pocket. After the couple kissed, the organ rang out with Purcell's trumpet voluntary. No cameras, except those appointed by Nicholas, were allowed in the service. As the couple made their way to the outside lawn, it seemed like the entire world had shown up to get a glimpse, a photograph, and the story of a couple who were well used to the press and the demands of the public. The bells rang out and the sun shone down on the blissfully happy couple. After witnessing an endless stream of flashing cameras, Nicholas and Davina were quickly whisked away to the reception hall in Nicholas's Rolls, driven by Reggie. Sabrina and James followed in Jeremy Soames's burgundy Rolls Royce.

Jeremy introduced his wife, Julia, who, like her husband, was tall and elegant and seemed to possess the same intellectual excellence as Jeremy himself.

They eventually arrived at Rowton Hall in Chester. There was adequate parking for the reception, which had an attendant on hand. Naturally, the press and photographers followed as the well-known couple had already made their entry. Great interest was also taken with the arrival of James and Sabrina.

James and Sabrina hadn't had an opportunity to meet up with his mother and her father as they arrived after them at the church. Claudia and Sir Thomas were also present as well as a number of people James recognized from his meeting at the Dorchester Hotel in London.

"James, you carried out your duties without dropping the ring, and Sabrina, my dear, you look absolutely exquisite in your dress," said Phillipa after the family hugged and kissed.

"Claudia and Thomas, it's great to see you both here," remarked James.

"You have to tell me all about his place when you have time," urged Claudia. "I would really like to know." After her short-lived romance with Nicholas, she was curious to know more about him.

The large room was beautifully decorated for the occasion. The sun allowed people to gather on the lawn outside the reception dining area. After the chats on the lawn with champagne in hand, people drifted into the dining room. At the head table sat Davina's parents, sister and maid of honor Naomi, best friend Donna, James and Sabrina, Jeremy and Julia, and finally Nicholas and Davina.

After the meal, James stood up to make his speech. "My lords, ladies and gentlemen. Nicholas only recently announced to me that he would like to give me the honor of being his best man, as apparently in his own words, he knows no one else." A cautious laughter wafted around the room. "As you all know him well, he spends most of his life at work. I have, however, found time to know what I believe to be the real Nicholas. Under all that wit and dashing humor lies a deeply considerate and talented man. As flamboyant as he is in his business life, he is equally as private in his personal life. He did mention that he should have actually had his best woman do the speech, but rethought the prospect in view of Davina's obvious objections." The entire room was reeling in fits of laughter at the outrageous suggestion, but they all knew Nicholas well enough for that comment. "So here I am, the last person he knew that would be even capable of such a duty. No, I didn't go to Eton, so I'm not at liberty to tell you all of his antics. But I am familiar with one of those stories which I was given the pleasure of hearing."

"Now hold on, James," Nicholas interrupted. "The only reason you got the job is you don't know a damn thing about me!"

"If I may be allowed to continue..." said James, bringing the audience to order. "As you well know, Nicholas was quite the prankster, and in my short time of knowing him, I can well attest to that. There happened to be a teacher known as Mrs. Parkins, who delighted in teaching English. I know this is not unfamiliar to most of you here. From the confidant that informed me of the story, she happened to be quite a stickler for detail." Jeers and laughter were going up all around the room as everyone waited in heated anticipation to hear the story.

"Well, for some reason, she always gave Nicholas a hard time because of his explicit essays. When I say explicit, I mean explicit. One essay in particular was seriously noted and remembered by all members of the classroom. The surprised look on her face as she came midway through his essay and discovered an extremely provocative woman taken from a pinup magazine. Nicholas at least had the dignity to remove the woman's head and replace it with a photograph of his beloved teacher, Mrs. Parkins. She stood there dumbfounded, not knowing what to say, as the rest of the class waited for the rest.

"Nicholas, you've finally found a way to put your talent to better use. This woman you have put here far exceeds your capability to describe one. My advice to you is stick to your father's business and take up fashion."

The entire room was on the floor with laughter as Mrs. Parkins said, "That will be all for today gentlemen."

"James, your duties as best man are now more than exceeded," said Nicholas, clapping with the rest of the guests.

"I now hand you over to the maid of honor, namely Donna!" said James, happy with the applause on behalf of his friend Nicholas.

"Ladies and gentlemen, it's going to be hard to match that one, but I will attempt to enlighten you to a most mischievous and exuberant side of Davina. Everyone knows that Davina can be quite expressive when the moment defines. We've known each other since our prep school days and afterward when we went to school at Roedean, in Sussex. Davina was always on the tall side and was noted for her scholastics, humor, and wit. None of us knew she would become the famous person we know her all to be today. She alights the world's magazine covers and pages with the same flare and dignity that she's always had. At every opportunity she would act in our school plays.

"I remember one such part in particular. It was the end of school term and our final summer at Roedean. As always, she had to leave her mark. And that she did. It was an unusually hot summer day...for England. Everyone watching the play, in a theater that seriously lacked ventilation, was beginning to become uncomfortable. In addition the actors, who had made themselves up to the nines, were playing the role as fashion models. Totally suited to Davina. Her part in the story was, of course, the lead role, as only Davina would have it. The dressmaker had to prepare the finest costume for the king's intended wife. I played the part as the queen-to-be, and sat on my throne, as the models passed one by one so that I could finally make my choice. The models would pass again and again and I couldn't make up my mind as to the dress I really wanted. This was all part of the script. As it was only an amateur school play, and the parents were there mainly to see their daughers act, no one was taking the story too seriously. Finally Davina walks on stage in a tight swimsuit, high heels, and fishnet stockings, much to the amazement of the audience! I sat there wondering what on earth she was doing?"

"She finally says out loud, as she passes in front of me, 'Look, I know the king will go crazy for you to have this outfit. This is not an option anymore. Choose it before we all die of heatstroke, and let's get out of here!'" The guests, who were now in a jovial mood from James's speech and the champagne, nearly fell off their chairs with laughter, not all knowing that side of Davina and just how direct and to the point she could be. "Needless to say, she got a standing ovation from the audience at school. She's continued to be not only the beautiful woman she is today, but never at a loss for making everyone laugh. I believe Nicholas and Davina are aptly suited to be husband and wife and I propose a toast to a long and successful life together." Everyone stood up, rose their glasses, and drank to the happy couple.

Davina and Nicholas sped away after the dancing to their yacht. James and Sabrina were taken back to the castle for one more night by Reggie before leaving to go back to London.

****

After their honeymoon, and as Sarah promised months later, Davina and Nicholas returned to Penbroke to have that experience on the Throne they so wished for.

Sarah was prepared. Nicholas had called ahead too make the appointment.

"So Sarah, am I ready to take the trip to the stars?" asked Nicholas in his usual manner.

Sarah looked deeply into him and evaluated his alignment. It wasn't perfect, but his fourth chakra had opened enough and she thought that the experience would do the rest. They walked down to the Throne Room followed by Davina. Nicholas was nervous, remembering his first encounter.

"Okay, here goes nothing." It took a moment as he sat on

the Throne and then he was gone. James and Sabrina hadn't arrived yet, but Sarah was prepared for Nicholas and Davina's arrival. It was now six o'clock on a Saturday night and the crowds from the day had already left.

Nicholas suddenly reappeared and awoke from being on the Throne. He looked so sad and unhappy that Sarah knew he needed to talk. So she ushered him back to her office and the pair sat down. Much to her amazement he was sobbing his eyes out.

"Take your time. You don't have to talk right now," Sarah consoled. "Regain your composure and then we can work through what you've experienced."

"You were right. My master revealed things to me that were deeply buried in my childhood. My mother had such a desperate existence at the hands of my father. How she could have lived with a man that cruel, I don't know. I was away at boarding school and then on to Eton. I sensed some of her anxiety but her fear and terror at the mercy of his wrath is the very reason I have found it difficult to connect with anyone since I met my Mary, who died of leukemia when she was only nineteen. After that, I just thought no woman would ever be right for me. I was instinctively terrified to be the abusive person my father had become to my mother. I had locked away all the screaming and rage that he pummeled on her. I don't know how she lived through it. No wonder she committed suicide. All that was kept from me. How he could have lived with himself, I don't know."

He then continued after regaining his composure, "It's something I had feared had happened all my life and yet I just didn't want to face it. I was afraid."

"It's what made you strong, Nicholas. As terrible as it was, you overcame your fear of him and proved your worth. In spite of all that, he was in a position of power. He'll pay dearly for his actions. The price of karma will be his to learn, not yours."

"I spoke with her because I loved her, and missed her so much. She died when I was only eleven. She told me she was beside me and gave me all her knowledge and encouragement in fashion from her early years as a designer and seamstress. She worked in my father's factory. They fell in love. She was much younger and because he found someone else he loved more, he wanted her to leave. He had trumped up some scandal that she was having an affair with one of his workers. In fact, she was helping that worker because he had fallen down a stairwell. When my father saw her trying to help him, he assumed she was having a love affair. When in fact she never knew the man, she just happened to be there and of course helped the man. She told me that she had her lessons to learn and that the only thing she regrets was taking her own life because that left me alone. She won't leave me again until I return. Sarah, I learnt how I'm able to do the things I do. I well suffered at the hands of his abuse and overcame him. No one should have to go through what she went through. No one!"

"Nicholas, you should be proud of yourself. Now you know why you weren't ready, and you must release all that pain and anger so that you can live your life with Davina and have the happiness you deserve. Stay here and regain yourself and I will now see what help I can give to Davina."

Sarah made her way back to the Throne Room. Davina was looking around waiting by herself in anticipation, apprehensive about taking the Throne. "Look, I can tell you, you are ready but it's a personal journey for each one of us," said Sarah with her usual calmness.

"Okay, I will do it!" said Davina with her pluck, in the way she would walk out in front of the crowds with the latest fashions.

She nervously sat on the Throne as others had done before her. Sarah could see the light that surrounded her, and an intense feeling of joy could be felt as she went. Moments later she was back and, unlike Nicholas, she was enthralled. She too was ushered back to Sarah's office to discuss her experience. Nicholas had left and had wandered back to the house to think about all that he'd encountered and learned how he could release something that had been locked up inside him for most of his life.

"So, my dear, how was it?" asked Sarah, anxious to hear what she knew already.

"I was with my master and guides and it was truly a special feeling to talk with souls that know you through and through. I was told how independent I am and that being on the stage was natural for me, as I had done this in so many lifetimes. My purpose is to inspire people to help them find self-confidence in themselves, so that they could become what their dreams tell them. I am a highly evolved soul and will not be returning to physical form at the end of this cycle of life. When I finish my career I will teach all the things I've learnt for myself and give back all the great opportunities that I've worked for and yet have been rewarded for through my faith. As a young woman I wasn't religious, but I believed in my God and had always felt a presence and a voice in my moments of fear before marching out in front of an audience. Now it has become second nature and it's that confidence that has brought about my success in what I do. It is a fascinating journey and I was told about the children we'll have. Also, it was to understand the man I'm with, for although he has come from privilege, he's had a very hard journey without his mother. I was told that he now knows she's always been with him. I actually wept when I heard some of what he went through, because Nicholas, as you know, is not one to explain his personal journey to anyone and now I know why. This whole experience will bring us even closer. I suspected something before but couldn't put my finger on it."

"You are indeed an advanced and beautiful soul who has

worked hard to refine yourself to the esteemed position you hold in the eyes of the world. You have helped to unlock that fourth chakra, which is now fully open. You are the reason he now understands what he needed to know, but not until this moment. You and Nicholas can now openly share your thoughts, which will bring you even closer to each other than you've ever been."

Nicholas and Davina didn't wait for James and Sabrina. The experience had been too traumatic for Nicholas and he needed time alone with Davina to talk and understand all that they had learned.

CHAPTER 15

THE GRAND OPENING

Over the next three years Sabrina had become a hugely successful model thanks to the support of Davina, Darlene Jenson of Fashion World, and of course, Sir Nicholas. She traveled everywhere for shoots and James went along when he could. They had planned this part of their life before making the next step—they both wanted to get their careers well launched before taking on the responsibility of a family. Both of them were apart more than they wanted because of business but they always knew that home was with one another.

John Higgins and James had replaced most of the fleet, and the building at Felixstowe had been constructed. The fleet was increasing above the 10 percent a year for the expansion that James wanted. They both knew that the immense future of containerization lay in the Far East. The ports of Shanghai, Hong Kong, and Singapore were producing a lot of the world's goods and the new larger ships were able to handle the cargo.

They now had routes to Los Angeles across the Pacific to pick up the lucrative trade from China to America and the Port of Nagoya in Japan. In Europe they were stopping more at Antwerp in Belgium and Rotterdam as well as all the traditional ports they shipped to in the past. They were a worldwide shipping company. Hong Kong proved to be the biggest growth area, and the staff was bursting at the seams waiting on the final construction of the new skyscraper to be built. John and James had done a wonderful job of collecting all the history and they had built a single-story museum next to the main building in Felixstowe so the public could visit for a nominal fee. Like the Throne Room at Penbroke, a lot of the souvenirs they had there were now sold at this museum. It was, of course, a proud place for the shipping history that had lasted for well over two hundred years, not only for the generations of employees, but to be shown to the public and their many customers.

Roger Bell had done everything he promised. Having invested heavily in textiles, related products, and commodities such as rice, silk, tea, spices, and herbs, he was well on his way to doubling the company's money. James was so pleased because the growth of the bank could now help support the investment in the new building. Roger had developed a full-time second-in-command and now had plans to return to England and accomplish the same thing on Threadneedle Street. Roger and Kate were married in England, and then returned to Hong Kong. They would now return for good so they could one day raise their children in England. Sandra had married; it was now James's turn.

James had bought out all the buildings Bannermans had owned in the world and was charging rent to each one of his businesses; now the revenue was being paid to the company his trust fund had set up in Zurich. It had taken a lot of work and a tremendous amount of thought and travel. Claudia had been instrumental in finding her accountant to help with the implementation of a new financial system with John Higgins, at Trans Global. He would be employed at the bank, but she would use him to keep a close watch on this account. The strict rule for dual-control signatures for all of James's businesses was firmly in place. The authority that had been given to Jonathan Park would never be given again. She also found the right man for managing the property in Hong Kong and the buildings in England. The bank would pay them, but James's business in Zurich would reimburse the bank for any employees and outgoing expenses. Claudia had one accountant assigned to keep up the accounting on the English properties, and Roger Bell in Hong Kong was doing the same.

Claudia was James's critical link and she had now taken on a secretary of her own. In a sense she was the one who connected all of James's worldwide operations to him. She was the senior and most important person in James's affairs. He had given her the title of group managing director. He could dive into any area of the business at will, but he never did so without learning all the up-to-date details from Claudia first, and if she didn't have the facts he was looking for, she knew in an instant how to get them.

From his shipping business, his properties, and the newly emerging energy of his merchant bank, he was well on his way at the age of twenty-six to becoming one of the richest men not only in England, but in the whole of Europe.

He was planning his wedding day with Sabrina for June, but first he had to be in Hong Kong for the gala opening of his new building with Nicholas. It was early March 1970, and the thought of being in a warmer climate made the occasion all the more welcome.

They arrived jet lagged and went to the hotel in Kowloon to get some much needed rest. The opening was scheduled for March 24; the governor of the island would be present as well as Alan Archer and many of the island's dignitaries. As it was Sunday, this would give James a chance to catch up with the new manager and Roger Bell on Monday.

Roger met James at the hotel for breakfast. Nicholas had his own plans and was going to meet James later as he planned to meet Darlene Jenson, who was planning on writing a story about Nicholas's store in Asia. He was also going to scout out the area because he wanted to move part of his textile plant to an area north of Kowloon that was growing fast.

"James, great to see you," said Roger.

"You too, Roger."

"Going to take a sneak preview before the big day?"

"Certainly, but I want to go over how the bank's doing. Then this afternoon I shall take time with our property manager out here, Gerald Davies."

"The bank is doing very well, as promised. I have taken the liberty of training Harold Cummings to take over my position when I return to England...of course with your blessing."

"So how's life with Kate?"

"She's a riot. Completely changed my life, James. She's got me into go-karts and motor racing, not to speak of horseback riding. She keeps me busy. She's done a great job at the bank. I once feared having a person you live with, at work every day. Might be a problem. She does her own thing and keeps to herself when I'm with customers and employees."

"So what about when you get back to London? Will it work there, do you think?"

"I'm not sure what duties Claudia now performs, if she's not directly involved with what I'm doing. I believe Kate could work with me or for Claudia."

"Good point. I've made Claudia group managing director. This is how I see it all working: You will be over the merchant banking in London as well as here, so you need to plan the staff when you return. Stephen Gates will be handling the properties we have here and in England, and Gerald Davies will be out here permanently and will report directly to Stephen. In the same way you've had Harold Cummings reporting to you. Incidentally, Stephen is coming in tonight. So we have, in essence, three entities: the merchant bank, which is you, Trans Global, which is John Higgins, and the property business, which is Stephen Gates. You three are not necessarily under Claudia but she is a senior partner, as it were, in being able to coordinate information, which I prefer to get from one person.

"If I'm going to build this business, I'll be doing a lot of traveling. So it's necessary that I have someone like Claudia. I've known her from childhood and we work well together. She will be up to speed with what you're all doing when I'm not in the office. In a sense, she's my assistant, and a very good one at that. So it's not a question of anyone trying to take up someone's space. I want there to be the fastest line of communication that I can have through one person. When I'm in town of course I'll be dealing with you directly, and Claudia, when necessary, will be part of that conversation, only again to keep up to date with what's going on. I believe in communication. I don't like gray areas and indecision."

James was careful not to tread on Roger's space, as he'd been an exemplary managing director with amazing talent. James wanted him to now do the same types of investments and trading that he'd done in Hong Kong in London too.

"James, it makes complete sense! You've made a good decision to coordinate all our efforts. I had no trouble working under Claudia when I was in London. We're both Cambridge graduates and have a lot in common."

James, looking at his watch, motioned to Roger that it was time they left to go to the bank.

As they drew up to the old bank building there to the left stood his giant gleaming modern dream of a building. He couldn't wait to take a look later.

"Quite a sight, don't you think, James?"

"It's spectacular. I can't wait to look it all over." James spent the morning talking to the staff and invited Kate to have lunch with him to catch up with her on a personal basis. The building was bursting at the seams and space had even been taken up with cubicles in the main entrance. After tomorrow, the big move would go into action.

Kate was excited to see James and take a moment to be with him. "Isn't that building fantastic? Roger and I almost wish we could stay but if we're going to have a family, we feel England is best. I think Roger wants the challenge of making things happen in London like he's done here."

"He's certainly a man of his word. I have a lot of respect for what he's achieved and no doubt he'll accomplish a lot more. So how are you? You look well, happy, and in love."

Kate swooned. "I never thought I would be lucky enough to meet a man like Roger. He's changed quite a bit, by the way. He's not the shy man we met on the boat coming over anymore."

They walked into a little café Kate knew, where they could eat quickly and get back at the bank for James's afternoon meetings.

"So how's the family doing?" asked James.

"I think Peter has to get away from Dad. Things are not going well at all and Peter is quite depressed."

"Well, he talked of some plans on this shot peen process some years back. I know it's something to do with blasting metal shot at the surface to shape and form metal, but it would be nice to know more about how and why it's so effective. I asked for more financial data, and your mother had said that your father didn't think Peter was a businessman and has taken him under his wing in the machine shop."

"I don't think Dad likes the fact that you would be owning

part of the business. He wants to teach Peter how to run it and pick up the slack. It's his son, so I can understand, but Peter's just not happy. Unless Dad retires, which he'll never do, I don't see a solution."

"I've been so busy the last three years with reinvesting in the shipping line that I've scarcely had time for anything. Sabrina and I have committed to getting our lives in order professionally. She travels all over the place modeling and my life's been similar, but after this building gets opened, she'll be more selective on the work she takes. Sabrina and I will be getting married in June. If you're over by then, you must come. Anyway, I'll send you and your family an invite."

"On another note the last time your mother and I spoke, she wanted me to share the fact that some of the gifts she has with all her insights and psychic abilities, you too have and could also develop. I've always felt that you shared those abilities too, and that's one of the reasons I felt your coming to Hong Kong would be helpful in understanding this environment and the people here."

"I've known that, too, but have always been careful not to share my insights. People can think you are a bit odd, don't you think?"

"You know I have those instincts too, but I have also worked hard to develop them. We don't have to share this with the world; it just helps in making good decisions and giving sound advice. Unless you want to take up your mother's role, do what I do. One day you must take your journey on the Throne and talk with your masters. You have a distinct purpose and I feel that very strongly."

"It's been so good talking with you. I love working for you, and Roger is in heaven. Don't worry about Peter. I'll take time to visit with him when I get back," said Kate as they parted.

James went over to the new building to meet up with Gerald Davies, who was busy organizing the festivities for the grand opening of the building.

"Your Lordship, it's indeed an honor to meet with you."

"Likewise. Please call me James."

"Yes, sir. I've been in touch with Stephen Gates, who's arriving tonight, and he's very excited to hear of the progress," said Gerald nervously. This was a big occasion and a lot rested on his shoulders.

James took a moment to walk all around the front lobby. There was a basement for restaurants offering lighter fare with a large seating area in the middle. The first floor, where James stood, had elevators running to the basement or ground floor and up again to the second floor. The first floor would be the main entrance to the building from the street. The basement would be the entrance from the underground car park and the main eating area for the inhabitants of the building. The first floor had around its perimeter space for showrooms and shops. The second floor would also have a combination of higher-end restaurants, and shops too. It was all brilliantly planned. James could see that a lot of money had been invested in the first three floors. Renters of the various businesses, which would be coming there, had made this investment on their own: from flower shops to what Nicholas had in mind for a dress shop, perfume shops, shoes, handbags, accessories, and jewelry. The variety of merchandise was impressive. The renters had clearly spent a lot of money to give the latest image to their products.

"So Gerald, for starters, what percentage of the building is now rented?"

"I can tell you more accurately when we get to my office," Gerald said. "Roughly speaking, between sixty to seventy percent."

"I'm impressed."

"People want to be in the latest building and have that spectacular view over the harbor. So many of the buildings don't have underground parking. The features we offer here allow a person to come to work and never have to leave the building 'til they go home. Every employer wants that, and that way, the minimum time is lost during the workday."

James and Gerald stepped into the elevator and it took off to the fiftieth floor. "Our elevator in London would take forever compared with this one," said James, still taking it all in.

Gerald led the way to James's quarters. James had his architects design him a penthouse suite and office for the times he was over.

The suite opened directly into the living room area, which was at least forty by thirty-five feet, covered with hardwood floors. It was large enough for a desk, dining area, and living room furniture, with a small kitchen at the opposite side to the bedrooms. The suite had two bedrooms, a master and a smaller one, both with en suite bathrooms. The grand feature was the huge balcony garden hosting a small swimming pool and lounge seating areas with a box garden holding a beautiful variety of flowers. Last but not least, was the best feature of all, the panoramic view across the harbor.

James started to feel the potential. These buildings with a complete facility to offer the customer would definitely be the way of the future. They made their way over to Gerald's office and there James could see that two-thirds of the building had been rented already and that his secretary had been giving him stacks of messages from prospective renters. He also ran down the list of companies that would be moving in at the first of the month. He thought that this property would be the first of many that he would want to build.

Gerald and James stopped at the many different floors and studied layouts for law firms, accountants, and shipping agents for other shipping lines. Gerald had reserved the top four floors for the bank and Trans Global. They were ready to move out of the front lobby of the old building into this new and more productive space.

James descended to the first floor and there he met Nicholas, who was busy showing Darlene Jenson the space he was going to take.

"This place must have cost you a bomb. Where's your hideout, my man?" Nicholas asked.

"Come on, I'll take you up and you can see my camping quarters. You can come too, Darlene."

Nicholas couldn't believe the speed of the elevators. "So this is your hideout?" he asked. "Pretty swank, James. I'll definitely be making a trip when you come out. Look at this, your own private patio. Darlene, take a look at that view. Hard to get any work done looking out at that. First class job, sport!" They went over to Gerald.

"Hey you guys, be my guests for dinner?" asked James, thinking of what Darlene had done for Sabrina and to celebrate Nicholas's entrée into Hong Kong.

They agreed and James had Roger take him back to the hotel. He was starting to feel a little jet lagged and took a quick catnap.

James met everyone in the lobby for dinner. They went to a restaurant they knew close to where he and Roger had gone for a drink one night.

"So did you find a suitable site for your textile manufacturing?" James asked Nicholas.

"I did. After your opening tomorrow I'm going to make a decision to buy the land and then work on setting up a place. There are a lot of old high-rise buildings in Hong Kong that could be used, but they require investment. There's no way those places would be allowed to operate in England. The codes for fire and electric are almost nonexistent. No wonder, with the cheap labor prices, they can blow us away. There's no way to compete with what's out here. I'll make a decision before I leave about being downtown for now. Later I'll probably move out toward the Pearl River Delta."

"Sounds like a good plan. With the expansion rate in Hong Kong I suspect it's only a matter of time before all those manufacturers will take a profit on their buildings and move further out where it's cheaper and probably more efficient. It's just tough to find flat land around here. I'm sure that's a big reason for people living in all these high-rise buildings. Darlene, I want to thank both you and Nicholas for all you've done to help Sabrina in her modeling career."

"Sabrina is easy to market. She has the body and those distinct looks that just sell magazines. We have plenty of good models, perfect bodies, but to find a truly beautiful, one-of-a-kind woman like Sabrina—that's rare. Super models don't grow on trees and to top it off, she's such a lovely person to work with. Claudia, Davina, and Sabrina believe me and have helped our circulation and Nicholas's business."

"Well that's nice to know, but we all have to start somewhere and I know how demanding both you and Nicholas are in getting that right product to the market place."

"So you're making a speech tomorrow?" asked Darlene, changing the subject.

"Of course. I've got to say a few words, especially with our name plastered all over the building." James thought he'd better work on a few words before retiring for the night.

"Well, look what you've done at twenty-five years" extolled Nicholas. "You had a great start, true, but you overhauled that shipping line. You're back to merchant banking with that wiz kid, Roger, and you're on the way to becoming a property tycoon. Tomorrow is living proof of that. Admittedly, it's one thing to have the cash, but there's always a risk; fools and their money soon part. You've handled the pressure of your company's reorganization extremely well. Can't ever rest on your laurels. Take my situation. There's always someone out there who's going to dream up something new. We have to stay ahead of the game. One way is to be more competitive, but if people don't like your product, you're dead. Always as good as your last purchase order, I say."

"I do admit the last three years have made me sweat at times," James said. "More employees, huge recapitalization, and creating a hierarchy that's lean, mean, and simple and has a good chemistry of people working together is a constant challenge. Now that this building has been built, it'll at least give me some time to marry Sabrina and start a normal family life."

"I was on my own so damn long it was an adjustment, but Davina's like your Sabrina, one of a kind. I can tell you that when I had my experience on that throne of yours it was a mind blower. I learned stuff about my father and mother I never knew, but only suspected. That's the first time I've cried since my mother died. What you have there is an absolute gift. From my own experience, I can only tell you it has changed my whole life. Davina so enjoyed learning all the things she needed to know. Who would ever believe something like that exists? I still have to pinch myself, yet it's real."

"It's nice to know that you can be vulnerable. I always think that a person has more soul when they can take a loss and get up and keep going. After all, we don't win them all. I think that Davina has changed you for the better."

"That's what Sarah McKenzie told me. So you thought I was impregnable?"

"Like a bloody fortress. I've always enjoyed your wit and persistence, but it's nice when a person feels comfortable to share their feelings occasionally."

"As Darlene will tell you, I'm not one to wear my heart on my sleeve. Darlene, you should go up to Penbroke and learn what I've learned. I could never repay James for what I now know today."

"I would love to experience that throne of yours. If it can

make a believer out of Nicholas, that's enough to sell anyone," said Darlene. "So I'll make the effort. I also agree with what Nicholas has said about you. Look at what you're doing with your business. Keep it up."

"So no plans for you just yet, Darlene?"

"No. But there is a significant other and Nicholas knows him well."

"Good for you. I believe we should all head back because I need to be at the bank first thing to ensure this shindig gets off the ground." James was remembering his speech and wanted to take a moment in his room to make some notes.

He had done his homework and met Roger after breakfast for his trip to the bank. He would take one last look at everything before the opening, which was to start at 10:30 a.m.

James made a quick detour of the building to see that everything was set up and then went over to the old building to the conference room to have a coffee and quietly go over his speech and thoughts before plunging into the spotlight.

****

James made his way over to the new building just after 10:00 a.m. and as he entered the main lobby, he was met with a barrage of press reporters. Television cameras were there busily announcing his entrance and giving viewers an account of who he was, his background, and a brief history on his involvement in the construction of the building.

James answered questions while anxious TV cameras followed. He then told everyone that after the ceremony, he would be delighted to sit with anyone who wanted to go over the plans they had for the building, and their future in Hong Kong. Like all ceremonies, it took almost until 10:30 a.m. to get everyone quieted down and for all the speakers to take their turn at the podium. James had spoken with Alan Archer and Sir David Trench, the governor of Hong Kong, and now they were about to proceed.

Jim Olders, who was the secretary to Alan Archer, made the introductions. He had made notes, in order that the attendees clearly would understand the background of each of the speakers. There were over five hundred people invited, including the press, to the opening, and all of them were now seated and ready to hear the opening remarks.

As the speakers rose to the podium, each speaker spoke with high admiration for the project and the ambitious size of a building that would be a trendsetter for the future. Their voices carried high up from the main floor and clearly echoed off the walls of this formidable structure. Governor Trench spoke about the great admiration he had for James's father, Collin Bannerman, as he knew him before becoming governor in 1964. He spoke of the sad loss of his life at such an early age, and how appropriate it was of James to dedicate the building to his father as the pioneer for the Bannerman family and in tribute to his foresight in starting the bank in Hong Kong. Alan Archer spoke proudly of James as well as the courage and determination he showed toward building this self-contained building. He spoke of all the new innovation that had been considered and how it would set a new standard for buildings of the future. It was finally James's turn and he was given a resounding standing ovation as he walked to the podium.

"Governor Trench, Consul Alan Archer, Ching Seng, managing director of the Bank of Hong Kong, and my esteemed lords, ladies, and gentlemen seated before me today, it is indeed an honor to be finally standing here so we can formally open the largest building ever to be built in Hong Kong to date. I know it won't be long before someone else will build a building to exceed this one." The crowd laughed, as they knew it was just a matter of time. He continued, "Such is the spirit of this great island and its surrounding territories. Literally, the sky is the limit. It is the enterprise and drive of many of you who are here today that has made this island almost unequalled in its growth and expansion over the past hundred years. We all know that this island and region toward the Pearl River Delta will continue to develop at an astonishing rate. We embrace this spirit of determination and the investment from the Western world and the support of the Chinese government, by allowing this trading capital to grow without restriction. We will continue to employ more and more people from our neighboring China and the islands that surround us. We compliment those that choose to invest and believe in what was once just a dream. I see no end to what can be accomplished here.

"Hong Kong sets an example to many other places in the world, to one of the greatest natural resources we have, the ability of the human being, which I like to refer to as human capital. This island is an inspiration to all mankind of what can be done by hard work, vision, and great minds.

"For those of you who know little about my family, we date back to 1704. We started in the shipping business, Trans Global Shipping Lines, in 1730. We have been shipping between London and Hong Kong for over two hundred years. In 1838, during the time of Queen Victoria's coronation, we started our bank in London on Threadneedle Street, the heart of the financial district of London. My father came here to start the bank in 1953. He was to me as good as any father could be to a son. He was loving but tough. He always expected excellence in all that I did. More importantly, he was a great teacher and humanitarian. To lose him at such an early age was a painful experience, but for what he taught me I can never be grateful enough. This building stands as a proud dedication to his life's work and belief in Hong Kong. Our family has a proud heritage that we've held for many hundreds of years. In our own way, we have been playing our small role in the development of these islands. It is people like us that have loyally and steadfastly stood by to develop Hong Kong that has resulted in what it has become today. I have a duty to continue that commitment, as I know many of you here today feel and share that same passion. May I thank you all for coming and please feel free to wander the building. Both Gerald Davies and Stephen Gates—please both stand up—are here to advise anyone who may have questions. After lunch we will have the formal cutting of the ribbon."

James, the governor, Alan Archer, and members of the staff all took part in the tape-cutting ceremony, which released a cloud of balloons. The string was pulled on the cover of a large prominent portrait of his father that was hung above the entrance to the elevators as the founder of the bank's beginnings in Hong Kong. Above the painting were the words, "In loving memory of Collin Edward Bannerman, ninth Earl of Penbroke, founder."

James took the opportunity to have books and souvenirs from Penbroke and his new shipping museum at Felixstowe available in the lobby at the side of the front entrance. He wanted to educate the invited guests as to who, why, and what they were all about. This was the factual evidence of what his family had stood for, from its early beginnings to the present day. The crowd all applauded and was fascinated with the story of a family that most knew little or nothing about. James knew that you couldn't buy this kind of goodwill. He wanted to use this fantastic marketing opportunity to promote the family's greatest achievement so far.

CHAPTER 16

THE FUNERAL

Quite drained after his long flight, James arrived back who was anxiously waiting to see him. Nicholas had stayed over in Hong Kong to secure his plans for his new showroom and textile building. Roger and Kate were due to arrive back by the weekend.

"It's so good to have you home; I've missed you so much," said Sabrina, wrapping her arms around James. "I just got in from Milan last night after working all last weekend. I'm sure you don't feel like going to have a bite, so I've prepared a snack at the flat. We can share a nice bottle of wine and catch up on all the news."

James told her about the building and how proud he was of it. He talked about the private suite he had built; on his next trip he would take her with him. They talked until James looked tired. They both retired early. They were so happy to be in each other's arms once again, and that was all the comfort they needed.

James slept late and woke up confused as to where he was and then realized he was home with his Sabrina. He went downstairs and she had cooked him a big breakfast, and after a few cups of tea, he started to get his bearings.

"Have we set the wedding date yet, my chief organizer?"

"June is a good time. It's hot in Italy and they'll enjoy coming here, if that's okay with you. What do you think?" she said, thinking Penbroke would make a nice place to host a wedding.

"We can always have a wedding in Italy, in say, late September. The question is, will that eliminate a number of people coming from Italy that are family friends?"

"No, I don't agree. The people we know can well afford to come to England and would love to visit Penbroke that time of year."

"Remember, your family is Roman Catholic, and I'm traditionally Church of England. Will that be a problem? I have no problem marrying you in a Roman Catholic church, but will your father have a problem with that?"

"You've got a point. I'll talk with him further. I'm not bothered by being married in your church but I can't see why he would have a problem; we must check that out."

"I must get to the office this afternoon and catch up on matters," said James. "Call your papa and we'll plan things when I get home tonight," said James, starting to have thoughts about other business.

"I'm going to meet up with Davina this afternoon, so see you later."

James arrived at the office to an anxious Claudia, who had all sorts of matters and questions. He also wanted to bring her up to date on how things went at the opening.

"James, Jeremy Soames would like to see you as soon as convenient. John Higgins and Sarah need to talk with you as soon as possible. She asked if you could call her at her home.

So how did it all go?"

"It was magnificent. The whole of Hong Kong's upper echelon was at the opening. I believe it was a tremendous opportunity to promote our business for the future. It's surprising that when we've been going to Hong Kong all these years, how little people really know about us. Anyway, they will know now and that's got to bring us more business. That building is something. Our architects and Gerald Davies have done a brilliant job. You've got to come out and see it, and bring Sir Thomas, too. I think I'll go and call Sarah. It's rare she calls; I hope everything's okay. I'll be back in a moment."

"Sarah, James here. Claudia said you called. Are things okay over there?"

"Yes, absolutely. It's a personal matter. Victor died yesterday so now I must prepare for the funeral."

"I'm so sorry. What can I do to help?"

"It would be wonderful if you could come for the day. I'm trying to arrange for the funeral on Tuesday next week."

"Of course. I'll be there without question. Were you expecting this?"

"In a way, yes. But it's still a shock. I'll tell you all about it when you come. I've called Kate so she'll be here as well, and I hope Roger can make it too."

"I'll see that they're both there. They're due back at the end of the week anyway."

"There's much to discuss. I look forward to your advice on some family matters, if you've got time," she said in her modest, polite way.

James knew that Sarah had a sense about things like this, and wouldn't see the event as most people would. He made his way back to the conference room.

"I just called Sarah; her husband died yesterday. I suspect a heart attack. Sarah's quite calm about it, but you can only imagine how she feels. The funeral's next Tuesday, so I'll go to Penbroke this weekend and leave from there. I'm sure it's a shock for Peter and Kate. Especially Kate, since she's not seen him much since she's been in Hong Kong with Roger. So let's see John tomorrow, Jeremy the next Wednesday, and what else?"

"There's lots of minor stuff, but we can sort all that out over the next few days."

"So how are you finding things with your accountant you hired and Trans Global?"

"We've spent a fortune on updating the fleet, but John's bringing in the business and we're staying above target for our ten percent growth per annum. With larger ships our sales are getting close to two hundred million and we're cash flowing around thirty-five million so we've more than recovered our investment. I never thought I'd ever know what I know now about a shipping line, but John is fabulous to work with. Stephen Gates is very quiet, but he doesn't miss a trick and he knows the price of every square inch of a building for rent and construction. We've got a great team and I believe we can build on them and continue a solid, sustained growth. Roger Bell, who, of course, will be back here soon, has definitely upped the ante. So last year we made with two companies here over thirty million after tax. The property company in Switzerland, which, as you know, has minimal tax for all the properties in the trust, made about four million. When that new building comes on line in Hong Kong you should see a huge change. So for your comfort, everything you thought up, and the small role I played in the implementation has absolutely worked. James, it's phenomenal what we're doing. And on top of that, I love my job. When you have team chemistry like we have, it makes life so much easier. Your father would be proud."

"We have a long way to go, but at least we've got the ball rolling. I love this container business. I think we got into it just in time. Now that we can afford a sustained growth, we can become a major carrier, and that's why I'm so excited to talk with John. The key now is to find good captains to run these ships.

"Tell me about the new accountant you've got coordinating Trans Global. You still haven't told me what you think."

"He's no Roger Bell, but he's doing fine. It took me some work in the beginning and I wasn't sure, but it's going on three years and I'd hate to train another."

"Roger Bell was a find. If I believed he'd have the talent he's got for investment and commodity trading, I'd have taken him off you right away. Nigel was a nice man, but compared with Roger, he's just an everyday banker. You wait and see. This guy is amazing, Claudia. I've only got to look at the figures to see that. Changing Nigel and Jonathan Park has transformed our banking business. Before that, my interest level was low. But with guys like Roger I can see why Wall Street looks up to talent like that and pays them the money they do. A person's got that light bulb or they don't, and I don't profess to be a banker or even close to his acumen. Speaking of which, since you have Nigel's old office, where do we plan to put him?"

"We have plenty of space on the floor below us. Let him sort out the way he wants to run it, like he's done in Hong Kong, and I'll support him any way I know how."

"Good. We'll put all the banking on the seventh floor and keep this floor for corporate business. Now that we've built Felixstowe, we've got plenty of room with most of the Trans Global guys having moved there. Cheaper homes and better facilities."

"Speaking of which, Stephen Gates has some space he can rent and he needs to get on that and fill it up. I'm sure you'll push his buttons," said Claudia, realizing they had space to offer now at the London building after the closing of their brokerage operation.

"Well I'm headed north tomorrow afternoon, after seeing

John, to check on the farm and Keith. It's time we talked again and then I'll be back here next Wednesday to see Jeremy.

****

The next morning John arrived on time and was waiting in the conference room.

"John, it's good to see you again. How's life in Felixstowe working out?"

"I'll tell you, it was a good decision to move there. My wife has a job in Colchester and we have a place close to the sea, so the kids love it. As for business, we can't grow fast enough. I've been punting around for prices on new and used ships and it's hard to beat the Chinese prices for shipbuilding. The growth of business there, and worldwide, is going at such a pace that I believe we'll place some orders. Since we have our business center in Hong Kong, it makes it easier to manage the progress."

"Something else I wanted to discuss with you," said James, getting right down to it, "is I know we are being faced with unions, especially at the ports. The number of container ships is growing so fast that it's moving toward automation with these cranes for loading and unloading and massive layoffs are starting to take place. A lot of employees have friends on land and at sea who could spread across to us. Strikes are not good for business. We need to start some stock option plan where a person can buy a Type B non-voting stock and can earn some type of value over the years. This can be offered in bonuses or something. Especially for all our officers, this will create loyalty among the staff and when others are having labor issues, we're sailing."

"We'll take a strong look at that with the accountants and arrive at something. I know I would appreciate stock options with a company like ours that's sure to keep growing, as would others."

"That was my main reason for seeing you. A dear family friend has died. So I look forward to dropping in at Felixstowe...soon." John understood.

****

James brought Sabrina with him so that they could go to Hampstead together and pick up his car.

James and Sabrina had settled on June 27 being the planned date for their wedding and Sabrina was busy talking all about the big day as they were driving toward Penbroke.

"Tomorrow I'm going over to see Sarah; do you want to come?" James asked.

"I feel sad for Sarah. He wasn't that old, was he?"

"Early fifties I believe. Yes, I must say it was a surprise to me. I know they must be in one hell of a state."

"That's okay. You can go, I don't know them that well and I'm sure you'll have lots of things to discuss with them about the future."

During the next morning Sabrina was busy looking around the house and planning the décor. James had been down to see Keith to get the latest on the farm. The new dairy was now being built and James was encouraged by how many cows they could milk so quickly with one man. The farm was being more strategically run. Keith could now hold back on grain and produce, until he felt it would be the right moment to sell. Claudia was keeping a close watch on the money; she had set up a new system where each week Keith would send her the list of payments to be made and she would transfer the funds into a zero-balancing account, which he was allowed to sign on.

James wandered through the new buildings that had now been erected for the Throne Room and admired the amount of space people could enjoy. Sarah's classroom was much larger. She had designed her office so that it was large enough to do her readings and write her books at a small conference table where she could meet privately with people on business matters and talk to select students. James was impressed with the facilities in the new tearooms, and the souvenir shop was at least three times the size of the little temporary building they had before.

The car parks too had been enlarged. It was quite a sight to see after seven years of operation. There were now films and new books on the Throne Room. Articles and pictures had been selected from newspapers and magazines. They had all been posted in frames around the shop. He thought Sarah had done a brilliant job. The whole area reflected the hard work Sarah had put into something she loved. James pondered over what decisions she would make now that Victor had gone.

"Sabrina, my beautiful bride, what have you been up to?" James asked.

"I've been planning the new Penbroke Court. I've been thinking, would you allow me to pay for all the renovations and updates?"

"That would cost you a fortune."

"I can afford it. I want to invest every penny on the home I'm going to live in," she said, sitting on his lap and putting her arms affectionately around him.

"This estate is part of my trust, which you will enjoy. I have more than enough to make all the alterations and updates you want."

"Can I work with the architects to plan the changes...of which you'll get to affirm?'

"Of course. Make this your project. God only knows I have enough things to take care of. I would love for you to take the lead."

"It's going to be hard to get it all done by the wedding. I think we should wait 'til afterward, don't you?"

"Absolutely. This is going to take at least a year or more. It'll be fun seeing the progress and choosing all the new items we'll buy." She took him through every room, telling him about all the alterations she'd make for the house and James let her continue with all her excitement. He thought of how many generations had done the same thing before him and had a strange déjà vu moment as she spoke.

****

James headed out on Sunday with Sabrina, not wanting to leave her alone. They arrived soon after lunch at the Lloyds' home in Banbury to see Peter opening the front door as they pulled in.

"Hey James, it's been a while but it certainly is good to see you at a time like this. Kate will be arriving with Roger later. They got in last night and are still trying to get over the jet lag."

"As long as you keep your spirits up! I remember when my father passed away. Just takes time, old boy."

"James, how lovely to see you both!" said Sarah. "I must give you a hug, dear Sabrina, looking so beautiful as always. Come on in and let's make a pot of tea. Then James, you and I can have a chat, if that's good for you."

"Of course."

The four chatted away with James and Sabrina bringing Peter up to date. All the news of the business and travels lifted their spirits and got their minds off of the moment. Then Sarah and James left to go to Sarah's office for a talk.

"Sarah, how will this affect our relationship at Penbroke? You've probably not had time to think it all through," said James.

"I've thought it all through long before today, in the event that Victor went before me."

"So what is it you'd like to ask me?"

"James, after the funeral I would like to buy or rent a cottage from you at Penbroke. My life for the last seven years has been there. It's what I love and this house I'm in has many memories. I want to move on and of course see my family when they're available."

"Please take time to think over your decision. I know this is a hard time for you right now, so don't act in haste. Whatever you decide I will work with you. Anyway, more importantly, what's your plan for Peter and Kate?"

"Victor left Peter and Kate fifty percent each of the business, and hoped that Peter would work hard to pay off his sister. The house and the land, which is at least two hundred and fifty acres, is mine. The business is on fifty acres and includes the racetrack, so that's included with the business. The difficulty here is that the business isn't making any money. Peter and Victor are very different in many ways and they had a hard time getting on at work. Peter prefers the bodywork and working with sheet metal and Victor was the machinist. Since Formula One car bodies reduced in size and are now starting to go to other materials, Peter doesn't have much business. Victor does have work but his machines are so old and outdated that it's hard to make money.

"The dilemma I have is that Peter is not a businessman like Victor. He's a shop man and very talented with his hands. He's like an artist with some of the work he does, but he doesn't have the personality to get out there and get business. With the right person, I know he could run circles round other people doing the same work. So the inevitable outcome is that he'll end up working for someone else and the days of having a family business with his father will be over. To sum it all up, if the business gets closed, then it remains for Peter and Kate to sell off the whole property and let the two of them split the proceeds and buy themselves a place, and as Kate's done, get on with life."

Something was disturbing Sarah. James was feeling a very deep connection to the vibrations she was giving him. He knew something wasn't right and by seeing her aura he knew she was very unhappy about something.

Sarah and James sat at her little table thinking and then James asked, "Sarah, we know each other well enough, so what is it that's bothering you with all this?"

Sarah then burst into tears. James couldn't help but be moved by a woman that he cared for so deeply. She had been such a great help in his life that he knew it was his faithful duty to help this woman. "I know you can read me like I read you. It's not Kate, it's Peter. What's to become of him? He's so talented and I believe the last years with Victor were so diminishing to him that he's lost all his self-esteem. He needs to get well. I know he loved his father, but nothing he could do was ever right. Victor never appreciated the skills he has for metal and because their thinking was so far apart it did affect Victor's health and it has done so to Peter. I carry a guilt of loving what I was doing at Penbroke so much that I lost sight of two people I love very much." Then the floodgates started to open again.

James got up and just held her in his arms and let her release all the feelings that she'd locked up inside. "You can't blame yourself for that. They were adults and they had conscious decisions to make for themselves. Peter is a sensitive guy. I know that. He needs to toughen up. We'll get him on the right track and that will be done for sure."

"James, he looks up to you. I feel you can help him a lot."

"Whatever happened to the plans he had for that shot peening business?"

"I've still got them, but he hasn't got a proper business evaluation done and I know why. Victor didn't like the idea and couldn't understand why he wouldn't get in there and learn his business. When he went to you with the idea of helping him with the project, Victor was furious and felt belittled. Not that he didn't have the greatest respect for you. He felt humiliated that he would even ask you. So nothing came of it. Peter needs a mentor, but it takes someone of different qualities and inner strength to make it happen."

"This house is yours. Are you just going to give it away to the kids?"

"I've made good money through the years with my writing. I have all a person could possibly want. I'm happy to let them have the place. It will be theirs one day anyway, and my life is at Penbroke, not here, anymore."

"Look, we have Roger, who is a brilliant businessman and accountant. It won't take him long to evaluate the situation. The choice comes down to Kate and Peter. If they want to do this project, then Kate needs to join up with Peter and I don't mind investing if it's a worthwhile business proposition. Then it's up to Kate and Peter. Who wants to live in the house?"

"Do you think Kate would leave you to do that?"

"Why not? She has a chance to have her own business, if it's a good idea and we have a strong business plan. She's got confidence and she's not afraid of hell itself. She loves that track and I think she'll want to keep this place. As much as she loves Roger, she's her own person. They could have a flat in London for Roger and this would be more than a lovely country home; a great place to bring children up for both of them."

Sarah felt a great relief after talking with James. She took time and collect herself, then decided to go back and join the rest. They had the basics of a plan. Now would be the time to throw the conversation open to her family. "Kate, so good to see you back. Roger, no worse for the wear?"

Kate looked sad as she too had a soft place in her heart for her father, and not having the chance to see him again was hard.

"This house won't be the same without Dad. What are we

all going to do?" asked Kate, concerned about the future.

"James and I have had a brief discussion and it really depends on what all of you want. I've told James that I'm quite happy to move to Penbroke and leave the house to you and Peter. Your father has left the business to you and Peter. So it all comes down to what the two of you wish to do," said Sarah, feeling more confident after speaking with James.

"Peter, do you want the business?" asked Kate, kicking off the discussion.

"At the moment, it's not making any money. If it were left to me, I would crank up the prices on the machining we've got left or send the work back. There's no money to be made on those old machines. As for the sheet metal, I can get by for now. I just need help bringing in more business because it's hard to do the work and market for more work at the same time," said Peter, not disinterested but lacking the confidence to say he could turn it around.

James seriously wondered whether Peter had the drive in him to run a business. He was beaten down from working for his father and thoroughly exhausted from frustration.

James tried to get to the point. "Kate, why don't you have Roger do a financial analysis of the whole situation? Peter, you had talked about this shot peening venture at one point. Is this something you want to do or not?"

"I would love to, but my father was dead set against it. Now I don't have the funds."

"Isn't that the reason you and I spoke about it, because you needed some financial backing?"

"Well, now that Dad's not in the picture, yes, I'd like to pursue it."

James turned to Roger. "Would you take the time to get with Peter and see what could be worked out here? If there's a viable plan and if these Americans are supposedly making a fortune at it, maybe there's room for competition."

"If that's what Kate and Peter want, of course," said Roger. "If you're happy to do without me for a few days, hey whatever it takes."

"So Kate, what are your thoughts on the matter?"

"I agree. I want to save this place. I love that racetrack and this is a lovely house for raising children."

James tried to motivate the group. "If that was the case, would you be prepared to pay for Peter's half of the house and give him some extra capital if needed to put toward the business plan? Let's honor your father's memory by making this business a success."

Kate turned to Roger, who agreed. Kate had some savings and she could easily get a mortgage with 50 percent equity. Roger had the cash and he knew as a businessman that for him getting a two-hundred-and-fifty-acre farm for half price was a no brainer.

"Okay. We have a plan, let's get it done this time," said James. As sad as it was for all of them to be there for Victor's funeral, the air was beginning to clear. Daylight was starting to creep in, and James could feel the relief coming from Sarah.

They all toasted with a round of drinks while Sarah had fixed up some light snacks. The tired group then went to their beds.

Roger would start in the morning and James would make his rounds to weigh up the situation as well.

****

The funeral was a sad affair as Peter stood at the pulpit and spoke with a quivering voice of the life of his father. Sarah shed her tears along with Kate as Roger and James watched the grieving pain of their family. Many other members of the family were in attendance, along with friends and Victor's employees. Victor Lloyd was loved for his work ethic, integrity, and leadership not only at work, but also within the community. To be taken at the age of fifty-two seemed unfair and was indeed a shock to a lot of people who knew him well in Banbury.

James and Roger had done their homework with Peter the day before and as suspected, the business was in trouble and must have been of great concern to Victor. He'd worked hard all his life, and to see the possibility of losing his business must have been a tremendous stress. Victor, after enjoying many years as a respected person whom many looked up to, couldn't understand why Peter had not come to him earlier to discuss and plan for the future, knowing the current state of affairs his father didn't need to know. Surely this outcome could have been avoided. He knew Victor had a lot of pride, but to lose one's life over something that could have been averted was something James found difficult to fathom. He then felt that Peter must have had a much harder journey than he'd previously thought. Victor just wouldn't listen to reason and the very part of him that was his strength became his undoing. James meditated as he sat in the little church, and as thoughts were coming to him, it was then that he felt Victor's presence. He saw him crying over his casket and wishing greatly to be part of the family he so deeply loved. James knew it would take him time to move on, but he wouldn't until he knew everyone was on the right road. It wasn't long before Victor suddenly realized that James could see him.

James, help my boy. I loved him so much. I was a fool not to realize the good in him. I was blinded by my own ego and look where it has got me.

James then answered in his own mind. *Victor, I am a friend to your son and I will stop at nothing until I see him on the road to a worthwhile future in the business you started and will always be remembered for.*

Victor started to feel at peace and the anguish he felt was

starting to leave. The last words James heard were, *You are a special man with gifts. I just never knew how much.* With that, he was gone. James felt, even though the business was far from being in good standing, he was going to make this new shot peen venture work. He thought that Victor would be talking to Sarah since she had those same gifts and could see him clearly. He would talk with her after.

Watching the coffin lowered into the earth after the vicar's eulogy, then seeing the dirt thrown onto the casket, was a defining moment. People then moved away with their heads held low in loving memory.

For the close family and friends, Sarah had catered some food to the house. The scene of discussion at the house was of a lighter nature as people started to talk about the future and make plans, having faced the inevitable. Sabrina had faithfully stuck by James's side through the last couple of days and was making polite conversation with Kate and Roger about their experiences in Hong Kong.

"Peter, you got through it all graciously," said James.

"Thanks. I appreciate that. As much as my dad and I had our differences, I did love the man and I'll miss him."

"I'm sure he feels the same way. I have a feeling things are going to go a lot better than you think. Why don't you grab your sister and Roger and let's all have meeting in another room, because I've got to get back to London right away."

The four of them made their way into a private room with a table to talk. James left Sabrina with Sarah to discuss their upcoming wedding.

"Okay, Kate, what do you want to do now that we have a business plan from Roger?" James asked.

"I want to stay and help Peter get started. We agree it's going to take at least five hundred thousand to get this off the ground. The selling off of the machinery could bring about one hundred of that eventually. We need two hundred and fifty thousand pounds to buy this shot peen equipment and then install it. So initially, Peter and I can get the ball rolling. After that, we're going to need help."

"Do you want to loan the money or have an investor that has equity in your business?"

"Peter and I have talked about that," Kate started. "I had hoped that Roger could help us, but he says he's committed to working at the bank and obviously he makes more money doing what he loves. He's in a position to loan us the money and he would expect to be paid back, but he doesn't want to be a shareholder."

"Is that correct, Roger?"

"James, I know you'd want to help, but I'm married to Kate now and her mother has provided us with a beautiful home at minimal cost. I just don't have your day-to-day leadership skills in a manufacturing service industry environment. I'm at best a financier, so helping them in this way is the best." Roger was being as honest as he could about what his skills were.

"Kate, do you think it'd be possible to hire someone to go out there and get the business?" asked James.

"I've given this a lot of thought," said Kate. "I feel I can run the administration side of things and Peter can handle the workshop. We both get on well together and yes, a marketing person would be exactly what we need."

"It just takes one of you to stay behind this man to get business and go with him when necessary," said James. "Kate, I believe you could handle that and when technical issues come along, that's where Peter would step in. I'll be around if you need my help, but I believe you can handle this and I feel that's what your father would've wanted."

Everyone agreed with James, who had enough on his plate. He would miss Kate at the bank, but in a way this was the best outcome. Victor would have wanted his family to run the business he had started. Roger was also in a financial position, to help out, if necessary.

James and Sabrina said their good-byes. James asked Sarah to see Keith and pick whatever place she wanted, then they could work out the rest between them.

CHAPTER 17

MAKING PLANS

James felt good about the positive plan and outcome to such an unhappy event in the life of the Lloyd family. He was now prepared to do whatever he could for Sarah and be there for her, after her loss. She was forty-seven and had lived such a routine existence that finding a new life outside her work would probably be the last thing on her mind.

"James, you're incredible," Sabrina said.

"Why?"

"Look at what you've done over the last three days we were there. You've got that family back on their feet and they have a new plan and direction because of you. I can see how you're so successful at work. The fact that you take action at a time when others are going through great pain is one of the things I love about you."

"Well, those people are like family to me. To see Peter beaten down was devastating. If we don't appreciate our friends, what do we have in life? No amount of money can buy relationships like that. Sarah felt guilty that she couldn't have done more to help the relationship between Peter and his father. Life is a challenge; we just have to know how to pick up the pieces and move on. You can reward me, by putting on that sexy lingerie when we get home, and I'll make love to you all night."

They arrived back late at the flat in London. As promised, Sabrina blew his brains away with her teasing, seductive manner that put him completely and totally under her spell.

The next morning James made arrangements for Sabrina, who had some available time, to meet with the architect. He then hurried off to the office to meet with Jeremy Soames.

****

"No doubt you've got a trendsetter by the tail," said Jeremy, referring to the new building in Hong Kong. "I've heard nothing but rave reviews from everyone."

"That's good to know. It was a big investment but I think it's going to do well."

"I came to bring you up to date with some unsettling news in the Middle East," started Jeremy, after taking a deep breath. "As you know, the Suez Canal's closed and no one knows who to pay whom. There're a number of ships that have been stuck in the canal since 1967. It also appears that the Americans' continued support of the Israelis is starting to inflame Arab countries against the West; the bottom line is oil prices could go through the roof. If the Arab league known as OPEC got together to limit oil production, panic would start. Oil prices are already affected by the higher shipping costs due to shipping around South Africa. Another spark could ignite serious inflation. It all goes back to our last conversation. Russia is behind all this inflammatory action against the West. Wherever they can strike at the heart of capitalism to weaken their so-called view of American imperialism seems to be the goal. Our agents inform us that although Russia is not directly involved, we do know they have their own hatred toward the Jews. This is causing us great problems in maintaining our alliance with Israel. If we lose Israel, we've lost a strategic point in that part of the world. The Arabs have been fighting each other ever since the Crusades, but a central hatred can make people forget their petty differences and align them toward a common enemy. Thank God the Americans are doing what they are against Vietnam and yet, the world is so blind to the realities we have on our plate right now."

James listened then had a thought. "What if I bought some ships from the Russians if you could help me?"

"Of course that would be welcomed."

"I could have an opportunity, if the order was big enough, to talk with a top official in a social way and hopefully meet the man himself, Leonid Brezhnev. I would be in a position to discuss industry and trade, potentially buy ships from the Russians, and get an inside view of how they see the world we live in. In exchange, if he were to invest in our bank in Hong Kong, then maybe a relationship could be built. Sometimes as an individual, one can build a relationship that is virtually impossible between countries. Being a businessmen, we can exchange ideas and views."

"I don't think it's going to stop the inevitable," cautioned Jeremy, "but there's certainly no harm in trying. You don't need money; you're not linked to any organization that would be viewed as political, you're just a businessman doing what business people do. I believe it's time we all had another meeting here at the bank, with your permission, and have a round-table discussion on the matter. In the meantime, now that you're back, do that training course I told you about. Remember, Jonathan Park could get out of jail with good behavior within the next two to three years. Nothing like improving your defensive skills to ensure having you're wits about you. Can't hurt."

"I've got a plan for him. You've paid us back completely, but he won't know that. So I can say that while he was in prison I didn't wish to hurt his family, so I made no attempt to recover the money from his textile business in order that his wife could manage her affairs. However, the amount of two million is still owed and has interest accrued. Giving him an opportunity to show his colors could allow us some leniency toward him and make him feel grateful."

"That won't stop him from defecting to the east, but it does offer him a hope of redemption. We shall have to wait and see when the time comes."

Jeremy then went silent changing the tone of his voice. "James, it's time you and I talked not about the affairs of the world necessarily, but more importantly your life's journey."

"How do you mean? Is there something I should be doing that I'm not?" asked James curiously.

"As we have discussed before you have an important part to play in the future of this country and with your role in the brotherhood. I applaud your dynamic enthusiasm for trade and industry, but you were put on this planet for a much higher destiny and purpose."

"Why? Am I headed in the wrong direction?"

"Not yet, but you are on the edge of that happening. Let me explain. You've come such a long way in such a short space of time. Your work ethic and ambitious drive are to be commended. You are surrounded by love and admiration for the journey you are headed toward, but remember this: However vast Bannermans becomes, and however successful you are, it will fall far short of the true journey and purpose you are here for. I as your guide here on Earth, and your masters, expect more from you and know what you are truly capable of doing."

"I thought I was doing exactly that, but obviously upholding the tradition of my forefathers is not enough?" James was disappointed in what he was hearing.

"James, this is not a competition for you to become the wealthiest man in the world; you have a much greater gift to give. Remember I was on Atlantis with you, and served you with the utmost loyalty, but for all your talents and hard work you fell short of one quality."

James was now starting to become frustrated. "Then pray God what is that?" he burst out with frustration.

"Doing what you're doing for the business is commendable, but are you doing it for the good of your people, your country, and mankind, or is there a slight degree of greed slowly creeping in? This makes you hunger for more and more, and then that desire will never be able to be satisfied."

"Okay, so what's your advice, Sir Jeremy?"

"Obviously continue with what your doing, but shift your focus slightly and be doing all that you are doing for a greater purpose. Our time is limited, like all of us on this planet. However, what you do for this world and the world beyond will be the lasting testimony to your life's work and future in the universe. In other words, to put it in your language, 'there are bigger fish to fry' than building an empire on mother earth! It will be what you do for mother earth and all its inhabitants that will contain a lasting legacy, and the key to fulfilling your true destiny that will bring you lasting fulfillment. You are still young, but there will come a time when you must grow above the need for materialism. This was your undoing on Atlantis and you now have a golden opportunity to choose the path that satisfies not only your creator, but in the end, you most of all!"

"I know I have a purpose, and thank you for reminding me not to get off track. I do tend to become obsessive over my goals and aspirations. I must realize the good and the destructiveness those qualities have in me."

"We are only at the beginning of our discussions. I will not stop until you have replaced me in the service of this great country that so honors you."

"Jeremy, checks and balances are good; I will reflect upon our discussion on my honeymoon and dig deeper into understanding God's purpose for my service to him, for the life that's been bestowed upon me. I thank you, sir, for shaking my rivets...and giving me a paradigm shift. I need those prompters," he said, laughing at himself as Jeremy shook hands to leave, also laughing to himself, knowing the invincibility of youth. It wouldn't be easy, but by "hook or by crook" Jeremy was determined that this time his initiate would come to understand.

****

James now had much to reflect upon. What Jeremy had said bothered him. He hadn't discussed the Dark Vortex with Jeremy, so he decided it was high time they talked, but in a different environment. So he decided to give him a call.

"Jeremy, as I am now progressing further with my studies and writings from the seventh earl, would now be a good time to meet up and receive some fine mentorship from that knowledgeable brain of yours?"

"It would be a pleasure. In this busy world of ours we've scarcely had time to talk at Nicholas's wedding...and even now on a personal level. As I have told you, we have a much more overriding purpose for our lives than the day-to-day activities we are so engaged in. The world we live in needs serious guidance if we are going to achieve and be part of correcting the direction we now find ourselves headed toward. So the answer is yes. How about dinner at your favorite restaurant, where we can have a more in-depth discussion without interruption. I am free, so meet you at say seven tonight?"

"Look forward to it." James was excited. This was the first time that he began to see a change in himself and a paradigm shift that was now taking on a stronger purpose in his life.

Jeremy arrived on time as usual at the Brass Bell, and after the usual discussions on family affairs they both started to analyze what James had just experienced.

"James, you are now starting to dig deeper into the way the universe works and how spirituality and our divine creation is actually part of this process. Mankind's impression of life on Earth, hell, and heaven are to some extent true but they are simple basic foundation points for those of us who have become more evolved to move forward. Good and so-called evil have always existed, but without the opposite how could we truly know the way, the truth, and the light?" remarked a more soulful Jeremy. His demeanor was different over an evening meal-less formal and more friendly.

"So you are aware of my journey to the Dark Vortex, obviously. It's as though the entire universe is a planned entity in which we are given the free will to discover. Even our many mistakes and failures or 'sins' as the Bible refers us to can be turned around if we so choose," responded a more thoughtful James.

"Yes, I am aware of your experience in what we call the in-between place, in the afterlife, or purgatory as the Catholics call it—but we digress—and this is where you were allowed to witness what Lucifer has to deal with. His job is to reform those of us who lose our way, but as you can see, this is no easy task. As great as some of his victories in restoring souls toward the upward path toward our creation are, he is always saddened like a parent, teacher, or anyone who tries to restore a soul back toward their true purpose, and for some reason that's not achievable."

"This was an experience I shall never forget. As crazy as it sounds when we sit here and discuss the matter, it all makes complete sense. The universe has a preordained journey, and even with the 'free will' we are given, in the end it is up to each one of us to learn the value of love. Without this recognition, we are doomed to digress. I can well see the importance that teaching values and principles to our children, fellow man, can affect and change the direction of our lives."

"Now you see what our purpose is; it is our destiny as we too grow within the universe. By helping others we gain renewed energy and a higher purpose to carry out special assignments. I can't say we failed on Atlantis. Others were so absorbed with greater and greater technology that they lost the true goal, which is not the gaining of absolute power in this dimension; rather, it's the acknowledgement that we serve a higher purpose, which is in fact far more powerful than anything that can be created here."

"I see how seductive power is in this world, but none of it lasts; it is forever changing. We only leave behind our true legacy and that is what kind of person we were and what contribution we made to mankind," remarked James.

"This brings me to a newer subject that I wish to make you aware of. When I just met with you, I was going to relate what I had on my mind, but thought I would wait...for a moment such as this. We are entering a new era, so to speak; technologies not yet seen, but are being experimented on, are among us. For example, as quoted in the New Testament in Revelation, you will remember the number 666. This alludes to some biotechnical code we have yet to discern, but I can tell you this: A biotech company is producing devices, chips that can be implanted into humans in order to exert mind control over certain groups of people, in order to carry out commands from a central source, which we believe to be in one of the Eastern European nations. In addition there are others working on drugs that can do the same. The only difference is that they wear off, so it's more difficult to trace and validate their existence."

That could be dangerous. An army of robotized humans? thought James.

"James, this is just the beginning. We experienced all this on Atlantis, and here we are again facing the same dilemma."

"So how do we combat this dreadful scenario?"

"That's where you come in; now you are beginning to see your destiny. The success you are achieving is no accident, and the financial rewards you will receive are all with a singular purpose."

"Which is..."

"This money must be used in order to buy up new up-and-coming biotech companies with innovations that can combat this eventual outcome. On Atlantis we created clothing to detect the chips and bracelets that can also read any type of electrical message from the brain through drugs and other materials that will be used."

"That's a whole new journey, about which I know absolutely nothing. My sister Becky would be a great resource with her medical background."

"Don't worry, you knew all this on Atlantis. A new age will begin, an age where crystals, prisms, lasers, and so on will bring about a new defense system. It's not now, but during the next twenty years this will become of paramount importance. I will support you through my authority and connections as judge over the 'Law Lords' in the house. You will be eligible for grants, for R&D, and a percentage for experimentation. This is high on our agenda, and our purpose, which will become yours and that of your son as we move into the twenty-first century. The difference this time is that we shall overcome this dark menace with a force that can change molecular generation through the brain, something that we never successfully concluded in our last civilization. We shall succeed; we have too."

James and Jeremy continued their intense discussion in the cigar lounge over a glass of brandy, cigars, and black coffee. He was now getting to know Jeremy better; the evening they spent together brought them closer and was indeed necessary for them to succeed in their primary purpose of implementing procedures that were not realized on Atlantis.

****

"Did you have a good meeting with the architects?" James asked Sabrina.

"Oh yes, we have a great plan; when you have time, we must go over what we discussed. I've mailed out all the invitations today since I must show up for work tomorrow. Nicholas will be going crazy without me, I know. I want us to talk about my modeling career because if I'm to be at Penbroke, there's no way I can keep working full time, mio amore!"

"Whatever you decide, being with you is what's most important to me," said James, not wanting to hurt her career, but not wanting to put any stress on the intended marriage. "If I were you, I would ease off until after the wedding and leave yourself free to go up there at your leisure. You can always stay with Sarah. She's there full time if you're lonely. You know I'll be with you on the weekends to help. That being said, it's high time I called my sisters. Becky would only be too happy to help...and maybe Flick."

CHAPTER 18

THE WEDDING

It was only two days before the wedding and Sabrina was growing nervous. This was a day she had waited for since they'd met on the lawn behind the house and gone to the Throne Room. The realization that this was now about to become a reality was overwhelming and she was not quite her normal self.

The Throne Room had been closed to the public for the weekend, as the space would make a convenient parking lot, giving their guests the opportunity to explore the Throne Room and tour all the facilities they now had to offer. The new classrooms, tearooms, and souvenir shop were now permanent buildings that had been designed to comply with the architecture of the house and its surroundings. Becky, Kate, and Sarah helped Sabrina with everything. Flick, as usual, was off on some whirlwind romance and would be there for the day. James's mother had also arrived.

The last big event that was held at Penbroke was for James's twenty-first, almost five years ago. The progress that had been made since James took charge after leaving his school in the summer of 1963 was clear and pronounced. In seven years the farm, the Throne Room, and the cottages had all but been rented. The estate was now a thriving entity. From a rundown, unprofitable business, the investments had turned the whole place into a worthwhile venture and no one was more proud than James to see all that hard work come to fruition. There was still the house to refurbish and he was close to getting his way for the planning permission he needed to expand the little church and the shops in the High Street of Penbroke. Under the excellent stewardship of Keith Pruett and Sarah, the place was moving forward. It now remained to have the main house occupied again and another generation to start a family and continue the tradition.

James was quietly perusing the guest list and noticed that Piero, Sabrina's brother, was bringing Gina, Marco's sister. Sabrin'a father would also be in attendance. James was pleased that he accepted her choice and that the painful wounds of Marco's demise had healed. He felt good to know that there was peace in the Tuscan valley and he had always wondered how people there might have reacted to Sabrina's choice. There were over two hundred guests and he was grateful to see the number of Italian families that had made the trip. It was probably a good opportunity to turn the event into a holiday during the hot summer in Italy. A marquee like he had at his twenty-first had been erected and the ballroom would be available for dancing, as before. The little church in Penbroke would have been too small, so James had made arrangements with the vicar to come to the house. The caterers, on the other side of the marquee, had put in place a platform for the service so that those who wanted to be inside or out, depending on the weather, could be satisfied.

"Sabrina, there you are," said James.

"James, I love all this, but I'm going to be glad when it's over. You know us Italians. We're just like you Brits; we have to have a grand event at these affairs. At least this time I've got tabs on you and you won't go running off like you did last time."

"Ah," James said with a smirk, "but I have to dance with the ladies and you with the men."

"Well a few, but I want to dance with the man I love." It was the first big event that she'd done most of the organization for. She well demonstrated her leadership in organizing all that had to go into the catering, bands, and hotels for visitors. James realized that she would have no problem running a household like Penbroke.

"James, come help me arrange the placing of the tables and chairs."

"At your service, madam." They planned between them for hours just where to put everyone, so that no one would feel disrespected.

****

The big day had arrived and crowds of people flocked in to the eleven o'clock service to be held on the lawn. People were lined on each side to represent the family they knew. The sun was shining and there wasn't a hint of a shower. Precautions had been taken to cover the seating and the ceremony where the vicar would join James and Sabrina. The awnings were adequate, but for the most part, the area was open.

The bishop of Lincoln had been asked to perform the service, but in view of his thoughts toward both parties, he decided he was happy to attend the event but let the vicar of that diocese have the honor. The different religious backgrounds on both sides of the family made holding the service at the house a common ground. It was an intimate ceremony between the couple; God and the vicar would provide the ceremony in the least offensive manner to the beliefs of any particular person present at the gathering.

Peter was the best man and Gina the maid of honor. The bridesmaids were Becky and Flick, and Piero was the head usher. All that remained was for the band to play the organ.

James anxiously awaited Sabrina and was standing on the platform below the vicar. Antonio proudly walked his daughter toward the podium to "Here Comes the Bride." The lawn chairs were packed and the clouds were now looming in the distance. The band added a little flair, playing a small piece of the Italian anthem as Sabrina rose to the platform to stand next to James. Her wedding dress was a work of art. Nicholas had chosen the finest silks and satin and the embroidery work must have taken endless hours of work.

Sabrina wore the immaculate ecru silk-and-satin dress, which had been perfectly matched by an inventive tiara. Her hair, pulled away from her face, showed the extreme beauty of all her features. Nicolas designed a showstopper as only he could. Rebecca and Felicity, James's sisters, held the train. James turned to wink at both of them in a way to say thank you as they smiled back. Gina stood on Sabrina's left while Peter, with ring in hand, stood on James's right. Antonio, Piero, and James's sisters stood quietly behind and below the couple.

The vicar made the effort to speak some Italian to the guests, which was greatly appreciated. The bishop's lack of skill in languages was another reason why it was decided that the vicar should conduct the service.

The moment came when the vicar asked James, "Do you take this woman to be your wife to love…?" Then a large bolt of lightening shot an enormous streak across the sky and within seconds the heavens burst open with a deafening thunder crack.

As yet, there was no rain. Out of politeness for the couple, no one moved. The vicar, who could not see what was happening behind him said, "Sabrina, do you take this man to be…?" and the rain poured down behind him. Then the final words came. "You may now kiss the bride." As the couple moved together to hold one another and take that most important ceremonial kiss, the sun burst out over the top of the cloud and a huge rainbow started to form. It was as though the entire audience was getting a show from the heavens.

James looked toward the rainbow and with his understanding of what was happening, heard the words from his master, *This marriage is blessed by the highest and sanctified by the heavens, we are here too, and just wanted you to know we have a few things we're allowed to do at appropriate moments.* Then James thought about the words his guide, Morphius, had said to him, *When stars collide!* James and Sabrina kissed again with tears of emotion falling from their cheeks. Before James dismounted the podium, he noticed shapes taking place in the clouds and the form of his master, Czaur, in the center and his four other guides became clear. They smiled and he smiled back as the wind started to pick up and everyone was now laughing, clapping and cheering, before making a beeline for the marquee.

James and Sabrina and the vicar also started to run and Czaur said, *We've baptized you both, too. A little water never hurt anyone!* James could hear him and all his guides laughing, as they too were enjoying the whole ceremony and had planned this moment to show them both that they and the heavens were there for them. The rain continued until the clouds had dispersed. The caterers carefully reorganized the seating while everyone was getting a glass of champagne. The rain soon passed and the skies were clear again. James knew in his heart that his guides had planned this firework display to let them know that they too were present, and in his thoughts he thanked them.

When the rain cleared, James and Sabrina stood by the entryway to all the tables so that they could meet each person as they entered. The afternoon was filled with the tremendous interaction of the guests as they all seated themselves at their designated tables. The food was incredible, thanks to Sabrina's careful selection of the menu. The moment came for the speeches and, of course, it was Peter who was the first to speak.

"James and Sabrina, thank you for the unexpected and dramatic firework display from the heavens. I wasn't aware of some of your abilities, but it did add some unexpected entertainment. James and I have known each other since our first meeting at Sterling Heights at the grand old age of thirteen, at our impetuous inauguration speech as new boys, where we stood up and got blasted by the old boys with countless objects and food at the dining room table. But we did survive. From that moment on, James and I became friends and he's always treated me like a brother. For those of you who don't know James, he's a man of many seasons, or I should say, *for* all seasons. Not only can he blast a cricket ball through a net at over one hundred miles an hour, but he also knows how to get down in the trenches and work his tail off.

"Few people in this room today could ever know the understanding and personal modesty this man has. For all that he has, there is no task or job that's beneath him. He's a pretty good horseman, not bad with a gun, but could learn a few things from my sister, Kate, on how to drive that car of his." People laughed knowing that he drove an extremely expensive sports car. "In truth, I've yet to meet such an awesome competitor. Losing is not part of his vocabulary and no matter how small the task, he will figure out a way to succeed. As his longtime friend, I believe his greatest gift is his dedication and work ethic for a man that believes in excellence and not the value of his back pocket—most of the time!"

Scattered cheers and titters went up. "James, my dearest friend and confidant, I wish you and your most beautiful bride, Sabrina, all the happiness a man and a bride could have. Ladies and gentleman, James and Sabrina." Peter raised his glass as everyone stood up to make the toast and to cheer and clap the newlyweds.

Gina then took the podium. "To my dearest friend, Sabrina, who I'm so proud of..." She paused. "I must start by remembering that fateful day, when my dear brother Marco departed from our lives. We're now able to enjoy today. To see Sabrina looking so radiant and beautiful is indeed a blessing and the success she's been able to achieve is truly remarkable. Life commands us all to have character in spite of the painful moments we all experience.

"Today has well proved that behind the clouds lies a silver lining. Any of you that could see that beautiful rainbow that stood out over the lawn tells us we must always believe that there is a God. There is love in our world, even though it sometimes takes us a moment to find it." She was referring, of course, to Marco's fateful journey. She felt that even though it was a very special day for James and Sabrina, it would be heartwarming to all the Italian families that had been invited and to her father, who had suffered such great pain with all of them, to say a few kind words. She continued, "Now if anyone knows a few things about Sabrina, I certainly do. We have been like sisters from childhood. As she never knew, or had a mother to raise her, she spent countless hours at our home working with us, cooking and laughing when my mother was alive. Sabrina has now become a fantastic cook. This lady, my sister, I'm proud to call her, has fed two men for most of her life. Piero and Antonio are already missing her since she moved to Milan. So now Lady Phillipa and I have become very close because she's learning all about our Italian dishes. And who doesn't like pasta?" A few roars and cheers went up, as everyone raised their wine glass to celebrate Italian cuisine. Gina spoke in Italian and some more laughs were clapped and cheered.

"I have to tell you a very special story about Sabrina just so you know she's not the little saint everyone believes she is. One day after school, when we were about fifteen, we decided not to go home because Sabrina had a plan. At the top of the hill that overlooks our vineyard is a small cabin. When school finished early, our parents never expected us home until about five each day. So we decided to form a club of seven girls who were our best friends. Each week we would bring a bottle of wine and a packet of cigarettes." The audience started to laugh, wondering where this was going. Gina's father, Bastida, raised his eyebrows with a smile, while Antonio couldn't wait to know what his mischievous daughter had been up to. "We would do this until we left school and we swore to be best friends forever. In those meetings where we had our little social club, we discussed boys and who we all wanted to marry one day. So now, I will describe the man Sabrina wanted to marry."

Sabrina laughed, embarrassed, as she put her head in her hands, clearly recalling the memory.

"He had to be tall, good looking, blue eyes, and someone who would be completely different from anyone she'd met. Most of all, he had to have a special quality about him. She wouldn't describe it to us. Knowing Sabrina she has found that something but she's not letting us in on her secret. I can tell by that grin all over her face." All the younger women started laughing wondering just what had truly captivated Sabrina. "Now all of you be good, not naughty!" Gina lauged. "She did, however, say she wanted a man that had soul...and loved her for what was inside her and not only for her looks. Well, Sabrina, I think you've achieved just that. Anyone who hasn't visited the Throne Room would have to know that James is the person who brought this room into reality and there is a very special story behind it, which I'm sure James can tell us about, if he would be kind enough to do so. But before that, I want all the girls of our little Tuscan sorority to stand up and give everyone your name and wish Sabrina, as I do, a long and lasting happiness with the man of her dreams, James Bannerman, the tenth Earl of Penbroke." Each of the girls stood up in the audience and did just that. Then they all shouted with Gina, "To our bella Sabrina, amore for James, and both of you forever." Everyone then stood up to raise their glasses to the couple. Sabrina was ecstatic and wept with joy.

So Gina, who had all the confidence in the world, had thrown down the gauntlet to James and everyone looked at him and shouted, "Speech! Speech!" thumping the table for him to arise.

He finally stood up with a big smile, his eyes wandering across an audience who wanted to hear about the Throne Room.

"My Lord Archbishop, lords, ladies and gentlemen, what can I do but respond to such an invitation? Well, Gina, you certainly don't mess around when you want the facts, so I'll start with the Throne Room as I know you're all anxious to hear about it. I will not go into a lot of detail as everyone here can read about that by taking a short walk to the room. My great-grandfather, the seventh earl, brought these artifacts back to England, each one with a very special story of its own. This happened over a hundred years ago. The Throne, of course, is the central attraction. Now I'm not here to preach the spiritual values of the Throne, as I am in the presence of my Lord Archbishop and his vicar. I will tell you, however, there is a very special energy to the Throne and many people have had questions answered that have made significant changes in their lives.

"However, this is not for everyone and that's why we have a

school. Please stand up, Sarah. Ladies and gentlemen, I present to you Sarah McKenzie. This famous lady, who has written countless books on the subject, runs our school. Her books and her teaching can help a person understand just what it is that this throne does. Personally, I am a person that has, of course, spiritual values, but believes life is to be lived, and while we're here, we must do the best job we can for our fellow man and ourselves. That being said, if the Throne adds to that journey, then we've done a very special thing by bringing about the opportunity for people to experience something that hopefully can be helpful for their lives."

People throughout the room stood up and clapped. They knew the story and had nothing but admiration for James's efforts to see this room restored. Whether they believed in what it could or could not do didn't matter to anyone; they believed in James and what he'd done.

"I do think this is an appropriate time for me to say how special this day has been for us," James continued. He pulled Sabrina up from her chair. "I could not be with a more beautiful woman inside and out, mia amore bellisima!" He then kissed her in front of a standing ovation. "Let the festivities begin."

At the cake-cutting ceremony, the press photographers were allowed in and had agreed not to impose on anyone with questions. Claudia had given them a press release, which would have been sufficient for any story they may want to print. The couple was extremely well known, as there were enough facts about them already in the press. The wedding photographer was under a firm contract not to release anything to the press.

James and Sabrina started the dancing and others joined in. James had picked the same group he had for his twenty-first birthday, the Adjectives. They had kept up to date with all the latest songs and, as usual, their performance dazzled. Unlike his twenty-first, James and Sabrina danced with only close relatives and friends so that they would have the opportunity to wish the couple their best. A room had been set up for all the presents in the dining room and before they left for their honeymoon they made a quick tour of the long dining room table. Sabrina couldn't wait to return home to take the time to appreciate all of their gifts. It would be the start of placing their memories throughout the house for their family journey, once it had been renovated.

People were now well into the party and it was time for the newlyweds to leave on their honeymoon. It was at that moment that James recognized that the person Flick (Felicity) was dancing with was none other than Gordon Petersen, his sworn enemy from his school days. James couldn't believe that his sister would befriend such a man. She had brought him to his twenty-first before, and now she had to add insult to injury by inviting him to his wedding. She didn't sit with him at the main table but had artfully invited him without anyone knowing. She knew James would be too polite to have him escorted off the premises so she took full advantage by agitating him.

James thought after his twenty-first birthday, she would have dropped the relationship. Their eyes crossed and Flick knew this was the best way to get under his skin. Gordon's grinning face, as he looked over Flick's shoulder, said it all. Flick's jealousy toward James appeared to be growing, not subsiding. James blew it off as they ran upstairs to change. He would face that situation one day and deal with it once and for all.

Their suitcases were already packed and the helicopter would be arriving at 4:00 p.m. on the lawn outside near the marquee. Sure enough they could hear the spinning blades as the couple excitedly ran toward the Bell 206 JetRanger. Sabrina had the bouquet in her hands as the crowds lined the way. Toward the end of the line stood Becky, Flick, and Gina. After giving them all hugs, Sabrina turned her back to them and threw the bouquet up over her head. She thought that Becky, being the tallest, would be the one to reach out and grab it, but Gina caught the bouquet. The couple looked down on the cheering and applauding crowd as the press photographers clicked away at the helicopter swiftly climbing up and away over Penbroke Estate and the waving crowds below.

****

They flew to the nearest airport close to Lincoln, where Nicholas had his Lear 25 awaiting them on the tarmac. The couple, with their baggage, was ushered onto the private jet that would speed them away to Nicholas's yacht that lay moored at the harbor in Monaco for their weeklong honeymoon. Nicholas and Davina would be joining them toward the end of the week.

Nicholas's yacht was luxurious. James and Sabrina had unpacked their suitcases and made their way to the veranda where an ice-cold bottle of champagne awaited them. The yacht had three bedrooms and Nicholas had given up his master suite so they could enjoy the very finest his yacht had to offer. The captain introduced himself and presented them with a written itinerary of their cruise. They would take the yacht through the waters between Corsica and Sardinia and then down to Sicily. From there they would proceed to Malta then onto the island of Crete. After that, he would head up to Athens where they would join Nicholas and Davina for the weekend. They would then journey through the Greek Islands and after backtrack their way to Monaco on a higher route to shorten the return.

The trip would take about ten days and the captain could stop wherever to suit the couple's needs. He told them he had a chef on board and gave them a menu for the days ahead. Also aboard they had two cabin staff members that would be available to take care of their needs. His experienced first crewman would also be happy to convey any messages they may have. He didn't want to bother the couple in any way. "We are here to make you have a wonderful experience and if you wish to sleep later, stay up late, we are here to serve whatever your needs may be."

"I've got to hand it to Nicholas," said James. "He certainly knows how to do things first class."

"I have to keep pinching myself. You're mine and I'm yours forever," gushed Sabrina.

"We'll polish off another glass of champagne and then we'll go and test that bed out."

CHAPTER 19

THE HONEYMOON

The couple retired early after a grueling week of wedding preparations. They relaxed and made love, slept and made love again, and it wasn't until midday that they finally made it back on deck. Sabrina had delighted in wearing her skimpy bikini and James his swimsuit. All they did was swim in the little pool and catch the sun and just sleep. They would eat, drink, and do it all over again. The thought of no agenda and the time to do as they pleased was what they wanted. James now had time to think over what Jeremy had said, and as much as he was driven toward his goals and achievements, he knew what Jeremy had said was right. But deep down he wasn't going to worry about it now. He would continue to build his world and then devote his time to the works of a higher purpose.

The captain finally made his appearance. "Tomorrow I'll be stopping in Malta to take on some supplies, so if you want to go ashore, let me know."

They both agreed that a shore excursion would be a good idea. The weather had been beautiful and the cool sea breezes were helping with the heat they would normally be experiencing.

Their tour guide told them a lot about the history of the island from the megalithic structures, known as some of the oldest surviving remnants in the world, to the time when St. Paul was stranded there. The island held a long Christian history that they both enjoyed learning about. Like all tours, one would have to spend a number of days to truly appreciate the history, but it had been an island well visited by tourists through the years. They bought some souvenirs for the journey, had lunch close to the harbor, but were quite content to get back on the boat and go for a swim.

The days were passing quickly and James and Sabrina were now so relaxed that by the time they reached Athens they were ready to go ashore and visit before Nicholas and Davina arrived. Both were fascinated with the Acropolis and the Parthenon. James, having spent his life surrounded by lush vegetation, noted the experience of an arid environment and the dry climate of Greece. They enjoyed hearing about all the history of Sparta and Macedonia and how the provinces finally became Greece, united under the famous Alexander the Great. They bought many souvenirs as tokens of their trip. They arrived back on the boat to meet up with Nicholas and Davina, who were having a cocktail on the deck. That evening Nicholas served up a sumptuous meal in his dining room and they all enjoyed enough wine to sink a battleship.

"How do you like life aboard a yacht?" asked Nicholas, pouring himself another glass.

"Anybody that couldn't get used to this would need their head examined," James said.

"You'd be surprised. It's not for everyone. Some people get seasick."

"We had a few nights where the surf was a little turbulent, but nothing to raise an alarm. After my trip through the Bay of Biscay on one of our merchant vessels with forty-foot waves, this was like floating on air."

"She's pretty stable and we do have outriggers we can use if the going gets tough and we need to stabilize things."

"Sabrina and I can't thank you both enough for such a lovely honeymoon and wedding dress. Nicholas, you know how to do things in an extremely exciting way. The whole trip to the yacht and being here has been out of this world."

"That's what friends are for. I had to come up with something after Sabrina's dad played that joke on us at Penbroke. I still laugh about that today. Now wait for the best part of our cruise through the Greek islands. We'll stop at a few places I know. I always love this part of the Mediterranean. The waters are nice and warm; we must go snorkeling and diving. Not like going for a swim up at Blackpool, eh?"

"You couldn't have said it better."

"James and Sabrina, I'm jealous. Look how tanned you are already," said Davina. "Tomorrow I'm going to do some serious sun worshiping. You guys are ahead of us. We need a day to recharge. Sabrina, look at you now. You're ready for a bikini photo shoot, and I've brought all my cameras, so beware!"

"By the way, I brought all the newspapers," said Nicholas. "You two made quite a hit with the British press and in Europe also. James, you're thought of as a tycoon. I better get my skates on if I'm going to keep up with you."

"That's just to sell newspapers. Nicholas, you've done alright. If you can do this a few times a year, I'm not sorry for you," said James.

James and Sabrina sat up in bed reading all the newspapers Nicholas had brought. She couldn't believe the publicity she'd received from the wedding. "Sabrina Rossi, now Lady Sabrina Bannerman, marries one of England's fastest-growing tycoons, the tenth Earl of Penbroke." *The Express, The Sun, The Daily Telegraph, The Daily Mail,* and *The Manchester Guardian* all had their well-proclaimed thoughts. All of it was flashy and verbal as newspapers tend to be, but none of it was in poor taste.

"Now you are a real celebrity. Not that you weren't before, my Sabrina."

"It's nice and I'm happy for the compliments, but being with you is all I care about."

He grabbed her in his arms and the rest of the night was shared in blissful oneness.

The next morning Nicholas had the captain set sail for the island of Lesbos. It wasn't the largest but it had an interesting history and was set in the most northern part of the Aegean Sea. Famous for its name from the poet Sappho for his attention to women, much to the chagrin of the islanders, it has always been a curiosity point for tourists. Its climate was temperate and there were lots of exciting islands and places to visit on the way. They would then travel south to Rhodes. From there they would start their westbound return journey to the island of Patmos. Then around Santorini at the southern point of Greece, on their way back to Monaco.

Sabrina and James had never been snorkeling, and under Nicholas's wise tutelage they all got their first sight at the wonders that lay below the sea's surface. That evening they sat out on deck and were served snacks as they anchored the boat in the harbor in order to visit the isle of Lesbos.

"I'm told the girls come out at night and frolic naked in the moonlit waters. That's another reason I chose this spot!" said Nicholas with his usual mischievous grin.

"Don't believe a word he says," said a spirited Davina.

"We must all fly down to Barbados one year and rent a boat and go out and view some of those incredibly brilliant colors you saw in those tropical fish," suggested Nicholas. "It helps me forget about work and everything else."

The next day they traveled south and slight west to visit the island of Patmos. Here John supposedly wrote the book of Revelation from his cave, escaping the Roman persecution of the Christians.

They then stopped at Rhodes to hear about the tallest statue in ancient times. The Colossus was built in commemoration of the battle they won against the Cypriots. After an apparent earthquake where it broke into many pieces, the history of its whereabouts was now unknown. It was carried off by nine cargo boats and probably sold piece by piece.

The seas were a little rougher as they headed northwest toward Santorini to see the white buildings in full sunlight against the dark blue waters of the South Aegean Sea. They now started to take the northern route west round southern Italy for home and up to the port of Monaco. It would be a honeymoon they would never forget.

They had both found a new hobby in snorkeling. They realized the great chemistry they shared with Nicholas and Davina, and the generosity he'd shown. Sabrina had her charm bracelet that James had bought her in Malta. She would continue to add charms in the future to remember all the places they would visit. More importantly, James was returning home with his wife, the love of his life, to a new beginning.

CHAPTER 20

THE NEWLYWEDS AS LIFE UNFOLDS

After returning from an unforgettable honeymoon, James and Sabrina decided they would work hard to restore the main house and would not have children for a few years. James had many more plans he wanted to implement for his business and Sabrina's modeling career had become so lucrative for her that she just couldn't turn her back on such a promising future.

James went on the course Jeremy Soames had made available. Now he was ready to take that trip to Moscow then onto to Beijing to have discussions about the buying of his ships to increase the size of his container fleet. James knew that this type of leverage would get his foot in the door. Also to understand just what this Communist part of the world was all about and to have a deeper understanding of what their intentions might be for the future.

Sitting at his office in London, he decided that to build the quantity of ships he needed would take time, so he went to have his discussion with Claudia.

"James, you certainly look tanned and rested after your honeymoon."

"It was a trip to remember. I don't think I've ever been so spoiled in my entire life. Nicholas certainly does everything with style. Let's go into the conference room and bring the latest financials on Trans Global. From what I see, we cash flow around three quarters of a million on average for each ship in a year. I'm thinking of placing an order for at least a hundred ships over the next ten years. So we're looking at spending between two to three hundred million."

"Well, that's certainly ambitious. Have you spoken to John about this?" asked Claudia.

"No, I wanted to talk with you first so I could understand the numbers. From what I see when I took over five years ago, we had thirty ships and we were cash flowing around twenty million. In five years we've doubled the fleet, our fixed cost has reduced, and we're cash flowing around forty-five million now. These ships can pay for themselves in less than three years if we pay cash. Prices will continue to rise and so will the cost of making ships. By 1980 I want us to be well on our way to having two hundred ships. The downside would be if the world market takes a nosedive. Then we can always push out the orders or let someone else take up the slack. If we don't fight to stay the leader, someone else is going to take away that spotlight. The newer technology will allow us to build larger ships that go faster which means faster payback, provided the world market continues to grow at the current rate."

"I, of course, am a little more conservative by nature than you are. But if you can have a clause in your contracts to pay a minimum penalty for any delays we might give, then I suppose you have less risk."

"I don't intend to have any risk clauses. If someone's going to get this amount of business, we all take the risks. We can see well in advance if business starts to slow down, then, we just push out the orders. Anyone with this amount of business has to work with us and we all take the good with the bad. That's part of doing business."

"You have a point, as long as John knows the way to negotiate and you see the contracts before one or both of you sign. Who's going to build all these ships?"

"Now, that's the question. As we're in Hong Kong, I want to support the ship-building industry there. It's good politics but at this time they don't have the skilled work force like the Japanese do. I'll spread the work around and it'll come down to an annual analysis by John to see who can produce what at the fastest pace."

"Two hundred ships..." Claudia paused. "Do you realize that you'll be employing over ten thousand people?"

"Well, not all at once," stated James. "We've got to grow the business. Certainly by the mideighties we'll have at least that."

"That's my competitive," said Claudia, shaking her head and laughing at him as though he were a little boy.

James did indeed visit with John and he would do a complete analysis of what James had planned so that the growth rate was predictable and accurate. The availability of trained personnel to run with the intended growth was also a key factor. He also asked about Vivian, whom he knew from his schooldays. He was impressed with how she handled Stephen Jenkins on his trip to China and told him that if she was still around, she would make an excellent lead for the medical staff on board their ships.

James had been thinking for a while about buying his own jet. After the experience he had with Nicholas's helicopter and jet, he ordered the same. He could now fly from Battersea Heliport in London and be at his estate in Penbroke in half an hour. The drive could take him up to three hours by car. He still kept his little Mini at his London flat, since it was easy to maneuver around the highly populated, ever-growing city of London, but left his Aston Martin at the estate. Oftentimes he would arrive by helicopter and just take the nearest cab to his office. This allowed him to move around Europe and to his buildings at Felixstowe in the fastest way possible. Frequently, he could be at a meeting on business in Europe and back home that evening. This gave Sabrina and James the maximum time together and yet accomplish their hectic schedules with greater ease.

****

The moment had arrived and James was taking off to Russia from the new landing strip he'd built at his estate. Andrei Kostov had been promoted to head of the KGB and was anxiously awaiting James's arrival. The hope of helping their beleaguered shipping industry that had devoted a lot of its energies to building nuclear submarines was a promising prospect. James would maximize his leverage with his purchase of the ships. He knew he was visiting Moscow at the best time of year. He'd heard about their cold winters, but he was looking forward to seeing the Kremlin.

"My lord, I'm so glad to see you," said Andrei. "We've looked forward to meeting you and you'll be pleased to know our General Secretary, Leonid Brezhnev, will be having lunch with us. His English is not perfect, so I will be there to assist." Jonathan Park knew Andrei but James wasn't going to bring that up just yet.

The long walk through the palace and up to the main dining room was a treat. Stalin had replaced all the eagles of the tsars with his star, but it still remained a spectacular sight with all the armed guards and long corridors. It took a while to get to the private dining room they had prepared for his visit. As the door was opened to their meeting and luncheon room, there, walking toward him was the future premier of Russia, Leonid Brezhnev himself.

"My lord, you won't mind if I call you James, I hope," he asked presumptuously.

"Of course not, sir. A man in your position with a nation to run is more than my equal." James thought people of power love to be revered and he knew just how to do that from the excellent training of his schooldays.

They started with a traditional glass of vodka, which they quickly gulped back and then recharged their glasses. Leonid spoke in his broken English and Andrei would always be there to translate more specifically as they talked.

"James, I hear many good things about you for being such a young man of great wealth and position."

"Having a birthright such as mine places a heavy burden on my shoulders that I must live up to. The nine previous earls worked hard to bring my family to where it is today and it's my duty to leave this life having improved upon all that was handed to me."

"How refreshing to hear words like that from such a young man! You know, if the Romanovs had thought like you I wouldn't be sitting here today. So you are on a mission to buy ships? Why would you come to us when the Japanese are the biggest and the best and your own country is also capable?"

"It's simple. They can't produce the amount of ships we want quickly enough."

"How many ships are you thinking of buying?"

"Over the next ten years, more than a hundred."

"That's certainly a lot. We could not produce that many but we could contribute. We are anxious to improve on our shipbuilding industry. We have many skilled workers in Russia and they need work."

They started their meal, while the staff attended to their

every wish, bringing them a bottle of wine as was requested.

"James, what do you expect in return for giving us this work?" asked Andrei, digging deeper.

"Well, we have a bank in Hong Kong. It would be beneficial to see that some of the people in Russia like yourselves are not opposed to making some money. On behalf of your nation, a little capitalist risk would be appreciated and most welcome."

"We have a businessman! Just because we have different philosophies and ideologies it doesn't mean we're opposed to Western ways. The values that were founded under Lenin, Stalin, and writers like Karl Marx are always under constant debate in order to evolve from a society of people who were controlled by the Romanovs and were helpless, poor, and starving. We have worked to provide better education to advance our people; we work hard to establish housing and give health care. Our people have a long way to go. There are many ways to run a country. Ours is just one, and believe me, we don't have all the answers."

"You have to understand that the West has fear of what Russian intentions are toward the rest of the world. Geographically speaking, you live in a region that's shut off from the West. The landmass you control, for whatever reason, doesn't seek to define its role or purpose. If I choose wrong words, forgive me. I seek only to understand, rather than to impose that a Western way of life is more transparent in its expression. The world you have developed brings fear because no one really knows what Russia's long-term intentions are. You're next door to China and both of you have Communist governments. The fact that you helped China against the Japanese in World War II does create apprehension. I'm sure you must understand that."

"James, you must understand that it's not Russia's intention to escalate adverse feelings toward ourselves. We have one major concern, and that is the United States and its drive to what we refer to as American imperialism. We define this as a need on behalf of the United States to not only have domination in the West, but want to be in a position of world domination. Their involvement in Vietnam is, in our opinion, an example of that intent and behavior. The rate of their defense buildup, which it has against the rest of world, is alarming. We know that this capitalist freedom you embrace is very unforgiving of other cultures, who don't play by your rules. For example, our commitment to China for South Vietnam is to protect the Communist beliefs that have separated the North from the South and the other countries in that region. The French gave up what was once French Indochina. It's only right that the people there should choose what they want for their country, not a minority of people in the South."

"You have a point, but where does it stop? What next, Laos, Cambodia, Malaya, Thailand?"

"Not at all. We have no interest in extending beyond the unity of Vietnam. I can't speak for China, but militarily they are not in a position to spend that kind of money. They have to build their own economy after the war, which Chairman Mao is working hard to accomplish."

"What we object to is that the average American has no clue of who and what we are. America is a country shut off from other nations by two vast oceans. It's easy for them to become paranoid. The news is fed to their people much like us, but with all countries, there is an element of propaganda. People create fear to give themselves a purpose to arm and protect. We indeed have those same objectives, but with nuclear power it would take an extreme act of stupidity to make war. At all costs discussion will always take place, but that doesn't mean we have to agree. We too are a superpower, and we believe in our way of life as much as the Americans do theirs. If there were more substantive facts rather than fear mongering among these isolation theorists, the world would have a greater understanding of how other cultures have evolved. We're not forcing communism on anyone unless it's the desired choice of the people. It's not a question of one system of government being better than another. It's a question of letting nations take their own journey and in time the best system will naturally rise to the top. One day it could indeed be a combination of both."

James could see that Leonid's thoughts were deeply rooted in what they had worked to achieve and it would be the same for any culture. In one luncheon he certainly could not compare the two systems of government; he would only seek to understand the thinking. "Sir, I thank you for being so open to discussing your government policies. Russia has indeed lived through a lot and lost more men in the war than anyone. I am richer for this meeting, and I look forward to having my staff, work with you to understand what can be produced. Over time I hope we can build a relationship regardless of our political doctrines."

"If only the world could work on building relationships and understanding, we would move at a much faster pace toward trust. It's been a pleasure to meet you and yes, we will work with you in Hong Kong. We like to work with families such as yours that have a long history of well-founded values. Unlike Chairman Mao, who has literally obliterated the ruling class in China, we do have those that come from privileged backgrounds and their insights and education do much to advance our way of life. Do recognize that just because of the unfortunate ending we had with the Romanovs, it doesn't mean we do not value certain aspects of our society in the new Soviet Union."

The meeting with Leonid Brezhnev was very different from what James had imagined. He was far more open to discussion and reason than James had previously thought. He'd answered James's questions frankly and now it would remain to see how true to his word he would be.

On the way back to the airport Andrei Kostov brought up the matter of Jonathan Park. "James, a subject that we did not discuss during lunch was the unfortunate occurrence with Mr. Park. I knew this man as a British agent and was shocked to hear what he'd done. Under the circumstances, leaving him with his business so that his wife could run things while he's in prison is more than magnanimous. I doubt that we would have been so considerate in the same circumstances."

"We know that he'll be out of prison soon and we have kept the debt open on the books. The two million that he still owes is accruing interest so he'll have an opportunity to negotiate repayment or we'll have to invoke tougher action. We believe that allowing him some time to recuperate from his undesirable ways will hopefully make an honest man out of him. However, I have my reservations. Time will tell of course."

James was inspired by his meeting at the Kremlin and he couldn't wait to get back to talk with Jeremy Soames about the encounter. James now had one more goa: on his next trip to Hong Kong he wanted to meet with Chairman Mao. James knew Mao was also anxious to build his shipping industry with the fast growth that was taking place in the mainland. His battle, unlike with Russia, would be the amount of skilled labor that could produce the number of ships he now needed.

****

Sabrina was remodeling and James would drop in on occasion just to make sure she wasn't changing the house into some Italian villa. Her taste was excellent and she worked with the architects to make sure that nothing would be changed as to go against the original heritage of the house. Just seeing a coat of paint in the hallways was refreshing.

James was now planning his trip to China and he wanted

Sabrina to go with him. She could pop in on the store Nicholas had opened there, and it was a chance for her to see a part of the world she'd never seen. They boarded the plane at Heathrow and were ushered into the first-class cabin for the long trip. Cathay Pacific was the airline to take as he'd done in the past with Nicholas.

Harold Cummings, the new managing director of the bank, was there to meet them. It was afternoon in Hong Kong and the tired couple, after the "red-eye flight," was pleased to reach their destination. James couldn't wait to stay in his new suite at his building. Sabrina was busy looking all around as they drove to the bank.

"Well, sir, I know it's been a long flight so I'll let you both go to your quarters and get some rest, then we can go over the latest numbers when we meet tomorrow," said Harold while driving from the airport. "How's business? Still booming?"

James answered, "Roger has an instinct that's built for investment. That being said, we're doing well," said James happy to have Roger now working back in London.

Harold continued, "You will be happy to know that Gerald has up to eighty percent of the new building rented. We had a few people move over from the old building. Now that we have vacancies we decided to leave Trans Global there and let them take over our space. We were renting up the new building so fast we thought that would be a better strategy."

The hall porter took their bags. Sabrina was starstruck with the size of this new building. She became giddy upon her arrival at the penthouse suite. "James, this is like living a dream. Look at that view! We have to come here more often. Your own patio and pool. I'm definitely going to be coming with you next time. There's nothing like this in London."

James laughed, delighted at her approval. "Well, I'm going to have a drink and sit out on the patio and maybe have a swim."

"Our own private pool. Now that sounds like the place to initiate our suite, mio amore!"

James couldn't wait. They both disrobed and the two jumped into the pool together. James and Sabrina hadn't been together a great deal since their honeymoon, so now was the time to make up for it.

"I could get used to this pad!" Sabrina said, splashing him with water.

****

The next morning James went to see Harold Cummings in his new office.

"Quite a view," said James, admiring the large window. "I'm envious. Our offices in London are nothing like this."

"My wife and I love it here. Working with Roger is great. He's so modest for being such a talented young man. I'm happy to report that we haven't slipped an inch since he left to go to England. In fact, we're doing better from a lot of the investments he started."

"Well, that's good to know. I thought about your plan of leaving the Trans Global staff over at the other building. John Higgins obviously likes paying a cheaper rent. If space hadn't filled up as fast as it did here, then the move wouldn't make sense. Gerald's done a great job of marketing. We're definitely paying our way, something that bothered me greatly in the beginning. Anyway, it looks like we're setting a trend for the future."

"As great a job as Gerald's done on pricing, the building really sells itself. Who wouldn't want an all-inclusive building with a fabulous view from wherever you stand? We have the latest high-speed elevators, great restaurants, underground parking, without ever having to leave the premises."

"You sound as though you could market the building yourself."

"Put it this way. I can certainly cover for him if he needs help."

"That's the spirit," said James. "Tomorrow I'm flying up to Beijing. The governor of Hong Kong and Alan Archer have wrangled up an audience for me with Chairman Mao. I have a problem because we need to build over a hundred container ships during the next ten years if we're going to keep pace with world market demand. The more ships we have, the more competitive we can be in a sector of the market John Higgins and I believe in. So I want to hear from the horse's mouth just what he believes his ship building industry can produce. The pace that China has gone with its industrialization leads me to believe that one day they'll outstrip Japan. The mainland has paid a great price with this industrialization because the farmers that were producing the food are now working in factories so they haven't produced the necessary amount of food. Starvation has been a problem and the Hong Kong authorities have had to beef up border control."

"Interesting. I've read up on Chairman Mao and he's had a hard life to get where he is. He's radically changed China from what it was to what it is now. Nor does he share the same ideology of communism as Russia."

"Well, I'm glad to hear all is well here. When we get this place filled up plus our other building, we may have to look at building another one!"

James left to go have lunch with Sabrina. He planned to meet her on the second level at a restaurant called the Steak Bar.

"James, guess who's here! Davina! She'll be here in a moment. She's helping with the fashions at their shop."

"Is Nicholas with her?"

"No. She's happy to be here on her own. She came out with an assistant. Nicholas works her hard. She's trying to start a family. She's three months pregnant and just getting over the sick stuff. So I have someone I can be with and keep her company while you go gallivanting around."

"That's great! We'll have to go out and have dinner tonight."

"Here she comes."

"I must bow to his Lordship," said Davina, approaching. "What a place!"

"Davina, I'm so glad we could meet up. We must go out to dinner tonight."

"Absolutely! Do you mind if I bring my assistant? She's worked so hard and a night out will do her good."

"Not at all. What man wouldn't want a date with three women?"

"Behave yourself, James. I'm here to keep you in order," said Sabrina, watching Davina being a little too flirtatious with her wink.

"I've got a big day tomorrow," announced James. "I'm off to meet Chairman Mao."

"Watch out, James. That man's killed more people than Hitler and Stalin put together," warned Davina.

"He's more contained now and has a president that's over the party," said James. "He's started to back off recently. I want to know if his country has the capacity to build our ships, and it's also an opportunity to get inside his head and make my own impressions."

"He doesn't speak any language but Mandarin Chinese, I believe," said Davina.

"How do you know these things?" James asked almost sarcastically.

"I like history. People like him always fascinate me, with his drive to overcome so much opposition at such a price. To be revered *and* hated by so many. Such is the role of public office."

"James, please be careful," begged Sabrina. "I almost feel like coming with you. I know you saw Leonid Brezhnev, but this could be a different kettle of fish."

They all finished their lunch chatting and laughing and promised to meet up at James's suite for a cocktail around six o'clock.

James returned to his suite to make some calls and prepare himself for his visit to Beijing.

"Alan, I'm so grateful for all you've done to make tomorrow's meeting possible."

"No problem, old boy. He's actually excited to meet you and has asked all about you and your background. For a man who's anticapitalistic, it's quite a switch. He liked the fact that you carried on your family heritage. You are considered a person of high integrity. You have to remember that China was once a very corrupt society and he's not familiar with people who have a position like yours and yet have good character. All capitalists to him are crooks. You'll have fun. Wish I could be a fly on the wall. You will have a pretty good assessment of who he is after you leave."

"I'll tell you all about it and it's my turn to buy dinner. I also look forward to you meeting my wife, Sabrina."

"Can't wait. Thanks for calling."

James made calls all afternoon, keeping his staff on their toes.

Six o'clock arrived and all the girls met up with James.

"Lisa, what a surprise!" said James. "So you obviously enjoy working for Sir Nicholas."

She came over to give him a big hug and kiss. She then stood back and looked at him, astonished. Her look was borderline seductive. He hadn't seen her since his twenty-first birthday, when they danced together. Davina and Sabrina stood there in his apartment absolutely stunned that James knew her.

"James, look at you. You know, my mom still talks about you and that twenty-first birthday bash, and Bobby is still waiting to get back his fiver he lost to you." Lisa was also extremely impressed with the man that once worked for her mother, and was now in a place of such elevation. She had never forgotten the night when they shared such frenetic love. Could it be more than a coincidence that they had met for some reason?

"Your brother's a good bloke. I've got to go down to the Jolly Roger some night and see him and his wife."

Sabrina and Davina looked at each other, not having a clue how they knew each other. Lisa knew from the newspapers that Sabrina had married James and had congratulated her on their marriage, but never took the time to tell her how she'd met James before with her mother. She had thought that Sabrina, who was a famous model, was here to meet up with Davina and that they had somehow planned to get together. The fact that James had business here in Hong Kong and owned the building never entered her mind. Lisa just thought he was an English lord whose family owned a bank in London and didn't connect the dots. Seeing that Lisa was an extremely attractive woman, Sabrina wanted to know the whole story. Lisa delighted in telling them how James worked for her mother in accounting and never knew who he was. They all laughed as they sat out on the patio overlooking the harbor, enjoying a glass of Chardonnay.

"How's that mother of yours doing?" James asked. "She's the best boss anyone could have. I still laugh at some of her jokes I remember her telling. If she ever gets fed up working where she is, I'd hire her in a second."

"I'll let her know. She would be so flattered to think that you still care about her."

The four of them went off to a fabulous restaurant on the waterfront. Davina had to take it easy, as she was pregnant. With Davina and Lisa the conversation was never dull.

Sabrina had seen Lisa at the shop many times but never knew her well enough to chat. Lisa, whom James had met back at the pub in England with her family and introduced to Nicholas at the Fantasy bar, was the last person James thought would be Davina's assistant. Lisa, like her mother, was smart and James wasn't surprised that Nicholas had recognized that. She now had a senior job at his shop and on occasion Nicholas did use her to model.

They parted after dinner and Lisa came up to thank James for the evening and then whispered in his ear, "Your sister Flick is keeping very dangerous company these days. Call me when you get back to London. I've got a lot to tell you."

"It was wonderful to see you again, Lisa. Please send my best wishes to your mother." James couldn't help but catch a glance as Lisa looked back at him. He was now curious about Flick. And he knew Lisa longingly wished that she would be going back to his apartment with him.

"That woman knows you quite well, I do believe," noted Sabrina.

"What gives you that impression?"

"I somehow wouldn't trust you alone with her. She's definitely got some kind of thing for you. A woman like that could make a man very weak."

"My Sabrina, you certainly have an extremely sharp antenna. I'm honored to think she likes me that much. I will do everything in my power to not be trapped by her persuasive charms," James said, laughing and teasing her.

****

James landed on time in Beijing. There to meet him was a chauffeur and Chairman Mao's trusted aide, Mr. Choi. "I will be the interpreter for your meeting," he said. "Chairman Mao would like us to go to his estate where we can talk in a more relaxed way. He is not a man that likes getting dressed up."

"I've brought him a bottle of fine old malt whiskey, which I believe he likes."

"Oh yes. He'll be very happy with that."

They drove through the large wrought-iron gates to a paradise of beautiful shrubbery and flowers. The colors were so brilliant all around as they parked under the canopy of his white columned building which was of classical Chinese design. There in the entranceway, to James's surprise, was Chairman Mao. A man who came from humble origins, he had no airs or graces. He had on his traditional silk tunic and sandals as they walked their way through the large hallway onto the back veranda to sit outside. James presented him with the whiskey, which he was happy to receive. Tea was brought and the conversation started.

The interpreter listened attentively, and then began. "Why do you want to see me?"

"I have many questions to ask. My first is that over the next ten years we are buying over one hundred ships, and I'd like to know if you think your people could build those ships."

"That's a lot of ships. We'd like to help and we need the work. I'm not sure we have the skilled labor yet to make all those ships, but I think we could make four per year and maybe with time we could increase."

"I believe with all your efforts in creating industry in China, the trade you will do with the rest of the world could be enormous. We see that just in Hong Kong."

"I do too. I watch very carefully how Hong Kong has grown and I ask, 'How is it we don't do that with all the people we have in China?' As you know, I am not a great believer in capitalism. I did read Adam Smith's *The Wealth of Nations* though, and he did impress me."

"Sir, why is it that you don't adopt some capitalistic ways? Look at what's happened in Hong Kong."

"Yes, I agree, I like the idea of free trade and healthy competition. But when I was a poor farmer whose father only had a little land, all the people that made money were so corrupt and dishonorable. They would treat us with such contempt.

We could not change our way of life without a massive revolution from within. When the Japanese took nearly half our country in World War II, I realized that they had industry and we were just peasants that had nothing to fight with. It took me many years because I was considered an outlaw with my Communist views. I lived in the mountains and people would say I was a guerilla fighter. I would say that I was a mobile fighter because they could never keep up with me."

They all laughed.

He continued, "If China was ever going to stand up for itself, we must make things, build things like the Japanese have done. We were a simple and backward-thinking country ruled by corrupt emperors and overlords."

"So you're doing just what Japan has done?"

"Yes, but we pay such a big price, because after I got rid of all those corrupt people we took the farmers out of the fields and so many people starved as a result. In reflection I should have embraced the transition more slowly, but with Russia as a powerful neighbor and American imperialism, we were afraid after what the Japanese did to us. So we had to build ourselves an army, a navy, and an air force to protect us for the future."

"Can you not let the farmers earn back their land and create enterprise for them to achieve more?" asked James.

"I've thought about that, but I have one big roadblock to my way of thinking. I like enterprise and competition, but I don't trust the capitalist element to it. Greed is what we had in everyone who owned land and had power. In the past they cared nothing for the people, a little like the French Revolution, the Russians, and so on."

"It seems to work for America and so far in Hong Kong." James knew he was taking a risk with that statement.

"I'm watching that and I've always thought that greed would eventually destroy capitalism. However, I'm learning that even if someone goes down, a natural order seems to take its place. I find that fascinating. The society of America is very different even from Europe. You have a more educated electorate. Because we were held back it was almost impossible to get an education. People with power didn't want you to have an education. It is this one thing that I've worked so hard to give my people so that we could have an educated electorate. My question to you is, how does one keep people in check without some governing force?"

"That's why we have to have belief systems that teach us that being a good citizen or person in life will provide a better journey. For example, it may be Buddhist belief, Christian belief, or some other. All I know, sir, is that I didn't make this planet. With all its problems and all the suffering, it's still a very beautiful place. I know how hard it is to achieve excellence in the simplest tasks of making something. To my way of thinking, what mind could have created this earth as an accident? That is why we must do good, and respect something that is greater than us and something I believe we're part of."

Chairman Mao stopped to think about what James had just said. "When I come back again, if I ever come back, I will ask your God to make me an Englishman and learn all the beautiful things you've just said. No wonder your family has made a success of its life through all these generations. It's that teaching of values that is the very essence of a society. It is something that I've had to cut out of our corrupt country. You've just stated the finest example of a value system, whatever your persuasion, belief, or religion. Why? The reason you've just given. Look at the world; it's out of respect for it that we must have value and do good."

James enjoyed the very best in Chinese cuisine as they continued their discussion over lunch. Chairman Mao, in spite of his controversial record, struck James as a man who truly sought to do the best for his people. Understanding the pragmatic choices one had to make for a nation that had the largest population in the world. His flaw in capitalist belief was that he saw only greed. He had failed to see that it was possible to have wealth but to also have values.

Mao saw James to the limousine and promised that China would invest with Bannermans and told James how much he enjoyed his visit.

"I think you impressed our chairman," said Mr. Choi. "He's not a very trusting man, but I believe you opened his heart to see something that he'd closed. He has watched with great interest the progress in Hong Kong, and one day I'm sure China will grow more and more to the ways of the West, because history has proved even with its ups and downs, as we have, it's the better system in the end."

James had much to think about after his visit with two of the East's most prominent leaders. What a different way, but somehow he felt with time Russia and China would slowly adopt the ways of the West. Not because they necessarily believed in them, but because economics would force them in that direction.

CHAPTER 21

A LOVELY ACCIDENT

"James, I've got some news," said Sabrina. "I hope you'll not be too angry with me."

"Well, let's hear it."

"I'm pregnant. I'm going to have a baby."

"Didn't we agree that we would wait a few years?"

"I know, but I think this happened when we were in the pool in Hong Kong, when I hadn't taken my pill yet. I completely forgot in the excitement of the moment."

"Well, I'm happy. I want to have a child with you. Now is as good a time as any. With the helicopter, I can get home more easily and you can stay at home more and oversee the work here. At least you won't be doing much modeling for a while. It all works out for the best."

"I thought you might be upset. But if I'm here, maybe things will happen faster and the baby will arrive in a newly renovated home!" she said, flinging her arms around his shoulders to give him a big hug and a kiss.

"I'm actually excited. Why should we wait? We're young and now's the time to have our children. It's not like we can't afford it yet," said James, laughing.

Then a thought struck him. He could feel his guide Serena close to him whispering quietly to him, *You're going to have a son.* James knew exactly who it would be. It would be his father. His old friend that had traveled many lifetimes with him would be back again, and they could now catch up on some of the life that they had missed together. What had happened as an accident was planned by something much higher than Sabrina and James.

James had been thinking a lot about his sisters since the wedding. Becky had just finished her years at Cambridge and had earned a degree in the medical field. Her ambition was to become a doctor and have her own practice. She lived comfortably from her inheritance but was not one to sit around. Having a lot of their father's traits, she liked to help others and being a doctor would be a great place for her to apply those qualities. James wanted to ask her up to go riding and take the time to reconnect since he'd taken over the bank.

Flick was still completing a course on journalism, which suited her controversial nature. She was the perfect person to write in newspapers and dabble in the world of politics. She, unlike Becky, was a real partygoer. Her constant relationship with Gordon Petersen had concerned James. He was anxious to see Lisa and find out what his sister had been up to. He couldn't understand what his sister, who was not unattractive, could see in a person like Gordon, who was not particularly appealing to the opposite sex. Gordon had to have something that she wanted, and was using his influence to help her in order to get back at James.

"I've been thinking about my sisters lately," James said to Sabrina, "and how little I've seen of them over the last few years. I guess we all grow up eventually and then we meet our own circle of friends and if we're not careful we lose touch with one another. I've always gotten along with Becky, but Flick can be a handful, and for some unknown reason wants to get under my skin. From the vibration I get, I think she's jealous of me."

"I remember she got quite tipsy at our wedding and definitely seems to attract men like flies. Men like Gordon Petersen are hardly in a circle of people she grew up with. She has personality and looks, and that's what attracts the guys."

"That's how you pulled me in, isn't it?"

"James, what happened between us I could only wish for my children or anyone. To fall in love like we have is so special and it changes a person forever. I can honestly say that since we met, it has changed my whole meaning of love and what you did in the hospital is something I couldn't describe to anyone."

"It was a life-altering event for me, too. I can see by your aura how you feel about me. Whenever we discuss us, you glow with energy, which is white at the edges and goes toward pink, and then red from your passion."

"I must practice how to learn that. It'll help me to understand people more and what they're truly feeling," confessed Sabrina.

"Now that you're going to be spending more time here, go see Sarah. She's the best teacher anyone could have. Speaking of her, see she has the accommodation she needs; I promised her that. Then I'll either sell or lease her the property. Whatever she wants."

Over the next few months James kept a watchful eye on Sabrina. He knew what had happened to her mother and he was not going to allow anything to upset her during her pregnancy.

****

All the orders had been placed for the ships after John Higgins's long and investigating journey to ship builders across the world. They had placed up to four ships a year with the Japanese, three with China, two with the Koreans, and one with the Russians. James wanted to place work with the English, but they couldn't come close to the prices he was being quoted. He would see how they would perform, and gradually increase production with whoever produced the best and the fastest. He turned his thoughts toward his buildings and wanted to buy or construct in New York and Los Angeles. They were now shipping all over the world and so he was planning his long-awaited trip to America. He'd always heard his father talk about going there one day. James had always admired their achievements within such a short period. He loved watching all the Western movies as a kid growing up. He would see his longtime school friend Kent Harkins in Texas.

"Sabrina, I'm planning to go to America, but I'm concerned with leaving you alone while you're pregnant," said James.

"People carry on with life. Just because I'm having a baby it doesn't mean you have to change all your plans. I doubt Nicholas will stop five minutes for Davina. Anyway, she can come here, or I'll go to her. Don't worry about me. I've got Sarah who's living here now, too. I'm sure my father and your mother will come to visit when they learn the news."

"I understand all that, but the thought of you being alone in this big house bothers me."

"How long will you be gone for?"

"At least a month, maybe a little more. I have big plans for my buildings there and I want to set up an investment firm as well as construct or buy some more high-rise buildings. I know there's money to be made there and, like Hong Kong, I want to get in on the ground floor."

the whole thing through."

"Are you talking about us? You know you can have me anytime you want. I don't care that you're married. I'll be your mistress; no one makes love like you do," said Lisa, looking so sincere, yet so unbelievably flirtatious and alluring.

"Believe me, if I was a free man I would be extremely tempted, but I'm not and if I was with you, Lisa, I would be the same way," said James. It took all his strength to stay true to his Sabrina. He knew he loved her, and as alluring as Lisa was, he didn't love her like Sabrina, and it would end up hurting them both.

"Well, the offer is always there. You know that. The one night I stole from you will remain with me forever and I will always cherish it. My feelings for you are true and you can always count on my loyalty for anything you may ask."

"What about your mother? Is she still at Smith and Barlow's?"

"She is, but she would like a change. Since Mr. Barlow senior retired, it's not been the same since the sons took over."

"Tell your mother she's got a job with me and I'll pay her more than she's getting now."

"James, she adores you. She could ride with me in the mornings."

"I'll tell Claudia Ringstone, our group managing director. Here's the number. Tell her to call Claudia and I'll have her set it up right away. I'll see her when I get back as I'm soon off to America on business."

"Now that's a place you could take me. I can be your traveling mistress and your personal secretary. Everyone will know that it's all proper and correct. Why shouldn't you have a nice-looking secretary who can take care of *all* your needs?"

"Lisa!" said James, grinning.

"Kidding." Somehow James doubted it.

The couple departed after a long good-night kiss she forced

on James, and then he relented and made the best of it. She could feel his apparatus firmly standing in his pants as she held him tightly. Lisa left knowing that she turned him on, which made her extremely happy.

CHAPTER 22

AMERICA

James spoke with Claudia about hiring Sally. He felt she would be the perfect person to oversee the accounting for Trans Global and lighten Claudia's load.

"I'll get right on it. She sounds perfect," said a delighted Claudia.

"Ask her what she's making and give her ten percent over the top."

Claudia had Rose organize James's itinerary after their long discussion. He would go to New York first, then to Houston, and across to Los Angeles. He then thought of crossing the Pacific again to Hong Kong. From there he would travel back home. He would take Stephen Gates and John Higgins with him to check out the building possibilities and probably leave them behind to lock up any deals they might make.

"I hear you're going on a trip to the States," said Roger. "Mind if I tag along? I've only been once before, but there are opportunities everywhere. If you really want to grow this bank outside Hong Kong, that's where it's at."

"Tell Rose and she can get you organized. We may split up in New York, but let's see how it goes," said James.

The flight over was a day long, getting them into Kennedy Airport around 10:00 pm. They made their way to the Waldorf Astoria in Manhattan. Being jet lagged, they agreed to meet up for breakfast at 8:00 a.m. the next morning.

"Okay, now Stephen and John, you're going to meet up with the architectural guys that are connected to our London firm and tour the complete area," instructed James. "I know they're expanding down in New Jersey the number of container berths. However, being in New York may be the best option for now. Certainly, property is not going to be cheap, but I don't think it's ever going down. Keep in mind we need space for our three main businesses: banking, shipping, and property management. That means staff. If we end up building in New York, Houston, and Los Angeles, we don't need a local guy. We need someone that can run things from this side. If he's a Brit, it would be a bonus, but we're in America now and we need someone who knows the ropes over here." Stephen had his plans and meetings worked out and although he never had a lot to say, he was extremely thorough, which James liked. John would also know the best ports to be located.

"Roger, what are your plans since you sprung this on me at the last second? Is this a joyride or do you have a real plan of action? Don't get me wrong. You've done a great job already and I'd take you along just to view potential opportunities."

Stephen Gates and John Higgins excused themselves after breakfast to get on with their day and left James and Roger to discuss what Roger had in mind.

"James, I've kept this under wraps until I felt like we were on the way to building up the business in London. Now that we have those two markets growing steadily, this is the one I want to go after. Here's what I have in mind. First, our main business is commodity trading, buying futures, like grain, textiles, steel, and oil, and we conduct a very thorough research into what we invest. Second, we obviously do a great deal of international money transferring and I'm dealing with banks here all the time. Third, we do the traditional hedging and insurance for business that companies and countries require in international trade. Lastly, we look out for smaller businesses with extreme potential that have grown beyond the smaller banker and venture capitalist. We invest, finance their expansion, and take them to the next level. What I want to do is IPOs. In a sense, we will do what investment banks do. Instead of investing in the stock market like we used to do, we'll take these privately held companies public, in which we have shares and loans. That's our exit strategy for realizing our investment." Roger stopped for a moment to take a sip of his coffee, and then sprang his next idea on James.

"I've also got some great potentials in the United Kingdom and Hong Kong, and I know that it's here, all over the map. Now, the final thing that I want is to completely analyze the credit card market. With the start of Master Charge, Diners, American Express, and Lloyd's Access, there's a huge future potential. These cards charge an annual membership fee and they can charge up to twenty-five percent interest per annum. Even if we do have a few losers, the upside is too great. This is how the world is going to be in the future. All those accounts at different stores are going to disappear and the credit card is going to be king. The customer gets cash right away, which he likes, and the cardholder has to pay monthly and/or pay interest on the unpaid balance. There's more to it, but that's the general idea and we need to get in on the ground floor. I'll tell you, this could be as big as your shipping company." Roger was so excited about the whole possibility that James just looked at him. He knew that his force and drive would make it happen. Although James didn't have a taste for investing in matters he had little control over, he trusted Roger.

"Well Roger, if you're that hyped over the idea, then let's get after it. I would just like to know what your marketing strategy will be to get this credit card business off the ground."

"Got it. We hit all the smaller banks who aren't doing this, and we grow it section by section, state by state, and that's how we get known. James, one day you're going to ask, 'Why in the hell didn't we get into this before?' I'll tell you that on going back to your grandfather's time, in a different way, that's exactly what he did, and he made a fortune. As your company became cash rich, the incentive for risk became less, and that's the reason for all the unnecessary stock market investments you had in the fifties, which you agree were superfluous. Now we are truly back in the game and you can proudly say we're on our way to becoming one of the leading merchant bankers in the world."

You're already a multimillionaire, but I have a feeling you'll have a lot more at the rate you're going!" said James, always excited by Roger's ideas.

"Wouldn't you be proud to have a credit card with your name not only at the bottom, but all across it as well? I can see it now: The Banner Card, with your family crest, and a commercial that says, 'The Banner Card, fit for a lord!'"

****

James left Roger to make plans for his day. He wanted to make a few calls and arrange to meet up with his old friend, Kent Harkins.

"Where in the hell are you, James? It seems like forever since we last spoke."

"I'm in New York, but planning to head to Houston soon. Can we meet up?"

"You can come and stay at our ranch. I'll pick you up, so don't worry about a car; just give me your flight details. Fly to Dallas Love Field and I'll pick you up; then you can make your way to Houston after you've been with us for a few days."

The flight down on Braniff Airlines was quite an experience. After the very polite protocol of the stewardesses flying with British Overseas Airways, he found the Texas stewardesses attractive and very talkative.

"So you have to be a Brit to talk with an accent like that?"

"You could say that," said James.

"With an accent like that you sound like those guys in the British movies I watch...with James Bond. He's so gorgeous I could just die and go to heaven if he ever spoke to me. Just keep talking to me and tell me where you're from. I could listen to you talk all day."

"Well, I have a home in England but I work in London, so I have to spend time at my flat there, since it's close to my work."

"So Mr. Englishman, what do you do?"

"I suppose you could call me a banker, but I'm certainly no James Bond."

"Well, you missed your calling. With your looks you could be a movie star."

"Tell me, are all Texas girls as friendly as you are?" James asked.

"Why sure, a girl's got to find her man and if you handle money, that's a pretty good place to start, don't you think? I need money to buy all those pretty things a girl needs and a ring or two doesn't hurt either!"

"I'm sure a woman like you won't have any problem finding all those things."

"For saying just that, I'm going to get you another glass of wine. If you need anything honey, just ask for Charlene."

James chuckled to himself; this was a whole new experience. What man doesn't enjoy being chatted up by a pretty stewardess? His discussion with her seemed to make the trip go faster. Before he left the plane, Charlene gave him a note with her telephone number and then gave him a wink. He was a married man now, but nothing beats looking at a beautiful woman.

Arriving in Dallas, Texas, in the middle of August, James found himself taking off his tie and jacket as he made his way to the terminal. There at the gate was his old friend. They walked together to pick up his suitcase.

"This has to be the hottest damned place on the planet," James laughed, enjoying the cool air conditioning inside the building."

Kent had on his jeans, cowboy boots, checkered shirt with pearl buttons, and, of course, his Stetson hat. "Now you're in God's country. Nobody can stay long with all those Yankees up there in New York."

"I can hear the difference in accent for sure. So where to next?" James asked as he grabbed his bag.

"I want to show you a little of downtown Dallas; then we'll head out to the ranch." James was fascinated with all the high-rise buildings, especially after spending time in New York. The States were way ahead in high-rise building design. England and the European world had its own charm, but he could feel the energy and dynamism that was part of being in America. The freeways and roads were so much wider and everything was so well directed by large signs. After passing the Texas School Book Depository building where President Kennedy met his fate, they traveled west toward the Dallas/Fort Worth Turnpike. Kent lived on the other side of Fort Worth in a town called Stephenville.

"You have so much space in this country; it would seem impossible to ever fill it up."

"We're not in rush hour traffic. This place gets pretty packed around 4:00 p.m." Kent was soon past Fort Worth, and within the next hour they were entering the driveway to his family's Sunset Ranch. It was surprisingly lush and hilly as the terrain varied a lot on their drive.

His mother, father, and the whole family were there to greet him. Kent drove his Cadillac under the high canopy of his beautiful plantation home. It reminded James of the type of house featured in *Gone with the Wind*. It overlooked a lake and stood high up on his two-hundred-acre property. From the upstairs balcony that surrounded the house he could see off in the distance the oil and gas wells that had made the Harkins rich Texans.

Mrs. Harkins had prepared a large evening dinner. They were a close-knit family. Kent had three other brothers. The oldest, Randy, was at university studying to be a doctor. The other two were still in their teens in high school. Mrs. Harkins was soft spoken, but seemed to have no trouble keeping the large family in their place when she had to. Her style was very feminine, quite unlike the younger woman he'd met on the way down from New York. Mr. Harkins was shorter than his sons, who were all above six feet.

"James, what do you think of Texas so far?" asked Mr. Harkins, who had an inquisitive look to his face.

"Well, sir, it's definitely the hottest place I've been to in my life, but apart from that, I feel a sense of freedom out here. I have a feeling that this is a very prosperous part of the world. My first impressions would be if a young man wanted to make something of his life, this would be the place to come to. The future appears unlimited."

"Tomorrow Kent can show you around our oil wells. As you know, Texas is famous for its oil and gas, but we do have good beef and dairy herds in the eastern part of the state. I understand you have a farm as well in England?"

James went into his usual dissertation about his family and heritage. Mr. Harkins struck James as a man who believed in education. The aura he was receiving from him as he spoke gave the essence of a very spiritual man that believed in the teachings of Christianity, unlike Kent, who had given James the impression he had a far more libertarian viewpoint of life when they were at Sterling Heights. Kent's father had a very approachable manner and had a modest countenance about him.

The family all joined hands to say grace. Mr. Harkins thanked God for James's arrival and welcomed him into their family with warmth. He was grateful to God for what he had and felt a deep sense of commitment to others for what had been given to him in his life.

"James, why have you come to Texas? Hopefully not to just see us," said Mr. Harkins.

"Coming to Texas to see your family would certainly be worthwhile in itself. I'm headed to Houston to understand the possibilities that we might have for our shipping fleets and whether it'll be a possibility to ship our containers through this port for the future.

"So let me understand. You have a large farm, a shipping company, *and* a bank?"

"Yes, and we've also developed a company that builds and buys buildings. We put our staff in a building we like to own wherever we go in the world, and then we rent out all the other available space."

"That's quite a lot for a young man to run, eh?"

"Well, sir, I have an incredible staff. I couldn't possibly manage a business that employs thousands of people throughout the world without a good team. Obviously, as our shipping business started in 1730, we have many great grandsons that work for us. The same goes for our banking. The property business is new and something that I'm developing personally, as I believe that's the way to go in the world marketplace."

"Watch that debt. Go slowly. If we hit a world crisis like in

1929, you'll need some reserves."

"You're very right. My father, having lived through it, never allowed me to forget it."

The next morning after breakfast, Kent took James out in his Robinson helicopter to fly over the wells and view the property and the surrounding land. They also flew over dirt bike tracks and the rodeo arena to give James an idea of what kind of things Texans enjoy doing.

"Kent, if you might buy land in the future, I might be interested if we could get some mineral rights, which I'm sure will only get tougher with time. Everywhere I look there are wells, so that tells me something must be down there."

"There's gold in them there hills," Kent said jokingly.

"So what's up for you? Going to stay here with the family or do you have your own plans?"

"Tonight I want to take you down to the stock yards in Fort Worth and we can have a beer and meet up with my girlfriend, Annette."

"So you'll keep me in suspense until then?"

"I like cars and I buy and sell them to make a little extra. Dad's still in charge and likes to run things his way, naturally. I did have plans to go to university but I think I just want to go off to California and learn about life and find my way. The business will be here and dad will keep it for us boys when his day comes to retire. The younger two can have a go at it when they get out of school like I did."

"So, what's the dress code for this evening, old chap?"

"Certainly not those stuffy old Brit clothes you've got on. They've got some Western clothing shops near where we're going so we can have you properly dressed. When you ride that horse of yours on the beach, you can imagine being here in Texas."

James and Kent went out for a ride on horseback to see the surrounding property. Coming from his background, the dress code was certainly a refreshing choice.

"Riding a horse here is very different," observed James. "You ride long in the saddle and it's actually a lot more comfortable. You just sway your arms and the horse goes in the direction you need. Our style of riding is a lot more formal. I like this, but we would have to retrain our horses from the beginning when they are lunged and broken in."

Kent was large enough to play American football, which he had told about when they were at school together. A big man like Kent needed a good strong horse to carry him. James could only imagine the hard work those cattle drives had to be. He thought how those men, after living on the trail night after night, would go and get blitzed at the local saloons when they reached civilization again and got paid. This was a tough way of life and not an ideal occupation for many men.

That evening Kent took James to his favorite bar in the Fort Worth stockyard area. It was a place frequented by tourists and reflected the flavor of a true Texas town from its origins, originally, a fort out west where soldiers were posted to conquer and tame the many warring tribes, like the Comanche.

After visiting a few shops to get James some Western wear, including boots but not a hat, he quickly changed and carried his slacks and shirt in a bag.

"Now, you look like you're ready to go party," said Kent.

Kent met up with his girlfriend and the three of them entered the saloon, with its swinging doors like James remembered from the movies. They then ordered a huge ice-cold draft beer, and a barbecue sandwich. The conversation started to liven up as the band started playing some old Texas songs.

"So James, Kent tells me you're an English lord, something I've only read about and seen in the movies. Do you live on a huge English estate where hundred of servants cater to your every need?" asked Annette in her very appealing Texas accent.

"Things have changed," James answered. "You could say that we do have a large home, but certainly not hundreds of servants. For example, we have a chauffer/housekeeper, two women that clean the house, and we're looking for a secretary to manage the affairs of the household, pay bills, and take care of the place when we're not there. The house has actually been shut down for the last five years, as my mother remarried and now lives most of the time in Italy and has a home in London. Now that I just got married to Sabrina, and she is expecting in the next several months, I have reopened the house and we are presently doing some much-needed renovations."

"We must go and visit, don't you think, Kent? This is the time of year to go, when it gets so hot here."

"I'm planning on it," Kent concurred. "We have to see how an English lord lives."

"Kent, look over there," said Annette, "it's Norman and Debbie."

Kent waved to them and they both joined the small group. After all the introductions were made, Kent said, "Now, James, here's your man for real estate. He knows every inch of this town. James is putting me in charge of his real estate purchases in the States."

"Hold on a minute. We haven't really discussed the issue," said James.

"Nothing to discuss. I've made up my mind; I'm going to run things over here while you're out shooting something out of the sky on that estate of yours in England."

"Really, you think you can handle what I want? What about your dad? What's he going to think?"

"He won't mind. He's happy running our place. It's time I got off my ass. I've learned a lot about the oil and gas business. He doesn't need me now. After all, he has my two younger brothers. He'll leave the business to us kids. I want a new challenge. I've been doing all the buying of property for my dad, who has a number of shopping malls around town and Norman over here has been helping me. Between us, we can get you whatever you want."

"Alright, you're on. At least you're the devil I know. I'll talk with Stephen Gates, who's my managing director for all our properties worldwide and is in New York now. I'll fly him down here and talk with you and then we can go from there."

"James, if I work for you, I want to work *directly* for you. I don't need some Brit telling me all about the country I live in. What I do, I'll do it for you."

"Kent, you have to realize that we have properties in Hong Kong and England. In each country we have a person that reports directly to Stephen. With the massive investments, like we have, I can't deal with too many people. There's just not enough of me to go around. Look, you'll be the boss out here and like you say, he won't know half of what you know, but don't underestimate his knowledge."

"I just want to be able to talk to you directly without going through someone I don't know." Kent was a pusher and knew how to get his way, which James liked. He would think seriously about it.

"Kent, let's get the guy down here and then we can make some decisions and go from there. You may know property here locally, but this is a big country and it's going to take a number of people to run this situation if we end up buying four high-rise buildings."

"You intend on purchasing four buildings? Wow, that's quite an investment," interjected Norman.

"I don't know what the costs are here, but we ended up spending over a quarter of a million for each of the fifty floors in Hong Kong. Also, there's underground parking, not to speak of the price of land. Yes, you're right, it gets up there. Then you've got to have someone who can get out there and rent that space."

"Now, James, that's enough business talk," said Debbie. "You didn't come all this way not to have fun, so take me out on that dance floor and show me how it's done." She wasn't tall, but had long blonde hair and beautiful green eyes. He could see why Norman found her attractive and appealing. Debbie knew all the moves and enjoyed warming up this slightly stiff Brit, in a more relaxed Texas honky-tonk bar.

"Debbie, do you come here a lot?" asked James.

"We like to come over after we've been to Joe T's, which is a Mexican restaurant not far from here, and just let our hair down and have a laugh."

"Mexican food is that good?"

"It's the best. Kent is not taking proper care of you, honey. I'll come and get you, and you'll taste the best food there is." There was no mucking about with Debbie; she was all action.

"I can see you've got me all figured out."

"Just stay close, I'll get you in the loop."

"I wish I was staying longer. You Texans like to have fun, and I'm sure you keep all the right company."

"You've got that right, partner."

James took her back to the table. "That was fun. Thank you." She gave him a wink. James was already feeling that a single man in a place like this could definitely have a good time. His thoughts always returned to Sabrina, wishing she could be here with him, but there would be a next time.

The bandleader asked if there were any requests.

"How about the 'Yellow Rose of Texas' for this fine lady standing before me," said James. Cheers went up everywhere as the two danced.

"My name is Susie and I know yours is James. So, will you take me back to your big castle in England?"

"It's not a castle, but it's been in the family for over 200 years and is a good-sized home."

"Wow, that has to be every girl's dream to marry an English lord. I'm sure you're taken, but if things change, always remember, there's Susie in Texas that would stand in line to meet you again."

"So, what does Susie do?"

"Well, my daddy has a ranch, quite a large one and I barrel race horses."

"So you ride round barrels and beat the hell out of all your competitors?"

"You got it. I'm the best in these parts. How do you know about horses?"

"Because I ride myself and we do have some racehorses."

"I'm not kidding. If I come to England, will you ride with me? I want to learn that English saddle and go really fast. I'll have my daddy take me there, so if I turn up one day you won't turn me away?"

"How could I turn away a beautiful lady that can ride a horse, like you say you do?"

Her father actually owned the saloon they were in, and she introduced her father to him.

"Daddy, I've just invited myself to this gentlemen's estate. He has horses and he's offered to go riding with me."

"Well, young man, that's mighty kind of you. We'll come and visit. I've always wanted to visit England and now we have a good reason to go." They exchanged addresses and telephone numbers.

"Anything for my princess. You know she's the best barrel rider in the state?"

"She was telling me all about it."

"Well, if you want to, the next time you come to Texas you come to our ranch and she'll teach you how to barrel race."

"Deal."

Susie hugged James and pointed her finger at him. "Promise you won't forget me?"

"My father knows him well," said Kent, referring to Susie's

father. "That's old man Parker. He's also got oil and he's loaded. His daughter has the whole planet after her, but she keeps her distance. She's quite a celebrity herself with all that barrel racing she does."

"Well, Susie Parker is certainly a looker, too," said James, thinking that people in Texas were so informal you wouldn't know who was rich and who wasn't.

"The fact that she danced with you is an honor. She doesn't do that with just anyone," said Kent, giving her a second look as Annette gave him a good thump in the ribs.

The next morning in Stephenville, James called collect to his London office.

"James, you're a hard man to keep track of. Stephen and John are now in Los Angeles and Roger is in Chicago. And don't forget to call Sabrina. She wants to know you're safe," said Claudia emphatically.

James got all their coordinates and called Stephen right away. He knew they were two hours behind so he would catch him in his room.

"James, good morning, sir."

"Sorry to wake you, Stephen."

"Sir, I was already up. With all these time changes, it's hard to sleep in."

"I'd like you to fly to Dallas. I have some people here that I think will prove helpful in what you're doing. I don't think we need John, so have him fly home when he's finished."

"I'm just about finished here, so I'll let you know when I'll be arriving."

James was going to spend the night in Fort Worth, and then they could organize their meeting the next day for everyone to meet up. Kent said he would stay there too, so they could all meet for breakfast with Norman who lived near the motel.

James spent the rest of the day at Kent's ranch and learned a lot from his father about the oil and gas business. They also discussed the possibility of Kent working with Bannernman's property business. His father agreed and thought it would be a great experience for his son.

On the way to Fort Worth with Kent they discussed Stephen Gates. Kent finally understood that he would have his hands full checking out the four buildings that James wanted. James told him that it wouldn't change a thing in their relationship. He could always call him and tell him his thoughts and Stephen wouldn't mind that they were old school buddies.

"Learn the way we do business, Kent, and if you want to move up, the opportunity will be there. If we're successful here, we'll buy more buildings and eventually it'll have a mind of its own. In all reality you have to see whether this is your cup of tea, too. You're like me. We're still young, and although I'm the boss, I listen to my staff. I'm the youngest member on my team. Nothing beats experience and we must respect that."

James and Kent went out to Joe T's that evening and, of course, whom should they see but Norman and Debbie.

"After two margaritas you can get really hammered. Those top shelf drinks are fantastic and never had one of those before." James was laughing as Debbie chose from the menu what he might like.

"Now, James, can you see yourself ever living here?" asked Debbie.

"Maybe in time. It's certainly the friendliest place I've ever been to. You feel so welcome here. My wife comes from Italy so we are able to get away from the rainy English weather. Your summers would take some getting used to. I will definitely bring my Sabrina over, because she likes the outdoors and I think she would love the people."

"So what does she do?"

"At the moment she's having our baby, so she's had to slow down. She's a model."

"What name does she go by?"

James told her.

"I know who she is. I've seen her in Fashion World. She's *beautiful*. But she doesn't look Italian."

"Coming from you, she would be happy to hear that. Her mother was Scandinavian, so that's where she gets her fair looks and she was a beauty, too. She died when Sabrina was born, and ironically, her father is married to my mother. So you could say we keep it in the family."

"So that's how you met."

"We met before my mother married Antonio, someone she knew when she was much younger. I met Sabrina when I was eighteen and had just finished school. The first time I laid eyes on her, she took my breath away. We just knew one day we'd get married and so seven years later, here we are."

"How very romantic. So now she's a countess? Lady Sabrina Bannerman."

"Yes, but after the baby she will continue her modeling career as Sabrina Rossi."

"She's known all over the world. She'd be an absolute hit here. I can't wait to meet her. Norman, did you know that James is married to Sabrina Rossi?"

"Who's that?" asked Norman, approaching the two with Kent by his side.

"When I show you a picture of her, you'll know exactly who she is.

"Sabrina Rossi is a model. My mother loves her and the clothes she wears. Even I know that," said Kent emphatically.

James then pulled out his wallet to show them her photograph. Norman and Kent said, "Holy cow! Susie Parker is hot, but that girl there would be a tough act to follow."

"Men," scoffed Debbie, shaking her head.

"You devil, James. You should've told my mother; she would have wanted to know all about her."

"Look guys, go easy. I'll be back, or you can come and visit me with Susie and y'all can meet everyone."

"That's a deal." Norman ordered drinks all around, on that fine decision.

James looked at his watch as since it was getting late and wondered if Stephen had made it to the motel.

The group split up and the men agreed to meet at the motel in the morning around 9:00 a.m. in view of the amount of alcohol that had been consumed.

****

At breakfast the next morning all parties were present; Stephen Gates had made the journey and had arrived before Kent and James got back from the restaurant. Norman had driven over from his house, which was near the motel.

"Stephen, this is your show," said James, "so first meet Norman Grindly, who is well known in the local real estate business in Texas, and Kent Harkins who works with Norman to buy real estate for his father. Kent and I went to the same school, so he can't be all that bad. He's had time to understand us Brits and our eccentricities. If you're short on a good laugh, he's your guy to go to. Stephen has a degree from Southampton University and is well experienced in building construction, rental, and estate management. So Stephen, take it from here and tell them what it is that we do."

"Very pleased to meet you all. It's always helpful when people have known each other before as in the case of Kent and James, and you, Kent, at least know something about our homeland even though we fortunately do speak the same language. At present, Bannermans Properties, of whom I am the managing director, has its head office in London where I work. It's the oldest building we have and it dates back to 1838 when James's family started in the merchant banking business. Stephen elaborated on the existing properties now held and then proceeded to discuss the plans for the United States. We want to build, or buy, or both, four buildings in the United States, all of which will be nearest to your country's largest container ports, namely, New York, Los Angeles, and Chicago. We may do some shipping through the Great Lakes, but primarily to be close to the commodities exchange for our bank. We could be interested in Houston as we are interested in shipping oil and manufactured products to and from that port. So all our properties have strategic reasons for their location. If we find the markets are good here, we'll invest further in other major towns. James may have told you all this."

"No. Please continue. Nobody here knows about your business," said Norman.

"The last thing is our managing director of our bank, Roger Bell, is extremely interested in looking at the credit card market. It's obvious this is the way things will go in the future, and the old way of having an account somewhere will slowly die out. This is, of course, an enormously exciting prospect. If this goes in the direction he feels it will, then we will be buying more buildings and be creating many more jobs." Stephen sat back in his chair, ready to listen.

"Wow, that's quite an undertaking you all are making. You're talking about enormous investments here. I like your way of thinking and if you have the liquidity to build up a credit card of your own, the sky could be the limit," remarked Norman, who had not expected such ambitious growth plans.

"Norman, you're a Texan," said James. "It's, y'all! We used to tease Kent when he was at school with us about that. We had to get back at him occasionally, because he certainly gave us a hard time and being as tall as he is, no one was going to take him on." This broke up the presentation and got everyone laughing, which is what James wanted the meeting to be.

Over the next two weeks the four traveled across the country to the various locations and made contacts there. James wanted to act fast as he had the liquidity from his trust fund in Switzerland. The bank with Roger Bell and John Higgins were making more than enough cash flow to kick off the credit card plan and pay for his ships. It was ambitious but achievable and James had calculated it all before making his trip to America. He had one ace up his sleeve and that was if the liquidity did become tight he would go as far as he could, then take Trans Global Shipping public with an IPO on the New York Stock Exchange. As he grew the company, he knew his cash flow would increase and his goal was to get into the 1980s. He would have close to two hundred ships and have at least the biggest percentage of the world container trade. Then, and only then, did he feel his shares would really take off in value.

CHAPTER 23

THE TEMPTATION FOR GREED

James was now on the final leg of his trip. He would check in on Hong Kong before returning to England. He needed the time alone. The long hours and the amount of new business he was taking on were starting to take its toll. James had met so many different people in the past few months since his marriage to Sabrina that something inside him was telling him to slow down.

He arrived in Hong Kong late at night from Los Angeles and couldn't wait to get to his suite and just sleep. The taxicab he took was quick and convenient. He didn't want to meet up with Harold Cummings until he'd had plenty of rest. He hadn't been specific about his arrival time and date and this he'd done purposefully. After paying the cab driver, he made his way to his suite. He would call Sabrina and let her know that all was well and he would be home in a few days. He had just put the key in the door to his room; the door slightly opened, when suddenly there came a pounding blow to his head as he collapsed onto the floor outside in the hallway. It wasn't until many hours later that he found himself lying on a cold concrete floor; his hands and feet were tied with a blindfold on his head and a gag over his mouth. The very thing he wanted to avoid by coming unannounced had happened.

He started to mumble and the would-be assailant, recognizing that he was starting to come around, said, "So now you know what it feels like when someone takes all your power and freedom away." James could tell that it was none other than Jonathan Park. James had calculated that Jonathan's insiders had mentioned that James was coming to Hong Kong and Jonathan had the airport carefully staked out for all arrivals from the States. Who the rat was that tipped him off would not be known at this particular moment. All James knew is that Jonathan Park could have him thrown into Victoria Harbor and nobody would ever know.

"Take off his gag and put him in that chair; I want him to speak his last words before we get rid of him."

"Now you're in the driver's seat, Mr. Park. Something I'm sure you've planned for quite some time," stated James, keeping his complete composure even though he had a splitting headache.

"James, I admire you. You've got guts. With the possibility of facing your death you manage to have some calm reserve. I've been in the Secret Service a long time and usually when a man is about to die he does at least wish to negotiate."

"What could I give you outside not foreclosing on your business and allowing your wife to make a living while you were in prison?"

"That was quite decent of you under the circumstances. However, I'm not as considerate and fair as you are. When you go missing I won't have to pay you back a penny. I will have an agreement to expunge the debt in return for me behaving as an honorable citizen in the future. Anyway, I'm sure the Secret Service has more than respected my debt. I've paid my price. Now you must pay yours. I've had the papers drawn up that completely release me, my wife, and my business from any obligations, back interest, and the entire debt of my business to Bannermans Bank Hong Kong and its worldwide subsidiaries. All you have to do is to sign. You will be a free man and so will I."

"Well, good luck with that, because I can assure you that one way or another, once I go missing your ass will be grass. This time they'll throw away the keys and don't be too sure of your own safety. The intelligence service has its own way of eliminating guys like you. Don't think they don't know you're out and about and let me tell you you're being watched as we speak. Your best option is to accept the offer; then we can both live in peace. You have a debt to pay. For all the trouble you've caused me and my staff, and the blatant way you have taken advantage of my father, the very least you could do is to pay back the principal on the loan if I forgive you the interest."

"Sorry, no deal. Total forgiveness of the debt or your days are over," said Park firmly. He thought James would crack and he'd get what he wanted. He thought with all the success he'd had, why would he risk his life for two million? "And the Secret Service would have to find you and prove that I was responsible."

"That doesn't bother me in the least. That entire building has surveillance cameras and they'll track you down." Not every building had cameras, so James was taking a big risk. Although he had cameras, it would be possible to evade them, as they were not everywhere, and James wasn't sure whether that particular corridor was visible or not. He just had to assume that it was.

"Take him away and carry out what was discussed. I've got

to give it to you, James. You would have made a damn good agent."

They approached the door to carry James off to his demise. Jonathan then told them to stop and leave him there for the night. He knew James couldn't be that confident if he was bluffing. He hadn't flinched an inch and for a man going to his death, Jonathan knew he had to be really sure before he executed his plan. A few hours wouldn't make a difference. He thought he'd make some calls and see if there was any validity to James having surveillance cameras in his new building. What Park also didn't know was that James had installed an alarm system to his penthouse, and as he had turned the key just enough to open the door a silent alarm notification would go off at the security room in the basement of the building. Without James entering his security code to turn the alarm off, this alone would be enough to alert the security staff.

Park also wouldn't have what he really wanted and that was James's signature. He knew forensics would be far too smart to not recognize a forged signature. James had outclassed him. He'd underestimated his resilience and thought he would cave in and write off the debt, as it wouldn't be worth the effort.

The moment they left, James went into deep meditation, and sure enough the kind of powers he'd been able to help others with now came through for him. He knew help was on the way. The security staff at the bank had noticed the abduction on the surveillance cameras and had called the police. The police had tracked down the thugs that carried James off and then they knew that probably Jonathan Park had to be behind this.

Detective Williams now knew that Park had been released and after the chief of police contacted him it didn't take long to organize an attack squad. They had been watching him since he left prison and his first guess was that he'd taken him to his textile factory where he knew there was a basement. He immediately organized an attack squad to enter from the top of the building by helicopter and another fully armed attack squad through the front entrance. If there was nothing there, he'd have to track down Park and haul him in for questioning. It was a risk and he knew he couldn't hold Park indefinitely. However, the other two assailants were well known to the police and they could be held and thoroughly cross-examined. Either way, the chances of finding a resolution seemed high.

"I bet he's at his business right now and they won't know we're coming," said the detective. "We must act quickly if we're going to catch him.

"We will, but I trust your judgment, Detective Williams. I'll get the attack squads on it immediately," said the chief of police.

They surrounded the entire building and its inhabitants. Park was caught red-handed and there, open on his desk, was James's brief case. Thanks to James's abilities in being able to see what his guides were doing for him, he was freed before the twilight hours of dawn. He had artfully outfoxed Park with the surveillance cameras and Park could kick himself for not having had the men kidnap him in some alleyway or street. Now it was all too late and this time James and the British government would show no mercy. James had given him a chance but it was now too late. The real suffering in all of this would come from Park's own family. After Park had been admitted James would go to see Park's wife and see if there could be any possibility of working with her for the future of her family's livelihood. For Jonathan Park, it was the end of the road.

James, after talking with Detective Williams, was rushed to the hospital. He'd received a severe blow to the head and needed immediate examination. He was cared for instantly and received stitches for the open area at the back of his head. The doctors X-rayed his head and thought they should hold him overnight because a concussion was possible after such a heavy blow.

News traveled fast of James's kidnapping and the next day he had to busily explain himself to Harold Cummings, who visited him at the hospital.

"That took a lot of nerve, James. Your life wasn't worth risking. We were in a position to write off the loan."

"That's not the point. A man like that will be back for something else. Once you give in to blackmail it's a matter of time before it rears its ugly head again. Anyway, I knew he wouldn't risk it. He'd have to forge my signature. It would all catch up to him, even if I was at the bottom of the harbor."

"You've got more nerve than me."

"I have a reputation to preserve and we're not giving in to people like him. I do feel sorry for his family and I will meet with them later in order to try and help them."

James's phone rang in his hospital room. It was Sabrina. "James, I heard from Harold about your abduction. Thank God you're alright. I'm coming out on the next plane."

"Is that wise with the baby?" asked James, though it would be nice to see her.

"Look, with a head injury like that you will probably suffer a concussion and if I'm there to help you recover, I think it would be wise. We can go to your apartment at the bank and I can at least see you have all the medical attention you need."

James slowly recovered. Sabrina felt she was there in return for the time he took to be with her when she had her accident. He had to stay in the hospital for almost a week before the doctor released him. He was now ready to go back to work and deal with the final saga of the Park family and their business.

****

"Mrs. Park, a pleasure to meet you and your daughter," said

James. His wife was half Asian and some other European mixture; the daughter looked similar to her mother, but was a little taller and looked sad.

"My lord, I can only give you my humblest apologies for what Jonathan has done. My name is Josephine and my daughter's name is Jasmine."

"Josephine and Jasmine, my name is James. I'm pleased to meet you. If I understand correctly, you run the textile business?"

"Yes I do, and since Jonathan has been in prison, he has transferred all the shares to me and my children. My oldest, Michael, is at school in England."

"Look, I seek no revenge. I understand what took place and it was extremely unfortunate. I offered your husband a deal where the principal could be paid back in order to help him with his future. That was not acceptable to him. So where do I stand with you?"

"That's more than generous considering the time that's been allowed on the outstanding loan already. You could have easily foreclosed on our business and why Jonathan has not respected makes me extremely angry. I, of course, could not pay the full amount right away. Would you accept giving us a five-year loan?"

"You must understand that the bank has not had a penny from you for this loan over the last several years since your husband last went to prison. I allowed this to happen so that your business could get on its feet and enable you to build a future.

"In order for me to see our risk level in affording you this privilege, as you can't pay the full amount now, we would have to see whether your company is capable of paying us back. There would be interest on the unpaid balance of the loan, so whatever amount you can pay now would save you interest in the future. After not paying this loan for this amount of time, you must have some reserves that you could pay now, right?"

"Sir, I'm not saying I'm the best businesswoman, but the costs of building the business and raising the family as a single parent has not let us build up much in the way of reserves," Josephine said, knowing that the family had extremely expensive habits, be it at the expense of Bannermans. James decided that he would have his auditors go through their company books and then devise a plan.

"Josephine, I don't wish in any way to impair your way of life. After what I've been through with your husband and, in essence, the free money you've been allowed all these years is beyond any normal situation of business. Let's look at the situation with regard to the company and then you and I can make a plan from there." James didn't like what he was hearing. If she was irresponsible with the money, he would have to act differently.

"Thank you, sir. I believe that would be the best course of action."

"We'll have someone over first thing tomorrow at your business; then we'll make a plan."

It took his two auditors from the bank a full day to get back to Harold Cummings with their findings. He then went over to James's office to discuss the preliminary findings.

"James, it appears the company is cash flowing to the tune of about one million per annum. Over the years they've been siphoning off money to a Swiss bank account, probably under the instruction of Jonathan Park. Over the seven years they must have at least four million tucked away. The mother only drops in two to three times a week. The daughter works at the business full time and is a fairly competent bookkeeper. Their expenses are through the roof because they have such a high standard of living. They write off every expense they can and pay themselves exorbitant salaries. The bottom line is the company is in need of investment in order to update their equipment. They have been living in fear of foreclosure as Park doesn't trust our bank, and they thought it would be just a matter of time before we foreclosed on them. Therefore, it appears they've tried to get as much money out of the business while they could for their own well-being. They knew the good times of not paying down on the loan and having no interest to pay wouldn't last indefinitely. They should have had a full and binding agreement with the bank which Park could have arranged when he was in charge. That would have at least protected them. They could have legally paid down on a term loan and still maintained ownership of the business. In the absence of an agreement they've just taken everything out of the business they could get their hands on."

"So you think it cash flows around one million a year?"

"Yes, sir."

"So the business is worth a maximum of six to seven million, less the two million they owe us and any other debts. If they've managed to squirrel away four million, in addition to all the other money he's got from his other dealings, I say we offer them three million for the business or we foreclose on them. We can't trust them with a loan. They'll spend all the money and we'd just be delaying the inevitable. The business needs to be run with tighter fiscal controls and the equipment needs upgrading to turn it into a more profitable enterprise. That way we're out of anything to do with the Park family, and they should have enough money, if they're wise, to do whatever they want. Maybe some good can come out of this testing situation after all. Have Mrs. Park come over here tomorrow morning and let's put this whole affair to bed."

James and Harold went out to dinner that evening and discussed Mrs. Park's situation in depth as well as other matters concerning the bank's present business.

"James, you'll be pleased to know since the placement of orders for ships with Russia, we've received an investment of near fifty million in Hong Kong dollars and over one hundred million from China. Your visits there were of great importance and they have shown great generosity. They believe in us, and in particular, you. This goes a long way toward bridging relations with two Communist countries."

"Excellent. We must show them a good return. No doubt Roger will put his mind to work and make sure we both make good from their investments. It's a start and I can see they appreciate our good faith in placing business with them. Once we get that building filled up, let's look around for another piece of property.

"James, I believe we're offering too much for the Park's business. Look what they've done to you and put you through. It's a wonder you want anything to do with these people."

"Yes, but knowing Park, his wife didn't have much choice. She was probably just as afraid as Ling Tak. When a person gets into a relationship like that, they make the best of it. We may have done her a favor for all we know."

"True, but you have the power to foreclose on the business right now through default. You have every right to take that business as it stands without giving them a penny. She has money tucked away in Switzerland. The fact that they have made a success has afforded them all they have now. Enough is enough."

James sighed. "You're right. The good part is we're taking over a business that has a good profit potential. The Parks have been lucky to save the money they've taken from the business. I'll give them a choice: one year's severance pay for Josephine and her daughter in return for the shares or we foreclose."

"That's the way, my lord."

The next morning a worried Josephine Park was shown into James's office. Her husband's behavior must have taken a toll on her and the stress of not knowing her future had to be quite emotional. She had a good standard of living and at one time had been very respected in the community.

"Josephine, thank you for coming to see me so quickly," said James as an assistant served her a tea.

"I know this situation has dragged on for both of us much too long and a conclusion is necessary."

"I thank you for your daughter's cooperation in making this as easy as possible for our two auditors. So in view of the generous loan that you've had over the years with absolutely no interest, and the money you've been able to save in Switzerland, we are prepared to offer the following: one year's severance pay to you and your daughter in exchange for the shares of the company."

"I know I'm not in a very strong position to negotiate, but I had thought of being paid more than that, based on what I know others out there would buy the business for."

"I understand, but the equipment you have is getting old and needs replacement. Since Mr. Park has been in prison, nothing has been put back into the business. I can understand why. Someone may offer more money but the company is in serious default with Bannermans Bank. After doing the calculations for the recapitalization of the business, you'll find my offer is more than fair, in view of all that's happened. I know in a sense you are victims of circumstance. I also know your husband to be a very strong-willed person, so I'm sure he's the one that has directed your financial activities from prison. Had the business, in honest terms, been kept up to date and profits reinvested, I would be prepared to consider an alternative, but that's not the case."

She was silent for a moment with her head bowed and then she looked up. "I accept. Thank you for being so considerate after all my husband has put you through."

James felt sorry for her, but business was business and the last thing she wanted was a foreclosure on the business. She had been advised by her lawyers and knew that not agreeing with the bank would put the business through foreclosure and into the bank's hands right away for the already outstanding default on the loan. The bank could then sell off the business to recover its loan and she would be lucky to get anything back over and above the outstanding debt. The business would go for bargain basement prices to the highest bidder. What James had offered was more than fair and the cheapest way without huge legal fees. She left sad but with dignity, realizing that matters could have been a lot worse if James had a mind to seek a very justifiable revenge for Jonathan Park's actions against him.

James sat and thought about the whole matter. He then decided to take a trip over to the textile factory and weigh up the situation for himself as to what he would do with a business he knew nothing about. He was, after all, now the owner of a textile factory and maybe after this dark episode there could be light, an opportunity that could be turned into a profitable enterprise.

"Come on, Harold. Let's go take a look at this business. Bring one of your auditors, and let's see what plans we need to make," said James. The auditor drove James and Harold to the factory. The mother and daughter were quietly clearing away their personal effects from their offices. James had ordered two security guards to be there to audit what they were removing and to see that Park hadn't organized any thugs to be around to take items that were no longer their property.

James wanted to know from Mrs. Park who ran the operations of the company. She politely took him to Charles Kin's office, while Harold and Robert checked out the operation.

"Sir, it's indeed a pleasure to meet you. I'm sorry for all you've suffered. My name is Charles Kin and I ran this company before Mr. Park and his family bought the business in 1957. I have been here for twenty years and would very much like to keep my job, if it is at all possible." James looked at him hard and wondered how much he knew about the finances of the company and the lifestyle the Park family led.

"I would like to consider your proposal and frankly it would be a lot easier for me if you did stay on, but how much do you know about the dealings of Mr. Park?"

"Over the last several years I've had no dealings with him at all. I've always respected Mrs. Park. Her daughter Jasmine has been a hard worker and very helpful in the administration of the business. In the years before I saw very little of Mr. Park, because he dealt all his business affairs through his wife. He's never been active in the day-to-day operations here, and never struck me as a man who was even interested. As can be seen by the old equipment and poor working conditions we have, I understood from Mrs. Park that we were only marginally profitable. I was actually at the point of resigning to go to another factory that makes T-shirts. Now I see you as an owner that gives me confidence. If you decide to keep me, I would like to know what your intention is."

"Well, Charles, if you can make a go of this place, I'd like to keep you and make those T-shirts here. I think there's a huge potential for that market now. I do, however, want to trust you; I'm sure you are aware of Mr. Park's activities. In my position I would be highly suspicious of anyone who was associated with his dealings."

"Yes, sir. I completely understand. You are in a position to take this business where it should have gone many years before now, and that is why I have offered to stay."

"If you can show me that you can make things happen in the next six months, I will keep you, but my fear is that people may have become a little slack without any serious leadership within the company."

"I have always enjoyed working with Jasmine, as she is a hard worker and always stayed late to help and listen to our problems. I can also say that there are no lazy employees here.

Under my direction they would be gone. You have good experienced people and with a little help we can make things happen and produce what we should, if we have the help we need for the machinery. We have around fifty employees, but we could double that amount if we had the machinery. The factory is in a poor state, as you can see. I have enjoyed a certain autonomy and that's the only reason I've stayed here so long. After twenty years, I know most of the employees very well and all of them are good hardworking people. I've been afraid that with new employment, I wouldn't have the status that I have worked so hard to have here."

At that moment Harold popped his head into Charles's office. "Can I come in, sir?"

"Absolutely," said James. "I've just extended Charles's job for the next six months, so we can get to know him better. Now Charles, prepare a wish list of what you need to grow this business. Tell us what types of products you're producing now, and let's get into this T-shirt business. I like the sound of that. When you've completed your report, hand it over to Harold and we'll go to work on making this place alive again!"

"Music to my ears, boss, music to my ears!"

"Know that I'll be hiring a general manager and probably a marketing man. If you do your job well, I will guarantee you that you'll have no interference, that is, if you do all that you say you can do."

"I would welcome the support, sir," said a grateful Charles Kin.

"For now you're the boss here. We have to put senior management in place so that we can take the company forward. Harold will have an accountant over here to take over the bookkeeping from Jasmine...until we can make long-term plans, okay?"

"Completely understand. So I will call Mr. Cummings if I need his support?"

"Precisely, and he will be here to check up on you from time to time until we get all the right people in place." With that, they all shook hands. James was going to take a shot at this textile business and loved the thought of being in the world of manufacturing.

"Harold, I really see a future in this business. Keep an eye on him. Any association with the Park family will be taken as an act of defiance outside seeing that they have all their belongings. Let him give us his report on what improvements need to be made and in the meantime find a good GM on this island that can run this business. When you have a group to interview, I'll be back to finalize the decision. We need a good bookkeeper for now and backup from our audit team. We also need to look into finding a good marketing man. It may well be that the GM can wear both hats for now. I'll leave that to your discretion."

"I'll get things rolling and contact you back in London and I'll fill Roger in on your plans."

"On another matter, fire Ling Tak. He had to be the person that leaked my coming to Hong Kong. I know he probably didn't have a choice, but it's time to move on and I want there to be an end to this whole Park affair. Treat him fairly, and let's move on."

That evening James and Sabrina went down to the Steak Bar.

"To come all this way pregnant couldn't have been easy."

"James, I would go to the ends of the earth to be by your side. I know you've got business to do. I've frankly enjoyed the past few days relaxing on the patio and reading my books. I've been thinking, it's good to have our baby experience the feelings we have had with our guides and what you've just been through. That soul I'm carrying will feel those metaphysical connections much more easily than us. They say young children can see things that we can't see. When they get older they may have nightmares, dreams, and imagine things we can't see, or simply discard as daydreams. We must always encourage our children to see and keep an open mind. We must not discourage them from expressing what they feel is real to them. Maybe it's like having an extra intuition that we lose as we become older? I don't know, but I want us to give this baby all the understanding we can give."

"Well, we have a whole throne room plus Sarah. You couldn't have a better start to the realm of the metaphysical than that!" James laughed.

"That's true. When you were away, I went to the Throne and had long conversations with my mother. We're going to have a son, you know."

"I know, and I know he's going to be the reincarnation of my father."

"James, you're always ahead of me. This week has ended well. To see you back on your feet is so rewarding. We have so much to look forward to and I can't wait to have this baby and get back to being more mobile."

"Sabrina, you actually look quite beautiful this evening. There's a glow that a woman has when she's with child. I can see your beautiful aura and I can also see the aura of the baby. He's very happy right now. He knows when we are together and he likes that."

"I know what you're thinking and we will. So let's pay the bill and snuggle up together and do what I've wanted to do for weeks; I know what you like, and I'll be that sexy woman you want again before you know it."

"Right now you look sexy enough for me."

The couple walked up to their suite arm in arm, feeling the warmth of their love at reconnection again.

****

After an exhausting few days, James and Sabrina were happy to board the plane back home. As challenging as the situation had been, he felt good about what he had accomplished. James knew he could ship products to the rest of the world with the new shipping fleet. He could start to strategically build warehouses in different countries in order to distribute his products at a price the competitors couldn't match. James sat back drinking a large scotch and soda, dreaming about his next new arm to the other businesses he had. The final general manager of the textile business would report to him directly. James thought he had a tiger by the tail and this more than excited him.

James and Sabrina parted after she stayed the night in London to get over the jet lag. The next morning he had her take a taxi to Battersea Heliport. The helicopter would be there to transport her back to Penbroke. She was anxious to see how the renovations were coming. James didn't plan to stay long but he wanted to take time at the office to catch up on matters since being away. Tired after all he'd been through, he was anxious to spend some time alone with Sabrina at the estate.

CHAPTER 24

THE SISTERS

James arrived at the bank to an excited Claudia who was anxious to bring him up to date on all that was going on. She was insistent that he call his sisters first, as they had requested to meet with him as soon as he was back.

"Becky, how are you? Claudia said you needed to see me."

"James, Flick and I would like to go out some evening with you. We have some matters we think should be discussed as a family. It's been a while and we need to totally understand our position with regard to the estate and the will. We want to move on with our lives and get back to being a family again," she said, as though she had some startling revelation about the will she'd just discovered.

"Okay, I'm in London for a few days before going back to Penbroke; why don't we all meet up at my flat and I'll take you both to the Brass Bell for a bite?" suggested James, anxious to know what was up.

"Wonderful. I'll tell Flick and we'll see you at your place at six o'clock tomorrow evening."

"Look forward to seeing you both." Had they just woken up to the reality of their inheritance? The girls had received the money from their father's will and been paid for the land that was deeded to them. Although not super rich, they were far from poor. They could live off their inheritance for the rest of their lives if they were wise. Having a good job wouldn't hurt either of them and, who knows, they were both attractive girls, and knew all the right people in order to marry well and enjoy a good standard of living.

"How's my little friend doing inside my beautiful wife?" James asked, on the phone.

"Oh James, I can't wait to see you! I have so much to discuss with you. The baby's doing fine. I haven't told you yet, I have a wonderful new woman to help run the house and take care of the administrative work. She's also helping me with the renovations. Also I'm not lonely. You were right; this place is large and lonely without anyone being here."

"I'll be there before you know it, Sabrina amore."

James got up from his office and walked over to Claudia's office to get an idea about what the girls might be up to.

"Claudia, you know everything. What have my sisters got up their sleeves?"

All I know is they've hired their own solicitor and he's contacted Sir Thomas over the will and asked for a copy. I think they're waking up to the fact that you're becoming very successful and somehow they might have missed out on something. God only knows they inherited what most people could only dream of."

"I know, but I would always be there for them in an emergency. That's what the family trust in Switzerland is all about. Our forefathers had carefully saved an appropriated amount of funds over the years, in order to have a support system in the event of some unforeseen catastraphe. This is an account to protect the business first, then the immediate family. Surely they must know that."

"James, when there's money out there everyone wants a slice of the pie. That's life and if you don't ask, you don't get, right?"

It was an intense day with Claudia going over Roger's visit to the States and Stephen's request that they leave the building unoccupied for renovations.

"James, it's Stephen and Roger's opinion that we need to renovate this building, and I agree with them. Roger's bank business is growing so fast that he's already taken another floor and it looks like that won't be the end of it. It's his belief that we keep the top two floors for corporate offices with a staircase between the two. We leave the rest for banking and the property business that's also starting to grow."

"We've concentrated so much on everywhere else it's about time we cleaned up this place. If they're not too busy have them come now, and let's get this ball rolling."

They all went to the conference room to have a discussion. After James's long absence he could see there were matters he must attend to.

"James, we all feel that this place needs a makeover," said Roger. "The lobby is passable but we are working back in the fifties. This place sits on one of the most valuable sites in the city. It's time we upgraded. We need to give our clients an image that's worthy of our progress."

"Flying all over the world is giving you all these fancy ideas," said James with a big grin.

"Is it essential? No, but the extra space is. I'm concerned with renting out space when our property business is growing, the bank is growing, and you'll be out of space on the top floor. Doing renovations won't be fun and we will all be playing musical chairs for a while, but I believe we are the starship and center of our business dealings, so to speak, and we should reflect that image," said Stephen, who made a valuable point about the need for more space.

"I agree. Stephen, get the architects in so we can do this renovation in a tasteful and well-organized manner," said James, convinced. If they were going to have to go to all that trouble, at least make the place look like the financial center it is.

"We really need a plan. Stephen, Roger, and Claudia, discuss what you believe you need among yourselves. At least see we have more toilets if we're going to be employing all these new people." The meeting broke up and a lot of happy faces left the room.

****

James had opened a bottle of wine and anxiously awaited the arrival of his sisters. He knew what they liked and had set out some cheese and biscuits for all of them to have a little chat, before going to the restaurant. What his sisters didn't know was that he'd not long returned from a very challenging trip to Hong Kong, and apart from having the occasional headache, he was lucky to be alive! He wasn't a complainer, so as always he wanted to accommodate family. It had been some time since they had got together, and this seemed like the appropriate moment.

The front door rang and James opened the door to his two sisters, who seemed happy to see him again.

After taking their coats and their being seated in the living room, James started in. "So Flick, I've seen so little of you over these past few years that it's like looking at another woman. You look incredible."

"Thank you. You used to tease me so much growing up that I had to get even with you."

"You were pretty good at the trade yourself, if I remember correctly, and definitely had a one-uppance on me in that department. Becky, you too. Look at you, my sisters are now ladies." Becky had no need to impress anyone; she was secure within herself. She was a saver and there was nothing flamboyant about her. Becky was nuts and bolts like their father, and a good, compassionate listener.

They discussed the lighthearted things of their youth and for the first time in a long while, started to reconnect. All felt how much they had really missed each other.

Later they arrived at James's favorite restaurant, which was within walking distance from his quarters.

"James, how is it you are always bringing such pretty women to my restaurant?" asked the proprieter, Livio Angeli, who had known James from his teenage years.

"These are my sisters!"

He started pouring them James's favorite bottle of wine and then allowing his waiter to take their orders afterward.

"So you're well known here, James," said Flick, enjoying all the attention.

"When I was learning to be an accountant, even when I couldn't afford it, I came here once a week just to have a decent meal. So they've all known me for years. In those days I ate alone and they thought it was time I brought young ladies to dinner. Now I bring ladies like you and he thinks I'm making up for all those lost days."

After a little laughter, Becky started right in. "James, both of us have now finished our education and have our degrees, mine in the medical field and Flick's in journalism. We could live off our inheritance and not do a stroke of work if we were wise with what father left us. However, we would like to know something about this trust fund that apparently we have in Switzerland."

"Why now all of a sudden do you need to know about something that was a private codicil to the will and has existed since we started in the banking business?"

"We just want to know how that impacts on us and to what benefit it may be to us."

"Money. That's why you're here."

"Not at all, James. As we are all trustees, you have at least an obligation to explain to us what this is." Becky was not forceful but was determined to know.

"From what I understand you have hired your own solicitor to investigate this. He's already been in touch with Sir Thomas. So you tell me, why have something explained when that has been done already?" asked James, becoming slightly irritated at what appeared to be avarice.

"James, we all know of your success and we applaud what you've done. It has taken guts and hard work. You're known to be one of the wealthiest people in the world. So why are you being so evasive and protective?" asked Flick in her usual candid manner.

"That trust was set up primarily to protect the business in the event of some political or world event like war that could severely disrupt or change the business climate. The trust was transferred in the 1930s in fear of the possibility of this country falling into the hands of Hitler and has remained there ever since. It was not set up for any of us individually. It was set up to protect the business."

"But you are the owner of that business, or at least it's largest shareholder, so that indirectly supports you and not us."

"You have your inheritance, as I do. This trust is something that the Bannermans have saved over the years to protect the business, which has indeed served you both well."

"James, we know all that. All we want to know is, if for whatever reason we confront misfortune, do we have a right to be supported by that trust?"

"That depends on the trustee."

"James, for God's sake. *You* are the trustee," snapped Flick.

"Congratulations, you've done your homework. So do you have any idea what's in that trust, or if there's enough there to even help you?" James was going to take them to the limit.

He knew they couldn't get the information they wanted from neither their solicitor, nor Sir Thomas. The trust was at the discretion of the sole trustee since its inception in 1838. This has been a tradition handed down to each successive earl over the years and was a most-guarded private tradtion. As much as they hated what they were doing, they had no choice but to corner him, as he was the sole source that could convey any information.

"No we don't, but we do know that the trust is being used to develop these buildings you've bought and constructed. So if you were to lose money, we want to know, how would that impact us?" asked Becky.

"It seems we're all going in circles here. You want me to disclose something that has been a private matter for over a hundred years and has only concerned the shareholders of the business and no one else?" said James starting to become emphatic.

"It appears that you think we've been rewarded enough with everything we have and that the right to that information is none of our business," said Flick, showing the very spicy side of her nature.

"Who put you up to this?"

"You know I've been seeing Gordon Peterson, your old school friend. He thinks you're using funds that are there to protect your business and the family in bad times, and that should be discussed. We are all trustees. Just because you're the sole trustee of this fund doesn't mean you can use those funds for your own self-serving reasons, which appears to be the case. You have an obligation to your business and us to be transparent and responsible by letting us at least know what you're doing. Especially when you appropriate funds that belong to all of our heritage."

"Now I get it. That Petersen you think so much of is a sworn enemy of mine by his own actions. I've advised you quite soundly not to have anything to do with him. He's hell-bent on trying to destroy my good name and place in the business community. In addition, you've been seen at an illegal gambling house with him. Do you realize what that man could do that not only spoils your reputation, but could also be misconstrued and turned into an absolute scandal for the whole family? Some unsavory character could blackmail you. These people Gordon is in with are gangsters and illegal operators of prostitution and barely legal strip clubs."

"I happen to like him very much! He's offered me a position in his father's newspaper, *The Statesman*, and he himself is editor and I welcome the opportunity."

"So you can write slanderous articles about your brother? He's using you, and the sooner you wake up to that, the better."

"I've had enough of this conversation. To hell with you, James! You're just a greedy spoiled brat that's had everything, and now you're using your inheritance to play with everyone. I've always had a problem with you and always will." She abruptly left the dinner table and left Becky staring at James.

"Wow, I never knew she hated me so much."

"She's hardly a character reference herself," said Becky. "Is it true that she was at an illegal gambling club?"

"I can't convey the source, but it's a very reliable one. She must be mad. This Petersen chap is not even her type; she's just using him to get up the ladder. If someone at this place has seen Gordon Petersen, he'd better be scared for his own reputation, I would think, especially in the business he and his family are in."

"God only knows I can't deal with her. Someone has to talk to her; she won't listen to me. I frankly want to get my own place. If that Gordon does have it in for you, he could be quite slanderous."

"She's already had the conversation with him, I'll bet on it. He's using this to put us at odds so that he can have his stupid revenge all because I beat him and his brother up when we were at school. Gordon swore he'd get his own back. They're not good people, Becky, but now I'm going to really watch my back, especially with my sister's knife stuck in it."

"Look James, I'm about to begin my own career in the medical field. Is it not fair that you, as a trustee with us for our father's estate, be upfront and truthful about such matters?" asked Becky, trying to restore some goodwill.

"I don't have to tell you a damn thing, but because I'm your brother and I love you both, I will. The trust is of considerable value and has been lying in Switzerland earning a modest amount of interest for many years. So I've formed a company that borrows from this trust in order to provide a better return than we're now getting. I have chosen to invest this money into income-producing properties, which will give the trust a far better return on the investment instead of lying in a bank. That being said, there's still plenty of reserves there to take care of the business in an emergency. I think you know me well enough for that. Now, as to my position as the sole trustee, this has been a tradition that's been handed down over the years by our forefathers. It's not something I asked for, and I frankly didn't even know about it until I turned twenty-one; I didn't even know about it at the reading of the will when I was fourteen. You know me, I would never see my sisters go without. You're my family, and yes, we've grown apart and we need to work on that. I for one miss both of you. Remember, we're family and family takes care of each other. To me it's all about being there for each other and I commit to being that person for the rest of my life."

Becky was so moved by what he'd said that she started to

sob and out came her handkerchief. "James, that's all I wanted to hear. You're the only brother I have, and you must make provisions with Sir Thomas. If anything happened to you, it would be devastating. I know this sounds selfish, but see that we're protected. We lost our father so we look to you. I know you see that, and at times we need that strong person in our lives to make us feel loved and welcome. Mother, as you know, is in Italy most of the time. Our parents are gone. All we have is you until we hopefully meet that wonderful person that comes into our lives."

James now knew she really had no ill intent. They had led a very sheltered life, and now they were about to go out into the world and make a living. James was flattered that she valued him.

"Look, Becky. That trust is still there and always will be. It was set up to protect the business. The business I have set up to buy or construct these buildings has debt owed to the trust. I have agreed to return a better rate of earnings than is at present being paid by the bank in Switzerland. With inflation expected to increase, it seemed to me an intelligent way to use funds that have been sitting idle to reduce debt and rebuild the businesses. I'm responsible for what we have and have worked hard to expand and rejuvenate what had been left to me in a somewhat rundown manner. These businesses have lacked any investment over the last fifteen years. Profits have been stuck in the stock exchange, earning little or no money. It has taken a fortune to rebuild a close-to-defunct shipping line. All these choices I've made have been to further the business and everything that we have available to us. I'm going to keep a bedroom at Penbroke for each of you, large enough to bring a man when the time comes. You can always feel that Penbroke is as much part of your life as it has been mine. We must get together for birthdays and Christmases and all the things that families do. We've all been too busy finding our way in the world. It's now time to reconnect."

"James, I have another request. I want to become a doctor and start my own practice. Would there be a position at your business to be able to use me to help with the medical side of say, Trans Global Shipping? I would be so proud to be working at our ancestors' business, and it would help me get started in my career for the life I have ahead."

"Nothing would give me more pleasure than to have my sister working alongside us, as long as you realize that we all come from a privileged background. It is our duty to integrate and be one with the people we work with. In other words, just because we are who we are, we expect no favors."

"Absolutely. I can possibly be helpful in talking with you about people you don't see every day. In a sense, I can be your ambassador," said Becky.

"I like that. It's hard to know everything that goes on, but understand, no politics, okay? I'll talk with Claudia tomorrow morning and when I've done that, make an appointment with her and she'll find you the job you want. You could be a great asset with the knowledge you now have."

Becky was delighted with the outcome as they hugged each other after leaving the restaurant. James offered her his home for the night, but she hadn't come equipped. He saw her into a taxi that would take her near Kensington. It was an evening that started out with a lot of tension. Now James had to deal with Flick and Gordon Petersen once again. At least he felt united with Becky and that pleased James more than anything. He knew in his heart that all he ever wanted to do is to see his sisters be the best they could be. But he knew that would not always be possible.

CHAPTER 25

A NEW FUTURE

The long-awaited moment had come. Sabrina was rushed to Pilgrim Hospital in Boston, South Lincolnshire, to have their baby. James was called and he flew up in his helicopter. It was late afternoon and he couldn't wait to arrive to be by her side.

"It won't be long now, James. I can feel the contractions every two minutes and soon you'll have your son. We still haven't decided what to call our young lord."

"I've been thinking about it and I've decided to call him Romeo," said James, laughing.

"*Romeo*? Have you gone nuts? It doesn't sound very British to me," said Sabrina, laughing then feeling the pain again. "Don't make me laugh. It hurts even more. Now I can't stop giggling."

"Well, he's half Italian…"

"Even if I was full Italian, which I'm not, I would never call him that." Then she started laughing again.

"Let's see, how about Samuel?"

"Samuel. I like that. It sounds solid."

"Samuel James Bannerman, it is."

At that moment the staff came to take her to the delivery room. James anxiously waited in the waiting room. To his huge relief there were no complications. The doctor informed him he had a beautiful baby boy. Sabrina had given him a son. James gave his son his first kiss and all the three shared that first special moment together. It was May 12, 1971, and the beginning of family life for the next generation of Bannermans. The family all came to stay with James the Christmas of 1971 to celebrate little Samuel's first Christmas and to have the christening of his son by the bishop of Lincoln. Piero was now his godfather and Becky was his godmother. It was a proud moment for both families to witness the anointing of the one day eleventh Earl of Penbroke. Samuel and James already had a deep connection. James could imagine how his father was as a child, and now he could see that same good-natured temperament in his own son.

The house renovations were completed in the early part of 1972. The newly stained floors, new master suite, kitchens, bathrooms, and updated decorations looked the way James and Sabrina had intended. They had put their personal stamp on Penbroke, which recognized their time. One day it could all change again, but for now it looked completely different and had a nice fresh odor of newly painted walls and floors. It was a new era in the house's long history, but still bore the antique heritage and paintings of years gone by.

In the early part of 1973 Sabrina gave birth to a beautiful baby girl, which James said she had the right this time to name as he'd named Samuel. They decided on Annabelle, having an Italian flair. They now had their two children, which they had planned. Sabrina still wanted to continue with her modeling career. The new woman they had hired to be with the children, Laura, would now be there to take care of them between the couple's hectic schedules.

****

During 1972 and 1973 all of Bannermans continued to grow. The London building had been completely renovated and as Stephen predicted they had used up all the available space for their own operations. Operations in the States were starting to prosper and Roger's "Banner card" was slowly making its way into an ever-growing number of people's wallets. It would soon be time to have headquarters in New York as the amount of shipping trade from China to the United States was exceeding their trading routes from China to Europe. A building needed to be purchased in order to handle the expansion. Many of James's management were in constant travel and he felt the need to reevaluate the structure of the whole business once more. It was becoming apparent that the US operation needed to be run as a separate entity. Logistically, it was becoming impossible to run it entirely from London.

The heated political scene over the Middle East and OPEC's tight grip on reducing oil to the West gave huge opportunities to Roger Bell once again. His ability to buy oil at the ports of Kuwait, Bahrain, and Saudi Arabia, where prices went through the roof when they arrived at Rotterdam and Shell Haven refineries, allowed them to make fortunes. When others would have shied away, Roger continued to have those amazing instincts in the face of crisis. The Middle East with the Yom Kippur War was a trouble spot and a sensitive area for shipping through much of the seventies. The Suez Canal had reopened in June 1975 after it was closed in 1967. Matters returned to the negotiating table to find a solution between Egypt and Israel. The Camp David Peace Accord talks were to continue for a number of years.

James, over time, was becoming more and more obsessive with his work. He was having dreams, which turned into nightmares. He kept having a repetitive dream that he was bowling the ball at Sterling Heights and somehow he could never bowl the ball fast enough. Then one night he bowled the ball so fast that it went clean though the batsman and through the heart of his faithful wicket keeper, Peter. He awoke with a cold sweat; Sabrina sat up next to him in their London home and asked him what was wrong. "Oh, it's nothing. Just a bad dream." He knew he didn't feel right. He had not heeded the words of Jeremy Soames, which he had completely forgotten in his obsession for his work.

In addition, the incessant demands of his work were overtaking his need to raise a family. He knew he must take to the Throne and spend time with his master to understand what was happening to him. Laura was doing a fantastic job with the two children, but Sabrina now felt a need to be the mother she hadn't been for her own children. She had decided to reduce her modeling career so she could now attend to those duties. They attended the local preparatory schools as James and his sisters had done.

****

In the summer of 1980 James arrived back at Penbroke with Sabrina for the weekend. Sabrina had discussed her change of direction and James was happy to hear that it meant a lot for her to be with the children and decided that he, too, must think about a change for himself.

On the Sunday morning before the crowds arrived, James went down to the Throne Room as he wanted to see his faithful Master Czaur and talk about his life's journey. He had become so embroiled in his work lately, but was not feeling the same satisfaction. Maybe he was just tired. It was time he reconnected to the things he truly valued, and wanted to take time to understand what he was feeling and discuss his thoughts.

He sat on the Throne as he'd done before and went swirling through the vortex. Much to his amazement, he didn't land on the beach, but on the lawn in front of a magnificent castle and estate. He was shocked and thought that maybe Sarah had changed the degree at the base of the Throne to another destination. The castle shone with light that reflected off the golden turrets. The gardens were filled with beautiful shrubbery and flowers that possessed the luminescent colors of the rainbow. He stood up and walked through the wrought-iron gates to a courtyard where he mounted the wide stone steps that led to large solid copper doors with brass studs. He knocked at the door and then pulled the long cord to announce his arrival. The bell rang out and echoed across the courtyard and inside the castle, and yet it seemed no one was there. He decided to open the door and walked into a beautiful hallway with white marble floors and a huge fountain in the center. The vast black granite columns with golden bases encircled the fountain and in three directions he could see wide marble staircases that led to the next floor. Still, there was no one. He called out to Czaur to no avail. He searched the castle, opening door after door, but still there was no one.

I must have made a mistake. I must be in the wrong place. This has never happened before, he said to himself. He finally went down to the lower level and sat down on the marble seat next to the fountain and put his head in his hands, trying to think what must have gone wrong and how to get back to the Throne Room at Penbroke.

At that moment, in a burst of brilliant, blinding light, Czaur appeared before him. "Beautiful, isn't it?"

"It is, but where is everyone?"

"I don't know. You tell me. This place is not of my creation," said Czaur, sounding extremely evasive.

"Then where am I? Did I go to the wrong place? How did you know I would be here?"

"Ah, indeed a question only you can answer."

"Czaur, you're talking in riddles. I'm completely lost."

"A little like your life at the moment, wouldn't you say?"

"My life has complete order. Yes, I have some questions, but this is not why I came to see you."

"Really? Then I'll help you back to the place you came from and you can continue on your journey. If you only have a few questions, then I could have answered those in your sleep."

"Well, it's more than that. I feel cut off and lonely, tired from all the things that have been started and are beginning to evolve. I now find myself feeling isolated and alone."

"Finally getting a little more honest, James. This place has nothing to do with me. This castle you're in is of your own making. Beautiful it is, but I don't see anyone here. Do you?" asked Czaur in his thought-provoking manner. "With all that you're doing, the more you build, the more you have, the more isolated you'll feel and will become. The joy and laughter you once shared with Sabrina and your children are slowly slipping away into the distance. You don't see anyone unless it's work. You don't socialize unless it's business, and worst of all, you have two beautiful children, one of which is your beloved father, Collin Bannerman. How much time do you take to spend with him? What about your wife and your daughter, Annabelle? Do they have any importance above your beloved empire? This house is you, your life, and what you are creating. Soon there won't be any gardens. There will be walls and after that it'll become a fortress and inside, at the center, all alone will be this wonderful and great magical genius called James Bannerman, the tenth Earl of Penbroke, who is revered by all the world's wealthiest people. You will be completely and utterly alone in a hell of your own creation of materiality.

Beautiful it is, but empty without a heart, wouldn't you say?"

"I don't think that's fair. I've always worked hard to help people and to see my family is taken care of. This is not who I am; you must surely know that."

"I do, but do you?"

"That's why I'm here to talk with you. If I didn't care, I wouldn't have come."

"Now that you've finally become honest with me I can talk to you and advise you. You have two paths you can take. The one that you're now taking is to the world of greed. Why not take the one road that leads to the world of love? The reason you don't feel any satisfaction at the moment is after the initial excitement of having done all that you have, it wears off and then there is the need for more. It's like taking a pill then after a while it wears off, and you need another one. All that you've done is of tremendous satisfaction to all of us here. You are right. You have helped many and opened dreams and opportunities by your vision and hard work."

He paused. "All that is good. But greed is empty. You cannot satisfy greed; it continues to want. My concern is you're going in the same direction that you did on Atlantis. You've become so obsessed with your life's work that you've become blind to everything else. This is the reason why we gave you what you needed in the material form so that you would develop your spiritual abilities. In so many past lives you have fought hard and failed in business, then you started to get the art of it. Now you've become so proficient at it, you take to it like a duck takes to water. In this life, instead of feeling blessed with all that you have, there's an underlying guilt that you didn't start from nothing like others have had to do. The seeds that you've planted will all flourish and continue to grow. Remember, in chess the king doesn't move too far from his original place and castles to protect his position.

"Have your company's staff come to you more often rather

than you always traveling to them. Take time for your family and concentrate on improving the world you live in. Love that beautiful wife who worships the ground you walk on, and get back in touch with the real James. The road you're on now will lead to further isolation and you will not join us at the end of your time on earth. You will be condemned to another cycle of civilization on Earth again. How many times do you have to do that? Bring all your talents and abilities and be with us and let's work with the 'divinessence,' to help form this beautiful universe we are part of."

At that moment the castle started to disappear and there they both sat in Czaur's little garden by the sea. He stretched out his hand and held him. "You were once my son and I will always love you. I can't bear to see you not come to us after all that you've worked so hard to achieve. Remember those conversations you've had with Jeremy Soames. You and he have a great purpose, far above this temporary need for wealth on this planet. Don't you see how nothing in the third dimension lasts? The written word has more power, and can at least cheat death and time!"

"Czaur, thank you for making me see, once again, my true purpose and the reason why I have what I have. I will honor all that you've taught me and I will change my ways, because it is my final goal to be with you and my other guides."

James found himself back on the Throne once again. The thought of being in that isolated castle all by himself had been a shock, and he ran out of the room to find Sabrina. She was just getting up to go downstairs to make breakfast, when he threw his arms around her to tell her how much he loved her.

"I've been such a fool. I've become so lost and obsessed with my work that I've lost sight of the very things that are important to me. It's because of you I have been successful in all that I do. It's that love you give me that helps me to excel. I've been such a fool. How could I've been so blind?"

"Thank God you're back," said Sabrina, then she broke down into a torrent of grateful tears. Nothing else had to be said between them as they held each other tight.

****

James picked up the Sunday paper to read after breakfast, as was his usual practice. There, much to his disbelief, on the front page was a large picture of him and a passage about him stating, "Tycoon James Bannerman, tenth Earl of Penbroke, misappropriates family trust funds from Swiss bank account for his own purposes. Story on page 3." James read in horror, an entire epistle on how he had absconded funds from a one-hundred-year-old trust fund set up by his forefathers, to build his property empire.

The phone calls came in immediately, first one by one then several at a time.

"James, have you read the newspaper?" said Claudia anxiously.

"I have, and I think I know who's behind this." James seethed. He knew that this was a lesson of life he would have to learn. He was now going to take the kind of forceful action where this type of vicious behavior would never happen again.

ABOUT THE AUTHOR

DAVID FRANCIS COOK

David Francis Cook was born and educated in England. In 1967 David immigrated to the United States. He started his own business in 1982, after having worked for major aerospace manufacturers to gain experience within the industry.

In November of 2003 he sold his business, which became the largest wing-forming company in the world, to a Belgian consortium.

In 2006, he built his own 2.5-mile road racetrack in North Texas, where most of his family and grandchildren now reside. He also spends time at his home in Canada, where he likes to write.

Throughout David's life he has been a prolific writer and public speaker within the industry he worked in. He has worked with many writers where he learnt and taught in order to one day fulfill his dream.

THE LEGACY SERIES

David's vast experience in dealing with high-ranking people in governments and different countries during his time at his own business, has given him the knowledge to write this series of books. He has always had faith and belief in the amazing universe we live in. In his travels all over the world, he's been able to capture thoughts about other cultures. His working years allowed him to make notes. He has used those experiences to apply to this all-encompassing set of books he has written and will write.

It is David's hope that his work will provoke the reader to thought and stimulate the imagination.